GRAVEN IMAGES

ALSO BY JANE WATERHOUSE

PLAYING FOR KEEPS

GRAVEN IMAGES

JANE WATERHOUSE

G. P. PUTNAM'S SONS / NEW YORK

This is a work of fiction. The events described are imaginary and the characters are fictitious and not intended to represent specific living persons. When persons or entities are referred to by their true names, they are portrayed in entirely fictitious circumstances; the reader should not infer that these events ever actually happened.

G. P. Putnam's Sons
Publishers Since 1838
200 Madison Avenue
New York, NY 10016

Library of Congress Cataloging-in-Publication Data

Waterhouse, Jane
Graven images / Jane Waterhouse.
p.   cm.
ISBN 0-399-14080-8 (acid-free paper)
I. Title.
PS3563.A812G73   1995   95-13104 CIP
813'.54—dc20

Book design by Jaye Zimet

Printed in the United States of America
10 9 8 7 6 5 4 3 2 1

This book is printed on acid-free paper. ∞

During the writing of this book I relied on the technical expertise, and plain kindness, of many people. Special thanks go to Manny and Arlene Haller; John Garofalo, Manager, State of New Jersey, Bureau of Coastal Engineering; Raymond A. Gill, Jr., Esquire; Katherine Cusack; and Gary Lotano.

A faithful team of readers saw the manuscript through its many drafts. My heartfelt appreciation goes to Carol Clayton, Alyce Rathburn, Carolyn Tvrdik, Jerry Donovan, Carol Gallager, Pat McLaughlin, and especially Michele Armour and my sister, Amy Waterhouse Lotano, who offered invaluable insights at every turn.

I will be forever grateful to my resourceful manager, Scott Shukat, and my astonishingly sensitive editor, Christine Pepe, for their un-flinching belief in this story of mine.

Finally, I want to thank Noelle, Matthew, and—most of all—my son, Baylen, for being an inspiration to me, daily.

For my mother, who gave me a love of mysteries,
and my father, who taught me to look
within the stone

Contents

"I like having the truth be the truth so I can't change it."

TRUMAN CAPOTE
ON WRITING *IN COLD BLOOD*
FROM *CAPOTE*,
BY GERALD CLARKE

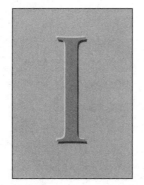

THE GHOST

BEFORE THE INTERVIEW GETS UNDER WAY, GARNER QUINN MAKES SEVERAL THINGS CRYSTAL CLEAR.

SHE WILL NOT DISCUSS HER FATHER (LEGENDARY DEFENSE ATTORNEY DUDLEY QUINN III), OR THE LAWSUIT HE BROUGHT AGAINST HER AFTER THE PUBLICATION OF *ROCK-A-BYE BABY,* HER STARTLING EXPOSÉ OF THE NOTORIOUS DULCIE MARIAH TRIAL. SHE WILL NOT ENTERTAIN ANY QUESTIONS ABOUT HER EX-HUSBAND (FLAMBOYANT MANHATTAN ATTORNEY ANDREW V. MUSCATI), HER DAUGHTER (TEMPLE, 14), OR ANY OTHER ASPECT OF HER PERSONAL LIFE. NOR WILL SHE COMMENT ON THE CONTROVERSIAL CASTING OF TOM CRUISE (AS PSYCHOPATHIC KILLER HAROLD BEECH) IN THE FILM VERSION OF HER LATEST BESTSELLER, *DUST TO DUST.*

WHAT SHE *WILL* TALK ABOUT IS HER WORK—TRUE CRIME.

AND ONCE SHE GETS STARTED ON THAT SUBJECT, IT BECOMES QUITE OBVIOUS THAT HERE'S A WOMAN WHO DOESN'T MERELY LIKE WHAT SHE DOES—*SHE BLOODY WELL LOVES IT.*

VANITY FAIR
(JUNE 1993)

1

Just a fly on the wall. That's how I always put it. Go on with your business, I'd tell them. Forget that I'm here. Pretend I'm a fly, just a fly. It always surprised me how easily people bought into the concept. Personally, I've never met a fly I liked.

Jeff Turner was my fourth. Fourth true-crime book, fourth trial.

I had the part down pat. Clothes serviceable yet subdued. Expression distracted. This distraction acted as a sort of tinted windshield. I could see out, but they couldn't see in. After years of practice I'd perfected slowing down my body rhythms like a person under ice. It's a conscious process, a sleight of hand of the outer skin. Inside, all your senses are going full-tilt: registering, weighing, filing, judging; but on the surface, you're a speck in a busy landscape, transparent as glass. A fly.

Sometimes I wonder if that's how God feels. Overlooked. Underestimated. Biding His time.

Turner's defense attorney, Nick Shawde, called the room to order. As the breed goes, I'd rank Nick in the top percentile. That's an educated opinion. My father was an attorney. Most of the people I grew up around were attorneys. My ex-husband was an attorney, too.

By then, you'd have thought I'd know better.

"Listen up, people." Nick tapped the edge of the desk with his clipboard. It was time for the pre-courtroom pep talk.

I enjoyed these lunchtime stratagems. I'd come of age in the sixties, before the dawn of girls' sports. Listening with the others while Shawde outlined his latest game plan for the defense—tie loosened, Doublemint snapping like a fast towel against a hard fanny—was the closest I'd ever come to high-fiving a huddle of palms in some sweaty locker room. Strangely enough, it made me feel at home. Or as close to at home as someone who doesn't feel at home at home can feel.

"Here's what we gonna do." Shawde cracked his gum. "Weinstein's gwan keep our boy and his mama real, real quiet. No talky-talky around the teevee cameras, yes? Leave that to Sistah Cox."

Weinstein shouted "Amen," and everyone laughed. I took a bite of my sandwich, focusing on Nick, trying to see him fresh, as though his every mannerism wasn't already indelibly etched in my mind. That adolescent habit he had of using any hard surface, including his thighs, as a drum pad. His braying *hee-haw* of a laugh. The way he squinted behind his wire rims as though he might need a stronger prescription.

Details that would make him really come to life on the printed page.

He glanced down at his clipboard. "Oh yeah—who the fuck slicked the kid's hair back, anyway?"

"He did it himself," Maria Lombardi replied, adding sarcastically, "They don't exactly have hairdressers in the Richland County Jail."

"In there long enough, they all turn hairdresser." Nick shrugged. More laughter, from everybody but Lombardi. "Slip him a note," he told her. "That choirboy cowlick of his works for us."

The woman attorney shot him a withering look. It came to me suddenly, like the jolt of a neon sign lighting, that they were sleeping together. I found it vaguely disturbing that I'd missed the signs before. I wondered if Shawde's wife knew. And, in spite of myself, I wondered why he hadn't hit on me.

As if reading my thoughts, Nick called out my name. "Hey, Quinn!" I looked up from my sandwich, uncomfortable with the attention. "Just sit back, babe"—he blew me a kiss—"and decide who you want to play your part in the movie."

That was the joke.

True crime meant big money in Hollywood. One of the legal assistants had started up a pool where you could bet your buckwheats on the cast, and a director had actually flown in from the coast to *do lunch* with Shawde. Nick had rolled his eyes and yucked it up. But he went. Which was more than I would've done, even for a free meal in the best restaurant in South Carolina.

Let them make movies out of my books if they wanted, as long as they didn't bother me with the details. In my view that was why, on the fourth day, God created agents and lawyers, along with the other creeping things.

"Humina, humina, humina." Nick Shawde's beady eyes scurried across the page. He ran a line through the last entry on his clipboard. "That about does it for me. Anybody else?"

A chorus of *nos* sounded around the room. He dropped his clipboard onto the desk with a clatter. "It's the end of the fourth quarter, folks," Shawde told his staff solemnly. "And we're gonna give the ball to Susie Trevett."

Susan Trevett Cox. The bombshell who would blow the prosecution's case apart, and set young Jefferson Turner free. But I didn't want to think that far, to the end of yet another project, to that hollow, empty feeling I'd be left with; so I closed my eyes, the better to pretend we were a team, and Nick was our coach, and we were ahead.

The snap of gum accentuated Shawde's words like the plosive pops of an African dialect. "Stay tight, stay sharp, stay tuned, because one way or another, by next week this pig'll done be crisped."

There was no dodging it, the sense of something big drawing to a close. Earlier in the trial everyone would've been rushing off in all directions—hustling over to the courthouse, making phone calls, fielding reporters, ferreting out information. Today, however, they hung around in the hotel suite, ambling over to see what was left of the cold buffet, kicking back the dregs of diluted Pepsi from plastic cups, trading barbs, nudging shoulders. Gone was the familiar litany of complaints. *There's nowhere to get a decent pastrami. Southerners are too fucking slow. Southerners are too fucking hospitable. The weather outside is too fucking hot. The air-conditioning inside is too fucking cold.* Days shy of turning the case over to the jury, on the verge of confirming their return flights, it was as though everyone had suddenly decided that these last six months in Columbia, South Carolina, hadn't been half bad.

A ukulele inexplicably materialized out of thin air. Shawde picked it up and, perched on the edge of a desk, began strumming "In-A-Gadda-Da-Vida." Maria Lombardi stood next to him, laughing too loud. For some reason the sight of the two of them acting like goofy teenagers ticked me off.

I forced my attention toward the midday news program playing soundlessly on the television set in the corner. A short, barrel-chested man in a uniform was being questioned by a reporter. Without warning, the hair on the back of my neck rose and tiny prickles cakewalked down my spine.

He was just a guy, weightlifter arms dangling parenthetically at his sides, a con-man squint; but it was as though I knew everything about him. This sometimes happened to me, this hyper-alertness at the sight of a stranger. It was as if an ever-vigilant, always-working part of my brain had already reduced him to six neat pages of print in a book I'd yet to write.

"Turn that up, will you?" I motioned for Weinstein to adjust the volume.

The sound popped too high for a moment, cutting short conversation around the room. Shawde stopped strumming.

"—we was carrying the artifact up these stairs in the art gallery, see, and it felt kinda funny," the man told the reporter. "So I says to my partner, I go, 'Ange, this statue don't feel right.' And, bango! The thing nosedives. Breaks into like a million pieces, an' inside there's this hand . . . a *real* hand . . ."

Cut to a woman, well dressed, lots of jewelry. "The piece was . . . ," her hands fluttered to her face nervously, ". . . is called *Lady Sitting*. It's an excellent example of Blackmoor's sculpture technique, in which he wraps a model with plaster bandages and lets them harden into a mold—"

"You hear this, Shawde?" Weinstein called.

Nick put down the ukulele. "Yeah," he said. "Word has it he's goin' for the Gold." *Diana Gold*. I'd heard that she and Shawde had shared an ongoing rivalry based on competition and atrophied lust since their law school days. "Wonder if ole Tight Thighs'll loosen up under the Blackmoor mystique?"

The television reporter's voice continued to drone on as the scene shifted to another location. A limousine was pulling up to a curb. The door swung open, and a man emerged, face down, his Armani raincoat cut for sudden movements. Some camera jostling. Reporters cried out like a crowd of hysterical teens in the presence of a rock star. Someone said, *"No comment."*

The raincoated man's eyes suddenly connected with the camera. I pictured reams of celluloid curling at the edges, searing frame after frame until it was smoldering ash, disintegrating the videotape, turning it into smoke.

If such a thing could happen from a simple look.

"He doesn't appear very upset for a guy just accused of murder," Maria Lombardi observed.

"Who said murder?" Shawde asked. Lombardi raised two perfectly plucked eyebrows. "A missing hand don't necessarily mean a missing corpse, chile," he reminded her. "Who's to say one of his models don't like it rough? Maybe she's walkin' around with a stump, not complaining."

"They'll find something in one of his other sculptures," Lombardi predicted.

"Ten to one it'll be the heart." The words tumbled out of my mouth before I could stop them.

"Oh, so you know him, Garny?" From where I sat in the back of the room I could see Nick's antennae going up.

"We've met."

He whistled low. "Ladies and gents, looks like our Ms. Quinn has found a subject for her next book."

"Forget that. Haven't you heard?" I managed a smile. "I'm retiring."

"Come on, Garner. You ain't no more retiring than you are shy," Shawde guffawed. "In fact, I looked up the word *driven* in the dictionary, and your picture was there. Right next to your daddy's." High praise, in Nick's eyes. To ruthless young attorneys like him, Dudley Quinn the Third was an icon, a living legend, someone to admire and revere.

I held a different opinion of my father, one which I kept mostly to myself.

"Check that dictionary again," I told Nick lightly. "Because once this case is over, you can kiss me goodbye."

"A tempting thought." He hiked his eyebrows suggestively, another of his adolescent mannerisms. The next moment he was glancing at his watch, all business. "Better get moving, folks."

I stayed put as they scattered, taking a last bite of sandwich, chewing thirty-six times while Shawde slid into his silk suit jacket.

"Admit it, angel face. As soon as I leave, you'll be on the phone, making your bid for a Blackmoor exclusive." He shoved a sheaf of papers into his briefcase. The metal hasps snapped shut viciously, like teeth. "You can't help yourself. You're insatiable."

"I don't have to bid for books, Shawde. Especially not his." I tossed my crumpled napkin at the wastepaper basket. It missed.

"I sense some personal history here." He stood over me, his glasses, his face, his suit, all shiny and gleaming. "Tell Uncle Nicky what happened. You slept with him, didn't you?"

"He was a guest at Dudley's beach house a couple of times," I scoffed, "a million years ago, when I was a kid."

At the doorway, Shawde stopped and turned. "The question still remains, Garny," he taunted softly, "—did you sleep with him?" I heard his laughter, out in the hallway, even after the door closed.

I waited a few seconds, then plopped myself down behind his desk and dialed the phone. I was surprised when Temple answered on the first ring. "What are you doing home this time of day?"

"I didn't go to school. Throat's sore."

"Did Cilda call the doctor?"

"Uh-uh. I'm better now," Temple croaked hoarsely. "What's the latest down there? Have they put Susan on the stand yet?"

"Probably not until Monday," I replied, impatient with the question. It frosted me how often conversations with my fourteen-year-old daughter centered around this damn trial. "I should be able to get an early flight."

"Can I fly back with you after the weekend to watch her testify?"

I sighed. "We'll see. Look, I have to go, honey. Buzz Jack for me, will you?"

"Okay."

"I love you."

"Love you, Mom." The connection was bad. She sounded very far away. When she put me on hold, there was so much static on the line, for a moment I expected to get disconnected; but then I heard Jack's voice, accentless and pleasant, "Hey, boss." I imagined him sitting at his desk, leaning back in the chair, his feet up.

"Temple doesn't sound too good," I said.

"It's nothing serious," he assured me. "Cilda's keeping an eye on her."

"Listen, book me on . . . ," I checked my watch, "the six o'clock, and arrange for a limo at the airport."

"I could pick you up."

"No," I replied, pleased just the same, "that's after-hours for you." He didn't pursue it. "Anything new?"

"An invitation just arrived," Jack said, "hand-delivered by messenger from Manhattan."

The place I called home, and its adjacent office, was a secluded estate in a small, out-of-the-way town on the Jersey shore, forty miles from New York. I wondered who would go to such trouble. "What kind of an invitation?"

"A gala at the Metropolitan Museum of Art this weekend," he said, then, inflecting a deeper meaning into his words, "The Dane Blackmoor retrospective." When I said nothing, he asked, "What should I tell them?"

I sank back into the cushioned leather of Shawde's chair. "Nothing," I said crossly. "I've got more important things than art galas on my mind—or have you forgotten I'm down here fighting for an innocent man's life?"

"Silly me." Jack's quiet sarcasm crackled over the telephone line. "And here I thought you were just writing another book."

2

I saw him at a distance, towering above the other people in the corridor outside the courtroom. There were only two alternatives. Payphone. Or the rest room. The phone was closer, but I was afraid it wouldn't give me enough cover.

"Hey, Quinn!"

I managed a look of surprise. "There he is," I said, pulling out the all-purpose phrase I used whenever a name escaped me.

"Just the person I want to see." He was one of those people who always seemed to edge you into walls or doorways.

What was his name? *B something.* Billy, or Bobby, or Brendan. He freelanced for *People*. A group of early birds walked by us. He turned to do a quick check in case someone more important was among them, and I used the interim to search my memory.

He'd interviewed me just before my third book, *Dust to Dust*, came out. The house was being built then; and that's where they took my picture—in faded jeans and a thermal undershirt, hair flying—standing under the newly framed entranceway as belligerent waves flapped over the seawall in the distance.

"Why build a house," he'd asked, "with the ocean beating down your door on one side, and the river on the other?"

"I like to live dangerously," I'd told him, hoping he knew good copy when he heard it.

He had. The article began, *True-crime writer Garner Quinn has built her home, and her career, on dangerous ground.* I still remembered those words, but his name was mostly a blank.

He turned back to me, satisfied that I was his best bet for the moment. "All over but the shouting, eh, Quinn?"

"We'll see." Something about him reminded me of a sardine. Long and sallow. Tapering at the head and feet. Oily.

"Of course, it probably doesn't matter much to you which way it goes now." He flashed a sardinish smile, teeth narrow and pointy. "Royalties being royalties." This was my punishment, I decided, for dawdling in the hotel suite, for wandering away from the pack.

"How's the Nickster bettin'?" asked the B Man.

"He thinks Pacino'll play him in the movie." I stepped back to let a young woman pass.

"Mmm-*mmm*, can't get enough of that South'n fried chicken." The reporter licked his lips in the direction of the girl. It pissed me off that he considered me one of the guys, someone he could cuss with, and leer at other women around.

"See you in court," I said.

He grabbed my sleeve. "Be a pal, Quinn. Come on, between us." I kept my face impassive, committing nothing. "No matter what she says, you don't really think he's innocent, do you?"

A loud commotion saved me from having to answer. Microphones waving, cameras jockeying for position, the press ebbed and flowed down the hall like a giant amoeba. At its nucleus, looking serene and untouched, was Susan Trevett Cox.

"Mrs. Cox! Susan—!" a jumble of voices yelled at once. The B Man from *People* moved toward the Susan Cox Story reflexively, like a weed toward the light.

Susan's face, stripped of all makeup, was spit-polished and shiny under the fluorescents. Her hair had been tied back so severely that the broken ends around the crown and neck frizzed out like a halo, framing a small upturned nose, immense lashless eyes, the pouty upper lip. It looked a lot different than it had that first time, almost a year before.

3

She was surrounded by reporters that day, too; blond hair tumbling in feathery wisps, eyes fringed with dimestore mascara.

I watched the wheelchair brigade as it passed out of Richland Memorial. Sitting within the confines of the big metal contraption, flanked by two bulky detectives and a gaggle of geeks from the prosecutor's office, Susan looked as small and defenseless as a child. It wasn't until one of the men took her elbow, assisting her toward a waiting car, that the illusion of fragility snapped against that taut reality of spandexed hips, and high, firm breasts—the kind women go to surgeons for—bobbing like buoys on the filmy polyester sea of her aqua-blue blouse. Susan didn't walk, she rippled.

Her glorious body strained against the garlands of gauze wrapping it as if to say, Let me out. In one slow, liquid movement, she poured herself into the car's upholstered darkness, the bandages playing peekaboo with the outer skin of her clothing.

There would be more linen dressing, I knew, winding its way around her shoulders, under the up-tipped breasts, across her belly, and down her buttocks. All in all, the knife had pocketed forty-seven crosses into the girl's flesh.

I stood apart as the reporters swarmed toward the departing automobile. There would be time later. I would have plenty of opportunity to talk, to listen, to become whatever and whomever Susan needed me to be—a sister, a mother, a friend, a confessor. It didn't matter.

I played them all very well.

All Through the Night, the Jeff Turner book, started out as so many of my books did, with a tip. Someone was murdering girls down in Columbia, South Carolina. The press dubbed the killer the Holy Ghost because he'd staged a funeral Mass for each of the women he attacked before raping and killing them. A friend of a friend knew one of the detectives.

I was lousy with those kinds of friends.

The call came one hot summer morning. "Thought you might be interested," the detective's voice was a whisper. "We got a live one."

Her name was just plain Susan Trevett then, a cocktail waitress who modeled lingerie at ladies' get-togethers and businessmen's lunches. She particularly enjoyed the latter, she told me, because she was able to pick up a little cash on the side.

"But I ain't nobody's bimbo, unnerstand?" she emphasized, her slow, southern voice clinging to vowels, the way the capri pants clung to her tightly rounded buttocks.

"Ever since I was a little girl, I wanted to make it big, you know." She stretched toward her toes in a gesture that was both catlike and contrived. "Wanted to have it all." Then, with one of the swift changes of emotions that I would learn to expect, her immense eyes clouded with tears.

"I coulda been in *Playboy*," she went on softly, "maybe even made centerfold." Susan looked down at the angry pink cross-hatched welts on her wrists. "Men used to tell me I had a perfect body."

"It still looks pretty perfect," I said, truthfully, "to me."

"Well, you ain't Mr. Hefner, now are you?" sighed Susan Trevett.

We were sitting in the bedroom of the apartment where Susan had been staying since leaving the hospital. In the middle of the room her open suitcase spilled its contents onto an old shag rug. She kneeled next to it, the way I'd seen Asian women kneel, not with a thud, but a gentle undulation of the body, like cake dough folding into a pan. From behind, she looked to be about eight years old.

"Here." She handed me a manila folder. Inside were several 8x10 color shots showing Susan Trevett in a sheer teddy with the laces completely undone. I leafed through the photographs, wondering if I would be expected to say something about how tastefully they were done.

"Guy I know took 'em," she explained. "But *Playboy* mailed 'em back." She continued, her voice earnest and introspective. "I think it was 'cause I didn't have an agent. That and the fact that Eddie wannit much of a photographer.

"Which is how I come to take the job over at Annalee's in the first place. To save up for my portfolio." She rose suddenly, landing in another part of the room like an agitated butterfly. Her fingers worked at lighting a cigarette. "How I ended up comin' home late that night."

"Can you tell me about it?" I wished she would face me again, but couldn't chance moving in her direction. The name of the game was unobtrusiveness. No tape recorder. No notepad. Just ears, eyes, and memory.

Susan Trevett sighed, or let out a drag of smoke. From where I sat, I couldn't be sure. "Yeah," she said, finally. "Why not?"

It was the sixth straight day of the heat wave. She remembered because one more would have made an even week. It had been a relief to report to work, Susan said, where it was air-conditioned. On her first break she'd had a fight with T. J. Shiels, the bartender she was dating, after catching him groping another waitress. To spite him, she'd started flirting with a college student from USC who was sitting at the bar. When her shift was over she left with the boy.

"What was his name?"

She shrugged, offering helpfully, "Mark, I think. Mark, or maybe Bart."

"So did he take you home," I prodded gently, "or what?"

Again, Susan shrugged. "We fooled around in the parking lot for a while."

"You had sex with him?"

"His car was too small," she explained, "so I just gave him a blow job."

I nodded, as though this were a perfectly natural thing to do under the circumstances. "And then he took you home?"

Susan stubbed out her cigarette in the palm of a big clam shell. "Hey, I may be a little wild," she said, "but I ain't nuts."

She'd had the boy drop her off a few blocks away from her apartment, she explained, so that he wouldn't know exactly where she lived. She lowered herself down slowly on crossed legs. "I always do that when it's a new guy, 'cause," she said, "you never know." Her voice shattered into a little laugh. The irony of this was not lost on Susan Trevett.

"You walked the rest of the way home?"

She began playing with the feathery ends of her hair. "Ye-ah. I walked."

"Then what happened?"

Susan arched her back as though it were stiff. "Look," she protested, "can't you just listen to those tapes the police got? I mean, I been over this a hunnerd times already."

"I can come back," I said, careful to keep my voice free of impatience and expectation. "We don't have to do it now."

She muttered, "Now, later. I guess it don't make a hell of a lot of difference."

Susan began telling the story, *her story*, again.

She'd started walking the two and a half blocks to her place. It was still hot. Her feet were killing her. She didn't remember hearing anything, except for the sound of the cicadas, like sandpaper rubbing against the night. "That's the way they do it, innit? They rub their legs against their wings?" she asked me softly. "Or am I thinking of some other kinda bugs?"

There was no one on the street, she said. She took off her shoes and stuck them in her bag, then peeled off her pantyhose and hung them around the back of her neck, like a towel. The pavement hurt, she recalled, so she walked on the grass, humming to herself, dancing a little in the dark. By the time she reached the duplex she rented for three and a quarter a month, she'd already had her key out.

"I remember everything suddenly being so clear," Susan said, "like it didn't matter no more about T.J., or any of 'em. I was gonna get in *Playboy*. Be a big name. It was gonna be all right. I remember feeling real happy." She let out another bitter laugh. "Innit a bitch?

"Here's the part that really takes the cake—the moon was out, and I closed my eyes and made a wish on it. Closed my eyes for just that little bitty second, but it sure was enough." The man had jumped out from between two parked cars, grabbing her from behind. Within seconds he was using the pantyhose around her neck as a garrote. She tried to fight him. Her pocketbook came loose in the struggle. The key flew out of her hand. It was later found in the grass.

Susan spoke without emotion now, as though these things had happened to someone else. Every once in a while she paused, seeming to see something in a small, dark space behind her eyes. She let it register and then went on, surprised, perhaps, at her own disaffectedness. I'd seen this before, victims detaching from the fear, the anger, the sense of naked helplessness.

She lost track of what she was saying. I prompted her gently. "Did you scream?"

"He put something in my mouth. A handkerchief, I guess. And he pounded my head down on the hood of a parked car." She was becoming fidgety again. "Slammed me real hard—hey, you got a match?" I reached in my bag, and tossed her a pack. Although I hadn't smoked for years, I carried it all—matches, butts, a store of gum, lots of tissues.

Susan walked over to a deco vanity, beat up but still a marvel for its rosy inlay and bold curves. I could see her face in the mirror as she lit up, then reached for a tube of liquid eyeliner and began applying it with a steady hand. "Next thing I know"—she was barely breathing, Kewpie lips parted, as though that were part of drawing the neat little line—"I was in the back of the van." *Beige. North Carolina plates. Blacked-out windows in the back. Gutted. Moldy carpeting on the floor.*

She blinked, her left lid rimmed smoky blue, startling the white of the eye, making the iris stand out like the target of a ball toss in a carnival game. She went to work on the right.

The man had thrown her down and pulled the door shut, Susan continued with her dull, loose-lipped delivery. He took a condom out of his pants pocket. When he tried to rape her, she fought back. Hard. That's when he started with the knife.

"You could see it was what he liked using," Susan told me, "more than his dick. And the whole time, he's whispering this mumbo-jumbo stuff in my ear. *Dominoes, Nabisco*—that kind of crazy shit."

"Latin?"

"I guess so, though I can't say I ever heard it spoke before then. All I know is it was weird, even weirder than his face."

"What did he look like?"

"White." Susan studied her handiwork in the mirror. "And I don't mean just that he wannit black. Like a Halloween face'us been painted on."

"The tests run on your blouse and skirt showed traces of grease-paint."

She shrugged. "A great big sweatin' moonhead, s'what he was."

"What were you thinking?" I asked.

"Thinkin'?" she snapped. "I wannit thinkin' anything. I was just tryin' to get the fuck away from the bastard—and I did, too, didn't I?"

I stayed quiet, remembering Susan's statement to the police.

How they'd struggled with the knife, how she'd managed to elbow him and break free. "Lord knows how I got outta the van. I just remember the fresh air hittin' me, and my bare feet on the blacktop. There was a lighted window down the street"—her voice had sounded heartbreakingly young—"and I made toward it like heaven."

I made toward it like heaven. I'd filed that phrase away.

Susan resumed work on her eye makeup. "That's when I started yellin' to beat the band, but mustn't abeen nobody heard me, 'cause they didn't come." We lapsed into a long silence, thinking of all those people on that block, not hearing, never coming. It had been almost morning before someone noticed her, collapsed in a row of hedges.

"Would you recognize this guy, if you saw him again?" I asked finally.

"With the gunk on his face, sure," she sighed. "Without it? I don't know. I just don't know." Under her eyes the liner began to run in inky wet blobs.

"Shit," Susan Trevett said. "Shit, shit, shit."

Less than a week later I sat with Susan in a small viewing room at a police precinct in downtown Columbia. The humid air was laced with tension, making it almost hurt to breathe.

"That's him," she said, pointing at the third man from the left.

The detective moved closer, his face almost touching hers, but whether from concern or downright lust, I couldn't tell. "Are you sure?" he asked her.

"Absolutely, positively." The wispy blond head bobbed.

Maybe we should try this chorus line in clown white now, I thought. *Mix 'em up, give her another go at it.* But then again, perhaps Susan Trevett had underestimated her own powers of identification. Because the young man was Jefferson "Bird" Turner, and he owned a beige van with North Carolina plates, blacked-out windows in the back, and moldy carpeting on the floor.

4

"Susan! Susan! Do you have anything to tell us?" the reporters called.

Susan's attorney, Tucker Morton, said, "After the defense rests, Mrs. Cox will make a statement."

Shelby Cox's arm tightened around his young bride. He reminded me of a possum—pink face frozen into preternatural stillness, eyes mesmerized by the headlights of an oncoming car that was about to steamroll him.

Susan shook off his sheltering embrace. "I have jus' one thing to say now"—her soft, childlike voice rose above the clamor—"an' that is—no matter what I said before—Mr. Turner is an innocent man." A few flashlights went off. Susan Trevett Cox put up her hand as though to shield her eyes. From where I stood I could see the rosy tracks of scars on her wrist and forearm. Then Tucker Morton ushered his client and her husband down the hall.

The *People* reporter edged back in my direction. "Did I tell you I got an exclusive? Cover story next week, and get this"—he nudged my arm with his elbow—"Susie put on *mascara and lipstick* for the photo shoot. I guess she felt the Lord would've wanted her to look her best."

You slime, I thought. Aloud I said, "I gotta get inside, Bryant," my tongue rolling off the name before I knew I knew it. I would have gotten away from him, too, if an elderly woman carrying a prayer-book, its leather cover grizzled like the lips of an old dog, hadn't been taking her sweet southern time passing through the courtroom doors.

"Hey, what about this Dane Blackmoor stuff?" Bryant dodged my heels. "Sex-y, huh? Very sexy."

"I really haven't paid much attention," I said, elbowing my way through the crowd as politely as I could.

"Oh, come on," he protested in a stage whisper, "Blackmoor's perfect for you! A match made in bestseller heaven!" He stopped suddenly, gesturing toward the section reserved for the press. "Well, this is where I get off. The cheap seats. See you around, Quinn."

I continued down the aisle, sliding into my usual chair just be-hind the defense table. Jeff Turner's mother, Varlie, was sitting with her sister in the row behind me. I turned around and flashed them a supportive smile. They nodded with faces set in the same sad lines, stone tablets carved with identical commandments: *Life shall be hard; the poor will be trod upon; nothing good can ever come of anything.* I doubted they'd show a spark of emotion, even when Jeff was set free.

Don't jump the gun, I reminded myself. We aren't out of the woods yet. Still, it was difficult not to anticipate a happy ending. I'd all but written it.

A tide of whispers lapped over the courtroom as the guards ush-ered in the defendant. Jefferson Turner had quite a following. Nick Shawde called them the Turnerettes, and insisted that at least two women on the jury were charter members of the club.

"He's got that little-boy lost thing going for him," the defense at-torney told me exultantly. "When he laughs, the ladies laugh. That hangdog expression crosses his pretty face, it's hankie time in the ole South."

I watched Jeff Turner, flanked by the two guards, walk to his seat looking sheepish and a bit disoriented, as though surprised once again to see all these people here, on account of him. He had on the same navy blazer, pale shirt, yellow tie, pleated khakis, and loafers he'd worn for most of the trial. His freshly washed hair stuck up in wavy little corn-colored flips around his ears where it had been towel-dried. The faint scent of Johnson's baby shampoo wafted toward me. After a moment, he twisted around in his chair. His handsome face brightened when our eyes connected.

We gave each other the high sign.

Nick Shawde turned to the witness. "Now I grant you, Jeff's scholastic record's mighty impressive, Miz Nadine," he said, blithely exchanging his New York accent for something softer, more comfortable, as though it were as easy as stepping out of three-hundred-buck loafers into warm, fuzzy slippers. He smiled benignly at the woman. "But, apart from that, what was he *like?*"

"Well, I'd say he was jest about the perfect all-American boy," Jeff's high-school guidance counselor told the attorney.

Darla Tate, who had met Turner when they volunteered together at the ASPCA, testified that he was compassionate, gentle almost to a fault. "And it wannit just the animals he was good to, either," Darla told the courtroom. "Why, Jeff Turner kept friendly with every girl he ever dated, even the homely ones."

Turner's former art teacher, a tiny, concave-chested woman of about sixty with the shrewd, sunken gaze of a rhesus monkey, declared Jeff to have the "pure, innocent soul of an artist." "I give private lessons, and take on very few *chil-dren*," she said, separating the syllables as if one was more distasteful than the other, "but in Jefferson's case, I just had to make an exception."

None of this was news to me, of course. During my early research, I spent a whole month in Turner's hometown trying to get somebody to say something bad about him. No one ever did. I took it with a grain of salt. The way I figured, so what if he drew pretty pictures, and his neighbors said he was nice? John Wayne Gacy's second favorite hobby was painting; and just about everybody I interviewed for *Dust to Dust* swore Harold Beech—the monster who buried little Dierdre Purdy alive, and left her to die—was an all-around, stand-up fellow. Jefferson Turner might have been the proverbial boy-next-door. But in the neighborhoods I frequented, the boy-next-door usually turned out to be an axe murderer.

It took me a long while to think he was any different.

5

That first day, visiting him in jail, there wasn't a shadow of a doubt in my mind that Jeff Turner was the Holy Ghost.

He sat on the other side of the plate-glass window looking even younger than he had in the lineup. "Can I get you anything?" he asked. "A Coke, maybe, or a glass of wine?" For a split second I thought, Oh great, here comes the insanity plea. But then he laughed, and his body realigned itself—head bowed, shoulders slumping—as though the sheer humiliation of this situation were weighing him down.

"Jeff, my name is—" I began, stiffly.

"I know who you are." He smiled. His teeth were straight and white. "I try never to miss *The New York Times* book section. Pretty lame, huh? Reading your reviews but not your books?"

"I get partial royalties for that sort of thing," I said, still trying to digest the fact that this farmboy in prison blue read *The New York Times* Book Review.

He seemed to relax. "You may not know this," he said, "but you and I once had a pretty heavy relationship goin' for, oh, I'd say, almost two weeks."

I decided he was loony-tunes after all.

"Yes, ma'am," Jeff continued, easily. "After I read that *People* article they did on you a few years back, I decided you were just about the most beautiful, fascinating female in the world. I imagined us meeting, get this, at one of your book signings. As you might expect, it was love at first sight. Yeah, we were quite an item for a while, in my head, at least—" The look on my face stopped him cold. "Ever do that?" he asked, a little sheepishly.

"Can't say that I have."

"You should try it sometime. See, that way, if you say something dumb, why, you just go back and replay the scene in your mind till you get it right. Like I wish I could now—" He ended with another embarrassed laugh. "No offense, but meeting you was a lot better in my dreams. At least I wasn't in prison."

"Do you often dream of meeting women you don't know, Jeff?" I tried to finesse the question.

"If you're asking me whether I live in a fantasy world," he replied, "the answer is no." He leaned closer to the glass. "Look, I'm not used to people putting a sinister spin onto everything I say, okay? All of a sudden, I tell you I had a crush on Chrissie Evert in the third grade, and it proves I'm some kind of psycho stalker."

He looked down at his hands. "It probably wasn't too smart of me, going off about you and that article, and my dumb fantasy. So I'm not smart. That doesn't make me a criminal. It was just my clumsy way of saying . . . I admire you."

"So what happened?" I asked. He looked puzzled. "You said our relationship lasted only two weeks."

"Oh. It was the age difference," he said, so naturally I was charmed in spite of myself. "You told me I had some growing up to do, then you kissed me and got into your big black limo and drove off into the sunset"—he smiled at this imagined memory—"and I went back to thinking that Jolie Brenner—who I happened to be dating at the time—was just about the most beautiful, fascinating female in the world."

We lapsed into an oddly comfortable silence. "Well, since we go way back, I guess you know why I'm here," I said finally.

"Yes, ma'am." He nodded solemnly. "I guess I do. But I didn't kill anybody. It wasn't me."

I pulled out the standard line. "I'm not a lawyer, Jeff, and I'm not a judge. I've got no more loyalties than that fly over there on that wall." Of course there was no fly, but he didn't look. They never did. "I'm just someone who'll listen to all sides," I told him, "and draw my own conclusions."

"Sounds fair, Miz Quinn," he said.

I said, "Look, I'm Garner. Or Quinn. Or hey, lady. Just drop the Miz, and don't ever call me ma'am again, okay?"

"Lady'll do." He smiled. "I'm Jeff. Bird to the folks at home."

"Where'd that come from?"

"Probably had something to do with the fact I was skinnier than all get out as a kid." He grinned. "That, and the way I am with animals."

"You have a lot of pets?"

"Used to. Most were just bad-off critters people dropped by. Sparrows. Kittens. Dogs with three legs, that couldn't see, that kind of thing. I'd find them in shoe boxes, or wrapped in bloody blankets on the porch.

"See," he went on, "back home, there's still pretty much a rural mentality. You know, animals are there to do something—to work, to produce, be useful. If they can't, then, well, the general thinking is, just kill 'em." A flicker of sadness passed over his handsome face. "But after a while, it got around about me, so folks'd leave 'em in the middle of the night over at our place."

"And you took care of them?" I asked.

"I took care of them"—he nodded—"the best I could."

The guard lumbered toward us, about as subtle as a digital watch alarm playing Dixie. Jeff looked panicked suddenly. "One more thing—" He was imploring with his eyes.

"Yes?"

"Anybody you write about ever turn out to be innocent?"

"Not yet," I told him.

He flashed his dimples. "Y'all believe there could be a first time?"

"I'll do my best to keep an open mind," I promised, watching as the guard cuffed him roughly on the shoulder and led him away.

6

Myrna, North Carolina, the town where Jeff Turner had spent the first twenty years of his life, was ninety miles south of Raleigh, and a million miles from nowhere. Whenever I picture it in my mind, the images I call up are always sepia-tinted, the hue of tobacco leaves hung too long to dry, of burnt fields, and paint-peeled barns. Even the sky, as I remember, seemed devoid of color.

Instead of booking a room at the Holiday Inn on the highway, I'd opted to stay with Turner's mother, Varlie. The minute I pulled the rental car into that dusty driveway, I regretted my decision. Jeff said his grandfather had once eked out a living farming tobacco here, but the fields that stretched before me hadn't been tended in years. Two curing barns appeared on the verge of falling down, and the farmhouse itself was a monument to neglect, as though decades of relentless sun and wind had dried up all the life inside, had just dried it up and blown it away.

Several chapters of *All Through the Night* are devoted to Jeff Turner's childhood, to Myrna, and the people I met there. But many of the most vivid impressions I have about that particular time, the month I spent with Varlie while doing my initial research, would never make it into the book. More than the interviews, more than anything anyone who knew Jeff said, I remember those long evenings at the Turner farmhouse—the sealed quiet of the place; the interior of rooms lit haphazardly by the cool, blue glow of an open refrigerator, by the flicker of a television, by yellow slices of lamp-light under doors. I remember walking with Varlie at night, out past the chicken coops, to the small cemetery plot where Jeff's grandaddy was buried. I also remember reading Jeff's letters at the desk in his old bedroom, surrounded by his pen-and-ink drawings, his posters and pennants, the long, linked row of his Sunday school pins. And I remember feeling strangely touched.

I'd asked him to write, and every day the letters arrived, mine and Varlie's, postmarked from the Richland County jail.

> Lady,
> Thanks for those art supplies. I've already done pastel por-
> traits of Bobby and Jimmy Harold, and the new guard wants me
> to copy a photograph of his fiancée. I keep flashing on how
> things'll change if I'm shipped off to some penitentiary. I don't
> want to have to spend the next forty years drawing tattoos on a
> long line of lifers just so they won't rape me.
> The people here have been very patient with my somewhat
> meager talents. I might not do so well with some dude who's
> serving time for shooting six people in a liquor store. Wonder
> how you tell one of those guys that the pen-and-ink of his
> mother isn't done yet? *Very tactfully,* I reckon.

I'd begun to like Jeff Turner, and that made me very wary, very guarded. The truth was, I wanted him to be guilty. I'd allowed the book to get ahead of me: *All Through the Night* was taking on a life of its own, with Jeff Turner as an integral part of the plot.

Even so, it bothered me that no forensic evidence linked him to the crimes. The Holy Ghost was into latex: latex gloves, latex condoms. Except for a residue of greasepaint and the presence of some black threads (the kind used to make priests' cassocks, the lab report said), he might just as well have been a real ghost, for all he'd left behind. Nor could I explain Jeff's apparent alibis for the murders. But whenever I was plagued by a misgiving, I reminded myself that Susan Trevett's identification of the boy was the ultimate clincher.

And yet it was Susan Trevett who troubled me the most.

Since the attack, she'd become tabloid journalism's flavor of the month. To the prosecutor's dismay, she appeared on a dizzying round of talk shows and sensational news programs, telling her story to whomever would listen, and—what worried me—changing it with every telling.

I asked Jack to keep track of her while I was in Myrna. "She whipped off her blouse during the Howard Stern pay-per-view," he told me during one of our phone conversations. "She let Howard run his fingers over the scars."

"Oh God," I sighed.

"Yeah." Jack's voice turned pensive. "It was quite a sight."

When I called the defense attorney's office, Nick Shawde got on the horn, ecstatic. "I love this girl!" he crowed. "I couldn't do a better job of discrediting a witness myself!" Then he sobered, adding, "When you gettin' back from the boonies, Garny? I miss you." I told him, in the most ominous tones I could muster, that in a few weeks he'd be anxious to get rid of me.

The Ghost's first victim, a nineteen-year-old French major at the University of South Carolina named Janna Mayer, had been murdered in the bedroom of her ground-floor apartment in the early-morning hours of September 17, 1993. Officers on the scene mentioned hearing an eerie sound emanating from the bedroom. Apparently a music box had fallen off the dresser during the struggle. The melody of a child's lullaby filled the room with false brightness, playing on and on, just inches from where the dead girl was found—

Sleep my love
And peace attend thee
All through the night
Guardian angels
God will send thee
All through the night—

At first, I'll admit, the music box thing was nothing more to me than a creative hook: the perfect title for the book. It wasn't until the very end of my stay at the Turner farmhouse that the lullaby began to haunt me. Just before sleep, I'd give in to it. I'd sit by the window in the boy's darkened room, and let it play through my mind—

Sleep my love
And peace attend thee
All through the night

I thought about Jeff, vehemently insisting that he couldn't have killed Janna or the other girls, that he'd been working in the printing plant all through those nights.

Guardian angels
God will send thee
All through the night—

I thought about Janna Mayer's last moment, when the terrible realization hit—that there'd be no guardian angels this night. I pictured the scene over and over again, until I was there with her, until I *was* her, and it was happening to me: the cold flash of blade . . . the clean tear of nightgown . . . the crosses etched deeply into flesh . . . the words roaring through my head—

in nomine Patris, et Filii,
et Spiritus Sancti . . .

I stared out into the darkness at the moon, willing it into a waxy, greasepainted face; and then I squinted, trying desperately to see Jeff Turner's fine features somewhere just beneath its cratered surface.

One night I returned to the farmhouse quite late. I let myself in the front door and found Varlie asleep in front of the television, stockinged feet up on the old recliner. Her legs were a knotted purple network of veins. Before I could tiptoe down the hall to my room, she sensed my presence and sat up, nearly upsetting the bowl of soup in her lap.

"Didn't hear y'all come in," she apologized.

I looked at her, wondering if this could've been my face, after poverty and despair cracked it into a thousand broken eggshell pieces. I said, "I didn't mean to wake you."

She moved her legs heavily off the chair. "Just restin' my feet." She held up her bowl. "There's some more Campbell's on the stove, if you like."

"Thanks, I already ate." I sat down on the sagging sofa, Varlie's abject loneliness reeling me in. For the first time I had a sense of how it must have been for her, living here after Jeff left for Columbia. His presence would have added color to these rooms. I imagined him walking down the long hall, toward his bedroom, whistling maybe, turning on lights as he went, unsettling the dust on the furniture with the steady clomp of his shoes.

Varlie picked up the remote, switching from a syndicated sitcom to "Inside Edition."

Susan Trevett's face flooded the small screen. It took me a moment to recognize her. For one thing, her hair was different, big and blown out, like pale cotton candy, and she was wearing thick, spiky false eyelashes. Oddly enough, this made her appear even more waifish than she had before.

The reporter asked, "How would you say the attack changed your life?"

Susan tilted her head, as though all that hair was suddenly too heavy. "We-eell," she replied, very carefully, "all in all, with the TV,

---

and the magazine offers, I'd say it was positive." She was speaking much too slowly. *Shit*, I thought, *the girl's loaded*. I felt ashamed to be sitting here with Mrs. Turner, watching Susan Trevett make a spectacle of herself.

Trevett looked into the camera and smiled. "I always knew I'd be famous," she said. "If it wannit for this trial, it'd have been for something else."

Varlie zapped the picture from the small screen. "I reckon I'm goin' to bed."

"Me too," I said quietly. "Tomorrow I'm going to head down to Columbia to see Jeff."

Jeff's letters were always so upbeat and positive, it was that much more of a shock when I saw him again. He'd lost a lot of weight, and there was a new listlessness in his voice.

"I keep having these dreams about Grandaddy," he told me.

"Tell me about him."

"Well, he just about raised me up after Daddy disappeared, and Mama started having to take on jobs. I suppose he was what people mean when they say salt of the earth." A flicker of a smile played over his lips. "Taught me everything I know about carpentry and machinery. Animals, too. Farmed tabacca with his own hands till he was seventy and never once took a puff off a cigarette. Wouldn't allow it in the house. Alcohol, neither.

"There aren't any more left like him now," he sighed. "His sort of small farmer. They're a dyin' breed."

"When exactly did he pass on?" I asked, pulling out the all-purpose euphemism as though it were the one I usually used, instead of *cooled . . . kicked . . . bought the big one*.

"I was twelve, I guess," he said.

"So from then on, you were the man of the family?"

"Yeah." He tossed his head back, as if trying to force the tears back into their allotted slots. "Botched up that job pretty good, didn't I?"

"I don't know. Did you?"

"Sometimes I feel like I'm trapped in an old movie, you know, *The Wrong Man,* and I'm Jimmy Stewart, and nobody believes me. Not even you."

I let that go by. "Tell me about your dreams," I prompted.

"Even now," Jeff said, "they seem so real. Grandaddy's always standing. Leaning over my bunk in the cell. I can feel him looking at me, and then I open my eyes, or at least I dream that I do." His voice sounded far away, like down a well. "He asks me how this could have happened. And I say, honest to gosh, Grandaddy, I don't know. I just don't know."

He pressed the heels of his hands into his eyes. "He always believed the Lord would provide, you know? That you could make yourself a life, if you worked hard enough. Even after it started turnin' on him, when the big government-run farms started killin' off his business, he never lost faith.

"But in my dreams, he looks so beat up. Sadder than I ever saw him. Like this is one thing he just can't understand. Over and over, he asks me, Did you kill those girls, Jefferson? and I say, No, Grandaddy, I swear I didn't.

"Then he comes real close, so I can just 'bout see him in the dark, with his pinstripe overalls, and the red hat he always wore, just like himself, and he asks me, he says, Then why are you here, son? And I try, Garner, I really do, but it's like I can't move my lips, like nothing comes out to answer him. Because I don't know. I just don't know . . . I don't . . ."

When he laid his head on the table and sobbed, I touched his shoulder. It was an automatic gesture of comfort, not meant to signal anything much; but he found my hand, quickly, without looking, and tucked it under him. I felt the cold metal of the tabletop, the texture of his skin against my palm. We stayed that way for several seconds before I slipped my hand away. Gently.

7

On my last Sunday in Myrna I accompanied Varlie
Turner to church. Looking back, this was something I
should have done earlier. Chalk my procrastination up to the fact
that I'm a lapsed Catholic—which means I have a sort of love-hate,
jilted-lover ambivalence toward anything that smacks of organized
religion. I was totally unprepared for the Myrna First Baptist.

Drab and boxy, painted mud brown, it looked more like a VFW
hall than a house of worship. A theater marquee with the words ARE
YOU FORGIVEN? spelled out in raised white letters announced the
time of the service and the minister's name, B bby H ward Brigham,
Past r, the church apparently being short a few o's.

The interior was another revelation. Jeff Turner's home church
had no altar, just a plain wood table topped by a vase of plastic
chrysanthemums. A metal lectern served as pulpit. There were no
stained-glass windows, no statues of saints, no crucifixes. Pastor
Bobby Howard Brigham turned out to be a florid-faced man in a
baggy brown suit, who looked as if he might sell used cars Monday

through Friday, which I found out later was exactly what he did.

My heart began to beat wildly. "Where's the Catholic church in town?" I whispered to Varlie.

"Can't say there is one," she whispered back.

"Where do Catholics go to attend mass?"

Varlie shook her head. "No Catholics around these parts," she said, "that I ever knew." Then, perhaps sensing my urgency, she added, "We had a Jewish family once. The Petermans. Stevie played on the baseball team over at the junior high 'fore they all moved back down to Chapel Hill."

All through the service Susan Trevett's words roared in my head. *He wore black*, she'd told me, and *he's whispering this mumbo-jumbo stuff in my ear, Dominoes, Nabisco;* so by the time I stood with the others for the final blessing, it was as though I'd experienced a kind of epiphany.

I called Jack from the nearest payphone.

"Garner, thank God it's you—" he began.

"There are no Catholics in Myrna." I cut him off, breathlessly. "Jeff Turner doesn't know Latin. He's never seen a Catholic mass."

"Yeah, well, get this." The excitement in Jack's voice matched my own. "I just hung up with some guy who says he's Susan Trevett's husband."

"What?"

"You heard me," he said. "Guy named Shelby Cox. He says he and Susan were married this morning."

"And here we weren't invited." I tried to sound flippant, but my pulse was racing. Instinctively I knew. I knew something big had happened.

"Yeah," Jack agreed. "Apparently it was quite an event. A second after the preacher pronounced them man and wife, the bride fell to the ground and started confessing her many sins. Topping off the list was that she once told a lie."

"What do you mean—?"

"According to the new hubby, Susan accepted the Lord as her personal Savior," Jack chuckled, "and all hell's broke loose. It sounds like you should get down there as fast as you can."

8

I found the house, an unassuming split-level in a vast,
treeless tract of unassuming split-levels, twenty miles
out of Columbia. Shelby Cox met me at the door. He was a big man,
with soft, pink hands and a jowlish chin. "She's in the family room,"
he told me, his voice an even mix of deference and concern, as
though I were a physician called to treat a gravely ill patient. I followed him down a set of stairs.

Susan was cowering on the sofa in the corner. She wore a calf-
length dress of cream-colored polyester and a limp corsage. Her face
looked as if it had been buffed raw in a car wash. Shelby dropped to
one knee and put his arm around her. I couldn't help thinking he
seemed unusually serene for a man who'd just discovered that his
wife of only minutes hadn't been disfigured by a psychopath, but had
instead confessed to a churchful of wedding guests that her past had
been one great big old sexual binge, that she herself had carved

crosses into her skin as some sort of bizarre penitence, and that—on a whim—she'd pointed a finger at a totally innocent man.

"The Lord forgives the guilty, and washes sin away from the blackest of hearts," Susan said, by way of a greeting, as she rocked back and forth under Shelby's steady arm.

"That's great," I replied. "I'm glad He does." I crouched next to her, turning over her hand to inspect the crosshatched scars, still puffy and the same angry pink as Susan's eyes. "But are you really saying you did this to yourself?"

"The marks are there because of me"—she rocked faster—"because of my lustful and adulterous life."

"Why would you cut yourself?"

"My body is the temple of the Lord," she responded. "The temple must be cleared of all that is unclean and unholy. *My house shall be called the house of prayer; but ye have made it a den of thieves.*"

This was going nowhere fast. I shot a glance toward Shelby, who had the desperate look of someone who could use a potty break. "Maybe Susan would like a glass of water," I suggested.

"Water," the poor man repeated, gratefully. "Yes, surely. Be right back, darlin'." He kissed his wife on the forehead. Her flinch was almost imperceptible. I watched him go back up the stairs before taking a seat beside her. "How long have you known Shelby?"

"What does that matter?" Susan cried, defiantly; then, the change, her eyes filling with tears. "He's *good* to me," she said simply.

"What about Jeff Turner?" I asked. "Are you saying he isn't the Holy Ghost?"

"The Lord knows Mr. Turner is an innocent man," Susan Trevett Cox said, her voice rising and rising. "Innocent as a lamb! I have seen the Truth and it has set me free!"

"But you picked him out of a lineup. You described his van," I reminded her, "the inside and everything."

Susan Cox stood, thrusting a scarred wrist in my face. "*And the Lord set a mark upon Cain,*" she cried. "*Resist not evil; but whosoever shall smite thee on thy right cheek, turn to him the other also.*"

Shelby had come back with the water. He stood to one side, his face devoid of surprise as his bride broke into a strange litany of nonsense syllables that sounded, to me, like a page of Dr. Seuss being read backward.

"Hey, Suse," I tried to joke, "help me out with the translation."

Her voice ebbed and swelled like the sea. *"Whether in the body, I cannot tell,"* she cried. *"Or whether out of the body, I cannot tell: God knoweth."*

"What does that mean?" I wanted to know.

She pointed a small, childish finger, the nail bitten to the bone. *"Judge not,"* she screamed, *"that ye be not judged!"*

For once, I could think of no snappy repartee suitable to the occasion.

"What happens now?" Shelby Cox asked quietly. The blind trust in his eyes made me want to cry.

9

I glanced down at my watch. Three forty-five. This would surely be the last witness called today.

"Could you state your name and occupation for the court, please?" Nick Shawde asked.

"Tom Kelland," the man on the stand replied. "I'm the, uh, night manager for Vickers Offset and Printing."

"You were Jeff Turner's boss?"

"Yes, sir," Mr. Kelland said.

"How did you come to hire Jeff?" Nick Shawde asked.

"Well, sir, uh, Loy Meachum, up in Myrna, wrote me," Tom Kelland said. "Mr. Meachum's the principal at Myrna High School. He and my daddy go way back. Anyhow, Loy said he had a boy graduated few years back was coming to Columbia to take up art over at USC and could we maybe use him at the print shop. Well, as it happened, Mr. Vickers, that's, uh, the owner, he was looking for a night pressman around then, and it worked out real well, with Jeff taking classes during the day and all."

"Did Jeff perform satisfactorily on the job?"

"Lordy, yes." Mr. Kelland broke into a smile. "Jeff was a hard worker! Always on time, meeting the deadlines. Nights is tough on some people. I mean, when it's busy, you're on your own with nobody to help you, and when it's slow, well, the tendency is to goof off. But not Jeff. He was always one for doing extra. Had an artistic touch about him, I guess you'd say."

"So you had no complaints?"

"No, sir. None at all."

"How long did Jeff Turner work at Vickers?"

Kelland had obviously rehearsed this part. "He came, uh, on the nineteenth of August, 1993, and stayed until they . . . you know . . . until the arrest." Everyone in the courtroom understood how critical these dates were. The first girl had been killed on September 17, a month after Jeff Turner arrived in Columbia.

Nick paced in front of the witness stand. "And what were his hours?"

"Ten to six," Mr. Kelland replied.

"That's ten P.M.," the attorney stressed, "to six A.M.?"

"Yes, sir, that's correct." This was a major point. All the murders had been committed between eleven at night and three in the morning.

Shawde looked directly at the jury, enunciating each word carefully. "And during all that time—roughly one year, from August to August—did Jeff Turner ever miss a night at work?"

"No, sir," said Tom Kelland, loudly. "Not a one."

Nick matched the man's volume. "Mr. Kelland, on the night that Susan Trevett was attacked, where was Jefferson Turner?"

"In the print shop, working."

"How do you know?"

"I seen him," Mr. Kelland said solemnly. "He signed in and signed out just like usual. His name's in the book for all them other nights, too—"

"Objection!" The prosecutor, Charlie Biggs, was on his feet.

Judge Stuart waved a hand, impatiently. "Sustained. You will confine yourself to answering the question at hand, sir," he reminded Kelland, before motioning Shawde to proceed.

"So you're saying Jefferson Turner was in the print shop working on the third of August, 1993—the night that Susan Trevett was allegedly attacked?"

"Yes, sir." The man nodded his head vehemently.

Nick Shawde smiled. "No further questions."

Charlie Biggs stood, halfheartedly. "Mr. Kelland," he began, "were you in the same room with Jeff Turner during the entirety of his shift on the night Susan Trevett was attacked?"

A look of impatience crossed Kelland's face. "Not the whole time, uh, no—"

"Where were you?"

"In my office," Kelland said. "But I come into the print room, regular."

"Then it would have been possible," Biggs went on, "for Mr. Turner to leave the building for, oh, say, an hour, without your noticing?"

"It weren't likely—"

"I didn't say likely," the prosecutor reprimanded, "I said possible."

Tom Kelland shifted in his seat. "Like my mama used to say, anything's possible, Mr. Biggs," he said sulkily. "I s'pose maybe even pigs could fly."

As he had every Friday since the trial had begun, Judge Nelson Stuart looked at his watch at exactly four o'clock, shook his head, sighed deeply, and called a recess until ten o'clock the following Monday morning.

"Come on, Garn, let me buy you a drink," Nick Shawde offered.

"Not today," I said. "I'm heading to the airport right after I talk to Jeff." I'd struck up an acquaintance with the guards who took

Turner to and from the courtroom. They usually let me have a few minutes with him before they transported him back to Kirkland.

"Hey, lady." Jeff waved his cuffed hands awkwardly as I entered the holding room. "What do you think?"

"Looking good," I told him.

"What about that last thing with old Tom?" His blue eyes were anxious.

"Biggs fumbled it," I said, annoyed that Shawde's sports metaphors were creeping into my own vocabulary. "The prosecution's just going through the motions. You'd be in decent shape, even without Susan's testimony."

Turner's face brightened. "Think so?" He leaned forward. "That's thanks to you, you know."

"Shawde's the one—"

"*You,*" he repeated. "More'n Mrs. Cox. More'n Nick Shawde, or Tom Kelland, or anybody. You were the first to believe in me."

"Don't get mushy until the jury has their say," I protested, uncomfortable with such unbridled gratitude. "That's the only thing that matters."

Jeff's gaze shifted to my leather tote. "Heading north to see your little girl?"

"Yeah. What about you?" It was a game we played.

"Aw, I thought I'd hole up in a little room somewhere." He grinned. "Bang out a few license plates, eat some greasy food."

"Sounds tantalizing."

"Got a few good books to tide me over, though." He was working his way through my bestsellers with a zeal I found almost embarrassing. "It's your descriptions of the way the victims must've felt that really blow me away," Jeff said, as though we were trading insights at a writing seminar, instead of waiting for the van that would take him back to jail.

"You put your readers right into the action," he went on, "make 'em feel all closed up and suffocated, like Dulcie Mariah's little boy, in that closet, and poor Deirdre Purdy from *Dust to Dust* after Harold Beech buried her alive."

"I'm drawn to crimes that play on my own deepest fears," I admitted.

He leaned forward, in that overly earnest way of his. "What is it about my case? What do you see in this one?"

"The chance to do some good, for once." It was the truth. If Jeff Turner hadn't attacked Susan Trevett, then the Holy Ghost was still out there somewhere. I didn't want the public to forget that.

The guard's walkie-talkie squawked. "Your chauffeured limousine's here, Jeffie boy," he announced.

I stood, shouldering my bag. "Keep your chin up," I told him.

"I'll be okay." He smiled. "Say hey to that Yankee daughter of yours for me, will ya?"

10

My flight was delayed due to weather conditions in
Newark. Because of some mix-up with the car com-
pany, I had to wait another hour while they dispatched a driver. By
the time the rented limo left the Garden State Parkway, golfball-
sized hail was hammering its roof; visibility cut off sharply at the
hood. I guided the driver down the winding roadway, talking him
through each curve, relying on a sense other than sight, mentally
counting off the distance between invisible town and invisible
town—a whole peninsula kidnapped by the mist—until we reached
Rumson. "It won't be much farther now," I lied.

When we finally reached my private road it was all but
impassable. The massive gate looked unreal, untethered to solid
earth, a manifestation of fog and sleet. "All the way to the end," I
directed.

The windows were fogged. The driver started to wipe the inside
of the windshield with his handkerchief. "Jesus," he muttered under

his breath; then, perhaps thinking of his tip, he added politely, "You sure are off the beaten path."

"Yes," I said. Tall pines hovered on either side of us, their drooping boughs forming a dark tunnel. I didn't tell the driver that conifers were the first to topple over in strong winds such as this. He was already nervous enough. As we emerged from the trees, I heard his sigh over the clack of the windshield wipers—relief mingled with something like awe. The house seemed a mirage, rising out of the massive stones of the seawall. Mist had flattened the roof, obscuring the guest house and office so that they looked like the tumbledown rubble of some ancient fortified city.

"Home," I said, more to myself than to him.

Cilda opened the front door in her robe and slippers. "The child's in bed," she said, in the accusatory tone I'd known her to use whenever she was frightened. Her strong arms bustled me out of my raincoat. "Fever a 'undred and two."

Years ago, in my father's house, Cilda's official title had been housekeeper; but she was also *my* keeper, my nurse and teacher, alternately the blessing and bane of my existence. She had abruptly quit her job at Dudley's the day Temple was born, showing up, unannounced, at my New York apartment, with two old suitcases and a large aloe plant.

I loved her for that. For leaving Dudley for me.

"Have you called Dr. Boden?"

"She won't 'ave none of 'im," Cilda said. "Says 'e's only a baby doctor." While I was covering Jeff Turner's trial, my daughter had outgrown her pediatrician. I stored this piece of information away, along with the many other milestones passed in my absence.

The nightlight was on in Temple's room. She was fast asleep, head crooked to one side, lips parted, her breath slipping through in shallow little rushes. I crouched at the side of the bed, trying to reacquaint myself with her face: the length of her lashes, the slope of her nose, her mouth, her skin. It never failed to astonish me. Every book

I'd ever written was the result of constant editing and revision. My daughter was the only thing that had come out right the first time.

Her forehead felt hotter than a hundred and two. I sensed Cilda's shadow filling up the door behind me. "You better get sometin' to eat," she whispered.

I waved her away. "I'm fine. Go to bed." She nodded. I listened to the squoosh of her slippers on the stairs, the wheeze of Temple's breathing, the faint crashing of waves, the tick of the clock.

Home.

That whole night I slept on the floor next to my child. Just as morning broke, I crept into my own room. She never even knew I'd been there.

"What'd the doctor say?"

"Strep. She's sleeping again." I'd waited for Temple to drift off before grabbing a sweater and heading out the back door. The rain had left the flagstones slick, but there was a patch of clear blue sky overhead; I was pleasantly surprised to find Jack in the office on a Saturday.

"Have you decided what you're going to do about this?" He handed me an invitation, bold black letters on white—DANE BLACK-MOOR—PAWNS, it said.

"Leave it for now," I told him.

"It's tonight. If you're not going, I should—"

"Leave it."

Jack pulled on his beard, a sign of mild annoyance. "Blackmoor's going to be our next, isn't he?"

"I'm not thinking about the next one yet," I said, pulling a Diet Coke from the refrigerator. "I've still got to finish *All Through the Night*, remember?"

He shrugged. "Seems in pretty good shape to me." I couldn't argue that point. Except for the ending, which would be provided by the jury, the book was virtually written. Get 'em out while they were hot was my editor's philosophy.

I sipped directly from the can. "Did you ever think I might want to take off for a while to hang out with my kid?"

Our eyes met. It was clear the thought of me as a stay-at-home mom didn't fly with him. He said, "Next book, I want more responsibility."

"Okay," I said. "From now on, you can also make the beds and do the dishes." I caught a glimpse of his face. "That was a joke, Jack."

He wasn't laughing. "These past couple of years have been great, but I want to be more than your personal secretary. I'm ready to do research, maybe handle a few interviews."

Jack Tatum always seemed to catch me unawares. He'd come into my life out of nowhere, simply showed up on my doorstep and somehow managed to convince me that—more than anything else in the world—I needed an assistant. One by one he'd shot down my misgivings. Salary wasn't an issue; he had some savings stashed away. He didn't mind giving up his Manhattan apartment; rents were cheaper on the Jersey shore. He wanted to learn to write true-life crime, he told me; he wanted to learn from the best. That was Jack—an oddly attractive mix of flattery and pushiness. I watched him do it again now.

"Obviously, any contribution I made to the book would be minimal," he said earnestly. "I'd do the donkeywork. It would free you up for other things."

I felt a surge of childish emotion, the sort of territorial instinct that makes eight-year-olds trace property lines in the dirt—*this is mine and you can't come over*. The expression on Jack's face was enough to let me know I'd better reconsider if I wanted to keep him.

"Okay," I said. "We'll see how it goes." I wanted to keep him.

Jack walked with me back to the house. Temple was sitting at the kitchen table, looking much better. We played three-hand poker until dinnertime. Cilda had made a roast, and Temple asked if Jack could eat with us. I said fine, if it was all right with him. By the time he left it was after seven, and Temple was running a fever again.

"Beddy-bye for you, kiddo," I told her. She made all the usual protests, but weakly. We walked upstairs together and I tucked her in, pulling a chair up beside her bed.

"I bet I know what you're gonna do," she said with a sleepy little smile.

Her words took me aback. "What?" I asked, trying not to sound guilty.

"You're gonna write a book about the hand they found in that statue." She edged herself up on her elbows.

"Who told you that?"

"Nobody. I just guessed."

"Well, you guessed wrong," I said.

She rolled toward me, one hand propping up her head. "Do you know him? Dane Blackmoor?"

"Temple," I said sternly, "just go to sleep."

But she wouldn't drop it. "Because I thought you might." She sat up now. "On TV last night, they were interviewing famous people, you know, about whether they thought he did it, cut off someone's hand, and Grandpa Dudley was on"—the old, familiar anger surged; this was the way she knew her grandfather, as a sound bite, a legal expert who occasionally popped up on "Larry King"—"and I could tell by the way he talked that *he* knew Dane Blackmoor, so I thought maybe you'd met him, too, at Grandpa's."

I wanted to ask what Dudley said; instead, I pushed her shoulders gently back onto the pillow. "Shhh." I stayed there until she lapsed into sleep.

It was ten after eight.

As though this was a sudden decision, and not something that had been in the back of my mind all day, I went into my room, peeled off my jeans and sweater, and pulled a very short, very tight, very red dress off its hanger.

I found Cilda downstairs in her room, knitting by the light of a television sitcom. The click of the needles punctuated the show's dialogue like a tiny, tinny laughtrack. "I'm going out," I said. "There's a thing I have to attend in New York tonight." A *thing*.

The Volvo was gassed up, the city a little more than an hour away. It wasn't until I reached the turnpike that I allowed myself to think about Temple's words—*I thought maybe you'd met him, at Grandpa's*—and to finally answer her question, silently, while she slept miles away, unheeding, unhearing.

THE STORY

THE NANNY FOUND LITTLE CHARLIE LYING ON THE FLOOR OF THE SMALL CLOSET, A BLUE FRINGED BABY BLANKET WRAPPED AROUND HIS ARMS AND TORSO LIKE A WINDING-SHEET. HIS ONCE CHERUBIC FACE WAS A CONGEALED MASK OF BLOOD AND TISSUE. HE'D BEEN BEATEN BEYOND RECOGNITION. . . .

IN HIS AUTOPSY REPORT, THE CORONER REMARKED THAT THE CHILD HAD SUSTAINED SEVERAL INJURIES IN THE MONTHS PRIOR TO HIS DEATH, NOTABLE AMONG THEM: TWO SCARS FROM CIGARETTE BURNS ON THE INNER FOREARMS, AND A CONTUSION OF THE RIGHT SHOULDER.

EXCERPT FROM *ROCK-A-BYE BABY:*
THE BALLAD OF DULCIE MARIAH
BY GARNER QUINN
(RANDOM HOUSE, 1981)

SOME PEOPLE HAVE QUESTIONED MY MOTIVES IN WRITING THIS BOOK. THEY SEE IT AS A SLUR ON MY FATHER'S NAME, AN ATTACK ON HIS REPUTATION. LET ME SAY THAT I NEVER SET OUT TO UNDERMINE DUDLEY QUINN'S INTEGRITY AS A DEFENSE ATTORNEY. I SIMPLY SET OUT TO FIND THE TRUTH. THIS BOOK IS NOT A PERSONAL VENDETTA. IF ANYTHING, IT'S LATE JUSTICE FOR A LITTLE CHILD. FROM THE BEGINNING, FOR ME, IT WAS ALWAYS ABOUT THE CHILD. . . .

EXCERPT FROM THE PREFACE OF THE SECOND EDITION OF
ROCK-A-BYE BABY: THE BALLAD OF DULCIE MARIAH
BY GARNER QUINN
(POCKET BOOKS, 1983)

1

He came during the summer of 1969, the defining summer of my life.

By that July, all the turbulence of a turbulent decade, the unrest of a restless world, seemed to have gathered forces like some Kansas twister, beating a direct path to our beachfront estate in Spring Lake, New Jersey—coming right up onto our front porch, rattling the house to its foundations, turning everything upside down before winding its way into the sea.

For me, it will always be the summer of the Mariah Trial. The summer I got the Change—as though my body had reacted to what was going on around me by stirring up some excitement of its own. And the summer of Dane Blackmoor. He showed up, quite unexpectedly, one weekend, returning again and again, through the end of August, as if drawn by the scent of blood: the blood of the sensational case Dudley was trying; and, in some strange way, my own.

That he should have come at all seems more astonishing to me now than it did back then. In 1964 Blackmoor's plaster bandage–wrapped sculptures had hit the art world with a force of a Mack truck. He was twenty-six years old, and an instant star. His face was everywhere you looked: on the covers of *Time* and *Life*, inside the pages of *Vogue*, the cold stare, the permanent scowl, a ghost of a scar run amok on his chin, the epitome of physical beauty tamped within violence.

Women, I was discovering, went in for that sort of thing. At thirteen, I myself was singularly unimpressed by the romance of imperfection. The pictures of Blackmoor that sparked *my* interest showed him hurtling from parked limos into clubs, dashing from secret lovenests into fast cars. I envied people who had places to go, and the means to get there. All year long, I stayed put in my father's summer house, like the wicker porch chairs, and the empty hammocks, like the household help—waiting for a time when the great Mr. Quinn would favor us with his presence.

Then Blackmoor came.

I was in the kitchen that morning, as usual, reading the newspaper accounts of the Mariah trial. Dudley's face beamed up at me off the front page, smiling the smile that was so much warmer in black and white than in the flesh.

"Get away from those cookies with them grimy hands," Margaret the cook barked. I wiped the newsprint off on my dress before swiping a chocolate chip off the cooling rack.

"Using her shirttail," Margaret snorted derisively to Cathy, the upstairs maid. "Not that that getup of hers could look any worse."

Cathy stretched lazily on her stool. "You'd think with all his money," she yawned, "he'd buy her some decent clothes."

They always spoke about me that way. As though I were deaf, or retarded, or not even there. When I was little it hurt, but as I got older I found out there were certain advantages to being invisible. If I stayed in the corner, quiet, eating or reading the paper, all sorts of astonishing information passed my way.

"Wonder which one he's bringing with him this week," Margaret said, with a sly wink. I knew she was talking about Dudley and his many ladyfriends. I kept thumbing through the paper, scanning the human-interest story. Dudley was in this picture, too, standing just behind his famous client, the pale halo of her hair obscuring his face. I tried to picture her here in the kitchen, Dulcie Mariah, leaning casually up against the stainless-steel counter, flanked by the pots and pans, the utensils hung in orderly rows, enveloped by the day-after-day tedium of this small world. I wondered if—offhandedly almost—she might let it slip. Whether or not she'd killed her little son, Charlie.

"Ga'ner! Ga'ner Quinn!" Cilda's strong arms pushed open the swinging doors. "What you doing in 'ere this long time?" she demanded in her mean Jamaican Woman voice. Without answering, I ran from the kitchen, into the dining room, through the hall, and out the front door. This was my new way of dealing with Cilda, the flight-not-fight technique. It seemed to be working.

I sat down on the steps, yanking navy pleats over my knees. I would have to speak with Dudley about the pathetic state of my wardrobe. The problem was getting him alone, especially now, with the trial in full swing.

Pete the Handyman appeared from around back, carrying a large black caldron of geraniums. "What's new, Pussycat?" he called, flashing teeth the color of a stained porcelain tub. Pete never just said hello. He said things like "What's the story, Morning Glory?" or "What's up, Doc?" Once I'd found it funny; but since I'd turned thirteen, it was wearing thin.

"Will you take me to the beach?" I asked.

"Can't, Garn." Pete shook his head. "Mr. Quinn's home tonight. Got to get these flowers out."

Mr. Quinn. That was the way they all said it—never "your father," "your old man," "your daddy." It was one of the reasons I'd come up with The Story in the first place. Looking at him today, hunched over and grimy, it was hard to believe that Pete the Handyman once figured prominently in The Story. I'd gotten much pickier since that first time, so picky, in fact, that I hadn't had a candidate in over a month. My longest dry spell ever.

The truth was, there just didn't seem to be very many men who could qualify as my Real Father.

First off, he had to be old enough. Mr. Kelly, my piano teacher, scored high on most counts. He was handsome, intelligent, and he had that fatherly way of putting his arm around me as he demonstrated the left-hand part. At Christmas, he'd even given me a card, not from a box, but the sort you bought separately, especially, at a shop. It read: "TO A SPECIAL GIRL." He'd signed it: "Love, Mr. K."

Love.

Mr. Kelly had seemed just about perfect until I figured out that he would have only been twelve years old when I was born. And there was no doubt about it. Mr. Kelly wasn't the kind of person who would have done It at twelve. Mr. Kelly didn't even seem like the kind of person who had done It at twenty-four.

And so it went. Candidates were either too young or too old. Father Barnes, of course, was a priest, and it just didn't feel right to involve him. Then there was the tutor whom I nixed on account of his strong body odor; and Dudley's partner at the firm, Geoffrey Nash— the biggest disappointment of all. That plotline came to an end the night I asked Dudley why Geoff wasn't married. "Because he's a homosexual, Garner," he told me impatiently. I nodded as though I'd suspected all along. Later, in my room, I pulled out *Webster's* and read:

homosexual

adj. of, relating to, or characterized by a tendency
to direct sexual desire toward another of the same sex

I lay on my bed, shoes off, bare legs up, the toes of my feet tracing designs on the wallpaper, trying to picture Geoffrey Nash as someone who would have such a tendency. I closed my eyes, imagining him kissing another man—Mr. Kelly, or Pete, even Dudley himself—but I could only get to the initial clinch before the camera in my mind stopped clicking. I decided I might have better luck if I found another homosexual to imagine him with. This project occupied much of my time in the days that followed.

But it was boring, always being on the lookout for—as Cathy called them—*queers*. What Geoffrey did in private didn't seem to have anything to do with me. It wasn't like The Story, which, after all, was my life.

Pete had finished arranging the urns of flowers around the porch. "Wanna Juicy Fruit?" He pulled a pack out of his pocket. I took a slice. It was warm and limp from being in his trousers, and its smell was so sweet I could taste it before it was actually in my mouth.

"What's your father like, Pete?" I asked.

He scrunched up his face. "Aw, my old man died a while back."

"Did you love him?"

Pete considered this for a while, then said, "He was just my old man, Garn. I didn't really know him."

I nodded, understanding. Then I told him, "See ya," and headed out toward the front gate. I wondered whether I should risk a run to the beach before Cilda noticed I was gone.

"Hey, kid, com'ere," a man hissed from across the street. I knew all about talking to strangers, but I was bored and lonely. I crossed.

The guy was Elvis-haired and paunchy, with a pale blue polyester suit and an open-collared print shirt, the kind that would pass for silk if you'd never actually seen silk before. He carried a black canvas bag. "You live over there in that big house?" he asked, his voice low and friendly. I suspected he'd offer a lollipop next. That would be time to let out the Tarzan yell.

For now I nodded.

"Listen," he said, "I happen to know that Dane Blackmoor is gonna visit here today." He took out his wallet. It was flat and greasy, embossed with the word *Swank*.

"You look like a smart kid," the man went on, "maybe you could give me a hand." He removed a wrinkled five-dollar bill. "All you gotta do is smuggle me inside the gate, and not say anything to anybody."

"Why?" I asked.

"It's nothin' illegal," he assured me. "I just wanna take some pictures."

I took the money, wondering whether I should shake hands to seal the bargain. Before I could, the guy slipped into a nondescript car. A rental, I noticed, as it pulled away. I tucked the fiver into my pocket and walked back to the house, thinking about what I'd buy with the blood money.

Cilda turned off the vacuum as I went by. "The car is carrying 'imself back tonight. See you do somethin' about that hair." I started hopping up the staircase, one step at a time. "Stop that! You want to wake the 'ouse?" Cilda hissed.

"And you won't?" I tossed my head toward the Hoover.

"About time they get up, sleeping all day," Cilda sniffed, snapping the machine on again.

I walked through the upstairs hall. There were no vacancies today. With the Main Attraction home for the weekend, the place would be swarming with what Dudley called *houseguests* and Cilda called *freeloaders*. Strangers in the house made Cilda nervous. Some mornings she'd come down limping, shooting black looks, warning me to stay away from the man with the 'at, or the woman with the evil little dog that put a spell on her back. I suspected what made Cilda's back hurt had more to do with floor scrubbing than men with hats or old ladies with poodles; but I liked to hear her tales about people who had The Way, so I kept this theory to myself.

I stomped down the corridor, making as much noise as I could without actually banging on the walls. My room was all the way on the end, set off by an enamel plaque with *Garner* scripted in rambling roses. I opened the door, steeling myself against an onslaught of flowers and bows. One of Dudley's women, a French lady named Simone, had recently redecorated the upstairs. She'd promised once it all came together I'd love the florals and chintz, but some pastel deficiency in my brain made me ache for the drab reds and browns of Dudley's study.

I pulled my journal out from under the pillow, sat cross-legged on the bed, and divided a blank page into three columns:

1. MY FATHER IS DEAD.
2. MY FATHER IS ALIVE.
3. DUDLEY QUINN III IS MY FATHER.

Until my conversation with Pete just then, I hadn't considered
that my Real Father might be dead. Under the "DEAD" column I put
a question mark.

I looked at the second column, "MY FATHER IS ALIVE," and wrote
Where? Do I know him? Does he come here? Then I drew a long arrow
down the page, ballooning one word. MOTHER.

Fitting this human trainwreck of a person into The Story was
never easy. I thought about the skinny woman Cilda let in the house
like a stray cat once a year when Dudley was on another coast, the
one who sat in the kitchen gulping tea as if it hurt her throat to swallow until Cilda said, "Kiss your mama goodbye," and I was forced to
produce a cheek, to feel her liquor breath upon it, musty and stale,
like a closet where some small rodent had died.

I leaned back against the headboard, trying to trace the plot
back further, to a time when my mother was young and beautiful,
the way she looked in the black-and-white photograph Dudley kept
locked in the armoire in his bedroom. What had happened to
change her? Had Dudley's coldness forced her to turn elsewhere for
affection? Was she swept away in reckless passion by the man who
was my Real Father? That would explain why Dudley never mentioned her. Why he acted as though she were dead.

My eyes wandered back to the top of the page, to the heading,
"DUDLEY QUINN III IS MY FATHER." For a long time I wrote nothing. As
long as I could remember, Dudley had acted as though I were a
household fixture, something to get *done over* during growth spurts,
the way one reupholsters a chair. No Real Father would treat his
daughter the way he treated me.

If it wasn't for that one time. My tenth birthday.

Cilda had made a cake. Geoffrey Nash came with a big teddy
bear. At dinner, I'd found a package wrapped up in shiny paper and
grosgrain ribbon on the seat of my chair. Inside was a white linen

nightgown with hand-crocheted lace around the collar and cuffs. The card read: "*Happy Birthday, with love from Simone and Daddy,*" at least that's what I thought at the time, though it might have been "*Simone and Dudley*"—when I went back to look it had already been thrown out, so I never knew for sure.

I wore the new gown that night. I remember it was uncommonly warm for May. I pulled aside the comforter and ate the piece of cake with extra roses that Cilda had left on the nightstand, letting the crumbs fall like snowflakes on the clean white sheets. Some time later I woke, aware that the lamp was still on.

Dudley was standing over my bed.

I shut my eyes and stayed very still, the way you would around a wild animal that could be easily startled off. My chest felt funny, just from trying to breathe normally, in and out. He stooped over the bed. Through the curtain of my lashes I could see the outline of his bent shoulders, huge, extinguishing the lamplight. He bent closer. His big hand brushed the hair from my face.

I thought he might kiss me. He'd never kissed me before, not that I could recall, and the very thought set my heart thumping wildly. Maybe he heard because he suddenly pulled back. I wanted to sit up, to cry out, "Daddy, don't go!" but something stopped me.

A tear had fallen from his face onto my forehead.

I let him switch off the lamp, turn the knob of the door, pull it tight. Down the hall I heard Simone's glittery blond tread over the carpet, then the low rumble of Dudley's voice, and her answering giggle. Only after they moved away did I move, running my fingers over my brow, tasting the salt of his tear on them.

Since that night, I'd left my lamp on, with the door slightly ajar every night Dudley was at home. At two or three in the morning, when the last guests had stumbled upstairs and I heard his distinctive footfall in the hall, I smoothed my hair over the pillow and waited.

I thought if he was my Real Father, surely one night he'd look in again. He'd sit at the foot of my bed and whisper all the things he couldn't tell me when I was awake.

2

I carried the five-dollar bill around all that day, waiting for Dane Blackmoor. Strangely enough though, instead of me finding him, he found me. It was about three o'clock, much earlier than the Headline Weekend Guests usually arrived, and I'd decided to steal away to the beach for a few minutes. I waded into the water, letting the coldness stun my bare legs and take my breath away, rolling the elastic waistband of my skirt up as I moved seaward—the horizon always drew me—standing farther out than I should have without a bathing suit, the thin material of my blouse wilting in the spray.

Suddenly, and this is hard to explain, I had the sense of being pulled by two tides—the undertow of the waves in front of me, and something else, just behind, on the shore. I turned, falling into Dane Blackmoor's eyes.

"Hello, Gabrielle's daughter," he said, swirling my mother's name around his tongue a little, as though he were tasting the first sip of a fine old wine.

A lapping wave stung the back of my calves. I took several long steps out of the water, nearly stumbling. "I'm G-Garner," I stammered.

Blackmoor held out his hand, very solemnly. "Pleased to meet you," he said. I stared after him as he continued walking along the packed ribbon of sand parallel to the ocean, his shirt billowing like a sail. Under the rolled-up jeans, his legs were hard and brown as lucky stones.

He was already at least twenty feet away when he looked over his shoulder. I realized he'd meant me to follow. "I'd just gotten out of art school," he said when I caught up to him. "I went to a party, and there she was, your mother."

He picked up a shell and moved into the water, washing off the sand. We stood together in the first rim of waves. My skirt was soaking, the pleats plastered to my knees. "This must've been after she gave up modeling. She was already married to . . ." His voice trailed off, as though the impatient mouth couldn't be bothered. What was he going to say? *Married to Dudley? Married to your father?*

"She was sitting in a corner, all by herself. She had on a hat. A hat!" Blackmoor sounded as though he wanted to laugh, but couldn't remember how. "I thought she was the most beautiful woman I'd ever seen. She came to pose for me a few times. I still have the studies. Never went further with them. Just torsos.

"I never wrapped her face." He handed me the shell. "Even I'm not that arrogant." His eyes seemed to dare me to say that I hadn't supposed he was.

I couldn't lie, so I looked away.

Later, as we walked back, I cut a quick sideways glance at him, at the sunken places on his cheeks where it looked as though the skin had been chipped away with a chisel. He was older than I'd expected him to be, close to thirty probably. Old enough to be my—

I trained my eyes on the sand in front of me, replaying his words in my head. *"I thought she was the most beautiful woman I'd ever seen."*

Next time my mother visited, I would be nicer, I decided. Next time, we would talk, girl-to-girl. I didn't know then that there would be no next time.

At the house, with me still clutching the shell that would remain next to my bed all that long summer, Dane Blackmoor said, "See you around, Garnish."

"It's Garner," I told him, seriously, all at once hating the hard edges of my name.

He took my chin in his hand, turning it this way and that, inspecting my face from all angles, then releasing it abruptly. "You have her eyes," Blackmoor said. He started up the front steps. Stopped.

"And it is Garnish," he called down to me, softly, "a little something good enough to eat." He went inside without saying goodbye.

My heart raced. I wanted to follow him, but just then I heard the man calling at the gate. "Psst! *Psst!* Girlie!" He was jacketless today, his shirt and slacks a dark brown, as though he were trying to blend in with dirt, or the bark of a tree. I walked toward him.

"That was Blackmoor, wasn't it?" The camera was unsheathed; he was fiddling with one of the lenses. "Look, honey, all's I need is to stake out a little place over there—" He pointed to the garage, visibly excited, hopping from foot to foot as though there were hot coals on the pavement, or he had to go to the bathroom.

I took the crumpled five-dollar bill from my skirt pocket. "Forget it," I told him, watching old Honest Abe sail toward his cupped hands. I started back toward the house, turning once to yell in my most annoying smartass voice, "And if I see you hanging around here again, I'll call the cops!"

I'd planned to use the money to buy a halter top like Cathy's. I might have lost a chance to get something decent to wear, but I'd found something much more important.

I finally had a leading man for The Story.

3

If Dudley, Dane Blackmoor, and Dulcie Mariah's trial shared the spotlight on weekends, weekdays belonged to the supporting cast in the kitchen. Because this was also the summer that I learned about sex, with some help from *Webster's Dictionary*, an underlined copy of *Lady Chatterley's Lover*, and Cathy and her boyfriend Jimmy, a bellboy at the Essex-Sussex Hotel.

Just about every Monday morning I saw a further installment in the backstairs melodrama revolving around whether Cathy was pregnant, or whether she had a "bad ting in the innards," as Cilda believed. And every Monday morning I would be there, effecting the look of jaded ennui I'd practiced in the mirror, as Cathy, her long legs stretched taut across two kitchen stools, pushed a lit cigarette around the saucer she used for an ashtray and talked about doing it on the beach, and in the backseat of Jimmy-the-bellboy's Firebird.

Cathy—who seemed to assume that I had a fuller appreciation of making love than was actually the case—helped me piece together the sexual act as an intricate dance with a highly irregular beat. My mind raced with the implications of a whole new set of technical terms—*skipped periods . . . rhythm method . . . pulling out. . . .* I had only a vague idea of their meanings (*Webster* being frustratingly unforthcoming), but something about the sound of them depressed me.

It seemed a bad joke that I, who the great Dudley Quinn had once called hopelessly clumsy, should one day be called upon to engage in an act where timing and coordination were obviously so critical.

"Of course, my situation is tougher than most," Cathy sighed, applying a smear of lipgloss from a clear pot that smelled like bubble gum, "with Jimmy having multiple orgasms and all."

At such times I had to actively suppress the urge to run to my room in search of the dictionary. While the kitchen conversation meandered in other directions, I would whisper over and over to myself so I wouldn't forget, *orgasm . . . orgasm . . . orgasm . . . ,* waiting for the moment when Cilda shooed me upstairs to change for dinner when I found it, right smack in the middle of *organize* and *orgeat,* a definition more promising than the usual. My imagination reeling, I vowed to find a way to get one of the Adults-in-Charge to walk me into the lobby of the Essex-Sussex so I could get a glimpse of this bellboy Jimmy, this freak of sexual stamina, this roll-in-the-hay Hercules.

It crossed my mind that Dane Blackmoor might have experienced multiple orgasms with my mother, but I tried not to dwell on such thoughts. When it came to your parents, I didn't think you were supposed to focus on the mechanics of sex; although if your Real Father happened to be a famous man, a man who lived surrounded by art and passion, a little censored fantasizing was probably only natural.

Even if I'd tried, there was no getting away from it. This was the world in which they all moved—Dudley and his blondes; Cathy and Jimmy; Geoffrey Nash; even Cilda, who had a husband and kids back on the island of Jamaica.

"When you go home to visit," I'd once asked her, "where do you sleep?"

"In bed with me 'usband. Where else should I sleep?" Cilda had answered, as though I were silly in the head.

Even *Cilda*.

And then, of course, there was Dulcie Mariah, the rock star accused of killing her son, Charlie; and Mr. C. J. Stratten, her rich husband; and Ben Slater, the guitarist in Dulcie's band. I knew for a fact what the newspapers only hinted at—Dulcie had been having an affair with Mr. Slater. I'd overheard Dudley talking about it, or maybe not even overheard it, because he actually seemed aware I was in the room when he said it.

This was big news, enough to boggle the imagination: married women, women way over *thirty*, didn't necessarily just do It with their husbands. I thought about Dulcie having sex with Ben Slater and Mr. Stratten on the same day. I wondered if it made you feel funny, or guilty, or sick even, like having too much ice cream, or sneaking a bag of cookies and then having to eat dinner that night as though you were still hungry.

When it came down to it, all of them, except me, had been . . . *initiated*.

Yet this summer, the most exciting of my life, they'd dropped the pretense of lowering their voices, of cutting off conversation when I entered a room. They were letting me listen. And that, I decided, was like being told that, in this grown-up game of May I? I could take two baby steps into the bedroom world they inhabited after dark.

4

"What's the story, Morning Glory?" Pete called.

"Nothing." I kicked off my canvas Mary Janes and put on the Flip Flops I'd bought with money I was supposed to use for nylons.

"Goin' to the beach?" Pete asked, as he pruned a rosebush.

"Depends on who's asking." I shrugged.

He sat down on the porch steps, wiping the sweat off his forehead with a dirty handkerchief. "Aw, they'll be too busy to notice on a Friday," he said, "with Mr. Quinn coming in and all."

"Yeah." I tucked the Mary Janes into a canvas tote, next to today's paper and the bottle of Johnson's Baby Oil. "But in case Cilda asks, you haven't seen me."

"Gotcha," Pete promised. "In a while, Crocodile." *Poor Pete,* I thought as I walked away. He was probably hurt that I didn't hang around with him the way I used to. The summer before, I'd spent all of my time out in the yard, bringing him lemonade, puttering in the shed, singing along with the music that always blared on his portable radio.

The thought of that radio made me stop in my tracks. A radio was just what I needed this afternoon. A radio would make the time fly. Tossing a quick glance over my shoulder, I saw Pete digging among the impatiens. I doubled back toward the rear grounds of the house.

It was there, exactly where I knew it would be. I spun the volume control to check out the batteries before dropping it into the tote. *Pete won't mind,* I told myself. *Why, I'd been like a daughter to him. He'd said so himself.* And, for several months, I'd taken him quite literally.

Of course, things were different this year. I wasn't a child anymore. And then there was Dane Blackmoor. He'd be coming again tonight. Maybe this would be the weekend he'd admit to the secret—who he really was. I imagined Dudley's face when I told him I knew. Or would we keep it a secret? Just mine, and my dad's. I'd have to work on that—in fact, there was a lot to think about, so many plots to picture in my mind, before tonight.

I stepped out of the shed, barely missing Pete as he dragged a curled line of hose toward the front. Before he could look up, I made a dash for the avenue. Cilda didn't like me to go to the public beach. "What you want to go mixing wit that riffraff," she asked, "when you got a big pool right in the back?" She sniffed. But mixing with the riffraff was exactly what I wanted to do.

The beach wasn't crowded, a hazy cloudcover having scared off all but the diehards. Later, when the wind pushed this sky out to sea and replaced it with an empty blue one, they'd come—the weekenders with their summer passes, their towels, their uneven tans. I removed the rolled-up blanket from my tote, shimmying it the way Cathy always did to catch the direct rays of the sun. Without a decent bathing suit to wear, I was forced to hike up my sundress all the way to my underpants, so I could baby-oil every inch of my legs. Baby oil gave you color quicker than tanning lotion, Cathy said. I rubbed it into my calves, marveling at their new smoothness.

Another thing Cilda didn't believe in was girls of my age shaving their legs. At the beginning of the summer I'd taken matters into my own hands with a manicure scissor. This was a long and ultimately unsuccessful process, leaving me with stubbly patches in places I couldn't reach. Then last week when Cathy was cleaning my bathroom, I'd caught her mooning over some scented soaps.

"Paris," Cathy read, turning over the cellophaned package and breathing it in like she did her cigarettes. "Cost at least ten bucks, I bet."

Seized with sudden inspiration, I shoved them into her hands. "Take 'em," I said.

"I couldn't." She shook her head. "Stuff from the mall, that's okay. But I don't ever lift things from people I know."

"It wouldn't be stealing," I insisted. "It would be a trade."

"What kind of trade?" she asked me, dubiously.

And that was how I'd ended up with the small, pink plastic bottle of Nair depilatory.

I dialed the local rock station on the portable and stretched out on the blanket. The sun danced on the surface of my eyelids, hitting my well-oiled legs like grease on a pan. I could almost feel them sizzling.

So much better to be here than in the big house, with Cilda telling me to mind not messing anything up, the whole staff in a tizzy because Mr. Quinn was coming in. Better not to care whether Dudley would acknowledge my presence; whether he'd pass me by, as he would a chair or a lamp—not expecting anything from it except that it should be there, polished to a shine, inoffensive to the beholder.

The sun fried on my greased legs, thrumming like a bass guitar. I willed myself into sleep. When I woke, the first thing I heard was the song on the radio—one of life's little ironies—"Do you believe in magic?" The rays were at a different angle. Someone was casting a shadow. A shiver traveled from the soles of my feet.

"Looks to me like you're about ready to get out of the sun," Dane Blackmoor said. His face was completely eclipsed by the spots in my eyes.

Focusing, I saw the flaming magenta stripes on my calves and thighs. Not even parallel stripes, I shuddered, one being a frontal line, the other running from ankle to hip. I sat up quickly, pulling the dress down over my knees. The light cotton might have been razor blades and barbed wire. "I'm fine," I lied.

Blackmoor sat back on his heels. "I brought you something." He produced what looked to be a folded piece of paper from his pocket.

I opened it, squinting against the sun. It was an old photograph of some people sitting around a restaurant table. To the left, almost out of the range of the lens, was a very young Dane Blackmoor. Next to him sat a beautiful woman. They were the only two who weren't looking into the camera; and it isolated them in a way, made them seem somehow a world apart from the others.

"Your mother," Blackmoor said. "I thought you might like—"

But I'd stopped listening. It was as if my mind wasn't big enough to contain the thought. *Dane Blackmoor is my Real Father.* He brought me this picture as proof.

"I—I—" The words stuck in my throat.

"Dane!" I looked over Blackmoor's shoulder at the young woman calling from the boardwalk. "I'm tired! I want to take a shower!"

He didn't turn. Didn't even let on that he'd heard. "You can have it," he said, pushing the photograph back into my hand, "if you want it."

I watched him as he walked slowly toward his companion. Even at this distance I could see she was beautiful, her yellow hair flying in the wind, the gauze of a white dress whipped like frosting against her lean body. When they were completely out of sight, I turned off the radio and carefully placed the photograph into my tote. Waves of chilly nausea swept through me. The rays seemed to find the burn on my legs even under the cover of my skirt. I moved across the sand, as if in a dream, wondering whether a person could die by fatally mixing a depilatory with too much sun.

It didn't matter, I decided. Because if I died now, I knew at least one person would mourn me.

I knew that my father would care.

5

There was no hiding my legs from Cilda. She took one look at them, ablaze in all their aching crimson splendor, and her mouth went into action. "What you cooking yourself dark for, girl?"

"I fell asleep," I said, sitting patiently while the old woman applied clean white dishtowels soaked in aloe. It hurt, but I wouldn't dare complain.

"'ow is it the only time you pull these things," Cilda growled, "is when 'imself is coming 'ome?"

"That's enough," I told her. "I'm okay."

"Yes, sure you okay," said Cilda, "till the sun go down in the sky and up on your t'igh." I jumped off the kitchen stool, knocking over my tote bag. Its contents spilled in a damning configuration all over the freshly mopped floor.

"Where'd you get that radio?" Cilda barked.

"Pete told me I could borrow it." I watched Cilda's round eyes travel from the baby oil to the photograph. I went for it, a beat too late.

"And what's this?"

I took it from her. "It's mine," I said defiantly. "Dane Blackmoor gave it to me."

Cilda's big hands clamped over my wrist. "You put that ting away," she hissed, her voice low and dangerous. "The big man see that, there's gonna be 'ell to pay."

Pete poked his head in the back door. "Hail, hail, the gang's all here."

Cilda let go of my arm, smoothing the front of her dress as she crossed to the door. "Put it away," she said in parting. "Now."

It was true, I thought, hurriedly stuffing everything back into the canvas bag. There *had* been something between Blackmoor and my mother, something that would be enough to set Dudley into a rage if he were reminded of it. Even Cilda knew. I pushed through the kitchen doors. Dudley's entourage stood in the entranceway amid a ton of luggage.

"I don't care if you have to track him down in the fucking steam-room," Dudley was telling his assistant, "I want him on the phone *now.*" The young man walked into the study looking despondent.

"Hi," I said, holding the tote bag behind me.

"Hello, Garner." Dudley turned immediately to Cilda. "Did those cases of brandy I ordered arrive?"

"Came this morning," Cilda told him.

He smiled for the first time. "Good."

"I wanted to ask you something—" I began. Cilda glowered. "—about what the prosecution said at the trial this week."

"Not now, Garner. Can't you see I'm exhausted?" Dudley headed past me, loosening his tie. "Bring me a drink, will you, Cilda, love?"

"But—" I started to follow.

"Really, Garner," Dudley said, stopping short as he looked down at my legs. For a moment I thought he was going to reprimand me. Instead he just laughed and shook his head.

For the first time in years, it didn't even hurt so much.

"Don't bodder 'imself, girl," Cilda clucked after he shut the door to the study. "The man bone tired. 'e need to relax." She bustled off to get his drink.

I wondered, not for the first time, how no one else saw it. All of them—Cilda, Pete, everybody—they all thought Dudley Quinn III came home to relax. But I knew better.

I knew he came home to practice.

6

I sat on the front porch steps staring at the darkening
sky. Behind me, the wooden screen door swung lazily
open and shut on its hinges. The air smelled of mosquito spray and
the coming storm, a heady aroma that made me almost too lethargic
to turn. Still, I knew it was Blackmoor.

"It's always worse after dark," he said.

I turned, looking up at him, questioningly.

"Sunburn." He sat down on the step above me, holding a
stemmed glass filled with burgundy-colored liquid. Reflexively,
I pulled my skirt over my aching knees. We stayed that way,
quietly looking at the sky. Inside, one of Dudley's houseguests was
playing "Eleanor Rigby" on the grand piano. The sounds drifted
out and were immediately muffled by the heavy air. They sounded
as though they came from a million miles away. From the moon,
even.

I stole a glance at Blackmoor's profile. This wasn't his good side.

I could see the bumps where his nose had been broken. The thought of him hurting, bleeding, made me want to cry. I had the sudden urge to throw my arms around him, to be cradled in his lap, with my head in the hollow between his shoulder and his neck.

He slid down a step, to my level. "You come out here a lot?" I nodded, not trusting myself to speak. What if I made a slip? What if I called him Daddy?

"What do you do?" he asked.

I managed a shrug. "I wait," I told him.

He laughed. His laughter was never happy. "For the show to start," he said caustically.

The indoor pianist ended the song abruptly, pounding the keys with his fists as though suddenly bored. Dane offered his wineglass. I glanced toward the door before taking it from him, swallowed a mouthful, and handed it back. That moment, the church word *Communion* took on an added meaning.

"What do you think about the accused, Lady Mariah?" Blackmoor asked. It was a question I'd heard formed many ways this summer, but it surprised me, coming from him.

"I don't know," I replied truthfully.

He feigned shock. "Aren't you supposed to say she's innocent as the day is long? I mean, you *are* the attorney's kid, aren't you?"

Was that a trick question? The wine and the sun flushed me from head to toe. I felt confused. It took everything I had to look right into his eyes and say, as evenly as I could, "Actually, I don't think of Dudley as my father."

Blackmoor leaned forward in the dusk. "What goes on in that busy head of yours, Garnish?" he whispered.

The screen door opened with a screech. "What you doing sitting out so late?" Cilda called sternly. "Move your behind before you notting but one big mosquito bite all over."

Dane stood. "We were on our way in anyway, Mrs. Fields," he told her. He took the last swig of wine and put out his hand, pulling me up. "Let the games begin?" I shot Cilda a *so-there* look, and followed him into the house.

. . .

I knew he was behind me from the way everyone's eyes shifted when I entered. The good seats were already taken. Blackmoor put his hand on the nape of my neck and steered me into the center of the room.

A shaft of lightning split the sky. Lights flickered. Heavy sheets of rain slanted in through the windows. The sudden violence of the storm jump-started people into action. Several women shrieked. Geoffrey Nash dashed about, closing the sills, calling, "Cilda! Cilda, darling, come quickly!"

"Mr. Blackmoor really knows how to make an entrance," Dudley remarked. Everyone laughed. Somebody offered Dane a seat.

"We're fine." He motioned me to a spot on the piano bench. It wouldn't have been my first choice. The baby grand was at the wrong end of the room. We would only be able to see Dudley in quarter-profile, dimly. When his voice dipped, or got pensive or sad, we might not be able to hear him at all.

Why should I care? I reminded myself. My loyalties were shifting, fast.

The blonde woman who'd called to Dane earlier on the beach was again trying to get his attention. She'd changed into a canary-yellow mini and swept her straight blond hair into a ponytail. When he ignored her, she plopped down on the floor, stretching out legs that were long, tapered, and chestnut brown like the spindles on the center hall staircase.

I stared at her, mesmerized. For some reason she reminded me of Pete's cat, Zoey, cleaning herself in the sun, leg hiked over her head, licking her privates. She was that uninhibited. "What's her name?" I whispered.

"Who?" Blackmoor shrugged. "Oh, Sherrie. Sherrie . . . Something."

There was a crack of thunder. Cilda hustled into the room, lighting candles with a kitchen match held unsteadily in her bent black fingers. She was spooked by the storm and the roomful of strangers, any of whom she feared were capable of all sorts of bad magic and treachery. I breathed a sigh of relief when she left. Dudley would begin any minute, and then I'd be safe. Not even Cilda would come looking for me when Dudley took the floor.

Once I overheard a couple of the women guests talking together. "Dinner and drinks are just foreplay to Dudley," one of them said, and they'd exchanged looks and laughed. Later I looked up foreplay. *Erotic stimulation preceding sexual intercourse.* Since that time that was how I'd thought of the space of time between dessert and Dulcie Mariah—Dudley's foreplay. Sex, I decided, must be even better than I'd imagined, if it was half as exciting as his stories about the trial.

This night, though, something was off kilter. It might have been Blackmoor's presence, or the sudden shift in the weather; or maybe Dudley was growing tired of the same old routine. He seemed edgy, distracted.

Rain hammered against the roof like pennies thrown into a tin box. I caught a glimpse of myself in the windowpane. Hair, Medusa-like, a tangle of unruly curls. Skin overly shiny, as though I'd been dipped in a vat of doughnut glaze. The singed flesh on my legs was making me shiver. When Blackmoor took off his jacket and put it over my shoulders, my insides crumpled like tissue paper.

Here, I thought, was the ultimate proof. To him, I wasn't invisible.

Geoffrey Nash began steering the conversation toward the trial, his voice straining over the clatter of the rain, but Dudley remained uncharacteristically silent. He sat in his usual chair, quietly nursing a gin and tonic. The pretty girl, Sherrie, flexed her magnificent legs, brushing the great man with the tip of a toe. "Aren't you going to tell us about Dulcie Mariah?"

I held my breath, surprised when Dudley's face softened into a smile. "Oh," he said with a self-deprecating shrug, "surely everyone must be bored with all that by now." *So that was it.* He wanted to be egged on. His guests obliged, coaxing, cajoling, pleading, until he held up his hands, his face beaming, in his element now.

That was when Blackmoor took his first shot. "Yes, Quinn," he said. "Tell us. How's the murderous little wench doing?"

I gripped the edge of the piano bench, feeling as though I might fall off. A sputter of nervous laughter went around the room. All eyes were pinned on Dudley, trying to gauge his response. He leaned back in his chair, ice chinking to the other side of his glass.

When he spoke, his tone was friendly. "Well, Mr. Blackmoor, you know where I stand in the matter. If you have a contrasting viewpoint"—Dudley tipped his glass in a mock salute—"by all means, feel free. I'm certain your opinion, however uninformed, will be far more interesting than the prosecutor's has been thus far." Congratulatory laughter all around.

I wanted it to end there. Knew that it wouldn't. Dudley crossed to the bar, talking over his shoulder as he took the cap off the gin. "Actually, I'd love to hear what you have to say. You know the lady in question, don't you?"

Blackmoor's lips twisted up at the edges. "*I knew her.*" Something about his inflection made it clear the conversation had taken a biblical turn. I watched Dudley pour, put the liquor bottle down—plop, plop, *thud*. Not happy sounds.

He turned, the very essence of charm—"Why do I get the feeling I shouldn't call upon you as a character witness?"—defusing the tension in the room, allowing everyone to breathe again. Sherrie Something picked up a cocktail napkin and began fanning her face with it. Two of the regulars—a country-and-western singer and a quarterback wearing a gaudy Super Bowl ring—stumbled over themselves trying to see who could open a window for her first.

Just when it appeared the room had quieted down, Geoff Nash turned to Blackmoor and said, offhandedly, "I'm just curious, Dane. You don't really believe she's guilty?"

"Yes," he replied, "I do."

Everyone began talking at once. "No, no, I want to hear this," Dudley said over the objections. He turned his chair around, straddling it. "Is your opinion based on fact, Mr. Blackmoor—or do you simply not like the lady's looks?"

"Oh, I've always liked her looks," Blackmoor said. They eyed each other intently, as if the conversation were continuing, telepathically. I felt too close to the center of things, marooned on a piano bench with the object of Dudley's scrutiny. *I'm a speck of dust,* I incanted, silently, *too small and insignificant for anyone to see.* The mantra seemed to work because instead of lighting on me, Dudley's gaze turned to the others.

"Well, sir," he boomed, in his best courtroom voice, "why don't you tell us your version of what happened?"

"Versions are your business, not mine," Blackmoor responded quietly. "I thought we were talking about guilt." He sat very straight beside me, perfectly articulating his words. I suddenly realized Dane Blackmoor was drunk.

"Guilt," Dudley repeated, as though considering the concept for the first time. He gestured to Geoffrey Nash. "Hand me that file on the desk there, would you, Geoff?" Nash picked up a manila folder. "On second thought," Dudley told him, "pass it to our guest, why don't you?"

Geoffrey handed the folder to Blackmoor. I watched as he slid out the contents: four 8x10 glossies showing Dulcie Mariah's son Charlie lying on the floor of a closet, with half his head missing. The close-ups weren't as bad as the long shots. In the long shots you could tell just how small he was. Blackmoor studied each photograph for a moment before stuffing them all back into the envelope. I couldn't see his face.

"Was the woman you *knew*"—Dudley blew out the word like a poison dart—"capable of *that?*"

A sudden bolt of lightning lit up the room, turning it surrealistically white. Then everything went black. "I tell you, don't mess with Mariah," Geoffrey piped up. The others laughed.

"Sorry, ladies and gents," Dudley apologized, setting a flickering candelabrum onto the coffee table. "Must've struck a power line."

Blackmoor's Sherrie sat back on her haunches. "Oh, Mr. Quinn, can't we keep going anyway? It'll be like telling ghost stories in summer camp."

"I always make a point of obliging lovely ladies," Dudley said, "but I must remind you. This isn't a campfire tale. It's something my client will have to live with, daily, for the rest of her life. The memory of that precious little boy, her only child . . . gone. Taken from her forever, in such a horrible, horrible way."

His eyes brimmed, accentuated by the glow of the candlelight. He blinked twice, shook his head as though embarrassed by his own weakness, focusing his pent-up suffering on a bead of sweat that wended a liquid path down his gin glass. I counted in my head—*one–one thousand . . . two–one thousand . . . three–one thousand*—waiting for the smile. Wistful. Brave. Juries ate this stuff up.

It was only gradually that he appeared to remember the rest of us. "I'm sorry . . . those pictures," he sighed, setting his shoulders square. I feared for Dane. I knew now Dudley would move in for the kill.

His voice reflected the change. "You were about to tell us why you think she's guilty, Mr. Blackmoor?"

"Forget it."

"No, really"—expansively, on the offensive now—"I'd like to know. There were over a hundred people at the party that night—not to mention the nanny, the caterers, the housekeeping staff. Several of the guests had a history of violence. Many were drug addicts." He turned to the others, anticipating their thoughts. "Granted it wasn't the smartest thing, inviting these fringe characters into her home, with her little boy there, but that's the music business for you, that's rock 'n' roll." Although he didn't say the words, they were plain in everyone's mind—*hey, she might not be the mother of the year, but it doesn't make her a murderer.*

"I bet it was one of them druggies," the quarterback said. "The bastard had to be strung out on some pretty bad shit to do what he did to that kid."

"I just can't fathom such cruelty," said another one of the regulars, an editor of a fashion magazine, "coming from a woman. We're simply not capable of it."

There had been a lull in the storm. The rain rustled like taffeta skirts. It was eerie, as though Dulcie Mariah were just outside, peeking in on us, wrapped in the wide, diaphanous scarf she'd worn on her last album cover. She'd been pregnant with Charlie in that picture. Even though I didn't have a stereo, I'd bought it. It was up in my room right now, still in its cellophane wrapper. "DULCIE: Knocked Up—Knocked Out."

"She couldn't have, she wouldn't have," Dudley said, to no one in particular. "There's no reason. No motive."

Blackmoor shifted slightly on the bench. "I don't know about that," he said. "Dulcie was always searching for the ultimate high."

"That's outrageous!" Geoffrey cried in his best *your-honor-I-object* voice.

Dudley cut him off. "Let me get this straight." He turned away from Dane Blackmoor, playing to the crowd. "You think once the party started winding down, Dulcie got *bored*, and—on the prowl for something new and exciting—she suddenly thought"—a snap of his fingers—"*Hey, why don't I just go wake up Charlie, and bash in the little bastard's head?*"

"I can't say whether she did it alone," Blackmoor replied, "or somebody else did, and she just stood by. What matters is, it happened."

"Buy why?" Dudley asked shrilly. "*Why-would-she-kill-her-own-kid?*"

"He was an innocent. For some people"—again, that telepathic locking of the eyes, Dane's to Dudley's, as if to say *for people like Dulcie, and you, and me*—"innocence is a mirror. What it reflects isn't easy to take."

I didn't know what he was talking about but somehow I had the feeling it went way beyond the Mariah trial, that it had to do with both of them, and my mother, and maybe even me. I thought about The Story . . . my Real Father . . . all those endless, silly plots. Looking at these two men's faces now, I realized I was not ready for nonfiction. Not tonight. Maybe not ever.

I tried to stand up, but Blackmoor took my hand. "Faced with innocence," he said, looking steadily at Dudley, "such people only have two choices." He pressed my palm to his mouth, a gesture that was something less than a kiss. His lips were dry, his five o'clock shadowed chin pricked me. "We can kill it. Or we can corrupt it."

It was one of those moments played out in a time zone where every second is a dog's year—*just Blackmoor holding my hand staring at Dudley staring at Blackmoor holding my hand staring at Dudley staring at Blackmoor.* Finally, Dane released me. "Of course," he said, "I'm not sure that killing isn't the kinder way to go."

I'd never seen a volcano erupt, but I'd swear this was what Mt. Vesuvius had been like, just before it blew. I pictured us frozen this way—Geoffrey Nash, his Tom Collins glass to his lips. Sherrie, legs tucked up, panties showing; the football player's thick brow drawn up in concentration, as though wondering who to tackle first—every last one preserved mid-breath, for all eternity, as the lightning-swift current of molten wrath washed over us, turning our suspended silence into ashes. I saw Dudley's lips draw together dangerously, cheeks inflating—*and I'll huff, and I'll puff, and I'll—*

But he never did.

Because that was the precise moment the man came crashing through the window.

7

Focused as we were on the unfolding parlor drama, the man's entrance seemed all the more fantastic. It took a few seconds for my brain to register that—no, the explosion hadn't come from Dudley, but from another part of the room altogether, a corner window through which a human projectile sailed, finally coming to rest, in a heap, on the Aubusson carpet, camera straps twisting around his neck like a noose.

Of course, I recognized the lump of brown polyester immediately. I could have said so, but I saved my breath. There were too many outcries, too many people talking all at once. Only Blackmoor seemed disinterested, which was ironic, because he was the reason the flying paparazzo had performed his feat of daring in the first place, as unsuccessful as it proved to be.

The football player and the country-music singer hunkered over the guy, two angry bulls pawing the carpet, steam coming from their noses, no doubt grateful for the opportunity to show off in front of

Sherrie. Quite amazingly—especially because I'd nosed through every inch of the room and I couldn't imagine where it was hidden—Dudley had produced a small, elegant revolver.

"Don't shoot me." The man cowered, clutching his camera to his chest. "I'm not a burglar, I'm a photographer." His eyes lit on me. "I just wanted to get a shot of Blackmoor. Ask the kid."

Once again I found myself the center of unwanted attention. "I—I saw him hanging around outside a few weeks ago," I stammered. "I told him to get lost, or we'd call the police."

"Which is exactly what we're going to do," Dudley said, training the gun just below the man's sagging belt line. Geoffrey Nash picked up the phone.

Dane Blackmoor stood up and stretched. On his way out of the drawing room he looked down at the frightened photographer, put an imaginary camera up to his eyes, and made a *click-click* sound with his tongue. Then, flashing enough teeth to pass for a smile, he headed for the door.

The captive photographer sat sullenly on a small wooden chair, press card in hand, waiting for the cops to come and rescue him. His sudden arrival had acted as a high-pressure weather front, pushing Blackmoor's stormy presence out to sea and leaving a party atmosphere in its wake. Everyone was mixing fresh drinks and talking. Sherrie sat on the arm of Dudley's chair, stroking the barrel of his fine gun.

Instinct told me this would be a good time to disappear. I didn't bother to say goodnight. No one would miss me, and I hoped Dudley would be sufficiently distracted by Sherrie's sculpted lemon-ice profile, the gun, the gin, and the trespasser to forget that I'd figured—although how or why I still wasn't sure—in tonight's aborted mutiny.

I slinked out, running into Cilda, carrying a silver platter of fruit. "You in big trouble wit me, lady," she hissed.

"Leave me alone," I told her wearily. "I'm sick."

She stopped hissing and started fussing. "Wait in the kitchen," she ordered. "I got me a good root for the burn."

"I need some air." I bolted out the front door, off the porch, and down into the bushes, where I threw up twice. For a few minutes I just stood there, in the shrubbery, on wobbly legs. The rhododendrons were black and wet with rain. I pressed a big, dripping leaf to my face, wiping first my mouth, then my cheeks and eyelids. The burn on my legs had seeped into my bones and turned them to scorched rubber. My throat ached from vomiting. Tomorrow I'd catch hell from Cilda, and probably Dudley, too, but it didn't matter.

Inside the house, the phantom pianist was playing a song I'd heard on the radio. I remembered that it was from a new Broadway musical called "Hair." Cathy had said she wanted to see it because the actors took off all their clothes onstage. Humming softly, I began to sway. The motion sent showers of rain down from the bushes. Fairy cups of water splashed off of leaves, onto my head, and down my shoulders. My hands moved independently, unbuttoning my damp dress and letting it fall to the ground. My underwear looked glow-in-the-dark white.

Sa-ba-si-be-sa-ba

I twirled around until I was dizzy, feeling powerless to stop— around and around, Saint-Vitus-dancing, half-naked through the wet garden. The stiff points of leaves and stems and branches flogged me, saturating my thin undershirt and panties.

Police sirens shrieked in the distance on their way to apprehend the peeping paparazzo. They were coming, and I had no clothes on.

It'll be okay, I told myself. *The guests are in the drawing room. Cilda's in the kitchen. All you have to do is tuck your dress under your arm, and calmly walk up the steps. Then open the big front door, climb the center staircase, and keep going until you get to your room.* No one would see me. No one would ever know that I'd thrown up and danced in the garden in my underwear. I'd wrap myself in a robe, slide between the sheets, and fall instantly asleep.

The cop cars were getting closer.

Move it, Garner, I ordered myself, *just move.* Surprisingly, my body obeyed. I emerged from the bushes, sopping wet, dress balled up in the palm of my hand. Steps first. *Fine.* Then the porch. *Easy.* Now the door.

A whisper ruffled the darkness. "We have to talk," Blackmoor said softly. "Tomorrow."

I froze for a moment, my back to him, so achingly, humiliatingly exposed. The sirens were approaching fast.

"Sleep well, Garnish," he called. They were like a blown kiss, those words.

I pushed the door open and fled.

8

But by the morning he was gone, and he didn't come back. At least not right away.

To compound matters, the trial wasn't going well, and Dudley began staying in New York during the weekends. One by one, the houseguests dispersed to other haunts—places where there were more laughs, less tension—until finally only an eccentric down-at-the-heels painter remained. I never knew his name, although he often talked to me, beginning each sentence in the middle, picking up the conversation exactly where it had been left off. He was always the first one in the dining room, eating every meal as if it were his last, rolling hunks of food into the table napkins and tucking them into his shirt with palsied, paint-stained hands.

Except for him, and Cilda, and the household staff, I was alone. I wondered how I'd stood it before, the life I lived here. Mornings in the kitchen. Sneaking off to the beach. Talking to Pete. Arguing with Cilda. The kitchen, the beach again. Had it always been this dreary?

Just to have something to do, I followed Cathy around while she changed the sheets. "If these ole bedsprings could talk, huh?" she said, tucking a fresh pillowcase under her chin.

"What do you mean?"

She slipped the pillow inside, tossing it against the headboard with a little spank. "This was Dane Blackmoor's room, silly." She touched the mattress, hissing as though she'd gotten burned. "The guy was hot." She sat down on the bed. "Wanna know a secret?"

I did. I really did.

"I came in here one morning, late, knocked and everything," she whispered excitedly. "And there he was sittin' in that chair, with his shirt off, drinking whiskey. So I go, real sweet, 'Oh, Mr. Blackmoor, I didn't know you was here, I'll come back later,' and he goes, 'Oh, that's okay,' and he holds out a glass, and he goes, 'Care to join me?'—you know, with that voice—I mean, I almost wet myself."

"What'd you do?" (With my father.) I asked, very cool.

"What'd you think?" Cathy laughed.

"So what happened?" (With my father.)

"Not a helluva lot," she sighed. "Just then the bitch with the tits walked in." I had to get out of that room, had to stop Cathy from going on and on—picture it, Dane Blackmoor, a bottle of Jack Daniel's, and a bed, whoa, whoa, whoa . . .

"Ga'ner! Ga'ner Quinn!" Cilda called from downstairs.

Thank you, God.

I took the steps two at a time, hoping to shake loose the chokehold of emotions around my throat. Maybe having Dane Blackmoor as a father wasn't such a great idea. For the rest of that day whenever I had a thought about him, I tried to drive it out of my mind. But by the following evening the bleakness of my situation hit me dead-on. I needed the comfort of The Story to get me through the long days and nights.

So what if he drinks too much? I asked myself. He's a sculptor, a creative mind. He probably did it for inspiration. That he did it for inspiration with the teenaged help was a bit of a stretch; but then, Cathy *had* walked in on him. My spirits surged. I imagined the dawn of a new era in kitchen gossip. With a nudge from me, Cathy might talk some more about Blackmoor. Just the idea of hearing his name from another person's lips was thrilling. That, and my daily fix of the trial in the newspapers would be enough to make life almost worth living.

Around the beginning of August, the headlines took a turn for the worse—NEW EVIDENCE IN MARIAH TRIAL, NANNY SAYS MARIAH WAS NO MOM, SEX, DRUGS, AND ROCK 'N' ROLL KILLED CHARLIE. Except for one hour on Sunday evenings, I was not allowed to watch television, so every morning in the kitchen I pumped Cathy for information.

"They say she never took no interest in that child," she said, thoughtfully sipping a Coca-Cola. "That once, when he was crying, she said to the guy in her band—"

"Ben Slater?"

"The cute one, with the moustache—"

"Ben Slater."

"Yeah, him. One of the backup singers heard Dulcie telling him to give the kid a hit of something to shut him up permanently." Outrage and Cover Girl Flamenco Ice eye shadow battled for domination of Cathy's eyes. "Can you believe it?"

Margaret grunted, "Rich bitch. They're all the same."

"What else?"

Cathy considered for a minute. "Well, they showed the people going out the courthouse, and guess who was there? Roger Daltrey and Neil Young. Swear to God!—I mean, can you imagine sitting in court right next to Roger Daltrey? I'd cream my pants."

I didn't know who Roger Daltrey was. "Was anybody else there you knew?"

Cathy rolled her eyes. "Lawyer types, I dunno." She shrugged. "Mr. Quinn kept saying how they were gonna prove the witness wasn't reliable. Then he put his arm around her, and they got into a big stretch limousine." Cathy shot a knowing glance to Margaret.

Her, I supposed, was Dulcie Mariah. But what the knowing glance was for I didn't find out until later.

9

The following Friday Dulcie Mariah came home with Dudley for the first time. I was asleep when they arrived. When, the next morning, Cilda made me go outside to play so I wouldn't wake "the lady," I assumed her to be just another in the long line of Dudley's blonde companions, and did as I was told.

Pete was raking the gravel in the drive. "Hey, Starstruck," he called, "seen Dulcie Mariah yet?"

"Dulcie Mariah?"

He kept raking. "Whatsa matter, ain't she up?"

I ran into the kitchen. Margaret was having her cup of coffee. She didn't like anyone, except maybe Cathy, talking to her while she was having her cup of coffee. "Is it true?" I asked breathlessly. "Dulcie Mariah is here?"

"Rich bitch," sipped Margaret. *A definite yes.*

Later I saw her with my own eyes. She came down the stairs with Dudley at dinnertime, looking as though she'd just gotten out of bed.

Her hair, so pale it looked silver, appeared to have been hacked instead of cut, and there were things stuck in it, long slender needles with enamel beads on the end, clips as big as rodent traps. But nothing—not the fringe of greasy bangs, the soiled camisole, or her dirty bare feet—took away from the splendid beauty of the woman. I glanced down at my perfectly ironed, spotlessly clean cotton dress and wanted to die.

"This is Garner," Dudley said, adding exultantly, "and *this* is Cilda."

The famous half-moon grin broke out onto Dulcie's face. "What a pleasure," she said, with a little curtsy that was somehow not mocking. They walked into the dining room. Cilda brought the sliding pocket doors together, cutting off the view and reminding me that, until further notice, I'd be eating in the kitchen.

After that first time, I was to see Dulcie Mariah only twice, although she spent many weekends at the beach house. Dudley opened up the largest adjoining bedrooms as a suite for his guest. Special linen was shipped in from an exclusive shop in Manhattan; and the list of what Miss Mariah would and would not eat made Margaret even crankier than usual.

I wondered where her husband, C. J. Stratten, was, and why he never accompanied his wife on these jaunts. Once I even asked Dudley.

"She's tired, Garner. She needs to be away from everything," he told me, adding, "And I don't want you pestering her, you hear?"

When I told Cilda how Dudley had answered my question about Mr. Stratten, she just laughed. "Tired? What's that one tired of, except maybe 'aving an 'usband on 'er back?" I noticed that while Dudley's guests always fawned over Cilda, she was seldom won over. Dulcie would not prove an exception.

I remained on constant Mariah-alert, loitering in the upstairs hall, in the foyer, outside the dining room. When I was chased away, I set up a chair on the lawn below Dulcie's rooms, hoping to catch a glimpse of her at the windows. But the drapes stayed drawn from morning till night.

After weeks of dogged vigilance, she turned up in the least likely place of all.

It was about four o'clock, a Saturday. Light rain had forced me back from the beach early. I climbed the stairs to my room, bored and disheartened, peeling off my sundress as I went, stripping down to my dowdy bathing suit. As soon as I opened the door, I smelled it—a sweet, pungent fragrance, which Cathy called *eau de pot*.

Dulcie Mariah stood, her back to me, looking at the bookshelves. If she heard me come in, she didn't show it. She just kept studying everything, the botanical prints on the wide moiré sashes, the ruffled curtains, the jewelry box painted with rosebuds.

"Very girlish." She broke into that ripe watermelon of a smile. I wasn't sure whether she referred to the decor or my bathing suit. Without another word she brushed past me, the tiny bells on her long print skirt tinkling.

She'd left me a souvenir. The "Knocked Up—Knocked Out" album was on my pillow. Dulcie Mariah had autographed the cover with my brand-new Bonne Belle eyebrow pencil: *"To Garner, xxx Dulcie,"* the Xs scrawled across her pregnant belly.

I picked up the record. The neat cellophane wrapper had been slit.

One night I awoke to the sound of voices beneath my open window. I got up without turning on the light. The outdoor floods illuminated the pool and the cabanas; with the moon I could see clear over to Pete's toolshed.

Dudley and Dulcie Mariah were on the gravel path. She was wearing a long, flimsy gown, the outline of her body completely visible through the material. A thin band, like a cigar-store Indian's, played peekaboo in her hair.

Even in the night, from a story above, she glittered.

"In mah midna-ight con-fes-sion," she sang at the top of her lungs.

Dudley put his hands out, as though he were a conductor signaling pianissimo. She ran ahead, waving him off with the neck of an opened champagne bottle.

He called to her, "Dulcie . . . Dulcie, for Christ's sake!"—Dudley Quinn III, kind and dutiful lawyer, the man who would patiently trail after his clients, soothing their fears, calming hysteria. Or was this something more?

He caught up to Mariah and swung her around by the waist. Her laughter was raucous. *"In mah . . . "* She tilted the bottle of bubbly until it sprayed, shooting foam down the front of Dudley's starched white shirt.

"Dulcie . . . Dulcie, for Christ's sake!" he said again, more softly.

A couple of weeks later I came upon Dudley sitting all alone in the library. There were dark circles beneath his eyes. He looked exhausted.

"I didn't know anybody was in here," I apologized. He said nothing. I turned to the shelves, half-expecting him to tell me to leave.

"What have you been doing with yourself this summer, Garner?" he asked.

Waiting for you, listening to you, doing anything I could to be a part of your life, my mind screamed. I said, "Nothing much." Then, "How about you?"

He stared for a minute, before summoning a beaten smile. "Oh, you know. Same old, same old." Leaning back into the wingback chair, he sighed. "I always knew I'd have to find out what it was like to lose one day, but I'll tell you a secret, just between you and me—" I moved closer. "I didn't want it to be with this one," he said.

He got up and walked out of the room without another word. I glanced at the rolled-up newspaper he'd left on the cushion of the seat. The headlines read: OUTCOME BLEAK FOR MARIAH.

. . .

No one stayed after that except for the old painter. During Dulcie's visits he'd eaten with Cilda and me in the kitchen. Later, we continued this routine. The dining room seemed too cavernous and empty.

Newspaper reports remained grave. Witnesses for the prosecution streamed into the courtroom, day in and day out, testifying to Dulcie's failings as a mother, telling of wild parties, outbursts of temper, erratic behavior. One evening, Cilda put the television set on the kitchen counter and plugged it in. After that, watching the news during meals became a ritual.

I sat quietly, looking down at my plate. I was afraid if I acted too interested, it might be taken away; yet every word registered in my head. *Twenty-two more soldiers killed in Vietnam . . . Vice President Agnew denies impropriety . . . One hundred arrested at antiwar rally.* There was a great big world out there, and they couldn't keep me away from it forever. When the report on the Mariah trial came on, everyone leaned forward on their stools.

The footage of Dudley shocked me. He looked like a decked-out corpse—manicured, groomed, arrayed just right, but with the lifeblood sucked out of him. He avoided looking directly at the camera when being questioned. Dulcie, on the other hand, appeared to be holding up just fine. Dressed in tapered Edwardian jackets, long skirts, and laced boots, she might have been the heroine in a romantic novel—besieged, but proud. On television you couldn't tell that her clothes were probably dirty.

"She's guilty, you know," the painter said, the stubble on his chin glistening with dribbled gravy.

"Why do you say that?"

He went on, chewing with his mouth open. "Her eyes."

Something inside me quivered. "What about them?"

"Look." The old man picked up a piece of china and held it up to my face. "See those highlights? Now to get them on canvas, you take the flat end of a number-two brush, dip it in titanium white, and you dab the eyes, see, to make the light come alive." He demonstrated, using his fork for a brush. "I once did a portrait of a woman who'd lost a child. There was nothing in her eyes. No light at all. Grief snuffs it out like a candle."

I watched him mash beets into his potatoes, staining them red. "Now, that Mariah woman." He took a big mouthful. "Ever notice how her eyes sparkle?"

So maybe they shine from drugs or from the inner peace that comes with innocence, I wanted to argue, but I let it go. I didn't want to think about Dulcie Mariah. I was thinking about Dudley. Seeing his drawn face on the news had reminded me of a tear I'd once tasted, of a soft voice in a darkened library. *"What have you been doing with yourself, Garner?"*

Dane Blackmoor was gone. Dudley was all that I had. Maybe this time, I told myself, it would be different. Maybe, in failure and despair, he'd look to me.

10

"Wake up, girl!" Cilda's voice roused me from a far-off place. She shuffled to the window, bringing the shade up with a snap so it spun on the roller. The light was weak, but unmistakable.

"W-what time is it?"

"Six o'clock." Cilda was in the closet now, scraping hangers over the rack.

"Go away," I protested. "Let me sleep."

Cilda wagged my best ugly dress in her hand. "What you sleeping for now that this awful ting is finally over?"

"What—?"

"The trial, girl!" she whispered. "The trial!"

I hurled myself back on the pillow. "The trial won't be over for weeks. They haven't even presented closing arguments yet."

"That's all you know," Cilda said, huffily. "But while you been sleeping the day away, Mister Benjamin Slater damned 'is soul to 'ell and killed 'imself." I sat up straight. "And 'e left a letter saying it was 'imself murdered the poor infant, tank the Lord."

"Mister Quinn 'as won." She grabbed my hand impulsively. "The big man 'as won again!"

The media couldn't get enough of it.

Rock guitarist and teenage heartthrob Ben Slater had put a gun in his mouth, spattering what was left of his brain cells on the kitchen walls of his Connecticut estate. In an unsigned, handwritten suicide note he confessed to having killed Charlie, saying he'd wanted to ruin Dulcie's life the way she'd ruined his.

I can't live with what I've done, he wrote, rather unnecessarily; then, *Dulcie babe, I'll see you in hell.* An autopsy revealed that Slater had taken a near-lethal mixture of heroin and barbiturates before shooting himself.

There's a Latin term, *deus ex machina*—the god from the machine—a device employed by classical playwrights when they need to clean up a lot of messy details fast, and tack a pseudo-happy ending onto what would otherwise have been a sorry state of affairs.

The first time I heard it, I thought of Ben Slater.

From the beginning I always felt there was something *tacked on* about the way Slater checked out. Years went by, Dulcie died in that plane crash, and still it nagged at me, like a pebble in my shoe. Finally, during the first awful months after my divorce, I went back and dug up all the old records. And that—contrary to what Dudley has publicly stated—was how *Rock-a-Bye Baby* came to be written.

Out of curiosity. Not revenge.

11

The house was suddenly abuzz with people again.
Dudley returned, thinner, but the old edge was definitely back.

"Was she surprised?" I asked him. "Did she know it was Ben all
along?"

He waved me away. "It's over, Garner. Can't you let me have
a day's peace?" Then he resumed conversing with the invited guests
about Mariah, and the trial, and how they'd been preparing to
tighten the noose around Slater's neck when news of his suicide
came. Everyone listened, fascinated.

I stayed quiet, allowing Dudley peace, his way.

The first hint of autumn blew into the air. Tourists had taken
over the roads and the beaches; strangers had taken over our house.
In three days I would be back at school, with the nuns. I sat on the
front porch feeling depressed.

"Hey, Pete."

"Gotta make like a tree and leave, Garn," he told me. They were putting up a tent near the pool. There were planters to fill, and day workers trampling the grass. Pete loped off, looking worried.

Et tu, Pete?

The sound of fast tires on gravel made me sit up straight. Dane Blackmoor sped by in the Jag. He beeped the horn once, pulling smoothly into the garage.

He seemed altered somehow, angry, as though he hated himself for coming back. This time, instead of a beautiful woman, he brought with him a large white bird, which he allowed to fly through the house. He never referred to the thing, never called it by name; and he ignored the hubbub that it made by landing on people's heads or plates with a flurry of white wings.

He barely spoke to me. "Blackmoor's different, isn't he?" I asked Cathy in the kitchen.

She raised a carefully drawn eyebrow. "He's on a real bender."

"What's a bender?"

Cathy mimed throwing back a drink.

I considered this. My Real Father was obviously a man plagued by personal demons. It made him even more perfect. Dane Blackmoor needed me in a way that Dudley never would. That's why he had come back. I resolved then and there not to let him go away again without telling me the truth.

By Labor Day weekend the house was filled with laughter and music. Hot and cold-running buffets had been set up out by the pool, where Dulcie Mariah songs blared over a rented stereo system. Dane Blackmoor appeared in the middle of a crowd, or not at all. On Sunday night I watched for a while as he did card tricks for a group of admirers. For some reason, the sight of his fast, graceful hands made my chest ache. I was tired of summer, tired of hanging around the periphery of the crowd, acting as though I belonged. I walked back to the house.

The downstairs looked like a cyclone had hit. Still, it was quiet, the noise from outside muffled by thick paneling and drapery. I took a sweater from the hall closet and headed for the porch. The grizzled artist was standing in the foyer. "Keep up that work," he said, holding out a palsied hand for me to shake.

"You're leaving?" I asked, surprised at the disappointment in my voice.

He adjusted the filthy canvas sack over his back. "All good things come to an end. Just wanted to thank the woman of the house—" He peeked into the drawing room. Cilda sat, sound asleep on the sofa, amidst a littering of empty cups and discarded plates. Putting a finger to his lips, he winked. "Tell her I said goodbye."

I followed him out to the front porch. "What work?" I asked. "What work should I keep up?"

"The watching," the painter said, cryptically. Then he limped down the drive.

I sat on the steps. All around me, on the wicker tables, wax candles burned with the spent brilliance of small, erupted volcanoes. Crickets chirped, signaling the demise of summer to each other in their own private Morse code. I felt alone, at the end of the world.

From the bushes came a wild *thwapping,* a swoosh of white. Blackmoor's cockatoo landed on the porch railing in front of me, screeching. *"Hihowareya, hihowareya!"*

"Stay away," I warned. The bird cocked its head, so that one glassy eye looked heavenward, the other at my leg. *"Gottalight?"* I shooed it with my skirt.

"He won't hurt you." Blackmoor stepped out from the garden, quiet as an Indian.

"I'm afraid of birds," I said.

Dane snapped his fingers and the cockatoo hopped off the railing onto the back of his hand as though it were stepping onto a bus. "She doesn't trust us," he told the bird. It squawked again, surveying the porch, walleyed. He opened the front door and flicked the bird off his hand. It flew upstairs, probably to crap on somebody's bedpost.

Blackmoor sat in a wicker chair, near one of the tables with the burning candles, playing with a wad of soft melted wax, rolling it in his palm, shaping it with his fingers. A shriek came from out back. Somebody had been thrown into the pool. The music was mellower now, though, quieter than the crickets.

"When you were here last time"—I didn't look at him—"you said you wanted to talk to me about something."

"I did?" He appeared totally engrossed in the ball of wax.

"Yes." *Don't you remember? You must remember.*

For a long while Blackmoor said nothing; then he handed his wax creation over to me in the darkness. He had fashioned it into the shape of my head. My profile. My unruly mess of long hair. It was the most beautiful thing I'd ever seen.

I told him so.

He stared levelly into my eyes. "There are people in Third World countries who would say that now I have your soul."

I wanted to say something clever back to him, but I couldn't even frame a simple declarative sentence. Frustrated, I burst out, "I don't even— I don't even know what to call you. . . ."

Blackmoor didn't break his gaze. "What do you want to call me?" he asked.

Father, I screamed inwardly, *I want to call you Father.* Out loud I said, "I don't know. I just feel like there's—some kind of connection—between us."

He looked at me for what seemed to be a long time. If it hadn't been so totally out of character for him, I might have thought he looked confused. Finally he said, "Yes," and then, "Yes, I suppose it's inevitable you would feel that." The hard lines of his face softened. *This is it,* I thought, *he's going to tell me.*

The front door swung open. Cilda's dark silhouette loomed over us. I waited for the word "Ga'ner!" to crack like a mean Jamaican whip, but it never came. Her silence was more ominous. Dane Blackmoor rose to his feet.

"Good evening, Mrs. Fields," he said politely.

Cilda glowered. "That bird flying all over some lady by the pool, and 'er screamin' to wake the dead."

"I'll take care of it." Blackmoor strode to the door.

"You know, Mrs. Fields," he said, coming to a stop next to her, "you have an extraordinary face." He went inside without saying goodnight.

"Past time you're in bed." When I stood at once, she added crossly, "What you tink you're looking at?"

"Nothing," I replied. But I *was* looking at something. I was looking at Cilda through Blackmoor's eyes, astonished to find that someone that old, someone way up in their twenties could still be, as he said, quite extraordinary.

The festivities continued early the next day. For Cilda, Margaret, Pete, and the rest of the staff, it was the final push. Tomorrow the outsiders would be gone. They'd pick up the mess, and, by the end of the week, things would be back to normal.

Back to normal for me meant exchanging frumpy sundresses for frumpy school uniforms. It meant listening to the nuns, going to Mass, and coming back to eat dinner with Cilda, alone—no more houseguests, no more excitement, no more Dudley. Most important of all, no more Dane Blackmoor. It had to be today. Somehow, some way, I'd find out the truth about Dane and my mother.

From the bedroom window, I could already see several women stretched out on chaise lounges by the pool, well-oiled bodies begging the sun to ravish them. I studied the style of their bathing suits, and the way they fit into them, then I went over to my bed, sliding my hand under the mattress where the snowy-white Maidenform bra with the pink satin ribbon was hidden. I put it on.

After all it had taken to buy the thing without Cilda knowing, the final results were disappointing. I stuffed some tissue inside, putting the palms of my hands against the outside of the cups and squeezing as tightly as I could. A thrilling swell of cleavage appeared.

Outside, a woman shrieked with laughter. I hid behind the folds of the frilly lace curtain, watching as a man chased her around the pool, zapping her behind with a wet towel.

Later on, there would be fireworks and dancing. Dudley had hired a band. I had a feeling it was going to be the most important night of my life. An occasion that demanded more than new underwear. I had things to do.

12

The music started at nine. I waited in my room for Cathy's knock—*one-two-one-two-three*—before opening the door, self-consciously.

"Absolutely-positively outtasight," she told me, adjusting the scarf around my hips, blousing Dudley's V-neck undershirt until it was several inches above my knees. "Here." She dabbed some gloss on my lips. "Now go like this." She made a sound like white gloves clapping.

"Look at you!" she cried, shoving me in front of the mirror. The white of the T-shirt made my light tan appear darker. I'd sewn the little satin ribbon from the training bra onto the front, where it dipped into a vee. My hair was the only failure. Cathy had rolled it with Campbell's soup cans, but instead of coming out straight, I was left with long, sausage-shaped spirals.

"I don't look dumb?"

"No," she assured me, not bothering to mask the surprise in her voice. "But you better hurry before old Cildo the Dildo gets a load." I took a deep breath, and walked to the door. "Knock 'im dead, who-ever he is," she called.

There was no time to explain that he was my father; and that I didn't want to knock him dead. I wanted to make him proud of me.

I wove my way through the clusters of people on the lawn. An older woman, a friend of Geoffrey's, stopped me—*Wait! Now turn around . . . Well, aren't you quite the thing!* As I walked away, I moved more confidently.

Dudley was holding court out at the pool. I felt sure he saw me, that he even looked twice before turning back to his guests. I couldn't find Blackmoor. His bird was sitting high up in the tent. Every so often it swooped down and picked something off a dis-carded plate. Geoffrey Nash came dancing by, very drunk. "Garner, my sweet," he cried, "come dance with me!" Ignoring my protests that I couldn't, I didn't know how, he pulled me onto the crowded patio dance floor.

I stood there, frozen for a moment, unsure of what to do. As a dancer, Geoff seemed more earnest than skilled. I started bouncing, the way everyone else was. Once I had that down, I copied the chug-ging motion they were making with their hands, a gesture that looked like what kids did when they pretended to be locomotives. Suddenly, it no longer mattered whether I was doing it right or not. I was having fun.

I tossed my head back and laughed out loud. Geoff grabbed me around the waist, spinning me so clumsily, I laughed harder. Everything—the night, the people, the crazy dance—was a neon blur. Tall garden torches hung on the darkness like diamond drop earrings. The bass rhythm tickled the bottom of my feet. When Geoff finally released me, it took a minute to focus. Out of the cor-ner of my eye, I thought I saw Blackmoor. I stiffened, self-conscious again.

The music ended. Geoffrey bowed low from the waist and wandered off to find another drink. I drifted in the direction where I'd glimpsed Blackmoor, but there was no sign of him now. The crush of people had started to make me feel almost seasick. I threaded through them, past them, toward the very edge of the garden.

Even though the air was cool, I found I'd perspired right through the T-shirt. My partially straightened hair had already started to kink, the sausage curls unraveling. I leaned up against one of Pete's massive planters and closed my eyes. On the patio, Dudley was making an announcement about the fireworks—*"ten minutes . . . so if . . . a place . . . near the tennis courts"*—sounding as if he were speaking into a defective microphone. I considered going over to claim a seat.

"Don't you like fireworks?"

"They're okay," I replied, my heart quickening.

"Noise, flash, sputter," Blackmoor said derisively. "Like life." He leaned up against the planter, next to me. I could smell the liquor on his breath. He offered me his glass, and I put it up to my lips without even checking first, drinking what was left out of real thirst.

The band was on a break. Over the stereo speakers, Dulcie Mariah's gravelly voice unsettled the night. "Come on," he said. "Let's get out of here." He took my hand, quite naturally, leading me back toward the house. As we were going in, Cilda was coming out with a platter of food. I pressed myself against Blackmoor, trying to hide. His shirt smelled of a steam iron and talc.

I had no idea where he was taking me. It didn't matter, I thought, as long as I could talk to him alone. He lurched up the center staircase, pausing at the top for a split second as though he were momentarily disoriented.

"And where does the mysterious Garnish Quinn live?" he asked huskily, swaying a little on his feet.

"There," I pointed to the door, to the flowery enameled plaque with my name on it. He turned the knob. I walked in first, remembering too late the altar I had made on my bedstand: the shell he'd given me that first day . . . the tiny wax sculpture . . . the picture of him, with my mother . . .

Blackmoor passed by it without noticing. "This might be where the mysterious Garnish sleeps," he said, "but no way is this where she lives."

"One of Dudley's girlfriends decorated it," I told him.

"Now why doesn't that surprise me?" He laughed; and I did too.

I sat on the bed. "I've never felt like it was mine. Any of it." The half-glass of wine had hit me full in the face, making my mouth move before my brain could stop it. "I've never felt like I belonged anywhere," I heard myself say, "until I saw that picture of my mother and you."

Blackmoor looked at me, his head cocked almost like the damn bird's. "Sometimes I think you know what you're saying," he said softly, "and sometimes I think you haven't a clue."

I stared squarely into his eyes. "I have a clue," I said. He started toward me. I thought: *In one more breath, I'll feel his arms around me, fatherly, comforting, strong.*

And yet, when it happened, it wasn't that way at all.

Instead of moving his head to the side, he approached me, full on. His skin was hot, much drier than my own, his breath sweet and grapey. Suddenly, he was on me, mouth to mouth, chest to chest, his hips thrust forward, with the obvious difference which made a direct match impossible.

I struggled. His head came up once, like a drowning man out of the water, gasping for air before going down again. "Stop," I panted. "Wha—what are you doing?"

When he came up this time, the light was totally out of his eyes. "What do you think I'm doing?" he whispered hoarsely. "You wanted this. Isn't this what you wanted?"

I pulled out from under him, squiggling back on my hindquarters until I reached the headboard. "No," I cried, shielding myself with a pillow. "I wanted a father!" I picked up the photograph on the bed-stand and hurled it at him. "*I wanted you to be my father!*"

Blackmoor said nothing for a time. Then he dropped off the side of the bed, onto his knees, laughing. Really laughing. "Oh, that's great," he sputtered, "that's . . . price—! A fath—! . . . S'great!" His words came out in ragged, drunken hiccups. I waited, watching him, still trembling.

From outside I heard *tat-tat-tat-tat-tat—ohhhh! . . . tat-tat-tat-tat-tat—ohhhh!* The fireworks had begun. After a while Blackmoor stood up and brushed himself off. He leaned the photograph against the lamp on the bedstand next to the shell and the shrunken wax head.

"Whether you know it or not, little girl," he said, his head so close his eyelashes brushed my cheek, "you're not looking for a daddy."

I started to say something. Didn't. He took my face in his hands, inspecting it under the light for flaws, the way he had the first time we'd met. "When you find out what you *are* looking for," he said, "give me a call." Then, very, very slowly, he leaned down and kissed me on the lips.

And the room exploded.

Dudley charged toward the bed, propelling Blackmoor backward by the collar of his shirt. Dane didn't have time to right himself before Dudley's fist hauled back and let go with a crack square to the jaw. He crashed into the wall, knocking botanical prints off moiré ribbons and onto the floor.

"I want you out of this house," Dudley bellowed. "Now."

Blackmoor rubbed the side of his face. His eyes had regained their old taunting light. He walked calmly to the door, where Cilda was on guard.

"Just in case there should be any question," he said before leaving, "it wasn't her fault." After he'd gone, we stood in stunned silence, the three of us, me shaking uncontrollably. I tried to stand. The scarf had been pulled loose from my makeshift dress, the T-shirt edged off my shoulder. Dudley took a step toward me.

"I'm sorry, Daddy," I cried, holding my arms out to him.

"You're a slut, just like your mother," he said. The door slammed behind him.

I sank to the floor, feeling Cilda's strong arms around me. "Ga'ner, Ga'ner. Ga'ner Quinn." She rocked, singing my name over and over into my ears.

And I thought, as my heart was breaking, *I'll get them back. Both of them. Someday I'll make them pay.*

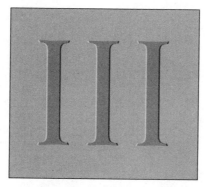

THE HEAD

THE HEAD WAS SEVERED AT THE NECK AND DIPPED IN AN ACRYLIC FIXATIVE, PRESUMABLY TO PREVENT MOISTURE AND ODOR FROM SEEPING OUT OF THE PLASTER CASING. IRONICALLY, THE LACQUERED SURFACE ALSO ACTED AS A PRESERVATIVE. THE YOUNG WOMAN HAS BEEN IDENTIFIED AS VICTORIA (TORIE) LYNNE WOOD, AGE 16. A SPOKESMAN FOR DANE BLACKMOOR CONFIRMED THAT WOOD HAD WORKED AS AN ASSISTANT IN HIS BUCKS COUNTY STUDIO, MODELING FOR SEVERAL OF THE SCULPTOR'S WORKS BEFORE HER DISAPPEARANCE IN MARCH OF LAST YEAR.

USA TODAY
(NOVEMBER 25, 1994)

ALTHOUGH DANE BLACKMOOR PROFESSED ASTONISHMENT AT THE RECENT TURN OF EVENTS, THIS IS HARDLY THE FIRST TIME THAT VIOLENCE AND SCANDAL HAVE TOUCHED HIS OTHERWISE CHARMED LIFE. IN 1977 A YOUNG WOMAN SHOT HERSELF AT A PARTY GIVEN BY THE SCULPTOR, IN FULL VIEW OF THE OTHER GUESTS. THEN, IN 1984, BLACKMOOR'S LONGTIME FRIEND, GALLERY OWNER CONRAD VESTRI, WAS CONVICTED IN THE S&M MURDERS OF TWO YOUNG MEN.

NEW YORK MAGAZINE
(NOVEMBER 28, 1994)

1

If the curators of the Metropolitan Museum of Art were embarrassed about hosting a gala opening for a potential murderer, you couldn't tell from the huge banner that fairly screamed Blackmoor and the title of the show, "PAWNS." A fine drizzle had begun, curling my hair until it swelled off my shoulders like some exotic fake fur.

The building was bathed in light. Spherical cones caught the raindrops within patterned arcs, silvering the pavement as if just for the occasion. At the main entrance, a bottleneck of glitterati trailed umbrellas like open parachutes. The rich and cultured apparently had never heard of the concept single file.

At the door, a uniformed guard asked to see my invitation. "I didn't bring it," I said. "My name is Garner Quinn—"

A small, very pale man dressed in white suddenly appeared. "It's quite all right, Derwin," he told the guard, adding, "Such a night! I do hope you'll enjoy the show, Ms. Quinn." He handed me a catalogue imprinted with the same logo I'd seen on the flag outside. I was about to ask him if he knew where Blackmoor was, but he slipped back into the crowd.

My eyes focused on the dazzling crush. Then they blurred and readjusted, like the lens of a camera. *Oh, no,* I thought. *Tell me I'm hallucinating.*

Everyone was in costume.

Fantastic ensembles. Black. White. Black and white. Women floated by wearing low-cut Josephine gowns, and wide, wasp-waist Elizabethan skirts. The men sported capes, ebony breastplates, cloaks, cowls. In the grand hall I passed a stunning girl in a short belted tunic and tights, whose face I recognized from the covers of magazines. Some carried the black-and-white theme to extremes: powdered wigs and powdered faces; lacquered hair; onyx lips and nails. I did a quick inventory—miters, crowns, scepters, swords, dark, light, checkerboard; rooks, queens, kings, knights, bishops.

Dane Blackmoor had staged his own flesh-and-blood chess game for the gala opening of "PAWNS." It occurred to me that the suggested dress for the evening must have been printed on the invitation, but to have read that far would've been akin to admitting I was going. My rain-splotched red dress stood out like a clot of blood. So much for blending in with the crowd.

A waiter clad in a velvet doublet and tights tipped a tray of fluted glasses toward me. I drained the champagne in one gulp. The properly attired invitees were making a show of not staring in my direction. I summoned up my reserve of brass and walked into the exhibit.

A woman in a skin-tight yellow polka-dot halter dress had stopped to pose for a picture, just inside the entrance archway. My first thought was, Thank God, another fashion faux pas. Then I did a doubletake. The blonde bombshell and the eager photographer remained perfectly immobile—fiberglass figures frozen in some picture shoot from hell; his finger on the button, her lips drawn up in a perpetually teasing kissy-pout.

The plaque read: "*Starlet,* Dane Blackmoor, 1979."

I stood as close as I could. Blackmoor had shaded the area around the eyes in order to make the plastic inserts appear more true-to-life. The starlet's nails were painted with crimson polish, and there was a growth of wiry hair on the photographer's wrists, above his shirt cuff. Nothing—not even the smallest of details—seemed to have escaped him.

The exhibit hall showcased some of the sculptor's most famous works. In the center of the room was a graffitied subway car. Its doors gaped open, revealing the passengers inside—a still-life of dead eyes and beaten, blank expressions. I glanced down at the plaque. This was *The D Train*, the work that had first brought Blackmoor to the public's attention.

Invited guests glided by, commenting in a low buzz, like large, exotic bugs in some rare species of insects. I had the feeling that if I stood still for any length of time, one of them would pause to coolly appraise the lifelike texture of my hair; so I kept moving, trying to search out Blackmoor in the crowd. I wondered how he'd be dressed. Dark knight? A king, caped in ermine? Or hooded bishop of black magic art?

I paused, drawn to a sculpture called *Crack*. A young black couple was seated at a Formica kitchen table, about to light up their pipes. The table was the kind Donna Reed had set to serve dinner to her freshly scrubbed family.

The small man in the white suit suddenly appeared at my elbow. "Have you seen Dane yet?" he asked.

"No. Actually, I'm not sure I'd recognize him, with all these costumes."

"Oh, you'll recognize him," he said. His skin shimmered with a light coating of powder. He wore mascara, too, I saw now. "You might try looking near *The Hospice*." He turned away from me to greet a large, pompadoured Marie Antoinette, burying his face in her bosom with a delighted whoop.

The Hospice was a frozen tableau of wasted young men sitting in the common room of a hospital, staring at a television. A video played continuously on the screen, President Clinton droning on and on about what he was doing in the area of AIDS research. This work seemed to be commanding a lot of attention, but I found no one who even vaguely resembled Dane Blackmoor.

Single-figure sculptures flanked the walls of the grand hall. Each piece had been placed in front of a mirror, creating an eerie effect— a roomful of silent, hollow people. Most of the figures were recognizable types. A Playboy bunny. A benched football player. A corporate executive hefting a briefcase. A drum majorette. A black Jehovah's Witness clutching a handful of pamphlets.

From the artist's perspective, pawns, one and all.

I started to feel dizzy. The line of plaster casts, refracted, then multiplied by the mirrors, crowded me, closing in on all sides. I've always been slightly claustrophobic; but usually the attacks came in closed, small spaces with a lot of people—not lofty, high places with no living person in sight.

I spotted a bench at the end of the hall. *Just make it that far,* I told myself, *and you'll be all right.*

Then, quite suddenly, I saw him, at the end of the row of figures, standing there, staring, in a charcoal Armani suit, a white shirt, a claret-colored tie. "I hear you've been looking for me." My voice sounded unsteady.

His came from behind. "Yes."

I spun around, too quick. "I—" That was all I managed, before the faint.

I came to, fighting. He was holding a glass of something to my lips. "What happened?"

"Your legs gave out." Blackmoor smiled with those ready-to-bite teeth. "The excitement of seeing me again, I suppose."

I struggled to sit up. My surroundings were gradually coming into focus. A cushiony seat. Low overhead. Plush, padded interior. "Where are we?"

"A 1933 Silver Shadow Rolls-Royce." Blackmoor tapped on the

glass panel. "This is Jeeves," he said, indicating the plaster-cast chauffeur behind the wheel, "and that is Mrs. Whittaker."

I felt the stiff, cool hardness before I saw her—a withered old dowager sitting on the seat right beside me, one gnarled hand clasped over the silver top of her cane. I almost jumped out of my skin. "Tell Jeeves I'd like to go home now." Blackmoor laughed. "I mean it."

He leveled a deadly gaze at me. "I suppose you would rather we'd met in another setting. Like perhaps prison. Of course, they haven't accused me of anything yet. But be patient, Garnish. I'm sure they will." He handed me the glass again. "Mineral water," he said, noting my hesitation. "Pure as the driven snow."

I drank it down, thirstily. He said, "I'm sorry about your mother."

That confused me; then I realized he was offering sympathy so long after the fact. I couldn't even say for sure what year my mother died, only that Dudley had shipped me off to boarding school by then. I might not have known at all, if it weren't for Cilda, showing up at my dormitory, in her plain wool coat and hat. "Ga'ner," she said, "you got to say goodbye to your mama now."

The service was held in Manhattan. I remember being shocked at the number of people trailing up to toss roses on the glossy white casket, some of them openly weeping—the whole world, it seemed, minus my father. The whole world, and I wouldn't have even known, except for Cilda.

Later I found out Dudley had paid for the funeral. It seemed too little, too late.

I handed Blackmoor the empty glass. "Why did you invite me here?" I asked.

"I thought that was obvious." He needled me with those eyes. "No need to concoct a complicated plot, unless it's out of habit." I reached for the door handle. He put his hand over mine. "Don't go. Please."

I slid out from his grasp, feeling the sculpted old woman's cane in the small of my back. From this position, I had an unobstructed view of Blackmoor's face. Something I saw there made me instantly relax—the sarcastic curve of his lips had tightened into a line of fear. "Where's your costume?" I asked him.

"I'm not a pawn," he said. "Where's yours?"

I felt his eyes travel over me. More than anything I wanted to pull my short red skirt down over my knees. I sat on my hands. "This is business," I told him. "I don't dress up on the job."

"Do you drink?" Blackmoor produced a bottle and two stem glasses from a paneled box on the door. "I thought we might switch to champagne," he said, "unless you feel another swoon coming on."

"Let's cut to the chase," I said.

He started to pour, the pale blond liquid hissing into the glass. "Things are heating up. There's talk of bringing in some sort of so-phisticated equipment to X-ray my work. My lawyer's fighting it, of course, but . . ." He shrugged, offering me the champagne.

"And if they do X-ray the other sculptures? What do you think they'll find?"

Blackmoor smiled sadly. "One can only imagine."

I took a sip of the drink, feeling cool and hotheaded all at the same time. "Where do I come in?"

The question seemed to fluster him. "I just thought," he said, clearly at a loss, "well, someone's bound to write about it. . . ."

"And you decided it should be me?"

"Yours was the name that came to mind." He topped his own glass.

The knock on the car door startled both of us. Blackmoor rolled down the window. A tall woman dressed in a white Juliet gown leaned forward to speak with him. With her heart-shaped face and braided dark hair, she reminded me of those doe-eyed beauties Errol Flynn had wooed in all the movies where he'd worn tights. "Excuse me, Dane," she said, "but they're ready for you now."

He waved her off. "So what do you say?" he asked, turning back to me. "If this thing turns ugly, as I suspect it will, do you want to come along for the ride?"

"I'll think it over."

Blackmoor opened the door and unfolded himself out of the car. He moved like a cat. A big, dangerous cat. "Next time, come to the Mill," he said, referring to his Bucks County studio.

I went for the handle on my side, but the sculpture of the old lady was blocking my exit. My dress caught as I lurched into the opposite seat. When I finally emerged from the car, I was once again feeling dizzy and faint.

Dane Blackmoor was nowhere in sight.

2

"Why can't I go down to Columbia with you?" Temple wanted to know. "I'm all better." People always said she took after me, but I thought she was the spitting image of Andy. Which was okay. By the end of our marriage, Andy's looks were the only thing I still liked about him.

I zipped up the tote and sat on the edge of the bed. "You have school. There's no one down there to take care of you, and besides, I'll be working. I'm going to need all my concentration."

"I wouldn't be a bother."

"Next time."

"You always say that," Temple countered.

I pulled her onto my lap. "It won't be long before I'm home for good." That was something else I always said.

Temple swung her legs off the floor, and snuggled against my shoulder—not an easy feat for either of us. She'd grown another inch since the Turner trial, and her body felt strange. Long and angular in some places, soft and round in others. Still, I tried to hold her as though she were four and not fourteen.

"It was on 'A Current Affair' that Heather Locklear's going to play Susan Trevett," she said.

"You know I don't like you watching those kinds of shows." I gently pushed her to her feet. I was tired of talking about the Holy Ghost, about Susan Trevett and Jefferson Turner. Jack had been right. For me, that book was as good as over. A flicker of Dane Black-moor's face passed through my mind. Dane Blackmoor, looking scared.

"Come on, we've got three whole hours before I have to leave," I said, giving Temple a playful slap on the behind. "Let's see how much junk food we can eat."

I took a whole stack of mail to read on the plane. Halfway down the pile was a plain envelope, square and white, addressed in a hap-hazard assortment of capital and small-case letters to *Miss Garner Quinn, PERSONAL*, no return address.

His name, he said, was Peter Michael Salvatore. Twelve years ago he and his mother had spent a summer in Myrna, North Car-olina, right down the road from where Jefferson Turner lived. *My fa-ther,* wrote Peter, *left us in March. I saw him at breakfast. We had oatmeal with butter and sugar. I spilt my milk and some got on his suit. For a long time I thought he didn't come back because I spilled that milk on him. My mother never said anything. She cried a lot. Then one day she told me we were going on a trip to visit our relations down South. We went by Greyhound from Newark to Raleigh. My mother's cousin met us in his pickup truck and we drove the rest of the way to Myrna.*

Up to this point in the letter, Salvatore's handwriting was small and precise. Now, with every handwritten page, front and back, it became bigger, sprawling from one margin to the next so that some-times only three or four words fit on a line.

He'd met Jeff on his first day there, Peter wrote, and over the next few months, the two boys spent every waking hour together.

His mother, he said, still cried all the time. The trailer where they were staying was very cramped, and he missed his friends back home. Jeff lived with his mom, just as he did. His dad had left him, too. He was popular with the kids and very friendly; but Peter added, he too was a lost soul.

The words *lost soul* were underlined three times, in thick, inky slashes.

The two boys spent most of their time, the letter went on, out by the railroad tracks or with the creatures Jeff kept in cages near the barn. Here Peter Salvatore began to digress—*I always wanted to be a priest*, he wrote, *I felt I had a calling from God.* He had been an altar boy, he said, and he went to parochial school. Peter Salvatore changed to flowing script—*Cardinal John Henry Newman, who I'm sure you know is now a Saint, Miss Quinn, tells us if we don't like being in church we won't like being in heaven. I will love heaven, Miss Quinn,* he assured me, *because I have always loved everything about church.*

That was why, Peter continued, his mother had made him the priest's robe in the first place. And that was how he and Jeff came to celebrate those funeral masses, after twilight, on the edge of Jeff's grandaddy's fields, so many summers ago.

In the beginning—Peter wrote in his fast, wild hand—he hadn't known. He'd thought that the little birds, the rabbits, and the cats simply died. Everybody dumped off their sick animals at the Turner place so Jeff could look after them. He said he'd just assumed they were a lot sicker than anyone figured.

Then one morning, he came up behind his friend, catching him unawares. Jeff stood halfway inside the cage where he kept the birds, his body bent in concentration. When Peter called him, he turned, and it was then that Salvatore saw.

Jefferson Turner was choking the life out of a small sparrow. Breaking its neck in his big farmboy hand. *He didn't blink an eye,* Peter wrote, *just smiled and said, "Looks like we got another burial tonight."* Then he put the dead thing into my hand and walked away.

· · ·

The letter became difficult to read, as though the writer's brain were spilling thoughts directly onto the page without the benefit of a hand to neatly contain them. Sentences were disjointed, entire words left out; the ones that remained jumped off the page like a message in Morse code.

Salvatore began talking about a salesman named George, and how George had condemned his mother's soul to damnation— "*A wife must not separate from her husband. But if she does, she must remain unmarried or else be reconciled to her husband.*" *Unmarried* was also underlined three times. However George fit into the picture, it was clear from the rest of the letter that Peter and his mother had left Myrna that September.

I have sinned, Miss Quinn, Peter Michael Salvatore wrote. He made a long list of his transgressions, using terms ranging from the biblical ("*coveting*") to the colorful ("*jacking off*"). Two words were offset by asterisks:

* LUST *
* GRAVEN IMAGES *

To further emphasize them, he'd circled these words with a red marker.

From the abrupt change in the penmanship, I guessed that Salvatore had stopped at this point, adding the last paragraph later. There, in a small, carefully controlled hand, he wrote:

> *I know who you are. I read that you are doing a book on Jefferson Turner. I believe you are a woman of Truth, and a Catholic. I tell you about the Monster that is Jeff, so I might be sent for perpetual Atonement and Penitence in Purgatory instead of perishing in the mouth of Hell forever.*
>
> Peter Michael Salvatore

At the bottom of the page, there were several postscripts.

P.S., Peter wrote. *The newspapers are wrong about the nickname. I was the first one to call him Bird, after the sparrow.* He added, *P.P.S.: Even after I knew, we buried a cat and two dogs.*

In the right-hand corner, Salvatore had printed *JMJ*, which I remembered from my parochial school days as standing for Jesus-Mary-Joseph; and then, perhaps as an afterthought, were these neatly printed words:

I still think of him as my friend.

The return address was on the bottom of the page. Whatever had happened to Salvatore in the years between his childhood encounter with Bird Turner was anybody's guess. At the time of writing this letter, he was living in a seminary.

Over the aircraft intercom the captain said, "Ladies and gentlemen, we are beginning our approach . . ." but I turned him out. I was thinking about Peter Salvatore and how, with a scribbled *JMJ* and some hand-sewn vestments, he had reopened a book I thought I'd shut for good.

3

I sat in my usual seat in the courtroom. Everything appeared much the same as it had only forty-eight hours before. But, in my eyes, everything was different.

"If what you're saying is true"—Nick Shawde's voice boomed—"how is it you described Jeff Turner's van in such detail?"

Susan Trevett Cox shifted in the witness chair. "I wish I could tell you that, sir," she said softly. "Everything happened so fast. The detectives kept asking for details, and somehow this van popped into my head. Maybe I'd seen it in the parking lot at Annalee's, or driving around town, and with all the pressure, it just came out, the description, before I even had time to think."

"And yet, you did later identify Jeff Turner as your assailant?"

"Yeah," Susan sighed. "Like I said, I was real messed up. My heart was hardened with sin."

Ask her why she said he spoke in Latin, Nick, I thought to myself.

Ask her how come they found greasepaint on the sleeve of her blouse. Things that had bothered me, tiny inconsistencies softened over time, once again nagged at me.

Shawde walked slowly toward the jury. "So you're telling us that Jefferson Turner is innocent of the heinous crime of which he's been accused?"

"Absolutely, positively." Susan's blond head bobbed, her voice as confident as it had been on that sweltering hot day a year before, when she'd first picked Jeff Turner out of the police lineup.

"I wish I could remember," Jeff told me, earnestly. "If you want me to say I do, I will, if it'll help you."

I don't want you to help me, I thought, *I want you to help yourself.* I said, "I only want you to tell me the truth."

"I'm tellin' the truth." He sounded hurt now. The guard glanced over in our direction.

"Like I said," he went on, "I vaguely picture a lady and a boy living in Teeny Lloyd's trailer. I might've been about twelve or thirteen, I don't know. But as for the priest stuff, and the funerals, that's something that this Salvatore kid must've dreamed up himself, in his head."

"Why do you think he'd make up something like that?"

"I don't know," he sighed. "My whole life I always brought home strays. Not only the four-legged kind, either, you know what I'm saying? I guess I felt sorry for the sort of people other folks made fun of. So I talked to 'em, treated 'em friendly. Which kinda made me their hero." He flushed, visibly embarrassed.

"But some of 'em were so lonely and mixed up, they started on imagining things. That I was their best friend, or their brother, or their sweetheart—and if I tried to set 'em straight, even if I was as gentle as could be about it, why, they'd like to turn on me." He paused, looking straight into my eyes. "That's what I think must've happened with this Peter Salva-whatever-his-name-was, don't you?"

I said I didn't know, but I was going to find out.

"I'm trying to reach a Peter Salvatore," I said, trying to remember what they called young men who weren't yet priests. "I believe he's a student at Saint Anthony's."

"Can you hold, please, while I switch you?" The operator didn't wait for a response.

"Father Podalski speaking." I repeated that I was trying to call Peter Salvatore. "Are you a member of the family?" Father Podalski asked.

"No, Father. My name is Garner Quinn. Mr. Salvatore wrote me a letter with regard to a book I'm writing. I hoped to be able to talk to him in person."

"I'm afraid that's not possible." I flashed back to the Catholic schooling of my childhood, wondering if Podalski had images of me as a lipglossed temptress trying to lure chaste young men out from cloistered walls.

"If he's in class"—or fasting or praying or putting on his hair shirt, I thought, irreverently—"I could call back at a more convenient time."

"There is no convenient time for Peter Salvatore," the man said with unpriestly candor. "The young man is dead."

When I called Jack that night, he sounded skeptical. "The guy was obviously one bead short of a rosary," he said.

I cradled the phone on my shoulder and walked over to the closet. The dark suit would do. I took it off the hotel hanger and draped it over a chair. "Maybe. But this isn't the kind of loose end I can afford to leave hanging."

"You want me to drive over to the seminary and check it out?" I heard the eagerness in his voice.

"Actually, I want you to book a flight to Columbia. Shawde's calling his expert witnesses tomorrow. I need you here." I was relieved when he didn't point out that it would have made more sense for him to go to St. Anthony's, a mere two-hour drive from the beach house. It didn't matter that my plan would mean a lot of extra travel for both of us. I wanted to handle the Salvatore situation myself.

"You know what to do. Keep your eyes and ears open. Pay attention to people. Not just what they say, but how they say it. Facts we can verify later, from the court report. There's a room already reserved for you." I threw a shirt and a pair of jeans into my leather satchel. "I should be back tomorrow night. Wednesday at the latest."

Before putting me on with Temple, he said, "By the way, a guy named Roberto called. Wanted to set up an appointment with you to go out and see Dane Blackmoor's studio at someplace called the Mill."

"I can't think about that now," I told him. According to the latest television reports, attorney Diana Gold had failed in her attempt to block investigators from X-raying several of her client's sculptures that had been completed around the same time as *Lady Sitting*. The noose was tightening around Blackmoor's neck.

It was the only good piece of news I'd had all day.

4

They'd found him hanging from one of the rafters in the choir loft, Monsignor Fahy said.

He reminded me of the priests I'd known as a girl—white-haired, apple-cheeked men with nicotine stains on their teeth and fingers, and a worldly knowledge of sports and entertainment.

"I saw your film," he said as we shook hands. "The one about the Mariah trial." He looked crushed when I told him I hadn't written the screenplay, visited the set, or met any of the actors. "Ah, well," he sighed, "but surely there'll be other murders." Then he caught himself, and laughed, his eyes telegraphing something more than simple ingenuousness.

He insisted I join him in a cup of tea, talking as we sipped about the history of the seminary, and how it had changed. When he was a lad, he said—using the word as an index to date himself to a gentler age—every good Catholic mother had one son who was marked as a designated hitter for God. Back then, St. Anthony's had been teeming with fresh-faced, strapping young men—boys who played football, and missed kissing girls; boys who were proud and humble, idealistic about the vocation to which they'd been called.

"It's different today," he said, offering a plate of scones. When I refused, he spent a moment choosing the largest, most perfect, with the air of someone who doesn't take the tactile pleasures afforded him lightly.

"We have twelve now, all told. Next year the Diocese is moving us to 'newer facilities' near the university." He shook his head. "The heating bill in an old monstrosity like this can kill you, of course, and then there are the grounds—"

The monsignor winked. "But I've always felt it was easier to find God up here than in some Formica-and-chrome classroom where you've got to take the crucifix down after your lesson so as not to offend the next teacher."

He lit up a cigarette. "Peter Salvatore," he exhaled, watching the smoke rise.

"Yes." I had the feeling I was back at catechism. That this priest was going to teach me something important.

"He was one of the troubled ones," Fahy said. "You could see it right off." He swiveled around in his chair, looking out the window at the carefully tended garden below. "In the old days, he wouldn't have made it through the door."

The monsignor shrugged. "Peter was right on the edge, all the way, I'd say. When his mother died two months back, well, that was the turning point."

"He had a breakdown?"

"Not a breakdown, exactly. If anything he became more wound up—reading and studying all night. At the chapel every spare moment. He acted like a boy who"—he paused, as though the thought were coming to him for the first time—"who had a lot to do, and only a little while to do it in."

I waited, studying his profile, backlit by the slanting sun. After a moment, the monsignor continued. "We were going to dismiss him at the end of term," he said quietly. "The words used, I believe, are that an initiate is not 'suited for communal life.'" Again he turned away, with a deprecatory little laugh. I wondered what he was feeling.

"The boy left a note. We released it to the police, of course."

"Can you tell me the gist of it?"

"It was a bit rambling. He talked of his mother, who'd divorced and remarried outside of the church. Said her soul had been damned. He wrote that he'd confessed his sins to God, to a priest, and to 'an Avenging Angel of Truth' who would proclaim them to the world." The monsignor looked at me, his fleecy eyebrows hiked high. "I believe that may be you."

I uncrossed my legs, trying as hard as I could to look like an angel of anything. "Was there anything else?"

"Not that I can remember," said the old priest. "Except for the pictures."

"The pictures?"

"Drawings," he told me. "All over the bottom of the page."

"What kind of drawings?"

"Birds, mostly," Monsignor Fahy replied, "small birds." He closed his eyes as though trying to picture them. "I took it that he meant them as Doves of Peace come to take his soul. . . ." His voice trailed off.

I leaned forward. "But you're not sure?"

"Well, they looked a little like doves," the old man said, weighing his words carefully. "But something he wrote under them I found rather unsettling."

"What was that?"

"Graven images," Monsignor Fahy said softly. "He drew an arrow to the pictures and wrote: 'Graven images.'"

5

Instead of returning to Columbia, I booked a flight into Raleigh and rented a car.

St. Anthony's had turned out to be for me what it was for Peter. A dead end. According to the detectives who'd investigated his death, Salvatore's parents and his stepfather, George Fazekas, were deceased. Fazekas was the salesman, the one Peter believed had doomed his mother's soul. As I drove along the highway I pictured them, stuck together for all eternity in some unnumbered circle of the poor boy's personal hell: the absent father; the weak-willed woman; the young suicide; and George, with a straw hat and a salesman grin, smiling the smile of the damned.

By the time I reached Myrna, the clouds were dark with pent-up rain. I pulled the rental up beside the Turner barn. The place was deserted. Varlie was in Columbia, at the trial. *Last stop,* I called to the empty landscape. *Everybody out.*

I'd made a few calls from the airport, enough to determine that a man named Lloyd, called Teeny in spite of the fact that he weighed over three hundred pounds, had kept a house trailer on the edge of the Turner property for many years; but Teeny was dead now, and no one I'd talked to seemed to remember anything about any Yankee relatives ever having visited him.

I walked past the chicken coop, toward the rows of empty cages at the rear of the barn. The wind blew up suddenly, rattling cage doors, sending up a swell of tiny feathers inside, as though the spirits of many dead birds were beating their wings against them before settling onto the faded newspaper at the bottom of the hutches, like dust.

I remembered walking with Varlie through the untended fields, toward the low wrought-iron fence that marked off the family burial plot where Jeff's grandaddy lay, next to his granny and his uncle Jarvis.

"Seems like the place is all fallin' to pieces now that Bird's not around," she'd said. "I never wanted him to go down there to Columbia. I knew somethin' bad ud come a that art."

"It must seem pretty quiet," I'd commented, "now that the place isn't filled with all of Jeff's animals."

She'd seemed surprised. "Ye-eas. I reckon it is."

On a sudden impulse I'd asked what had happened to them. "Well," Varlie said, "I guess they most of them just passed on." She pointed to a patch of land about a hundred feet from the coops. "He always gave 'em Christian burials. Said they was goin' to a better place with Jarvis, and Granny and Grandaddy."

Her words echoed through my head with new meaning. I came to the exact spot where we'd stood together, fighting an incredible urge to sink my nails into the dry dirt, to paw the ground until it gave, to dig until I reached—what? a tiny skeleton? a chalky patch of nothing, the remains of something small and frail? Or a cigar-box coffin, lined in faded purple and marked with crosses?

A sudden sound came from behind me, high, unearthly, causing the hairs on my arm to stand up straight. A cat sprinted by, so close it brushed my calves. And then the sound again, same pitch, same frequency, like a hoot owl in the darkness.

From around the side of the barn, the girl slipped into view. She wore a light cotton dress sprinkled with flowers, her long brown hair freshly brushed. I raised my arm, the way a movie Injun says, "How." It was the only thing I could think of to do. I knew the girl was deaf.

"Hello, Jenny—remember me?" I said slowly as she came closer. "Garner Quinn? I spoke to you and your mom about Jeff Turner a few months back."

"I'm looking for my cat," she said, in a high, consonantless monotone, each syllable melding to the next.

"I saw him. He ran past me. Over the fence."

She smiled shyly. "Maybe he's going home."

I pictured the neat little farmhouse Jenny shared with her mother—every threadbare inch of sofa decked with a quilt and a cat. "I'll walk with you," I offered. We set out across the field together. Ahead of us, rain clouds the color of a day-old bruise spread across a pale skin of sky. When we reached the place where I judged Teeny Lloyd's trailer had once been, I touched her arm.

"Did you know Teeny?" Jenny nodded. I went on, pausing a little after every word. "I got a letter from a young man who said he was a relative of Mr. Lloyd's. He said he and his mom stayed here one summer, about eleven or twelve years ago." Shadows masked the girl's face, rendering it unreadable.

"His name was Peter," I told her, "Peter Salvatore. He must have been about your age. He said he was a friend of Jeff Turner's." Jenny nodded again. "Yes, you understand?" I asked. "Or, yes, you remember?"

"I remember," she said. "I saw them."

We'd stopped walking. The Price farmhouse was only about fifty yards away. There was a light in the front window. "Playing together?" My heart was beating fast now. Again, the nod. "What else, Jenny? What else did they do?"

Jenny's eyes widened. "I don't know," she cried, her voice somewhere between a wail and a computer tone. "I didn't see the other things!"

And then she ran inside, leaving me to wonder about the things unseen.

In the moment it took to follow the girl into the house, everything changed. Jenny would no longer speak to me, except through her mother.

No, she signed to Mrs. Price, who in turn told me, she couldn't remember any more about Bird Turner and the Yankee boy. The words "graven images" had no meaning for her, besides what was said in the Good Book. She knew nothing about strangled birds or Catholic funeral masses.

When I suggested that perhaps the prosecutor might have more questions for Jenny, Mrs. Price immediately became suspicious. "What for? There isn't nothin' else to say." She stood, ready to walk me to the door. "Bird was like a brother to that girl, Miz Quinn. Always watching out for her. Carryin' over baby kittens. Makin' drawings. Bringin' books." She turned to her daughter. "Bird treated you real special, didn't he, honey?"

Jenny's head bobbled up and down. "Ye-sss," she said. The word came out sounding like a foghorn, insistent and mournful. I would've liked to ask the girl a few more questions, but I was put off by the look in her eyes.

She was obviously still afraid of me.

6

Nick Shawde was on a roll.

"Now I don't know if you good people are believers in the Christian faith," he said to the jury, when, of course, he did, "but you have heard Susan Cox testify . . . No"—he gently reprimanded himself—"you have heard Mrs. Cox witness to the fact that on a fateful Sunday in April of last year she accepted the Lord Jesus Christ as her personal Savior."

Juror Six, the Pentecostal, whispered "Amen" under her breath.

Shawde went on. "And for those of you who may not know," he said, as if with the exception of himself, there could be an agnostic within direct earshot, "to a Christian, being born again means shucking off one's sins as a reptile shucks off his skin." His voice lowered, sadly. "And we have heard here, in this courtroom, that Susan Trevett Cox had, in her young life, many sins to count, and to account for—

"We have heard testimony, from members of her family, and

from those who knew her best, that Susan was robbed of her innocence at an early age." The defense attorney turned away from the
jury, his shoulders sagging a little under the impeccably tailored
suit—American-made and purchased especially for cases tried in
venues such as this.

"Molested by her stepfather and her brother from the age of
four"—he looked down at the floor, and then up again, all hellfire
and damnation—"from the age of four—a survivor of the most dev-
astating breakdown of trust and protection that any child should
have to suffer, is it any wonder that Susan grew up thinking that her
only worth was in her sexuality?"

Shawde strolled confidently over to the jurors' box. "Mrs. Cox
has told us how years of guilt and shame over past wrongs done to
her, and from years of promiscuous behavior which—try as she
might—she could not control, drove her to the brink of a complete
emotional breakdown." He sighed, letting his clipboard slip onto the
railing, then looked up from it directly into Juror Three's eyes.

"And, when you think about it," he said. "isn't that understand-
able?" Juror Three nodded, almost imperceptibly.

"The newspapers that spring and summer were filled with stories
of a maniac on the loose." Shawde picked up the pace. "A monster
who attacked young women. Carved crosses into their skin. Raped
and murdered. A sick man, yes, but he held a strange fascination for
this fragile young girl, because he was a man who made women *pay*."
Nick paused. "Made them pay for some deep, dark, perhaps carnal,
sin.

"And so this disturbed young woman," he continued, building
momentum, "after yet another one-night stand with a nameless,
faceless person picked up in the bar where she worked, fell apart.
Literally went over the edge. And, using a paring knife on her own
flesh, she carved crosses into her skin as some sort of bizarre atone-
ment for the life she had led."

He spun on the jury. "Afterward, in the throes of shock and confusion, she gave police the description of a van with North Carolina
license plates—a van she had seen before, in the parking lot behind

Annalee's. A van that belonged to a young man, a college student, not much more than a boy, who'd never in his life gotten so much as a parking ticket."

Nick let his gaze travel over the faces of the jury. "Is anyone ready to cast the first stone at an abused and tortured girl for an act of self-hate, an act—warped as it was—of repentance and contrition?

"Is there anyone here who can doubt her when she comes here to finally tell the truth? That Jeff Turner did not attack her on that August night. How can we question her testimony when she stands before us—no longer a mixed-up, guilt-ridden child, but a happily married woman, and a new person in the eyes of her accepted Savior?"

Shawde looked up at the chandelier. This was one of Dudley's tricks. I did a ten-count, watching as he struggled not to blink or swallow. When he finally turned toward the jury again, there were tears in his beady little eyes. "Susan Cox has come to believe that the truth shall set her free. Is there anyone here who would deny her that truth? Especially, when by doing so, it would mean condemning an innocent man?"

Nick's voice rose toward the ceilinged heights, bounced off the palmettoed cornices, and fell like spent fireworks to the courtroom below. He was building to an emotional close now, ticking off, point by point, why the jury should find Jefferson Turner innocent of all charges.

Make me believe again, Nick, I pleaded inwardly, *make me believe.* But I'd stopped believing in lawyers long before I'd stopped believing in Santa Claus. Cynicism was one of the only gifts my father had ever given me.

"If the State had any other witnesses who could connect my client with those terrible murders, we would have heard from them by now," Shawde was saying, "but we haven't.

"One person, and one person only, was responsible for his arrest," he reminded the jury. "And she has willingly admitted that she

lied." Nick looked out into the courtroom, challenging the specta-
tors. "I ask you—is there anyone here, anyone at all, who can call
Mr. Turner anything other than a victim of the cruelest of circumstances?" He let the answering silence sink into the jurors' minds.

Peter Salvatore might have, I thought. But the way things stood,
we'd never know.

7

On the eve of the prosecution's summation, I visited Jeff in his jail cell. I knew this would probably be our last interview together before the verdict was read. He'd been sitting on his bunk, sketching; but he stood as soon as he heard us coming, waiting politely as the guard turned the key.

"Thanks, Bobby," he said.

"No problem, Jeff." The guard locked the door behind me. I heard his shoes squeaking all the way to the end of the corridor.

"Have a seat," Jeff said, pointing to the bunk, "please." I remembered his words to me the day we met—*Can I get you anything? A Coke, or a glass of wine?*

"You've done wonders with the place," I said, referring to the dozens of pen-and-ink drawings he had taped to the wall.

Jeff laughed. "Yeah," he flushed, eyes settling on the rusty commode, "all the comforts of home. Sure won't miss it." One way or another the boy knew he'd be leaving here in a matter of days. I could tell he was banking that his next destination wouldn't be prison.

His expression turned serious. "I'm sorry what happened to that fella over in the seminary," he said. "I guess it just proves he was a pretty messed-up character."

"I guess."

"Look, I hate that this has put doubts in your mind. I just want you to know, I'll understand if you feel you have to pursue it, even if it means it takes longer for me to be completely vindicated." He sat on the far edge of the bunk, across from me. "Do what you have to do."

It was a more supportive sentiment than I'd gotten from my agent. "Don't be anal, Garner," Max Shroner had said when I told him about the letter. "You're not a detective, you're a writer. People out there want to know about this Holy Ghost thing? Fine. Write a bestseller. Readers don't expect you to solve the fucking case. Leave that to the cops and the goddam lawyers." When I'd started to object, he'd put his arm around me. "So what, maybe two years from now, they find out the handsome farmboy really did it?" His face lit up. "Then you write another book, you know, like whosits and the-stranger-Ted-Bundy-among-us? Make a few more million."

I said to Jeff, "Nick thinks Salvatore was trying to hone in on the publicity. Even the prosecutor's office is treating it like a crank letter."

"Tell me about that." Jeff smiled, shaking his head. "You should see some of the stuff I get." He reached under the mattress and pulled out a sheath of papers, fanning them out on the cot between us. When I leaned forward I caught a whiff of wintergreen Life Savers, and something dusty and sweet, like lilac sachet. Jeff Turner's fans wrote to him on scented stationery. "Listen to this," he said, his voice lowering conspiratorially. "*Dear Jeff,*" he read. "*Everytime I see your picture in the paper, I cut it out and put it in my scrapbook.*" He looked up and shrugged sheepishly. "*I think about you in bed at night, behind bars, all by your lonesome. My pussy gets wet just imagining the things we could do together—*"

"I get the idea," I told him.

Jeff held up a photograph. "They send pictures. Naked, just

about." He sounded amazed. "Get a load of this one." He handed me a Polaroid. A woman was crouched on a bed, wearing a string bikini bottom, no top, her hands cupping her immense breasts.

"Looks like a class act."

"Maybe you could use some of them for the book." I realized with a start that he was serious. He began reading again, his voice barely above a whisper. "*I dream of taking you in my mouth. I want to swallow your hard cock, to feel you going down on me, lapping my clit with your tongue—*"

"Hey." I stood suddenly. My voice must have been louder than I'd thought because down the hall I heard a metal chair scudding against the wall. Bobby the guard was on alert.

"Sorry," Jeff stammered, "I embarrassed you, didn't I?"

"You didn't embarrass me," I snapped.

His eyes were guileless, a perfect blue. "I didn't mean to." He gathered up the pictures and the letters. "I just wanted you to see how much they love me," he said, "is all."

8

The deliberation lasted three hours and eleven minutes.

Shawde called to let me know. "Your voice is frogged," he said. "What've you been doing, sleeping?"

"Thinking," I told him.

"Forget that shit." For once he sounded sincere. "It's too late."

Inside the courtroom it was like the first hour of an Irish wake, before the mix of alcohol and closely pressed flesh have had time to do their trick. I spotted all the telltale signs. The bright eyes. Over-loud conversation. Movements much too big for these cramped, hot quarters. I knew there'd be booze and bodies combusting together, real soon.

Maria Lombardi met me in the corridor. She'd changed from the suit she'd worn earlier into a dove-gray silk dress with a linen blazer. The jury coming back so soon had evidently interrupted a quiet little dinner for two, and it wasn't hard to guess the name of the other party. "Nick's nervous," she said, giving herself away. "I told him, the earlier the better, but he just gave me one of those what-do-you-know looks."

She sighed. "I'm sure it's going to be okay." I gave her one of those what-do-you-know looks, then went in to find my seat.

When Shawde spotted me, he leaned his head back. I could smell anchovy on his breath. "It's showtime, kid." He winked, with a vestige of the old bravado.

Varlie Turner and her sister were already there, as were the Coxes—Susan looking pale and ethereal, Shelby in his usual state of stoic bewilderment. A side door opened. Two guards escorted Jeff into the room. The lapping tide of whispers again—Bird . . . Bird . . . Bird . . . I thought of the narrow cot covered with small squares of writing paper, the scent of lilac, and mint.

"I wanted you to see how much they love me," he'd said.

"Has the jury reached a verdict?"

"We have," the foreman said. "We find the defendant, Jefferson Turner, not guilty of all charges." Thunderous applause broke out in the courtroom. Susan Trevett Cox cried out, "Praise the Lord!" Several people laughed.

I had my eyes trained on Jeff, but just then Nick leaned over, blocking him from sight. From behind me came the sound of crying. Jeff's aunt was sobbing into her hankie. Varlie remained dry-eyed and motionless, as though she had no comprehension of what had just happened.

The judge made a closing statement; but his soft-spoken drawl was no match for the onslaught of emotions in the courtroom. New Year's Eve had broken out. People were on their feet, embracing, waving, calling from all sides. I fought my way through the crush, bumping into Bryant, the reporter from *People*, who picked me off my feet and kissed me violently on the mouth. "This ending," he said, "oughta translate well in Hollywood."

I had the urge to slug him, to leave him howling in pain, but just then the crowd parted so that all at once I was facing Jeff Turner for the first time since the verdict had been announced. A man I'd never seen before stood with him, pumping his arm up and down, clapping him on the back. Jeff looked dazed.

"Congratulations."

He pulled me close. The heady bouquet of Brut and Life Savers was almost overwhelming. "How can I ever thank you?" he whispered.

"I didn't do anything," I said. "It was Susan, and Nick."

"No." He shook his head. "What mattered most was you believing in me."

I tried to think of something to say. But what? *I don't know if I really do believe in you, Jeff.* I wasn't sure of anything anymore. The lights in the courtroom seemed unusually bright. They hurt my eyes. I put up my hand to shield them, but Jeff grabbed it.

"Look, I know things have been a little tense recently." The lights were affecting him, too. Little beads of sweat formed on his upper lip. "I just hope now it's all over, we can—"

I lost his train of speech. The room had turned liquid, lapping at my legs. Out of nowhere, a hand slipped around my waist. Nick Shawde shouted into my ear. "Whatsa matter, Garny? You look like shit."

"Nothing a year in total seclusion won't cure." I managed a smile.

"You?" Shawde dug an elbow into my ribs. "Never happen." Someone grabbed him; when I looked up again Varlie Turner and her sister were standing next to Jeff.

I started to edge away. "Well, good luck to all of you."

"We sure do appreciate everything, Miz Quinn," Varlie said.

"I didn't really do anything."

"Well, we thank you, anyway." Her voice was bereft of warmth or gladness.

Before I could leave. Varlie's sister spoke up. "Miz Quinn? I almost forgot. Did Bird tell you?"

Turner ducked his head, sheepishly. "Darn, Aunt Dot. With all that's been going on, it slipped right by me."

The woman opened up her purse. "That young assistant of yours?"

"Jack Tatum?"

"I believe that's the one. Well, he called about that boy and his ma, come to stay with Teeny?" My heart thudded. "And I got to re-membering that was about the time my husband first got his Po-laroid?"

"Just show her the picture," Varlie said impatiently.

She handed me a small black-and-white snapshot with perfo-rated edges. "It's Bird and that boy," she said. "I run by it when I was home yest'dy, and it set me to thinkin'." She turned to her nephew. "It start comin' back to y'all, too, don't it now, Bird?"

He flashed a dimpled grin. "Yes, ma'am. Guess now I see it, it does."

I looked down at the picture. Two young boys were standing near Turner's barn. The tall, nice-looking one held a cat under its front arms so that its hind legs were dragging. The small, fat one had some sort of scarf around his neck. Something was embroidered at each end. I couldn't tell for sure, but it might have been the sign of the cross.

I stuffed the photograph into my pocket and quickly said good-bye.

As I reached the door, I looked over my shoulder in time to see Jeff Turner posing for photographers, his arm draped casually over Susan Trevett Cox's shoulder. "Smile!" someone called.

And they did, on cue.

9

I sat alone in the darkened suite that had once served as the defense's war room, pressing the back of Nick's swivel chair against the wall, my feet up on the desk, scuffing the expensive blotter. In the hollow of my lap I held the snapshot. I couldn't actually see it, but I knew it was there. I ran its sharp edges against the pads of my fingers.

The door opened a crack. Some of the light from the corridor spilled inside before a hand hit the switch on the merciless overheads. I sat up straight, blinking away the brightness.

"Goddammit, Garn." Nick Shawde's voice was husky. "You trying to give me a coronary?"

"I didn't think anybody'd be around this late," I said, truthfully. "How come you're not out celebrating?"

Shawde shrugged. "I was." He crossed to the desk and removed a bottle of Jack Daniel's from a bottom drawer. "I am." He took out two shot glasses, setting them down so hard the sound echoed in the empty room. "And I will be."

I shimmied the chair forward on its casters, watching as he poured the golden liquid and handed it to me. We drank without looking at each other. Then he took out a pressed handkerchief, blew his nose, and went over to the television.

The news was on, the headline story, Jefferson Turner's acquittal. We watched for a while. Nick doled out another round and we stared at the set, sipping. When the segment was over, I expected Nick to switch the channel and check out the other network coverage; but he didn't. Instead we sat through a report about a car accident on Route 20 that had killed three motorists; the weather report; and a special feature on a soup kitchen for the homeless run by kids.

During the commercial Nick raised the Jack Daniel's again. I shook my head. "What if he's guilty?" I asked finally.

"Not my problem," Shawde replied. "The law has just found him an innocent man."

"That's not good enough for me."

"What are you, on some fucking crusade?" His small dark eyes taunted. "Garner Quinn, Seeker of Truth? *Pul-lease*." He sat on the other side of the desk, propping up his feet, one at a time, as though sublimely bored. "Get off your high horse, Garny. My job is to represent the guy to the best of my ability, and yours is to write about what happened. Period. I mean, the books you write are supposed to be nonfiction, right? You think you got some kind of poetic license? Let me clue you in—the ending's the ending, toots."

I tossed my shot glass on the table, where it rolled around with a marbled cat's-eye sound. "Spoken like a true lawyer."

"Sure, go ahead, keep playing the self-righteous act," he said, his voice surprisingly angry. "But you know, I'm gonna sleep tonight. I'm gonna go out, have a late dinner, get laid if I'm lucky, and then I'm gonna dream sweet, like a baby. What about you? When's the last time you got any? Or was that the question that landed the Birdboy in deep shit for asking?"

I slapped him. On the television, four young black kids were singing a rap song about burgers and fries. Nick managed a smile. "I'd heard you never ended a case without slugging the attorney. I was beginning to think you didn't respect me."

He walked toward the window, rubbing his cheek. "You know what the difference is between us?" he asked. "You never stop digging. Me?—once something's over, I'm ready to fuckin' bury it."

I went over to the small refrigerator and wrapped an ice cube in a paper napkin. "Here," I said.

He took it. "You must be a tiger in bed, Quinn."

"You're a pig."

"Yeah," the attorney agreed, "ain't it the truth?" Something on the television caught his eye, and he looked past me. A pretty young reporter was speaking directly into the camera, a picture of Dane Blackmoor over her shoulder.

"—Diana Gold, attorney for the sculptor," said the reporter, "issued a statement today saying that Blackmoor's art was being, quote, manhandled and destroyed, as investigators searched for additional body parts. A human hand was discovered just last week when—"

"I tell you, Garn," Nick said, "your next book."

"No effin' way, Shawde."

"Not even if they found the head?" He smoothed out his suit jacket and adjusted his tie.

"Not even then."

"Well, see you in court, Quinn. Unless you want to do a little partying with Lombardi and me?" The eyebrows went up twice.

"Oh darn," I sighed. "I'd love to, but I've got to wash my hair."

"You staying?"

"Yeah. Thought I'd run up your phone tab a bit."

"Heads it's Blackmoor. Tails it's your daughter." Nick pretended to flip a coin in the air. "Oops."

I caught him at the door. "Wrong on both counts. It's your wife." He stopped dead in his tracks for a moment before slipping into the hall.

10

The pale marble floor of the hotel lobby gleamed like the deck of an ocean liner. Although it was after midnight, the atrium was well lit and shadowless, a place with no dark crevices or corners. This reassured people, helped them forget that they were far away from home, sleeping in used rooms, on sheets where strangers had slept, one launder ago.

I'd thought about grabbing a nightcap in the bar, but now that I was down here the idea no longer appealed to me. I headed back toward the elevator banks.

Jeff Turner was sitting in one of the silvery-blue wing chairs. "Hey, lady."

"Jeff," I gasped. "What are you doing here?"

"I wanted to give you something." He held out a rolled sheet of paper. "Open it up. Please." I unfurled it gingerly.

It was a drawing of a bird. He'd used thousands of delicate, controlled pen lines to create a feathery texture. There was something unsettling about the dead-on perspective—beak forward, black eyes so wide apart.

"It's lovely." I stared at Jeff Turner, trying to imagine him sheathed in black, his fine features blurred under a shimmer of greasepaint; but somehow the image got sucked up into the fern-lined heights of the atrium. There was only an attractive young man in a navy blazer and a pale button-down shirt, standing at a respectable distance, in a well-lit, shadowless place.

"I guess you're already onto the next thing," he said. "Thinking about another book."

"No. Not really."

"Well, I'd better let you go," he said. "I have a friend waiting out in the car for me." This surprised me. Many people had claimed to like Bird, but now that I thought of it, only Peter Salvatore had said he was his friend.

I rolled up the drawing, and extended my hand. "Good luck, Jeff."

He pressed it to his lips, gently. "I'll never forget you, Garner," he said.

11

I was on my knees, digging with a small spoon. The earth felt moist. My arms were streaked black with it. Little clots of packed dirt, laced with earthworms, stuck between my fingers.

I hit upon something hard.

One. Two. Three. Four. Five. Six. A perfect row of animal caskets, each lid marked with words in a language that seemed strangely familiar. Almost against my will, I began prying the first coffin open. Inside, I found a dead sparrow. Beak forward. Eyes set wide apart. Its body shrouded in purple cloth, marked with crosses.

One after the other, I opened the other caskets. A mouse. A rabbit. A cat. A dog. A feeling of dread built inside me as I worked my way toward the largest box. This one was nailed good and tight. I wedged the spoon under the lid. A surge of hot, acrid air wafted out, filling my nostrils.

I almost had it, when I sensed the shadow on my back. A slow, soft voice said, "Open it, Garner. Open up the big one," and I saw, without turning, the face, white as the moon, the rut of dimples like craters. . . .

The phone pealed. I pushed my way up from the depths of the dream. The numbers on the clock read two forty-five. Another pretty little ring. I groped for the receiver. "Yes?"

"The bars are out," a voice said on the other end.

"Nick?"

Shawde's laughter was like a whooping cough sucked inward. "What's going on?" I demanded. Then my heart sank. "Has something—?"

"Relax, babycakes," he drawled. "I just wanted to give you the news."

"What news?"

"The bars are out, did I tell you that?"

I heard giggling, and wondered whether he was alone. "Yes, you did," I said, impatiently.

"Well, that's where I saw it. Big as life, on one'a them giant TV screens. And I said, shit, I gotta call her. I gotta call the G Woman."

"What are you talking about?"

"Sharpen your pencil, kiddo—'"

"You're drunk. I'm going back to bed."

"You can't sleep now, Garny. That's what I'm trying to tell you." Nick let out one of his enormous, donkey-boy hee-haws. "They found the head! Did'ja hear me? They found the fucking head!"

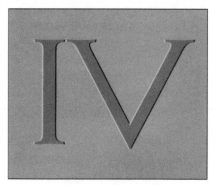

THE MILL

"PRAISE THE LORD, GO HOME WITH MY HUSBAND, AND
HAVE LOTS OF BABIES."

SUSAN TREVETT COX
ON WHAT SHE WAS PLANNING TO DO NOW THAT
THE TURNER TRIAL WAS OVER
PEOPLE
(NOVEMBER 14, 1994)

"WELL, MA'AM, I WOULDN'T BE SITTING HERE, EXCEPT
FOR THE GRACE OF GOD, AND GARNER QUINN. WE GOT
REAL CLOSE DURING THE TRIAL, BUT OF COURSE I
HAVEN'T SEEN HER RECENTLY. SHE'S OFF WRITING AN-
OTHER BOOK ABOUT THAT SCULPTOR. . . ."

JEFFERSON "BIRD" TURNER
WHEN ASKED ABOUT THE SOON-TO-BE-PUBLISHED
BOOK *ALL THROUGH THE NIGHT*
"TODAY SHOW"
(NOVEMBER 22, 1994)

1

The studio was in an old gristmill. Blackmoor's assistant said I couldn't miss it, and he was right. In a countryside smattered with picture-book farmhouses and ivy-covered saltboxes built on the tippy-tops of winding roads, it loomed like a Druidal monument—strange, mysterious, a little frightening. Bare trees lined the driveway, limbs outstretched like the hands of surrendering men. In addition to the main structure, I counted at least four outbuildings. A brick chimney served as a sort of watchtower.

Or a crematory, I thought. Maybe that was where he'd disposed of the other body parts.

I followed a series of small painted signs that read simply: THE MILL. The place was a relatively new acquisition for Blackmoor. According to my research, he'd moved his entire Manhattan operation here shortly after the Vestri scandal broke. There was a parking lot behind the main building. I pulled my trusty old Volvo 190 into an empty space and shut off the ignition. From here I had a good view of the mill wheel and, beyond the bluff, the steel-gray ribbon of the canal.

I got out of the car and strolled toward the water. My attention was immediately drawn to the three large, lumpish shapes that lurched on the embankment before me. They looked almost like tombstones—tombstones that had been blanketed with stiff, heavy coverings. I leaned over to touch one. It was hard. Ungiving as granite.

I turned backed toward the Mill, squinting the morning sun out of my eyes. Given all his money, the properties he owned, and the fast life he led, I wondered why Blackmoor had chosen to live in the middle of nowhere.

Of course, if his hobby was chopping up young women, this would make an ideal location. Nobody but the crows would hear the screams.

A young man with long, sandy hair tied back into a ponytail answered the door. "Can you believe this is November?" he asked. "Hey, if this is global warming, I'm all for it. You're Garner Quinn, right?" He beamed proudly, as though he'd just given the correct answer on a game show. "I saw you at the museum gala."

I felt my cheeks flush as if I'd been drunk that night, singing lewd songs on the top of a table, instead of simply wearing a red dress. The young man ushered me into a small, drafty foyer. Narrow beams of light spiked the floor from slits in the stone walls. A bleached pine table held an earthen bowl of white tulips.

"You know, you look a lot younger than those pictures on your book jackets," Mr. Ponytail chattered.

"Thanks," I said. "Remind me to fire my photographer."

He snorted, and held out his hand. He had a way of shaking without grasping. "I'm Roberto. We spoke on the phone."

"Nice to meet you."

"Everybody's in the studio," he explained. "Dane's starting a new piece on Thursday, so it's scamper, scamper, busy, busy." He turned the latch on a thick wooden door. "Come on, I'll show you around."

I followed him into a vast open space. Massive stone walls rose to vaulted heights. On one wall, a walk-in fieldstone fireplace glimmered with copper pots. Tall wrought-iron candleholders trailed a lifetime's worth of wax onto the brick hearth.

Everything was much brighter, and less gloomy, than I had expected it to be. Natural light fell in tubular shafts from skylights, or slanted through the tall, arched windows. A theatrical lighting grid had been suspended from the ceiling. Several men were hanging on scaffolds, adjusting barn-door flaps, so that they shone down in brilliant patterns on the raised platform that was in the center of the room. From invisible speakers, a singer crooned—*Ohhh! I love to hate you.*

Other scaffolds, decked with chicken wire and bolts of muslin, vivisected the studio at odd angles. A tall woman stood on the platform, giving directions to the technicians. I recognized her as the pale-faced beauty in the Juliet dress who'd come to fetch Blackmoor from the backseat of the Rolls that night.

She cupped a hand over her eyebrows, calling, "Roberto?"

"Duty calls." Roberto shrugged cheerily. "Please. Make yourself at home." He sprinted away. *Scurry, scurry. Busy, busy.*

The music was too loud. I had to keep myself from moving in time to the beat. Mr. Ponytail and the Amazon lady huddled on the platform, conferring. She reached down to her belt and drew something up to her lips. A walkie-talkie. I had a sudden vision of Blackmoor sitting in some dark, paneled room, with a Persian cat on his lap, waiting for the signal from his beautiful-but-lethal henchperson. *"She's here, boss."*

I forced myself to concentrate on the room. Twin winding staircases provided access to galleries above, where, I assumed, there were additional workspaces. Roberto had said to make myself at home. I decided to take him up on the invitation. I sauntered toward the closest set of steps, half-expecting alarms to go off, angry voices to yell, "Excuse me, you can't go up there!"

But I heard nothing.

The upstairs gallery had been divided into several garage-doored storage rooms. I pulled an old-fashioned counterweight sash. The metal shutter flew up with a clatter. Before my eyes adjusted to the light, I moved inside, immediately tripping on a body.

The floor was littered with them. Torsos. Limbs. Feet. I'd stumbled into a junkyard of hollow plaster casts. Or, at least—I reminded myself—they *appeared* to be hollow. Just by looking, a person wouldn't have guessed that *Lady Sitting* was a sarcophagus for a human hand. Or that *Woman at a Mirror* contained a severed head.

I kept moving.

In one corner of the room, something had been draped with a muslin shroud. I pulled off the cloth, carefully. A young boy lay on the floor, mangled and bloody, his neck crooked, part of his face caved in from being beaten to a pulp. A scream bottled up in my throat, but no sound came out—luckily, for me, because it was at that moment I noticed the small brass plaque.

"*Gang War*, Dane Blackmoor, 1991."

My heart had just about regulated itself when, from high up on a wooden shelf, something fast and white lunged at me.

Thwap-thwap-thwap.

I toppled into the pile of stiff hands and unyielding breasts, triggering an avalanche of body parts. They jabbed and poked, assaulting my nostrils with a dusty, medicinal-smelling smell. I fought to get out from under them.

"*Hihowareya, hihowareya!*" The cockatoo whistled past, with a flap of wings.

"Stay away," I warned the bird.

A pair of strong arms, one under my shoulder, one behind my waist, lifted me up, setting me back on my feet. Even with hair hanging in my face, and my eyes stinging from the pungent chemical smell, I could clearly see Blackmoor, with the big white bird on his shoulder. They were cocking their heads, giving me the old sideways once-over.

"When are you going to learn that we don't bite?" he asked softly.

Blackmoor crouched, Indian style, on the platform, surrounded by a circle of people who seemed to be hanging on his every word. Only the cockatoo affected disinterest. Perched on the rung of a ladder, it pared its pointy toenails with a sharp, probing beak.

"It has to be at more of an angle." He rubbed his hand over the floor, erasing some blue chalk markings. "And tell Kyra I'll need her early," he said to his sidekick with the clipboard. "Where are we with the clothing?"

"I've put together a couple of different looks you can choose from, Dane," a voice piped up. I zoned in on the speaker, a doughy-faced woman with rhinestone-clustered glasses edging up at the sides like sly smiles. She was wearing an orange smock over leopard-print stretchpants that managed to be both too tight and too loose at the same time. *If that's who's in charge of wardrobe,* I thought, *I pity poor Kyra, whomever she might be.*

"Which mirror are we going with, Dane?" This from a gaunt man in his early thirties who hung slightly back from the others.

Blackmoor shrugged off the question. "Let's see them both." He strode from the platform, stopping when he saw me.

"In case you're wondering," he said to the others, "this is Ms. Quinn. She writes books about murderers, and she's come here to find out all about me." He smiled without showing any teeth. "Make of that what you will."

I looked down the line of mostly hostile faces, keeping my voice friendly, but firm. "For the next few days, I'll be hanging around the studio, watching how things run, asking a few questions," I told them. "We could start with some introductions."

Blackmoor barreled through the amenities. "Elizabeth Rice."

The leggy Juliet. "Richard Lewan." *The thin man.* "Lucy Moon." *The leopard lady.* "And I believe you've met Roberto." *Mr. Ponytail.*

Elizabeth Rice extended her hand. Like Roberto, her shake was all style, no substance. "If you have any questions, please don't hesitate to ask." Under these lights, I could make out the first signs of creping on her neck, and more lines around her eyes. She wasn't quite the ingenue she'd masqueraded as at the museum gala. Elizabeth Rice had been around the block a couple of times. In the rain. During humid weather.

Blackmoor touched my arm. "I'll speak with you in my office now." He turned and walked briskly through the studio. Everyone watched as I made the decision to follow.

It was a very public surrender.

2

By the time I reached Blackmoor's office, he was already comfortably seated behind his desk. To achieve the unique ambience, his interior decorator had apparently pillaged several old European churches. Leaded glass windows varicolored the sunlight. Religious antiquities were being used for mundane uses—an open-armed statue of a saint held a stack of *Architectural Digests*; an ornately carved, canopied baptismal font was filled with bottles of Evian water.

Blackmoor looked up as though surprised to see me. "Oh, there you are." I took a seat without being asked. "Tell me," he said. "How's Dudley?"

"Fine." I wasn't about to admit to him that I didn't know. That I hadn't a clue as to how, or even where, my father was.

"And your daughter—Temple, isn't it?" Blackmoor smiled. It made me nervous, those same lips that could smile that smile, forming my daughter's name. "I like the name," he said. "It's very Faulknerian."

"Look, this isn't a social call."

"No, I guess it isn't." He picked up a lump of clay and began pressing it in his palm. "I was somewhat surprised when your young man called." The way he said *your young man* insinuated Jack was something more than my assistant. Or maybe I was overly sensitive on that point. "I didn't know whether you'd want to take on another book so soon. I found it flattering."

"Don't," I said bluntly. "I decided to do this because it fits in, logistically. I can do most of the work from home."

I didn't tell him the other reason. That Jeff Turner had left me with a bad taste in my mouth. If I'd sat home, plagued by unanswered questions, haunted by the specter of the Holy Ghost, I'd have gone crazy. A book about Dane Blackmoor presented no moral dilemmas. He was guilty. I knew it, and he knew I knew it. It would be my swan song—a perfect circle, beginning with Dulcie and Dudley, and ending with him.

"I'd like to ask you a few questions." He pointed a loaded finger at me as if to say, *Shoot.* I did. "When did Torie Wood start working here?"

Blackmoor leaned back in his seat. "The detectives wanted to know that, too. I explained to them that I couldn't say, exactly.

"Originally, I believe Roberto brought her around. He'd met her somewhere, at a club in Manhattan, I think, and she started showing up at the studio. One day I asked to wrap her. She had a good head. Strong bone structure." He kept working with the clay, glancing up only occasionally. "Later I discovered she had a knack for sculpture."

"So you put her on staff?"

"Yes, but only in the office, for odd jobs. I wasn't interested in creating a clone of myself. I wanted her to stay on the sidelines so she could develop at her own pace." His fingers had fashioned the lump of clay into a small figure. Suddenly he squashed it flat. "And that was that."

"Torie modeled for both *Lady Sitting* and *Woman at a Mirror*," I said. "Do you remember anything unusual about those two sittings?"

"You mean like whether I severed her head?" He glared at me. "No. I think I'd recall if that had happened."

"But shortly afterward she disappeared?"

"Yes." He'd started to massage the clay again, thoughtfully.

"And you didn't think her dropping out of sight was unusual? That it might be worth mentioning to the police?"

Blackmoor sighed. "People come and go out of this studio all the time."

"But you said Torie was special," I reminded him.

He threw down the clay. It landed with an angry *whomp* on the desk. "She was a free spirit. If you're suggesting I should have suspected she'd been chopped up into small pieces, I'm sorry"—the wolf grin again, intent and dangerous—"maybe I'm not that imaginative."

I walked over to a case displaying miniature models, maquettes for larger pieces, and caught a glimpse of my reflection in the glass. I had a smudge of plaster dust on the tip of my nose. *What a charge this arrogant prick must be getting out of me.*

"I'm going to be your shadow for the next three weeks," I told him. "I'll cover the legal proceedings, from arraignment right on through to sentencing. If it goes that far."

"I'm expected before the judge tomorrow," he said softly.

"I know. I spoke with Diana Gold."

"She seems to think they will set bail." For the first time I thought I heard the tiniest trickle of fear wash over his characteristic ennui.

"It usually goes that way," I said, "when the person's in the public eye."

"If not"—he lapsed back into a mocking tone—"will you come visit me in jail?"

"You can count on it," I told him.

"I've arranged it so you can take over the guest quarters."

"That won't be necessary," I replied. "I'll be commuting every day."

"The offer stands, if you change your mind."

"I won't."

"Well then," he said. "I guess from here on out I'm at your mercy, Garner Quinn." *You got that right,* I thought. Blackmoor stood. "I'm starting a new piece on Thursday, if they don't lock me up. So, unless you have any other questions . . ."

He stopped me at the door. "You know, a long time ago, I told you to call when you knew what you wanted from me. All these years I've been curious"—his voice faltered—"but I think I've finally figured it out. You want to nail my ass," he said, "don't you, Garnish?"

3

It was after seven when I pulled the Volvo through the gate, but lights were still on in the office.

"Early day," Jack observed.

I plopped myself down on the chair opposite his desk. "It was only a rehearsal. To get the hang of things."

"So how *were* things hanging?"

"It's obvious he killed her. The only question is whether he acted alone. There are some real characters working in that place." I stifled a yawn. "What's new on the home front?"

He opened a file folder and slid a picture toward me. "Show and tell."

"Torie?"

I scanned the snapshot. Two kids. The boy was darkly handsome, with skin the color of a brown M&M, the tawny kind. A girl sat on his lap, holding an open bottle of beer. Her hair was tinted purple, rather like the skin of an eggplant. It was slicked back in a style that would have been ugly had it not been for her almond eyes, high cheekbones, and straight nose—the good bone structure that had attracted Dane Blackmoor. "Who's the guy?"

"Victor Pearce." Jack checked his notes. "British. Calls himself a performance artist. Torie hooked up with him when she touched down in the big city.

"Supposedly he did a lot of drugs," he continued. "According to the people I talked with, he knocked Torie around on a regular basis."

I looked down at the picture of the young couple again. Sloe-eyed with liquor, with drugs, with lust, their attractive faces appeared blurry and unusually soft. "Was he enough of a sicko to have sliced her?" I asked.

"Unfortunately, Victor went back to London right after Torie started hanging around with Blackmoor." I felt relieved.

He pushed some 8x10s in my direction—Torie's head encased in its polyurethaned mask, plasticized like some obscene driver's license. *My God*, I thought, *she's only a little older than Temple*.

"I know," Jack said. I wondered if I'd spoken aloud, or whether he'd been struck by it, too. He pulled the pictures back like playing cards. "The parents are from Scarsdale. Upper-upper-middle-class home." He stared down at the glossies. "Pretty high price to pay for getting out of the 'burbs, if you ask me."

"Well, you sure ran circles around me today," I said.

"That's not all." He was chomping at the bit, obviously pleased with himself. Somehow I liked it better when he was just answering the phones.

He leaned across the desk. "I spoke with one of Torie's girl-friends. She had nothing but good things to say about Dane Black-moor. Said Torie told her she was really happy at the studio. Blackmoor was very good to her."

"I bet."

"For what it's worth," Jack said, "she didn't think they were lovers. Right before Torie disappeared, she called, all excited. Said Blackmoor was going to pay for her to go to art school, that he be-lieved in her talent—"

"Yeah, right."

He shuffled a few index cards. "This is a direct quote. Torie told the girl that *Dane Blackmoor was like a father to her.*"

I shot to my feet. "How would she know?" My voice cracked. *"What would a fucking adolescent know about a man like him?"*

I saw it in his eyes. The mixture of shock and curiosity. "You got me." He shrugged. "I was just following instructions to keep an open mind and listen to what people said, boss."

"I know you were," I apologized. "How about coming over to the house for a beer?" A beer would help me to unwind. Two or three and I might just drink past my defenses.

Jack looked surprised. "Not tonight," he said. "I'm pretty beat." He sounded pleased, though.

"Some other time, then." I offered him my hand. "Great work today."

He took it, and held on. "Thanks."

Suddenly it felt all wrong. I punched his chest with my other fist. "See ya, Jack."

"See *you*, Garner," he said. "Soon."

Outside, a fine mist had begun to fall. I walked through the kitchen door shaking rain out of my hair like a dog. Cilda was at the table, warming her crooked hands around a steaming mug of hot chocolate. I glanced at the clock on the wall. It was after eight, and she might or might not talk—her method of reminding me that no matter how long we'd been together, we weren't family, we weren't roommates, Cilda Fields was my employee, and any time after eight was her own, so she'd speak only if she felt like it, *t'ank you very much.*

"Where's Temple?"

"Where would she be now that she got a phone in her room?" Naturally Cilda would have to get that little dig in. During the trial I'd succumbed—mostly out of the guilt of an absentee mom—to Temple's pleas for a line of her own.

"Everything okay here?" I asked lightly, sensitive to the fact that most weeks of the year it was *"Everything okay there?"* But somewhere during my careful framing of the question, Mrs. Fields had retreated behind her checked-out, locked-up, after-eight face. She looked down into her cocoa as though reading the sworls of chocolate, like tea leaves, which said, *Everyting's fine. Go to bed, Ga'ner Quinn. I got it all under control, as usual.*

I heard Temple jabbering on the phone as I passed her door. When she saw me, she said, "Gotta go," and slapped the receiver down with a clang.

"Who was that?"

"Emory."

I said, *Oh,* trying hard to remember whether Emory was a boy or a girl.

"She's having a party on Saturday. Can I go?"

"Sure," I said, relieved. "I'll drop you off so I can meet her parents."

"You don't have to," Temple said helpfully. "Emory's brother said he'd drive."

"Nice try." I grinned. "Tell him next time. Like when you're twenty-one."

"*Mother,*" she cried in mock annoyance. "Just promise you won't come to the door when you come pick me up. Stay in the car and beep, okay?"

"Maybe I should wear a paper bag over my head." I leaned back against the headboard, contentedly surveying all the teenage clutter.

"So how was Dane Blackmoor's studio?" Temple asked, excited.

"It was okay." I watched as she lugged a thick scrapbook over to the bed. "But I'd rather talk about your day."

"My day was boring. Take a look at this." She shoved the book into my hands.

I opened it, almost gasping at what I saw. Neatly glued to the first page was a Xerox copy of an old *Life* magazine spread on Dane Blackmoor. His face stared back at me, moody, recklessly young.

Quickly, I thumbed through the rest of the album, turning page after page of newspaper clippings and magazine articles; scanning photographs of sculptures, personal interviews, and more recent reports about the hand, the head, Torie Wood, and the grand jury trial.

"What the hell's this supposed to be?" I demanded.

Temple shrank at the tone of my voice. "It's research," she said. "I thought it might help you with the new book."

I swung my legs off the bed. "I have enough help, thank you." I fought to control my emotions. "I have help coming out of my ears. I'm tripping over the help I have."

"So don't use it." She grabbed the book from me. "I'll keep it for myself. I think Dane Blackmoor's cool—"

I snapped. "He's not cool. He's a dangerous, manipulative man who in no way should be the idol of little girls."

Temple stood toe to toe with me. "Well, I'm not a *little girl*." She pushed past me, bounding down the stairs.

"Temple, wait—"

By the time I caught up to her, she'd already swiped her jacket off the coatrack near the kitchen door. "Where are you going?"

"To the beach."

"This late?" I cringed at my own shrillness.

"*You* do it," my daughter told me, slamming the door.

Cilda sat at the table keeping her eyes averted in a rare, gracious gesture that was supposed to allow me to save face. I crossed to the window, watching Temple traverse the uneven ground outside, as though it cost her young legs nothing. Light rain was still falling, and there was no moon. I flicked on the switches that triggered the outdoor floods. Flat-domed lights popped up in neat rows from the house to the sea. Spotlights played over the outlines of heavy machinery—the crane, the backhoe, the bulldozer, and some additional equipment I hadn't noticed before.

"I didn't know they'd started work again."

"Man come by today." Cilda shuffled over to the dishwasher. "Say they can't wait until spring on account of what 'appened with that last storm."

Temple had climbed the rickety metal ladder up the seawall, and was now walking across its rocky shoulder. She'd pulled up the hood of her jacket. From this distance she looked so small.

I thought about the scrapbook she'd filled with Dane Blackmoor's pictures. Then I thought again about Torie Wood. I wondered if her mother had stood like this, watching the back of her rebellious daughter retreating from her—spine stiff and straight, eyes pinned forward—so young, and yet so determined to walk ahead, on a hard path of her own choosing.

4

Diana Gold had the kind of skinny, sculpted legs that screamed Personal Trainer. She belonged to that elite group of women who could wear light-colored hose with a dewy sheen without looking either elephantine, or as though she were about to launch into a sugarplum-fairy dance. Her suit jacket was celery green, cut broad at the shoulders. The matching cashmere sweater skimmed her hips, successfully masking the fact that she, like most women, in my experience, with good, skinny legs, had no waist to speak of. This slight flaw was more than made up for by an incredible butt, with no hint of hiney hang, swathed within an inch of its muscle tone by a short, cream-colored skirt slit up the back, stopping just shy of provocative.

When the Honorable Julia Fallon summoned the attorneys to the bench, you could almost feel the watchers in the courtroom shift forward in their seats. I knew it was as much to catch an eyeful of

Diana Gold from behind as it was to catch an earful of the judge's instructions.

"I see where you're going with this, Mr. Richardson," the judge told the prosecuting attorney, eyes straying to her watch, "but save it for the trial, shall we? At this point, the evidence connecting Mr. Blackmoor to the murder is purely circumstantial, and you know it."

Gold and the unfortunate Richardson walked back to their seats.

She was born looking smug, I thought. A jury—particularly a predominantly male jury, which the PA would no doubt be trying for—might lust for her, but they wouldn't like her.

The judge tapped her gavel twice.

"Bail is set at one million dollars. The defendant is released on his own recognizance until jury selection begins"—she consulted calendar—"eight weeks from this day."

I glanced at Avery Richardson, who seemed about to object, and then thought better of it. Eight weeks was not a hell of a lot of time to build a case against someone like Dane Blackmoor, but Richardson must have known it was all he was going to get.

During the hearing, Blackmoor had sat with his hands folded on the table in front of him. Whenever anyone spoke, he turned ever so slightly in their direction, a polite but detached onlooker of events. There had been no sign that he'd noticed me; yet a split second after the hearing was adjourned, I felt a shoulder tap.

"Dane wants to know whether you'll be riding back with us, in the limo?" Elizabeth Rice inquired politely.

"I have some business here," I told her. I could have said, *No, I'm having lunch with his attorney;* but I enjoyed being evasive around curious people.

Rice pulled a folder from her smart, thin shoulder bag. "Here are those employee names you wanted. It's as complete a list as I could compile. Before I came on the scene, the personnel records were pretty spotty."

"Thanks. It'll give me a place to start." I took the file from her. "By the way, what time does the sitting begin tomorrow?"

"That depends on how Dane's feeling." As if on cue, Blackmoor walked up behind her. Rice sensed his presence before she actually saw him. The tension that was ever present in her face dropped suddenly, sensuously, as though an invisible hand had snipped a knot of muscles at the top of her skull.

"Well, that's over with," he said. "Are these things always this boring?"

I said, "I'm sure the trial will keep you on the edge of your seat."

"Garner won't be riding back with us to the studio," Elizabeth told him. "She has another engagement."

Diana Gold stepped into the small space between Blackmoor and me. "I won't be able to make lunch, Quinn," she announced, "but I might be able to squeeze you in for tea."

I bowed from the waist. "I live to accommodate," I said.

"How about the Yale Club at, say, three?" Gold put her arm under her client's and steered him away. Two or three steps later, Blackmoor shook the attorney off as impatiently as one would a flea. The gesture was enough to make me almost like him.

If anyone had asked, I would have probably said I'd met Arvin Meek on a case. It would flush, him being a librarian at the Library of Legal Medicine over on First, where all the forensic journals are kept. But the truth was, I'd met Arvin at the opera, years before I wrote my first book.

One of Andy's clients had given us the tickets. I hadn't wanted to go. We were fighting every other night at that point, mostly because it was only every other night that he made it back to our apartment. Each day—pushing Temple's stroller in the park, lining up at the grocery store, walking down the street—my exquisitely reasoned and perfectly argued case against his behavior, and for our marriage, played like a long-playing record through my head. But every evening, after the baby was in bed, all those brilliant thoughts shattered into the same strident, hard-edged questions—*where were you? why didn't you call? what's happening to us?* Questions to which Andy very shrewdly pleaded the Fifth.

Yet, for some reason, he'd liked the idea of these tickets. We should go, he'd said. We'd never been to an opera together. We never went out at all, anymore. (Go ahead, say it. I dare you. Say, since the baby.)

"It'll be good, Garn," Andy had said. And, in the end, I'd gone because I desperately wanted *something* to be good between us.

He never showed.

It wasn't the first time he'd stood me up, but it seemed the most humiliating. I felt as if every one of the smug, stylish people sitting around me had been in on it, from the start. I imagined them tittering behind their Playbills, shaking their heads over the empty seat that told the tale, like a gaping grave.

The tears started the minute the lights went down, washing brand-new mascara down my cheeks. On the tube it had said *water-resistant*. *Water-resistant*, maybe, but not *Andy-resistant*. I rubbed my face with the back of my hand. The black smear on my knuckles was enough to make me sob.

I felt the nudge of an elbow. The man sitting in the next seat handed me a handkerchief. He was very short, and quite old, and seemed neither smug nor stylish. I took it and blew my nose.

At the intermission, I sat in my seat, crying. "I'm sorry," I sniffled to the little old man, "it's just that I think I'm going to have to get a divorce."

Everyone in our row had risen. They wanted to use the bathroom, or have champagne and strawberries, or whatever the hell people did at these high-toned halftimes. They started in my direction, saw me there, and backed up, taking the long way out to the aisle.

"I, I guess I've known for a long time it wasn't working," I confided to this complete stranger, "but it didn't hit me until just now that I was going to be . . . a . . . a . . . a . . . lone. And, and that's why I'm crying."

He nodded. "I didn't think it was the opera," he said gently. "*Carmen* is really relatively happy, as they go." We sat together not speaking until the interval buzzer went off.

"By the way, my name is Arvin." He produced a small white card from out of his pocket. *Arvin Meek, Librarian*, it said.

"Nice to meet you, Arvin. Are you a . . . a . . . a . . . lone, too?" My voice sounded garbled from crying.

"Oh, no," he said, quite happily. "My wife is here." I looked around for a little old lady, but there didn't appear to be one. *Great. Arvin Meek, Librarian. One book short of a stack.*

"On stage," Mr. Meek explained. He smiled broadly, an elfin smile that made his eyes sparkle. "The third old gypsy from the left."

I pressed the elevator button for the sixth floor. The car paused on three and two women and one man, all wearing white jackets, got on. They stood in silence, hungrily eyeing the bags I had clutched in my hand. Maybe they didn't feed them, here in the Forensics Institute. Or maybe they'd assumed I was carrying a different kind of treat—a body part floating in a jar of preservatives, or some vials of human secretion. Who knew what these people went in for? When they got off on the fifth floor, I was relieved.

At the sixth-floor reception desk, I told the guard who I wanted to see. There was nowhere to sit. No coffee table stacked with old issues of *Consumer Reports* and *Newsweek*. It wasn't that kind of place. Still, having a friend who worked here had proved useful to me over the years.

Arvin Meek knew more about the science of killing than just about anyone I'd ever met. Poisoning, gang rape, garrotting, decapitation, mutilation, gunshot wounds—if it had to do with the medical or legal issues of dying, Arvin had the answers.

"Garner!" he cried, opening his arms for a hug. When we embraced, the top of his head brushed my nose. It was bald and whitish-gray, like undusted milk glass. "Would you mind sharing lunch in the stacks? We can be private there." We always shared lunch in the stacks.

He led the way. From behind he could have been taken for a young boy in his father's suit. Jacket sleeves covered his knuckles and his trousers skimmed the floor. We stopped in an alcove, totally enclosed by shelves of bound books. I sat at the wooden table, across from him, and began unwrapping sandwiches. "You still like pastrami, don't you?"

"Oh my, oh yes," Arvin sighed. "Although I'm afraid it doesn't much like me."

"How's Sylvie?" I asked, removing the lids from several plastic containers of potato salad.

"Fine, fine," he replied, his mouth already full.

"Enjoying *La Bohème?*"

"It's one of our favorites." Arvin nodded enthusiastically. "She gets to do a little bit in the café scene, you know, when the lovers meet"—he hummed a few bars while moving his hands—"and then there's that marvelous break . . ." He sighed, momentarily transported.

"I'd love to see her."

"Oh, you must," Arvin agreed. "Especially since this will be her last performance of the season." The other productions were smaller, he told me, and nonsinging roles—old gypsies, bohemians, and beggars, the supers, who were nothing more than human scenery for the immense stage—were the first to go. But for Sylvie Meek, who did it for free, just to hear the music up close, there would always be a next season, I supposed.

"How's Temple?"

"You won't believe it." I showed him the photograph in my wallet.

"Beautiful," he exclaimed, "just like her mother." Old men were so gallant. The pace of our eating had slowed. I removed the tops from two Styrofoam cups of coffee and passed one over. Arvin lowered his head over it, breathing in the cooped-up steam. "It's the Blackmoor case, isn't it?"

"How'd you know?"

He smiled. "When I first heard, I said to Sylvie, that's one for our Garner." He took a sip of coffee. "You've seen the ME report?"

I nodded, feeling vaguely guilty. My connections were high up these days. "What do you make of it?" I asked.

"Troubling." His eyes drifted off into space, then back, bright as buttons. "There are several problems one would encounter in hiding a body, or a body part, within a piece of sculpture such as the ones Mr. Blackmoor creates. First, is the process itself." Arvin stirred his coffee slowly. "Have you seen him work?"

"Tomorrow."

"I imagine it's all quite performance-oriented," he said. "The plaster he uses dries quickly. Minutes at most.

"The victim would have been wrapped while still alive. After the plaster hardened, seams were cut in the cast. That's probably when she was killed—although the means of death, as I understand, are not presently known." Arvin looked up at me for confirmation. "Ah well. Then the severed portions of her body were re-encased in the plaster shell."

"Sounds like a lot of work."

"Oh, it isn't just the work," Arvin said cheerfully. "It's the planning. You see, Blackmoor is famous for two different styles of sculpting." He took a pen out of his pocket and began making little drawings on the empty paper bag. "With some of the pieces, the so-called plaster-bandage figures, what you're really looking at is the outside mold.

"For his more lifelike, painted pieces Blackmoor has developed a high-tech version of the lost-wax technique, which sculptors have been using since ancient times." Arvin tossed this out as if it were everyday knowledge, like the price of eggs.

"The outside cast is filled with a flexible mold material, and reinforced by something like fiberglass, I believe." He sketched a diagram with his pen. "Then the positive mold is removed from the negative mold, thereby being destroyed in the process."

"In other words"—I tried to follow—"he couldn't hide a body part in one of the painted pieces, because there's no outside casing."

Arvin nodded. "Even the positive-mold figures are probably

eventually filled with some sort of quick-drying industrial material to strengthen them. But since they're most likely worked upon piece by piece, it's not inconceivable that a body part could be substituted for the filler." He looked up from his paper-bag drawings. "Does Blackmoor do all the casting himself?"

"I don't know yet," I admitted. "A lot of people work with him. Still, if he wanted to get rid of someone—"

"But was being rid of the body the point?" he challenged softly.

"What do you mean?"

"Well, the trunk and legs have never been found. Nor have the upper arms, for that matter." Arvin's whisper hung eerily between the silent shelves of books. "Just a severed head and a hand."

He shook his head. "If getting rid of the body was the reason for putting them in the sculptures, where is the rest of the corpus delicti?"

"Maybe they just haven't found it yet," I suggested.

"Maybe." He didn't sound convinced. "Or maybe the reason for putting them in there in the first place was so that they *would* be found. They'd been treated with an acrylic fixative, you know. It prevented the natural decomposition of the body from seeping through the plaster surface of the sculpture."

I jumped on this. "So whoever did it wanted to make sure no one knew what was underneath, right?"

Arvin Meek neatly refolded his paper napkin. "Perhaps," he said. "Although there was some seepage from the head, which, as I understand, led to the opening of that particular work."

"Meaning?"

"Meaning that fixative may have been used less to prevent the body from being found, than to preserve the identity of the victim."

According to Blackmoor, Torie had a good head. I wondered how far he would have gone to see that it remained—at least in some way—intact.

5

At the Yale Club, waiters of color served tea with white-gloved hands to suited men of a certain age who tried to pretend that they didn't resent the presence of women in their quiet, paneled, old-boy midst. A few of them nodded to me, patronizingly, as though I were here to join Daddy for tea.

I'm old enough to be your ex-wife, I thought, shooting one of the codgers a black look. Dudley had occasionally brought me to these kinds of places. That was probably why I disliked them so much.

Diana Gold breezed in, fifteen minutes late: short of flat-out rude, but enough to show who was in charge. She sat down at the linen-clothed table, so in sync with the hovering waiter who held out, then pushed in her chair, they might have been dance partners. "Sorry," Gold said, remorselessly.

"That's okay," I replied. "I was just soaking in the ambience." *Bitch.*

Diana turned brightly to Mr. White Gloves. "I'll have a pot of tea and some scones, please." He looked at me and I shook my head.

"By the way, congratulations on this morning."

Gold brushed off the nice-nice. "Oh, that was a skirmish I knew I'd win," she said. I noted the *I*. "The war is just beginning." She leveled a celery-green gaze (*God, she color-coordinates with her eyeballs*). "And I'm going to win that, too. Make no doubt about it."

I had a choice here. I could ignore the implication. Or I could meet it head on. I waited until the waiter had poured her tea. "You know, there's this nasty little stereotype about two strong women not being able to work with each other." I gestured around the room with what was left of my tea biscuit. "Come to think of it, it was probably started by some of the boys in this room—" I smiled. "I don't much believe it myself."

Diana Gold buttered, elegantly. "Strong men. Strong women"—saying a word with every little swipe—"they're all the same to me." She put the rounded knife down, like an exclamation point. "As long as we're working toward the same end."

"The truth, right?"

"Fuck the truth, Quinn," the attorney said bluntly. "The only end I'm fighting for is seeing my client walk away a free man."

"That's your job," I said. "I won't stand in the way of it."

"You bet your life you won't," Diana hissed, sweeping the nearest tables with her icy peripherals before continuing. "So let's get this straight right off the bat.

"I'm no Nick Shawde, who'll sit around shooting the bull with you. You won't find me discussing the fine points of this case just because I like to hear myself talk. You want something from my office, sit and watch, or work for it like the rest of us." She leaned forward in her seat. "It's no secret that I advised Dane against this book. I don't see the point—what? To make you and your agent richer than you already are, and have half of America thinking they know who done it, just because they saw it on 'Geraldo'?"

Diana let out a harsh little laugh. "Look," she said, "I have no idea what kind of hold you have over Dane. But whatever it is, you're crazy if you think I'm going to sit back and let you destroy him for the sake of one of your hot little bestsellers." She groped for the pen that was in a small tray.

"He's *my* client, so keep your distance." She scribbled her signature on the bill. "I don't care what kind of suicidal impulses you bring out in him. I'm gonna save his ass whether he wants it saved or not."

As usual, I'd won points by staying quiet. Diana Gold had made the mistake every seasoned attorney seeks to avoid—she'd said too much. She'd given me a glimpse into her own weaknesses, and that was never smart. It didn't matter what demons drove her—ambition, power, lust, even love. Once the question was posed, Dane Blackmoor was the only answer.

She threw the pen down, pushing her chair out so suddenly the poor waiter was caught with his gloved hands in his proverbial pants. "Have another, on me, if you'd like," Gold said, managing a curt smile. Then, tossing her straight, honey-colored hair back, she strutted her nigh-unto-perfect posterior out of the room, leaving a wake of half-dazed old men, their conversation frozen for a fluttered heartbeat.

I was on my way to the ladies' room when I saw him, seated in a wingback chair in one of the scores of fake little living room areas around the great clubby room. He was talking to another man whose back was to me. For one crazy moment, I thought I could keep right on walking.

"Garner?"

"Hello, Dudley."

He kissed me lightly on each cheek, European style. "Of course, you know my associate, Trace," he said, with an expansive sweep of his hands toward his companion, who was now on his feet.

Trace pumped my hand. "Of course, of course," each of us politely keeping up our end to the masquerade of having been one jolly little threesome at some point in the past. *How long has it been, Father dear?* I thought. *Six, seven years?*

"Well, I'll leave you two to catch up," Dudley's associate was saying, rather nervously.

I wondered if Trace was his first name or his last, finally settling on a simple, "Good seeing you again."

"You too." He shook Dudley's hand. Perspiration had broken out on his top lip. I couldn't tell whether he was sweating because my discomfort was catching or whether it was simply a part of the job description as one of The Great Man Quinn's associates.

Dudley watched him go. "One of the new partners," he said, his lips curled in distaste.

I suddenly thought of Geoffrey Nash, pale and wasted, barely able to speak through the pain of the cancer, which had started in the liver and spread throughout his body. "At least it's not AIDS," he'd croaked. And we'd laughed, me holding his ghost of a hand. Had it really been only two years ago?

Dudley sat back in the wing chair. "Do you have a moment?" He motioned to the sofa as though it were his own, with that way he had of suggesting he owned the whole frigging club, the whole frigging world, for that matter.

"Sure." I perched on the edge of the cushion. *You will note, I am not settling in.*

"So," he began softly, "what have you been doing with yourself, Garner?" I stared at him, trying to find a shred of tenderness in that perfectly ridiculous question he always insisted on asking. He didn't wait for a reply. "You're looking well." He cast a look at my pleated skirt. "Very . . . *gamine*." The word, and his perfect French pronunciation of it, made me suddenly furious.

I'm a writer now, Dudley, haven't you heard? I know what all your fancy vocabulary means. Don't expect me to go running off for my Webster's. I said, "You look tired," without a shred of kindness.

"I am tired," Dudley Quinn III admitted. His honesty made my heart drop.

"Are you in town for long?" I asked.

"To stay, I hope," he answered. "Of course, you knew I sold the place in Portugal." *No, actually. The little birdie carrying that piece of news must have expired on his way across the Atlantic.* Three men walked by with wide-load briefcases in their hands. They called to Dudley, in hushed clubby tones, and the old charming grin broke out on his face, melting the years away.

When he returned his attention to me, he said, "I hear you're working on a book about our friend Mr. Blackmoor."

A jumble of paranoic thoughts flooded my head. *How had he heard? Who told him? Had Cilda been spying for him all this time?* Then I remembered. It had been in the papers. "Yes," I said.

Dudley looked amused. "Well. You must surely let me know when that one comes out."

"Yes," I said.

A roaming White Glove came over, dipping his head next to Dudley's. "Would you care for anything, darling?"

"No, thank you. I just drank a pot of tea and my back teeth are floating." I knew that would embarrass him.

Dudley dismissed the waiter with a nod. There was a long pause. "How is my granddaughter?"

"Fine," I replied, making no move to open my wallet.

"You must give her my best." Not *I'd like to see her someday*, or *Might I drop by sometime?* but, *You must give her my best.* For the millionth time I wondered where he kept it hidden. The best part of him.

"I will," I said, holding out a hand in defense of more kiss-kiss. I didn't think I could stand one more show of phony, forced affection. "It was good seeing you."

"Yes," Dudley said. He looked puzzled, suddenly, in the way that old people do when they're abruptly roused from sleep.

Out of nowhere a thought flew into my mind, that maybe it would have all been so different if I'd turned out to be Diana Gold. I had a mental picture of Dudley, beaming with pride as I made my way toward him, a vision in celery green with a screw-'em-all, confident look in my eye.

"Perhaps we could—" he was saying.

"Yes." I nodded, blinking away tears. Then I turned and fled, without saying goodbye.

6

As I rounded the curve, Elizabeth Rice appeared in the pale moons of my headlights. Dressed in a dove-gray running suit, her hair caught up in a cap, she blended into the gray of early morning. If she hadn't waved, I might've taken her for just another fanatical jogger, instead of a fanatical jogger I actually knew. I considered backing up and offering her a ride, but decided she'd probably turn me down. Rice looked like the type who'd *want* to limp along in the frigid dawn until her nylon jacket and tights were soaked through in places where I myself had never sweated.

I pulled into a space in the parking area behind the Mill. Roberto was standing outside, cheerleading two hefty men as they hoisted a lacquered table on their backs. I checked my watch. *Six forty-five*. Evidently Blackmoor had gotten into the mood early today.

The young man threw his head down on my shoulder. "First, he wants the round mirror, then he wants the square. So is it my fault the props for one don't work for the other? Why is it my fault?"

I felt unequipped to answer this. "Where can I get a cup of coffee?"

"There's a setup in the kitchen," Roberto said. "Help yourself." Then, casting a panicked eye toward the grappling furniture movers, he wailed, "Slowly! Slowly! Use your gentle hands, please, boys!" I left him to his second or third nervous breakdown of the morning.

Inside the studio things were happening, fast and furious. At first glance, it was a verse from a happy children's song—*this is the way we go to work so early in the morning*—but as I got closer, I realized I hadn't seen this many red-rimmed eyes since Max scheduled one of my book-signings in a drug rehab center. I was walking toward the kitchen, when a voice shouted, *"Watch out!"* An electrical cord swung down from the lighting grid, coming to rest a few feet from my head.

"Sorry about that," the technician on the ladder apologized.

I kept moving, past a Hispanic muscleman who was capturing the goings-on with a hand-held camera. Roberto had said some producer was shooting a documentary on Blackmoor. Two large video projection screens had been erected on either side of the stage area, where Lucy Moon roamed, a staplegun poised in one hand. Today's fashion statement was an angora sweater set in basic black and a pair of droopy neon-green stirrup pants.

Bing-bing-bing shot Lucy's staplegun.

"Excuse me." I heard a timid male voice. "Could I get by?" Richard Lewan stood behind me, carrying two large boxes.

"Can I help?"

"If you wouldn't mind. They go over there." He tipped his head toward the stage. I took one of the boxes, surprised when it weighed next to nothing.

"Thank you," Richard said gratefully. He had a sickly pallor, like women a hundred years ago who wore their corsets too tight.

As we reached the dais, music started—Bonnie Raitt, belting out a ballad across the wide-open space. People were moving a little faster now, *heying* and *hi-ing* each other in surprised voices, as if they had only just become aware of the presence of other living bodies. A steady main line of coffee had apparently kicked in, trip-switching the room with a pleasant little caffeine buzz.

I set the cardboard box down, next to Richard's. The Abbott and Costello moving team I'd seen outside were presently attempting to attach a rectangular mirror to a lacquered dressing table. Roberto danced around them, covering his eyes, while Lucy Moon circled slowly, her stapler in the ready position. I hoped, for their sakes, the movers didn't drop anything.

"Ms. Quinn?"

I turned, "I'm Garner."

"Garner," the girl repeated. "Oh, this is so cool! I've read all your books." She held out her hand. She had a nice, firm grip. "I'm Annie. Annie Houghton. Sort of everybody's personal slave?" She had straight, ash-blond hair, and a darting lizard's face with small, quick eyes and a thin-lipped smile. "Beth wanted me to give you this," she said, fishing a key out of her trouser pocket. "For the guest quarters. Dane thought you might need a quiet place to write, or use the phone."

"Thanks." I took the key.

"If there's anything you need—"

"I wouldn't mind a cup of coffee."

"Come on. Hadary's got a buffet in the kitchen." I fell into step with her. "Have you met him? Graham Hadary? Little guy, lotsa makeup?" She rolled her eyes.

"I think I ran into him at the gala. What does he do?"

"That *is* the question," Annie said in deep Shakespearean tones. "On paper, he's sort of a business rep, but mainly, he does the catering. Go figger." She pushed through the double doors. The industrial-sized kitchen was white, trimmed with gleaming metal. We poured coffee into china cups. I selected a muffin from the sumptuous buffet. Annie put three grapes on a plate.

"God, what I wouldn't give to be a writer," she said. "If only it didn't entail so much—well, you know, writing."

"So, are you an aspiring sculptor?" I took a sip of coffee.

"Hardly." Annie giggled. "I'm an actress. Which is to say, I'm out of work."

The little man called Hadary appeared suddenly at the table. "So good to see you again," he told me. "A smashing evening the other night, wasn't it?"

"Yes. I was hoping we might talk—"

"And we will, of course. Anytime. You must let me know." His small, quick eyes spotted something on the other side of the room, and then he was moving again, toward no one in particular.

"Does he always swoop in and out like that?"

"Uh-huh." Annie popped a grape. "Just like the fucking bird."

I found myself relaxing, for the first time. "Did you know Torie?"

"Yeah. I loved that girl."

"We all loved her." I recognized the voice without having to turn. Elizabeth Rice sat down, freshly showered, in a cashmere sweater and skirt.

"Oh, Annie," she asked, almost as an afterthought, "did you find those receipts?"

"Yeah, sure, Beth. They're in the office."

"Do you think you could get them for me?" While Rice's smile was sweet, she might as well have had the word NOW painted on her front teeth.

"Nice meeting you, Garner," Annie said, extending her hand for another forthright shake.

"Thanks, honey," Beth called. Then she turned to me. "I bet you're excited."

"Excited?"

"About seeing Dane. Or isn't this your first time?" She packed as much meaning as she could into the question.

"As a matter of fact, it is," I said.

She bit into a wedge of orange. "I still get chills watching. But then, you're an artist yourself."

"What I do has nothing to do with art," I said. "People commit crimes. I write about them. It's pretty cut and dry."

"I'm sure you're being modest." The conversation had obviously begun to bore her. She checked her Rolex. "Well, better get back to work."

"Any idea of when he'll start?"

"We have a few problems with the props," she said. "At this point I'm guessing noon. Did Annie give you the key to the guest quarters?" I assured her that she had, and that I needed no assistance in finding my way. Out of the corner of my eye I caught a glimpse of Hadary, watching me watch Rice tippy-tap away in her red suede Chanel pumps.

An enclosed walkway led from the Mill to the guest quarters, a self-contained unit with a view of the canal. The walls were painted a bright shade of marigold. Tangerine swags hung from the windows. There was an artfully cluttered sitting room with a bleached pine desk; a tiny kitchen; a large bath; and a bedroom, decorated with paisleys and plaids, in decidedly unfeminine colors. Mason jars held bunches of fresh flowers.

I counted three telephones—one by the bed, one at the desk, another in the bathroom. The armoire concealed a small bar, a television, and a compact disc player. A note on the writing table said: *"Let me know if you need a PC—E.R."* I picked up the phone on the desk and dialed the office. "Hi. How's it going?"

"I'm working my way through that list of employees," Jack said. "Already I've found two no-shows."

"No-shows as in you haven't been able to locate them, or no-shows as in they've vanished?"

"Both listed as missing persons. Both—surprise, surprise—females under the age of eighteen."

"Jesus."

I heard the sound of papers shuffling in the background. "First girl's Donna Fry, seventeen, originally from Spirit Lake, Idaho. Then there's Kimberly Arnette, fifteen, Independence, Kansas."

I wrote the names down. "Think we can draw a line from Blackmoor's studio to the vanishing point?"

"It won't be easy. They were both drifters. Runaways. The detectives I spoke with think they may have just moved on and don't want to be found."

"Maybe," I said grimly, "or maybe they're part of a sculpture exhibit in some gallery."

"I'm not sure I like you being alone out there."

"What's he going to do? Even if he'd like to chop me into little pieces, all this notoriety has to have cramped his style."

"One hopes."

"Listen, there's something else I want you to check," I told him. "Graham Hadary. He's Blackmoor's business rep."

"Got it," he said. "Hey, Garn, watch your back."

"Relax." I laughed softly. "He goes for the younger ones." After I hung up, I did a fast scan of the cheery little room, looking for hidden cameras, bugs, microphones. I found nothing; but the wildflowers and paisleys seemed—suddenly, impossibly—to have eyes.

7

Blackmoor's study was deserted. Something on the desk caught my attention right away—a clay maquette, not more than eight inches high, of a scantily clad woman applying lipstick in front of a vanity mirror. There wasn't much more to it than that; yet, even in miniature, the piece was oddly disturbing. The woman's legs were splayed provocatively, her torso twisting forward, almost into the looking glass. This was vintage Blackmoor, a freeze-frame of life's darker side, where violence was only a footfall away, somewhere behind, down an empty hall.

The piece was called *Role Play*.

I thumbed through a stack of sketches. Except for a crimson gash of lipstick across the woman's mouth, it appeared as though this figure would remain as unpainted plaster. The better to hide something? Or did the painted fiberglass molds house secrets as well—hands and heads, shellacked to a shine—unholy relics of runaway girls?

"There you are," a voice said. I spun around. "I didn't mean to frighten you," said Hadary, "but I thought you'd want to know. He's getting ready to begin."

The model sat on the edge of the platform, stringing odd-looking beads and charms onto a necklace of safety pins. She was a stunning woman—part Afro-American, part Asian, with maybe one wild, drunken encounter with an Irishman thrown in somewhere for luck—but all the crossbreeding appeared to have watered down the blood. Her face was a beautiful, troubling blank.

"Kyra, could we try you in this?" Lucy Moon held up a pair of leather bicycle shorts. The girl stepped out of her kimono. Underneath she wore only a sheer black bra and a matching bikini. She hiked the pants over her slender hips.

Lucy Moon shook her head. "Let's see what Dane says about the bodysuit." Kyra peeled off the shorts, threw the kimono loosely around her shoulders, and went back to stringing her necklace. Blackmoor's cockatoo sat on the lighting grid, watching the action as though it were a guard in the watchtower of a prison camp. Occasionally it chewed on its feet.

Roberto trundled in, pushing a trolley with a big empty tub in the middle. "Once Dane's ready," he told me, "this will be filled with warm water." On one side of the basin were neat piles of bandages in varying sizes. On the other gleamed an array of mat knives, razors, and small, mean-looking blades with rows of wicked teeth. I picked one up.

Blackmoor suddenly came up behind me. "It's called a claw," he said. "The sharp edges produce a cross-hatching effect."

I tossed the tool back onto the tray. "What about these knives?"

He studied me for a moment. "Would you like to see the really good stuff?" He grabbed my arm, propelling me up the staircase. Lucy Moon, her arms filled with small leather garments, stopped what she was doing to watch. Beth Rice paused in her instructions to the technician hanging lights. Kyra ceased stringing. Even the bird laid off its beaky pedicure. All around us, people were looking up and taking note.

When we reached the upper gallery, Blackmoor released my arm. He continued walking, past the metal door of the torso grave-yard, to another open workspace. "Here." He snapped on a light. "You want deadly? Take a look at these—" He pointed to each item as he went by it. "Mallets. Hammers, of course. Bourchardes—they're used for bruising and pulverizing." He was talking too loud. "Power tools. Drills, saws. Rasps. Files. Rifflers. Gouges."

He lifted one. "This one they call a body grinder."

"Are they all necessary for the kind of sculpture you do?"

"I'm known for the plaster-bandage technique," Blackmoor re-sponded. "But I've dabbled in metals. Even marble, once or twice." He opened the doors of a large metal cabinet. "Oh, and just in case you should think I'm holding out on you, this is where we keep the joining and glueing materials. The heated tools. Polystyrene. Polyurethane. The foamed plastics." Plastics. Materials to encase, protect, preserve. I remembered Torie Wood's severed head in its clear, form-fitting sarcophagus.

"Snoop around to your heart's content," he invited, coldly. "And if you have any questions, don't hesitate to ask."

I had a couple for starters. *Is this where you did it? Is this where you took apart that little girl?* But instead I just said, "Don't worry. I will."

Blackmoor prowled around the perimeter of the platform, studying Kyra from every conceivable angle. She appeared totally oblivious to him. He'd decided upon a leather brassiere and match-ing girdle, with net stockings and high heels; but the costume was for later, after the plaster cast was assembled. She would be sculpted in the nude.

He posed her in front of the vanity, eyes looking vacantly into the mirror. The expression seemed suspiciously easy for Kyra.

It was three forty-five when Blackmoor finally gave the go-ahead.

The cameraman got into position. Roberto held a Nikon. The pictures, both video and still, would be used later, I'd been told, during the reassembling and casting.

A young man entered from the kitchen with a bucket of steaming water, which he poured into the tub on the trolley. Blackmoor kneeled next to Kyra, whispering into her ear. She got up, stretched, did a few neck revolutions and shoulder shrugs. Then she slid out of her underwear and sauntered back to the vanity, as though she weren't naked, on a stage, in front of a dozen people.

Don Henley wailed over the speakers. I moved closer, taking care to stay out of camera range. Blackmoor suddenly appeared on the twin projection screens, magnified, multiplied, larger than life. I felt momentarily torn between his live and his video presence. Somehow, his every movement was hypnotic—the way he pushed up the sleeves of his sweater, his hand as it dipped into a large plastic jar.

"Petroleum jelly," he said aloud, turning to slather it over Kyra's legs. "It coats the skin and makes it easier to remove the cast." He rubbed it between her toes. Around her heels. Up her calves, to her thighs. Kyra blinked her eyes slowly, *open-close-open*, like a cat.

Blackmoor submerged four bandages into the basin, then molded them around the girl's feet. He moved swiftly, without hurrying, modeling with his fingers. Roberto sat on his heels, focusing the Nikon. *Click-click-click.* Blackmoor was swathing Kyra's legs, his movements larger now, but just as sure, finding the line of muscle, kneading it with his palms, like an expert masseur. "I've set the knees at this angle to offset the tilt of the shoulder," he said, speaking just loud enough so that his voice carried over the music.

"Each line—how long it is, how wide it is, where it fits in relationship to the other parts—affects how the work will be interpreted. If I move one leg closer to the other, I alter the scenario." He'd been working for about fifteen minutes, although it seemed like far less.

The young man standing next to the trolley shifted his weight, and water sloshed from the basin. Elizabeth Rice whispered something to him.

Blackmoor leaned back on the floor, looking up at his model's long, encased legs. "You okay?" he asked. Kyra said yeah. They stayed that way for a few more minutes, Blackmoor seeming to be completely lost in the music. Then he drew up on his knees, touched the bandages in several places, and nodded.

Richard Lewan handed over a mat knife the way a nurse hands a doctor a scalpel. Blackmoor took it and scooted around to the back of the girl. I moved with him, watching as he cut a seam in the plaster from heel to thigh on Kyra's left leg. He did the same with the right. Sitting on his haunches, he worked his hand upward, prying the cast loose with his finger until it split all the way to the waist. If the girl minded all the groping, it was impossible to tell. She had the bored expression of someone who was mentally compiling a grocery list.

Lewan took the knife and handed Blackmoor a red pencil. He made some quick arrow markings, showing where the seams needed to be realigned, then began removing the plaster cast in sections. When he was finished, Kyra stood up and stretched. Richard carted the plaster legs and lap away.

Meanwhile, the guy manning the trolley had brought in more hot water, pouring it into the tub with a loud splash. Elizabeth motioned to Annie. They talked quietly together, with Annie nodding, and taking notes.

Kyra was in position again. Blackmoor spread more petroleum jelly over her shoulders, down her arms, to the tips of her fingers. He applied it to her back, working it into the archipelago of her spine. She did that cat blink again—*open-close-open*—as, very gently, from behind, he smoothed some under her breasts and over her perfect nipples. I found it increasingly hard to swallow.

Holding out a long, moist strip of bandage, Blackmoor began to shape it down the long curve of the girl's torso. *Click-click-click-click-click.* Roberto, with the Nikon, was out of control. Blackmoor's hands raced over Kyra's body, smoothing the wet plaster into sinewy lines. The music seemed to climb a few decibels, Don Henley raging.

No one except Blackmoor appeared to be moving, even breathing. By now he'd stopped talking, as though he were channeling all
his thoughts into his hands. When the plaster dried from neck to
waist, he took the knife again, slicing the shell confidently, ruth-
lessly, splitting first the right arm, then the left. With one deft motion he cut down the model's back, loosening the plaster cast, and
removing the torso in halves. She flexed her muscles but stayed
seated. Blackmoor whispered something, and the girl nodded. I saw
the first glimpse of a connection between them. Kyra was getting
into it.

Click-click-click-click.

The music changed from Henley's vocal to a floating, freewheel-
ing orchestration. Blackmoor's lips were moving; I could see him
talking steadily to Kyra, but I couldn't hear what was being said. He
took three strips, placing them across the bridge of Kyra's nose, her
mouth, her eyes and forehead. His hands traced the bandages, over
and over, until I could almost feel them harden from where I stood.

He was sealing the girl's head inside.

The studio began a slow turn. Sweat sizzled to the surface of my
skin. I wanted to cry out—*Stop him! He's covering her up . . . plastering over her air passages, her pores. . . .* Blackmoor placed thin strips
of bandage between Kyra's nostrils, shaping them around her nose,
to the prominent cheekbones, and brow. I wanted his hands to
hurry, but instead they dawdled, caressing the model's skull, playing
across her blank irises.

The camerman had zoomed in. Overhead, on the projection
screens, Kyra's face stared stonily, like some ancient eyeless goddess.
Inhale, I commanded myself. *Exhale. Inhale.* My body was going
through all the right motions, but it seemed to be a dry run without
oxygen.

Click-click.

I wanted to smash that camera. Only now I realized the sound
had actually come from Blackmoor, snapping his fingers; and there
was Richard again, with the mat knife.

Good old Richard.

The blade flashed in the light as it dove toward Kyra's neck. Blackmoor sliced a deadly perfect seam up to each ear. She cat-blinked again, letting out a nervous little laugh. The hush in the room splintered like the plaster cast. I sank down on the edge of the platform, watching the sculptor lead his model to the tub to rinse off her face. Lucy Moon covered the girl's bare shoulders with the kimono.

Blackmoor was looking at me. "I hope you found it useful," he said.

"Yes," I croaked.

Behind us came the sound of angry voices. Elizabeth Rice was arguing with the trolley assistant. "There's no excuse." She pointed to the puddle on the floor. "It's careless. It's sloppy. It's unprofessional."

The guy shrugged. "I don't see what the big deal is."

"You're out of here, mister." Rice's voice had become strident. "That's the big deal."

The young man looked around the room for support, but everyone had scattered. I turned to say something to Blackmoor, surprised to find Graham Hadary standing in his place. He inclined his pale head toward Beth Rice. "She's very protective of Dane," he explained in a confidential tone. "She'd do anything for him."

By the time I pulled in the drive it was almost ten-thirty. The lights were off in the office. The house was also dark, except for the lantern that hung over the back entrance, which Cilda always kept burning.

When I opened the kitchen door, I heard something fall—a large manila envelope with *Garner* written across the top in Jack's cramped, irregular printing. The sight of my own name in familiar handwriting made my heart drop. I felt lonely, and inexplicably sad.

I poured myself a glass of wine, dumping out the contents of the packet onto the table. More photographs of Torie Wood. Baby pictures. School pictures. A chubby little Torie in a pink tutu. An adolescent Torie sitting cross-legged with the girls' soccer team. She was easy to pick out. Like Temple.

The wineglass in my hand began to shake.

I stuffed the pictures back into the envelope, turned off the kitchen light, and moved through the empty great room. The long wall of windows reflected the ocean. Tonight the waves were as black as pitch.

Temple's door was open a sliver. I tiptoed toward the bed, taken aback, as always, by her total perfection in sleep—the thick brush of her lashes, the sheen of her skin, the curve of her upper lip. I touched her cheek.

She turned over. "Mom?" Her voice was thick and groggy. "Hi, Mommy . . . " then, as I hugged her, "You're getting me all wet. . . ."

I hadn't realized I was crying. "I just wanted to say goodnight," I told her. She grunted sleepily, her eyelids already twitching with re-membered dreams. Sweet ones, I hoped.

So much sweeter than my own would be.

8

I listened as Annie Houghton diplomatically explained to the shopkeeper that, while Mr. Blackmoor
had positively adored the glass bottle, he had gone with the enamel
box instead. The box would have been her choice, too, the woman
nodded with approval. Maybe the glass one would work next time.
Anything she could do for Mr. Blackmoor. Such a brilliant man!—
and, oh, she would be getting a poster-sized print of the finished
piece, wouldn't she?

Annie smiled. "I'll drop it off myself." She joined me on the
other side of the display counter. "This is the absolute best part of my
job," she whispered. "It's like playing hooky."

I could relate. As we maneuvered past the browsers in the nar-
row-aisled shop, glimmering rows of goodies teased me from every
direction. I had the urge to buy something frivolous.

Wind chimes tinkled pleasantly as we pushed through the shop
door. The balmy November weather had brought early holiday shop-

pers out in force. New Hope was packed. Couples strolled arm in arm brushing shoulders with young mothers and children. Packs of handsome gay men in jeans and leather jackets sauntered down Mechanic Street.

"I have to go in here." Houghton motioned toward another storefront.

In the front window a paint-chipped mannequin had been decked out in a paisley mini and white ankle boots. A vivid image of my old friend Cathy, the upstairs maid, flashed through my mind: her tanned snub nose, her streaked blond hair (*"With Sun-In they'll think the sun did it!"*), her lips slickered in something that smelled like strawberries and looked like pink Vaseline. The mournful wail of vintage Patsy Cline tugged me inside by my heartstrings.

Annie was already at the counter, delivering her routine to a tall, thin girl in a print granny dress.

"You like this?" I asked after she concluded her business. I held up a silver peace sign suspended on a black satin rope. "I mean, would you wear it?"

"Sure," Houghton replied. "I have one I wear all the time."

The salesgirl rang it up for me, putting it in a tiny, once-white box that was now as gray and battered as everything else in the shop. I felt exhilarated, as though I'd just done something adventurous.

"I told Nicholas we'd be there about noon," Annie said when we were out on the street again. "Would you like to get some coffee first?"

We found a little café that overlooked the canal. "Order whatever you want," I told her. "I'm paying."

Annie sighed. "I'll just stick with coffee."

"Don't you ever eat?"

She drew up her small pointed nose and sharp chin. "It's this thing with me. Yesterday I tried on a pair of size 0 jeans and they fit, but today I feel like, fat." She carefully poured a drop of cream into her cup. "Anyway, we're here to talk about Torie, not eat, right?" She smiled, eager to please.

"You said you were friends."

"Oh, everybody loved Torie." The quicksilver tongue darted out and back in. "Except maybe Beth. She really doesn't give a flying fuck about anyone but Dane." She stirred the coffee with the one measly drop of cream in it.

"Did Blackmoor treat her differently?"

"Not really." The girl thought for a moment. "He treats everybody mostly like shit." Then she corrected herself. "Not that he's a bastard, or anything. In fact he's real polite. Icy polite, you know? Very detached." She took a sip. "Very passive aggressive. He lets everybody else do his dirty work."

"Like Elizabeth?"

She nodded. "Elizabeth. Hadary. Lucy. Even Roberto, if you can believe it." Then, although I hadn't said anything, she added, "Beth is an easy target, but we get along okay. I feel sorry for her. Evidently she had a shitty childhood and a shitty marriage, so she probably can't help being a little screwed up."

I wondered if people said that about me. "She's heavy into therapy and these Twelve-Step programs," Annie went on. "Anything that's, you know, healthy. She jogs. She meditates. She fasts. She's always at an exercise class, or the manicurist."

"Is she involved with anyone?"

"I don't think Beth's had a date since her marriage broke up four years ago." She sighed. "I mean there's Dane, but that's like in her dreams. I think that's why she channels all her energies into this nurture-yourself crap. She's almost got herself convinced that an herbal wrap is as good as getting laid. Scary."

"Tell me about the sculptures."

"You got five minutes? I'll teach you all I know."

I looked down at my watch, and gave her the go. "What happens to the plaster casts after a sitting?"

"Oh, actually, that's pretty cool," Annie said. "The parts are stored upstairs in the workshop until they're ready to be reassembled. Then they dampen the seams, you know, where Dane splits them with the knife? And they rejoin the sections, piece by piece.

"It can be a bitch, too, because the wet plaster gets all gunky and shapeless, and you really have to know what you're doing to get it to align so it looks like it's supposed to." The girl paused. "They have to work really fast."

"When you say they, who exactly are you talking about?"

Annie considered. "Usually Richard, or one of the apprentices."

"What about Blackmoor?"

"It's not really his thing. Unless it's a figure that's going to be painted and dressed. He could care less about the plaster-bandage ones once the initial sculpting is over."

"If they don't interest him, why does he do them?"

Houghton drew up all the sharp edges of her face into a mock-serious expression. "You want the party line? It's an artistic statement." She dropped her voice theatrically. "*The unpainted-plaster technique captures the sterility and emptiness of modern life.*" She giggled. "But if you want to know the truth, it's a money issue. The lifelike figures take a couple of months to complete. They're not cost-effective. Dane can knock out a plaster-bandage job in a couple of days, and there's always a market."

She paused for a minute, checking out the faces around the café before continuing. "In my opinion, he's just going through the motions—like he's lost the passion for it, you know? Back in the studio in New York, he was supposed to be like totally fried. Ripped out of his mind pretty much all the time. Lucy Moon and Richard were doing most of the work. Signing his name to stuff. That's sort of a requisite of the job. Even I could do it if I had to. It's so bogus—people peeing in their pants over original Blackmoors?—*pul-ease.*"

"Is it still like that now?"

"A couple of years ago, he went on the wagon. That's when Beth came in to manage the operation. She convinced Dane it would be good to move out here, get a fresh start." She drained her coffee, looking longingly into the empty cup. "Still, sometimes we don't see him for weeks at a time. He just barricades himself in his quarters, and everybody covers. The official word is Blackmoor's better than ever." Annie rolled her eyes. "Shit," she said, "I really shouldn't have told you that."

I motioned to the waitress for the check. Houghton shifted in her seat. "You know, when I talk about him, it makes it sound like Dane's pretty weird, but he's really not, considering."

"Considering what?"

"Well, the life he leads, the sicko art crowd, and the fame." She paused, then said, earnestly, "I don't think he could ever kill anybody, though. Especially not Torie."

"Why not?"

"For one thing, the only time I've ever seen him act really excited about anything was when he saw her work."

"Did she ever say anything to you about him?"

"Like, if they were fucking, you mean?"

I felt my face flush. "Whatever."

"I think she would have told me if they were," said Annie. "I mean, I knew about her and Richard."

"Richard Lewan?"

"Yeah, do you believe it?"

"He seems too . . . breakable . . . for sex."

Houghton cracked up. "That's a kind way to put it. Although I wonder whether his wife would agree."

"He's married?"

"What a heartbreaker, huh? Torie used to say he was on a higher plane spiritually, but what she didn't know about men could fill a set of encyclopedias. I guess that's why she was so devoted to Dane," she mused. "He was probably the only guy who was ever nice to her."

I tossed a ten-dollar bill on the table to cover the $3.50 tab. "Let's go," I said. "It's stuffy in here."

When we were out in the fresh air, I turned to her. "One more thing—how did you start working for Dane, anyway?"

"Oh, I used to go clubbing with Roberto and his boyfriend," Annie said. "He knew I needed money, so he brought me around."

It was Roberto who'd brought around Torie Wood. Another question came to mind. "Did you ever hear of anyone named Donna Fry, or maybe Kimberly Arnette? They did some modeling for Blackmoor, before your time."

Annie shook her head. "Do they have something to do with Torie?"

"I'm not sure," I admitted. "I'm just hoping they won't turn up as body parts." Annie Houghton's sharp little face suddenly paled.

Torie Wood's friend Nicholas owned a small antique shop on the hill near the railroad station. He was talking on the telephone in hushed tones when we walked in. "No," he said softly, "I was at the hospital last night."

A friend with AIDS, I thought automatically.

Annie waved and blew him a silent kiss. We let him wind up his phone conversation as we looked around, Annie humming to the classical music that played over the speakers. Moments later, she made the introductions.

"This is a real pleasure, Ms. Quinn," exclaimed Nicholas. "I think your books are absolutely brilliant."

"Thanks."

"How's Howard?" Annie inquired solicitously.

"The same." He explained, "My friend has AIDS." I wished I hadn't guessed.

The young man's eyes misted over. "Torie," he said, "was Howard's favorite." The past tense hung in the air over all of us.

I was pleased when he suggested that I go up alone. The narrow wooden stairs had been painted a madder brown. I breathed in the musty smell of the place.

The room that Nicholas had lent to Torie Wood (lent, not rented, he'd reiterated carefully, because they were friends) was at the right rear of the building. It was barely bigger than a walk-in closet. A twin mattress, neatly made up with printed sheets and co-ordinating pillowcases, took up most of the floor space. In one corner stood a rust-stained pedestal sink; in another, a cheap, four-shelf bookcase. One nicely framed nude photograph of Marilyn Monroe hung on the wall. A Madonna poster had been tacked up next to the sink, probably to cover a wandering crack in the plaster. If I stood on tiptoe to look out of the one small window, I could see the canal, and beyond that, the railroad.

This was where Torie Wood had slept during the last six weeks of her young life. When she wasn't sleeping with Richard Lewan. Or maybe Dane Blackmoor.

I checked out the bookcase. There were a couple of books on sculpture, one by Frank Rich, another by Stewart Johnson; an unauthorized biography of Dane Blackmoor and a coffee table–sized book of his work; two photography books, one Gordon Parks, one Annie Leibovitz; and some Disney Goldenbooks—*The Little Mermaid, Peter Pan,* and *Bambi.* An upscale Sears-type family portrait in a simple wooden frame showed Torie and her two sisters with their parents. From the looks of it, it had been taken fairly recently. Torie's hair was slicked back in a vain attempt to disguise the blatantly fuchsia highlights. I felt my throat constrict.

One shelf of the bookcase was filled with a row of ugly little dolls with pastel-colored hair and heads too big for their bodies. "Torie's Kiddles," Nicholas said, behind me. I nearly jumped out of my skin. There's something unnerving about having someone sneak up on you when you're looking at a dead person's things.

"She collected them," the young man explained. "Actually the ones with the boxes are worth quite a bit."

But I'd stopped listening. I knelt down to get a better look at the objects on the lower shelf—small figures in wax and clay. A little boy. A horse. A naked woman. A Native American head.

Nicholas and Annie moved into the room. The shadows they cast over the tiny sculptures made it somehow difficult for me to catch my breath. Even after I excused myself, running down the madder stairs and out the front door of the shop to breathe in the moist, cool air, I still wasn't sure whether my physical response had been to the claustrophobic little room, or to the uncommon beauty of the extraordinary creations that Torie Wood's hands had fashioned.

9

We had arranged to meet in town, at a restaurant tucked off the main drag. Elizabeth Rice rushed in, a half hour later, but glowing. "I feel wonderful," she said. Not *Sorry*, or *Have you been waiting long?*, but *I feel wonderful*.

"Gee," I said.

"I just had an aromatic massage," Beth sighed. "Have you ever had one?"

"No," I said. "Gee."

"You have to," said Beth Rice. "You can just sense all the toxins pouring out of your body. We could go together, sometime—there's a spa not far from town."

I made all the appropriate sounds that might pass for indicating that this would be a swell idea, all the while waiting for the woman to settle in so we could get down to what I wanted to get down to. Beth ordered a bottle of mineral water. I caught the disapproving glance she'd given my glass of chardonnay.

I brought the wine to my lips, rebelliously. "How long have you been working with Blackmoor?" No sense in postponing things. For all I knew Rice would have a Reebok Step class in half an hour.

"It's been three years," Beth said, adding, "God." as if she couldn't believe it.

"How did you two get together?"

Rice drew her chin into a perfect heart, dimpling it on each side. It was a practiced, but effective, move. "As odd as it may sound"— she lowered her voice—"we met in recovery."

"You mean like AA?"

Elizabeth's smile flickered, then stuck. "Yes." The waiter brought her water. "Could we have just a teeny bit more time?" she asked.

"So you met in recovery," I prompted.

"Anonymity is one of the Twelve Traditions," she said, matter-of-factly. "But, of course, I knew who he was right away." She smiled at the memory. "I was managing a gallery on Fifty-seventh Street at the time, really terribly unhappy." She said this as though it were an unusual state of affairs; and I added another feature to Annie's description: shitty childhood, shitty marriage. *Shitty professional life.*

Rice went on. "One night, I just walked up to him and told him how in awe I was of his talent. Well, right afterward, he stopped coming to the meetings." She realigned all the silverware on her side of the table. "You have to understand that there was—and is—a great deal of self-loathing in this man. It might seem incredible to you or me, but, for some reason, Dane has never quite accepted his own genius."

"He hasn't?"

Elizabeth had relaxed into her subject. "Oh no," she said. "I sensed that about him, right from the beginning. That's why, when he stopped working the program, I summoned up the nerve to go to his studio. You see, I knew what I would find."

"What was that?"

"He'd started drinking again. The place was in absolute chaos. Graham and Richard had been trying to keep things going, but commissions were down. I immediately saw that something needed to be done."

"And you did it."

Beth smiled modestly. "Dane did it. I just provided the necessary support."

"He owes you a lot."

"Oh no," she demurred. "I owe him. He gave me a sense of purpose."

The waiter came back and asked if we were ready. Elizabeth went into lengthy instructions as to what should be cooked without butter, and what made with balsamic vinegar. I ordered a multilayered sandwich with Russian dressing.

When we were alone again, I shifted direction. "What can you tell me about Torie Wood?"

"Just that she was a sweet child," Beth said, adding, "and Dane thought she was very talented."

"Do you know of any reason why someone would want to kill her?"

"You mean someone at the Mill?"

"Who else could have sealed her body parts into a Blackmoor sculpture?" I lobbed the question across the table like a tennis ball.

This bluntness seemed to ruffle her. "I see what you—" she sputtered. "But it's just too awful to think about."

"Yes, it is," I agreed. "By the way, did you know Donna Fry or Kim Arnette?"

"The names sound familiar."

"They were on that list you gave me," I told her. "Only now nobody seems to know where they are."

Elizabeth's hands fluttered around her water glass. "I think I remember Kim," she said. "She wasn't one of Dane's regulars. She might have posed for him once, maybe twice."

"Could you find out the titles of the sculptures she modeled for?"

"I'll try," Rice said stiffly, "but I'm not sure we kept records like that back then."

The waiter returned with our food. As I bit into my sandwich, I noticed a visible change in Elizabeth's demeanor. The top layer of her face, the brittle, sugary one, had cracked, giving a glimpse of something softer underneath.

"You're going to hurt him with this book, aren't you?" She looked down at her food as though she didn't know what to do with it.

"That's not my intent," I replied. "I just want to find out the truth."

Rice nodded—one of those quick genuflections of the head that an athlete might give to an opponent on another team—then she dug into her salad, and began reciting the benefits of aromatic massage.

"Hello?" I called out into the empty studio.

A halfhearted echo bounced back at me. "—lo?"

The worklights were on, but the place looked deserted. Everyone had probably jumped ship early for the weekend. Upstairs, I noticed a light was on in one of the bays. I climbed the steps, noisily, as if a brazen approach might scare away all the bogeymen who might be lurking. I passed several shuttered workspaces, stopping at the one open door. "Roberto? Lucy? Anybody here?"

A middle-aged woman in a short-sleeved print housedress was on her hands and knees, scrubbing the floor. Unflattering folds of dimply flesh hung at the back of her big arms and legs. She wore a Walkman, the pack tucked in her pocket. "I'm sorry, I thought—"

The woman didn't respond. *Maybe the music*— I came closer. The plaque read: CLEANING LADY.

These sculptures were really getting on my nerves. They made me feel like a voyeur—fascinated, and yet ashamed—as though just by looking I'd entered into some kind of dark pact with Blackmoor. I turned off the light on the painted washerwoman and headed toward the last bay.

The door clammered open easily. I hit the lights, relieved to be among these workaday tools, free for a moment from the creepy, black-eyed staring faces, the unanswering mouths. I picked up implements, one at a time, feeling how heavy they were, testing their sharpness, their hardness, their cutting edges, trying to remember what Blackmoor had said. *Which ones were for pulverizing and bruising? Where was the gouge? The body grinder?* I counted four power saws and one hacksaw. Scores of razors. The place was a potential chamber of horrors.

A noise came from outside, in the gallery. I turned in time to see the door swinging down. "Who's there?" I called hoarsely, making my way around the worktables. Before I reached for the counterweight pulley, I picked up a mallet.

The gallery was empty.

"Hello?" I leaned over the railing. "Anybody?" My voice swirled around in the vaults of the deserted studio. I checked my watch. Six-ten. The weekend stretched ahead of me—time enough to learn all about sculpting tools and their uses; and to imagine what these implements could do when applied to flesh and bones.

I replaced the mallet, snapped off the light, pulled down the door, and hit the steps, taking two at a time. Rounding the platform in the dark, I ran slam-bang into another warm body.

"Jesus, Garner!" Annie gasped. "I didn't know you were still here!"

I laughed a little hysterically. "Were you upstairs a minute ago?"

She shook her head. "No, I was just heading there now to make sure the lights were off. As far as I know, I'm the only one left."

A sound came from the skylights, muffled but frantic, like fast feet in an empty gynmasium. The big white bird dive-bombed, landing on the edge of the platform, where it whistled a snappy, "*Screwyou . . . screwyou . . . screwyou . . .*"

"I say we kill it," Annie whispered.

"He's much too fast for you," Blackmoor said.

Annie spun around, stammering, "I was just going upstairs to—"

"I'll take care of it."

"Well, see you Monday." The young woman backed out of the room.

I stood my ground. "Were you up in the gallery a little while ago?"

"No," the sculptor replied. "Why? Did you get scared?" He moved past me, not waiting for a reaction. The cockatoo flew to the edge of the platform, sharpening its claws on a manila envelope. Blackmoor shooed it away.

"From yesterday," he said, removing a stack of photographs. "A good one of you." He held up a shot.

"What happens to the videos?"

He slid the pictures back into the folder. "We label them and put them on a shelf."

"What about Torie's sittings? Did you tape them?"

"I tape them all."

"I'd like to see those cassettes."

"So would I," Blackmoor said. "Unfortunately, they're missing." He began walking away.

"That's convenient." I ran to keep up with him.

"Depends on your point of view," he said. "Personally, I think it's a pain in the ass."

I followed him into his office. "How about Donna Fry? Do you have tapes of her? What about Kim Arnette? How many have there been?"

"Lost tapes?" he asked. "Or lost girls?"

"How come you didn't tell the police that more than one of your models had disappeared?"

"I didn't know myself, until today," he said. Before I could ask, he added, "My staff is very loyal." Beth Rice, I thought. Or at least I hoped.

"The ones who are still around," I noted. "By the way, I saw some of Torie Wood's work this afternoon." I gestured toward the glass display case. "Those are hers, aren't they? The two on the bottom?"

"What an eye." His voice sounded bitter.

"Was it difficult being around that much . . . natural ability?"

Blackmoor laughed. "You mean for someone like me?" He walked over to the shelves of miniature maquettes, and studied them for a moment.

"Do you know what my critics say, Garnish? They call me a fake. A con man. Would you believe that some have actually had the nerve to suggest that it takes little or no talent to do what I do? *The P. T. Barnum of sculpting,* one of them dubbed me. That's my favorite"—his mouth twisted—"that, and the one the gossip columnists use all the time—*celebrity slash artist.* What the fuck do you suppose a *celebrity slash artist* looks like, Garnish?"

"Like you."

He laughed. "Well, since you're the one with the eye, I'll ask. What do *you* think of my work?"

I thought for a moment. "I think it's startling, disturbing." I said the words slowly. "I'm just not sure I'd call it art."

He stared at me for a long moment. "Good," he said finally. "Now come over here." I hesitated. "I promise not to slice you up. Or kiss you."

I walked as casually as I could to the display case. "Want to know how I think of them?" He was standing so close, his breath tickled my face. "I think of them as my little graven images."

My knees almost buckled. I didn't like hearing those words again. For some reason they frightened me. "I know who I am, Garnish," he whispered. "My work is in every major modern museum in the world, private collections, you name it. They don't buy those." He pointed to the models. "They buy *me.*"

Blackmoor lifted one of Torie's pieces out of the case. "This, of course, is different. There's a purity here, a nugget of truth." He turned it over in his hand. "And the sad part of it is, it doesn't mean shit.

"The people in the marketplace aren't looking for truth, Garner. They're too busy worshiping the golden calf. Lucky for me, too. I hammered one out just yesterday." He leaned closer. He smelled more like a color or a taste than a fragrance. I wondered how that could be. I watched him carefully put Torie's maquette back on the shelf.

"So to answer your question. Was it difficult being around that much natural ability?" Blackmoor looked me squarely in the eyes. "No. Talent doesn't scare me. I just keep on doing what I do, as fast as I can do it, all the time looking over my shoulder for the guy who can gilt a better cow." He moved away suddenly; and I found myself working for my next breath.

His self-contempt had nearly suffocated me.

10

I spent most of Saturday with Temple, shopping for
something for her to wear to Emory's party. She didn't
mention the scrapbook or Dane Blackmoor, and neither did I, but I
had a niggling feeling that I owed her some kind of explanation. To
offset my guilt, I paid more for her outfit than I should have.

When we returned to the house, I noticed Jack's car. "You had a
couple of calls," he said as soon as I walked into the office. "Ms. Gold
buzzed at eleven to say that under no circumstances would Blackmoor's videocassettes be made available to you." He made a face.
"Five minutes later, Blackmoor's on the line. He wants you to know
you may be getting a call from his attorney, but you're to disregard
what she says. You can look at any tape he has."

"Generous of him, especially since the only ones that really matter happen to be missing." I walked over to the refrigerator and took
out a Diet Coke. "How'd it go with Torie's parents yesterday?"

"They were pretty heartbreaking. They said they didn't file a missing-persons report because Torie had been disappearing repeatedly for months ever since she was twelve. Anyway, it's all here." He pushed over a stack of papers and a micro-cassette. "I taped the interview and took notes."

That was not my way of working. I popped the can. The carbonation fizzled, dribbling over Jack's research packet. He had a funny expression on his face.

"There's something else, isn't there?"

Jack leaned across the desk eagerly. "On my way back from Scarsdale, I stopped in Manhattan to talk to a friend of mine down in Soho." He paused. "I hope you don't mind me taking that kind of initiative."

Initiative was good, I reminded myself. So why did I suddenly feel so pissed off? "Tell me what you found out," I said.

He looked disappointed. I knew he'd been hoping to draw out this moment, but I had forced his hand. "The upshot is," he said, "before he started working for Blackmoor, Graham Hadary was employed by none other than Conrad Vestri." Vestri was currently serving a life sentence for the sadomasochistic murders of two young men.

A ragged line of adrenaline zigzagged through me. It must have shown, because Jack picked up the thread of the story, more confidently. "Hadary was never implicated in the deaths of those boys, but it came out at the trial that he was the talent scout. He'd meet some young stud at a disco or a bar, and then invite them to one of Vestri's glittering affairs."

"Did you happen to find out anything about Roberto?"

He flipped through his notes. "Roberto Jurgensen—or as his mommy and daddy originally named him, Robert Jackson. One of Hadary's protégés."

"Who happens to the the person who introduced Torie Wood and Ann Houghton, and who knows how many others, to Dane Blackmoor." This was sounding all too familiar.

It was sounding really great.

Dressed in her expensive new togs, with the silver peace chain I'd given her around her neck, Temple could've easily passed for seventeen. The thought was somehow depressing. I was glad she hadn't put up a fuss about me driving her to and from the party.

The phone rang as I was getting my keys. I picked up the extension in the hall. "Hey, lady," said the voice. "We went dancing last night in my head. I apologize for stepping on your feet."

"Jeff?" My heart dropped through the floor, wedging itself into the foundation of the basement. "Jeff." I sounded disoriented, even to myself. "Is . . . is everything all right?"

On the other end, he laughed easily. "Of course. Why wouldn't it be?"

"I'm sorry," I apologized, "it's just—you got me at a bad time."

"Well, I won't keep you. I just wanted to tell you I'm going back to school."

"That's wonderful," I said, tenatively.

"Majoring in industrial engineering, with a minor in art, like I always wanted to."

"Great."

"I've got my portfolio up at Pratt, and MIT, and they wrote me back and said they're really impressed."

I tried not to sound shocked. "Those are good schools," I said. *Good northern schools. Good schools up here, in the north.*

"The best," Jeff agreed. "But I'm going to need a letter of recommendation. From someone who can vouch for my character. And, of course, you're the first person—"

I don't know whether it was actually Jeff, or all the stuff with Blackmoor, but I suddenly felt avalanched by the past. Buried alive by it. Outside, in the car, Temple leaned on the horn. "I really need to go," I said, my breath coming in little gusts. "I'll have to get back to you—are you in Myrna with your mom?"

"No. Let me give you my new number," the boy said.

I pulled out the drawer in the hall stand, poking around for a pencil. "Look, I don't have anything to write with here—"

"That's okay," Jeff Turner assured me. "I'll be in touch."

The horn was blowing again. I stood looking down at the receiver for a good two minutes before walking out to the car.

11

When I returned from dropping Temple at the party, Jack was sitting in his car, with the hood up. The engine whined low, and then spluttered. I parked alongside.

"So, what's the inside dope on Emory?" he asked.

"The parents seem nice."

"Does the brother pack a valid license?"

"She told you about that?"

Jack smiled. "She tells me everything."

I tried not to let this rattle me. "Yeah, well, Emory's brother is definitely well past driving age. He'll even be *more* past the first time I let my daughter ride with him."

Jack leaned up against his car. "Think maybe he'd want to drop me off at my place?"

"Hop in, mister." I smiled. "Just so happens, I'm going your way."

. . .

We traveled the winding road that followed the old seawall, stopping for dinner at one of the restaurants that dotted the peninsula. The dining room boasted a great view. In the summer months, it would've been packed, but on a Saturday evening in November, it was open season on tables. The maître d' discreetly checked out our jeans and sweaters, awarding us with a deuce by the window.

"Getting cold out there," Jack observed, looking down at the water.

The waiter brought a wine list. Jack ordered a good year of the Mondavi. It tasted delicious. "I wouldn't worry about the call," he said, reading my mind.

"But how did he get my home number?"

He swirled the wine around in the glass. "Probably that low-life Shawde."

Nick, I thought. *Yes, that would fit.*

"So are you going to write the letter of recommendation?"

The wine made me feel suddenly beneficent. I liked Jack; I liked this restaurant—the smiling waiters, the rows of lit votive candles winking at us from the windowpanes. "Hell, yes." I raised my glass. "To Jeff's life in art." We drank to that.

"I made a few more calls this afternoon," Jack said. "Talked to Beth Rice's ex-husband."

Even this didn't bother me. "What's he like?"

"A nice guy." That was the difference between us. Jack thought they were all nice guys. I started out assuming they were bastards.

"Name of Erik, with a K. Erik Karsh. They were college sweethearts. The relationship lasted seven years, with Beth hanging on by bloody fingernails for the last two.

"He owns a golf club in Maryland now. It took me a while to get him talking about Rice. At first, I thought he was being evasive, but it turns out he was more embarrassed than anything. According to him, the marriage was rocky from the start. The last couple of months, he was living with another woman, and coming home only for fresh clothes. Which Beth washed for him."

"Gee, he *does* sound like a nice guy," I commented wryly.

"He still feels crappy about it. Says he was afraid of what Rice would do if he left her cold turkey. She'd tried to kill herself a couple of times in high school, and once in college, when he tried to break up with her."

So. Elizabeth Rice is a little too intense about the men in her life. What a surprise. "Lucy Moon is another case." Jack was on a roll now. "She hung out with a really rough crowd in the city. S and M clubs. The role-playing scene, with a heavy emphasis on violence."

"Don't tell me." I laughed. "And Richard Lewan is a convicted axe murderer."

"I haven't found anything on him yet."

"Sounds like you've been busy enough."

He tugged on his beard. "I like being busy. It keeps me out of trouble. By the way, Ann Houghton seems to be exactly who she says she is. Would-be actress. The secretary in her agent's office is very chatty. Says little Annie sees an older man, married, an actor on one of the soaps, who takes good care of her financially. She wouldn't give me his name, but it shouldn't be hard to track down."

"Leave it for now."

"So what's he like?" Jack asked. "Blackmoor?"

"Manipulative. Narcissistic. Arrogant." I shrugged. "Nothing special."

Jack cupped his hand over the back of mine, covering it completely. "Good," he said. We sat that way until the waiter came to clear our salad plates, when I took advantage of the opportunity to rest my hands safely in my lap.

The temperature had fallen during dinner. We ran to the car, huddling against the cold. Ocean Avenue was deserted.

"I see they're finally getting around to restoring our part of the seawall," Jack commented.

"Yeah," I said, coasting along on the *our.*

Jack's apartment was in a private home fronting the public beach in a small honky-tonk seaside town. Although I'd never been there, I knew the general location, slowing down only when we reached the right block. "That one over there." He pointed to a boxy Cape with a ship's anchor set against a piece of driftwood, in lieu, perhaps, of pink flamingos. I put the Volvo into park.

"Come in," he said. It was not a question, but not a command, either. I switched off the ignition, following him through the cold, over the gravel, up the stairs.

He didn't fumble. Not with the keys. Not with the lights. Not with anything. "This is it," he said easily, flooding the small room with a snap of the overheads.

It was an unmarried man's apartment. Impressively neat and well kept, but for all that, hardly lived in. All the furniture was beige. The prints on the wall were the kind you see in sports bars. "It's nice," I said.

He walked to the window, peeling off his sweater as he moved. Underneath he wore a pale blue turtleneck. His shoulders had muscles you can only get from working out on certain machines in the gym; his waist and hips were small and hard-looking. "It's always so damn hot in here," he said, cracking open the window.

There was a decent-sized television set and a compact disc player on the shelves. I moved toward them, as though I were really interested in what kind of music he liked. He met me halfway, pulling me close, making light contact with my lips.

I let him.

The second kiss was a more complicated affair. He moved his tongue. I moved mine. His beard rubbed my skin, soft in some places, bristly in others. Somewhere along the way we had stumbled backward, against the wall. His body hadn't appeared as though it could possibly be as heavy as it now felt, on top of me.

I opened my eyes and looked up. It was a strange perspective. Jack's eyes were shut, his mouth gaping like a fish, his head bobbing, as though guided by some inner sexual sonar that could find me, blind. The kisses were nice, the feeling was okay, but for some reason I wanted it to stop. I pulled away. He kept coming. I pulled away again. He persisted for a while, then stopped.

"What?" His voice was raspy.

"I have to go," I said, "pick up Temple." Jack tried to straighten up, and we almost fell on the floor together. I held him for a moment. "I'm just not sure this is right. For me."

"When will you know?" His face looked very young.

I laughed. Then felt sorry I had. "I need some time."

He walked me to the door. I let him kiss me slowly, passionately. He was lobbying hard for this.

On the long ride home, I rolled down the windows and cranked the radio up loud. The frigid air blew through my hair. I remembered Jack Tatum and his earnest, fish kisses, and tried desperately to drive all thoughts of Dane Blackmoor out into the cold, dark night.

12

By the time I reached Hopewell on Monday morning
it was already snowing and the road was a slippery ribbon of ice. Newscasters were being cautious about the storm. The
first wave would leave only a slushy glaze, they said; but, later on
tonight, the tail end of the system could dump as much as six inches
of white stuff. I gripped the steering wheel with gloveless hands, and
gentled my foot on the gas pedal. Jack had telephoned early, my own
personal Willard Scott. "It's going to be treacherous on the roads." I
told myself he was only being nice. Thanked him, and promised to
buckle up.

The bridge into New Hope was slick. Up ahead, a car swerved. I
had less than ten miles to go. No snowplows had passed through this
part of Route 32. The Volvo's skinny wheels pulled longingly toward
the ruts of ice on the side of the roads. I held the wheel so tight my
hands felt cramped and sweaty.

The sleet dropped a sheer, glassy curtain between my windshield and the surrounding landscape. When I finally spotted the Mill it appeared to be in another dimension, sealed and unreachable, like a snow scene in a domed glass. Shake it, and tiny sequins would swirl around the make-believe castle. I maneuvered the car up the drive and parked on a fresh carpet of snow. The granite tombstones were capped in white. I'd forgotten to ask Blackmoor about them.

Roberto opened the door before I could knock. "Love your hat," he sang. "Are the roads too awful?"

"They're pretty bad."

"Do you believe it? It's my parents' fortieth wedding anniversary, and we're throwing them a big party in Frenchtown. Well," he said, as if I had just convinced him of something. "I'm just going to have to leave early, that's all." Someone had put a coatrack near the door. I stamped the snow off my boots and hung up my coat and hat before following Roberto into the empty studio. "Where is everybody?"

"Dane's on the phone, talking to his attorney." Roberto made a face. "Lucy Moon and Richard are up in the workshop. And Ms. Beth is around, spreading her own personal brand of sunshine, probably to Annie. Better her than me."

I found Richard Lewan in the second bay, dipping his hand into a small basin of water and moistening the split seams of a plaster torso. Kyra's, I guessed. It was unthinkable that there could be more women around with waists that small. He didn't look up when I came in. I watched him for a while. His fingers moved swiftly, as Blackmoor's had during the original shaping. Enlarged photographs of the midsection were spread out over the table, but his eyes never strayed toward them. He obviously knew what he was doing.

"Do you usually assemble the figures?"

"We take turns depending on the project."

I moved closer, never taking my eyes off his hands. "Happen to remember who assembled *Lady Sitting* and *Woman at a Mirror?*"

He worked the plaster into a smooth curving line. "Might have been Dane."

"Don't you keep records?"

"No." With every question he seemed to startle anew, as though he were surprised to find me still there.

"I heard you were sleeping with Torie Wood," I said. *Take that lump and smooth it, buddy.*

The hands stopped, then started again, moving a tad slower. "I'm married," Richard said.

"I'm not interested in your personal life," I told him. "I'm just interested in anything you can tell me about Torie."

"I didn't know her well." I shot him a scoff, which he caught between clenched teeth. "It's true," he said stubbornly. "Torie fucked like other people shook hands. There was nothing personal in it."

"Was she shaking hands impersonally with anybody else around here?" I asked. "Like maybe Blackmoor?"

Richard stopped working. "Dane doesn't get it on with women who work for him anymore."

I considered that word, *anymore*. "Was there anyone else?"

"Lucy Moon, maybe," he said, hunching his shoulders over the plaster form. "You'd have to ask her."

I was still reeling from this when Elizabeth Rice walked in. "Garner! You made it! We were worried, with the roads so bad," she cried. She had on a red wool pantsuit with a dazzling white blouse that exploded into tiny little pleats at her throat. Annie Houghton stood obediently by her, like a house cat that only pretends to like its master.

"What a great jacket," Rice chattered on. "You know, not everybody can get away with that style." Her delivery left reasonable doubts as to which category I belonged.

Annie made some notes on her clipboard. Richard Lewan concentrated on his work. Their efforts to mesh with the landscape seemed to lull Elizabeth into the false impression that we were alone. "I really enjoyed our lunch the other day. As soon as I get back, we should spend a day together at the spa, doing decadent girl things."

"You're going somewhere?"

She flashed the dimpled smile. "Oh, didn't you know? Dane and

I have a meeting in Chicago about a new commission. We'll be gone all week."

Like the snow, Rice blew in and blew out, turning the rest of us into frozen, ice-sculpture people. Annie turned on the heat. "She's at her most obnoxious when she's cheerful," she remarked.

"She must be excited about the commission," I said.

"Having the boss all to herself is Beth's idea of nirvana." She ticked off items on her clipboard. "She'll sit at his right hand when they meet with those stuffy old curators, then go back to her hotel room, straddle the bidet, and pretend it's his face."

Lewan snorted, but his fingers kept molding, shaping.

It was a frustrating morning. Blackmoor's office remained closed. Elizabeth said she'd given him the message that I wanted to see him, but that was all she could do.

To top it off, the weather reports were off base. No daylong lapse occurred between the comings and goings of the storm. Somewhere around noon, there was simply a gentle blurring between the angry, wet sheets of ice, and the soft, silent flakes of snow. They covered the skylights in the studio, tumbling mutely and irrevocably, one upon another, until the outside world was totally obliterated.

I felt muffled, as though someone had put a thick woolen scarf up to my face. I tried to remember what it was they said about the size of the flakes—*when they were big, the cloud was emptying out and it would soon be over, or . . .*

I met Roberto in the foyer, dressed as though he were ready to trek to the Pole with Peary. "You getting the hell out of Dodge, too?"

"Just checking my engine"—I tucked my hair into my hat—"to see if it starts."

We tramped outside, our footfalls echoing in the silence. "I wouldn't wait too long, or you might end up getting stuck here." Roberto shivered theatrically. He began to clear off his windshield. The snow fell off cleanly, in thick shirrings like the winter coats of sheep. I opened the door to the Volvo and let the engine run while I helped him.

"Hey, Roberto," I said. "What's the story with you and Hadary?"

"He was in love with me once," he said. "You know how that goes. Now we're just friends."

"Was he also a friend of Torie's?"

"Graham adored her." He kicked the excess snow off his fur-lined boots. "Listen, a lot of years back, something happened—"

"With Conrad Vestri?"

Roberto nodded. "Hadary never forgave himself. Since then, he's been especially protective of the kids in his charge. Torie's death devastated him."

And probably scared him shitless, I thought. Roberto threw the shovel into the trunk of his Toyota. "Hope your parents have a nice anniversary."

"The surprise is probably going to be that no one but me shows." He sighed, tucking himself neatly into the front seat of the car. I waited until he pulled safely down the drive before turning off my car's ignition and going back inside.

Blackmoor was standing there, watching me.

"You're not leaving already?" he asked.

No, but you are. So why should you care? "Just checking the engine."

"Oh." He seemed to be getting altogether too much enjoyment from my hat. I took it off, letting my hair tumble, and tossed it on the rack.

He said, "You're cold. I have some coffee in my office." I followed him, but didn't sit.

"I hear you're taking a business trip." The cockatoo was sitting on the window ledge, one grizzled foot stuck in its beak, chortling. "The least you could've done was to let me know."

Blackmoor handed me a cup. "I don't want your coffee," I said.

"And I'm not going anywhere," he replied. "I've been telling

Elizabeth for weeks that it wasn't going to work out, but she has a way of only hearing what she wants to hear. So"—he bowed slightly—"I'm all yours."

His cockatoo suddenly squawked, *"Waaak! Needadrink . . . needadrink!"* The intercom buzzed.

"Sorry, Dane," Annie's voice said. "A guy named Kislin is on the line. Says he knows you."

"He's a reporter. Get rid of him." He slammed down the receiver.

"I'd like a set of keys," I said.

"Searching for the spot where I stashed the body?"

"You. Or somebody else." Blackmoor looked genuinely touched. I added, spitefully, "Or you *and* somebody else."

His face hardened. "Of course." Rice appeared in the doorway wearing the same red suit, but looking different somehow, like a double of herself in a wax museum. "Ms. Quinn needs a set of keys, Elizabeth."

She reached into her shoulder bag and tossed me a key ring. "Knock yourself out." Then she settled into a chair as though she planned to be there for a long time. "If I'm going to Chicago by myself," she said to Blackmoor, "you and I have to talk."

I stuffed the keys into my pocket and shut the door.

Annie peeked out the kitchen window, clapping her bony hands with delight. Her boyfriend was coming in this afternoon from Manhattan, she said. Maybe tonight they'd go skating on the canal.

"If you can find it under all the snow," I grumbled, adding, "Do you know if Torie had a special place at the Mill?"

"Just the studio and the workshops. We'd come in here on breaks, mostly."

"Is there a floorplan I could see?"

"Lucy Moon might know." She nodded toward the kitchen door. Lucy Moon had just entered. Today, perhaps in honor of the snow, she wore a blue crushed-velvet baby-doll dress atop metallic-silver palazzo pants. She peered at us over her rhinestone glasses. "What might Lucy Moon know?"

"If there was a floorplan to this place."

"Got me," Lucy replied. "All I'm sure of is that Dane keeps the prisoner chained in the tower, and the torture chamber is still under repair." Her glasses looked like gondolas under the moons of her eyes. She turned to me. "Of course, if you're interested in seeing where I keep my own personal collection of whips and restraints, I'd be happy to oblige."

"Lucy Moon," Annie hooted, as though she was just the biggest kick around, "you are too weird." Coming from her, it sounded like a compliment.

I sat at Rice's desk, putting my feet up, just because I knew that it would piss her off. I'd learned nothing new from the files and log-books. While each sculpture had its own three-ring binder detailing a work from inception to completion, the information was geared toward design and propping. I could find no written system telling which person had assembled the piece. Even the names of models were omitted, except for cryptic notations—*Otis 552-3401*, or *Jessy, size 22 dress, 9 shoe*.

I tossed aside the binder for *Lady Sitting* and studied the tidy desk in front of me. Telephone. Tulips in a bowl. An expensive leather desk set. Two messages tucked into the blotter—*Mr. Bruce (312) 555-0940 WCB; Kyra (212) 555-2259—where is her check?* The notes were torn from a preprinted telephone log. Near the bottom, next to the date and time, the message-taker had printed her bold initials—*AH. Ann Houghton.*

I wandered over to Annie's desk, leafing through a logbook of pink carbons, the secretary's record of incoming calls. Peppered among the young woman's scribbles were notes in a more artistic hand. I didn't have to guess. This person had signed her name in script: *Torie Wood*—with a squiggled scroll under it for emphasis. I thumbed through the pages quickly.

The last entry written by the dead girl was from the previous March. March 15. *The Ides of March.*

My eyes wandered to the window. Graham Hadary was scuttling into the snow, mackintosh flapping. I watched him clear the windshield of a black BMW and drive away. I pictured him traveling through the storm to haunt some local gourmet shop, his alert little eyes in search of the perfect baguette. Or later, after nightfall, perched on a stool in one of the neighborhood bars, a small, pale man with a tall, clear drink, scoping out young flesh.

The lower section of the Mill seemed to be a maze of cellars, some no more than earthen traps, others with stairways and partially finished subterranean rooms. I started down a flight of old steps, equipped with the flashlight I'd found in a kitchen cabinet, breathing in the dank air, feeling nothing more than the vague sense of urgency I'd been carrying around since morning. At the bottom was a dark little foyer. A hooded overhang sheltered yet another door. I turned the wooden knob and trained the flashlight on more stairs, thinking this would be the last stop on my itinerary for today.

That thought stayed with me as my foot went through the first of the rotting stair treads. There was no railing. Somewhere during the long descent, the flashlight flew out of my hand. I kept falling downward, while it went up, on a course toward the low ceiling. I caught shutter-quick illuminations of sagging beams, cobwebs spreading like fairy wings in the darkness.

That was the last I remembered, until they were around me, and I heard Dane Blackmoor's angry voice, demanding, as from a far distance, "Who took the sign off the door? Who took the sign off the door?"

13

Richard Lewan slowly brought up my arm. Joint by joint, limb by limb, his gentle, ever-moving fingers carefully probed, bent, and twisted. "That left wrist may be sprained," he said, "but I don't think anything's broken." *If it were, there'd be no shortage of qualified hands here to whip up a plaster cast.* The thought was enough to make me laugh out loud.

"She's in shock," Elizabeth Rice said.

"Where's Annie?" barked Blackmoor. Houghton rushed in carrying a glass of water and a small white tablet. *As if I'd really swallow some nameless pill and surrender consciousness in this godforsaken place, in the middle of a blizzard, surrounded by a group of people, at least one of whom may want me dead.* I shook my head. "I'll pass."

"Who took the warning sign off the door?" Blackmoor asked again.

Silence dropped like an egg and rolled around without shattering. He went over to a cabinet and brought out a bottle of whiskey.

"If you don't want the Valium," Dane muttered, "at least take some of this." He poured some into the water glass. I kicked it back.

Everyone suddenly started to talk. Elizabeth suggested that the limousine, which would be here any moment to take her to the airport, could instead drive me back home.

"Or you could stay with me," Annie chimed in helpfully.

"There are plenty of wonderful bed-and-breakfasts around," Lucy Moon said.

I stood, to prove how steady I was on my feet. "I'm perfectly fine. I'm just going to warm up my car."

"No, you're not," Blackmoor said. It was as though someone had turned on the overhead sprinklers in the room. Everyone scattered.

"Let me know if you change your mind." Annie gave me a little hug.

Richard sounded disappointed that no drastic measures were called for. "You should put some ice on that hand," he called from the door.

Elizabeth was the last to leave. "My flight will probably be canceled, anyway," she told me. "Why not just take the limo when it comes?"

"No. Really, I'm fine."

When we were alone, Blackmoor tipped some more whiskey into my glass. "I'm driving," I insisted, sinking into a chair.

"No," he repeated. "If you want, I'll make arrangements for a room in town." He sat on his heels next to me. "Or, you can stay in the guest quarters. Unless, of course, that thought frightens you."

I said, "I'll call home, and let them know," calmly, as if it were my idea in the first place.

I was surprised to discover that Temple wasn't there. "Didn't you get any snow?" I asked Cilda.

"What'd you do, fall on your 'ead?" she huffed. "It's a blizzard out!"

"Well, where is she, then?"

"She call after school, say she stuck over Emory's, and please can't she stay because Emory's modder don't want to drive in all the ice."

"Oh. That's okay, I guess." Cilda's disapproval crackled over the line. "What?"

"Not'ing. Just she got boys on 'er mind, more than weather."

"What boys?"

"Emory's brodder, 'e's a boy. And 'e probably got friends are boys, don't 'e?"

My head hurt. My wrist hurt. "Look, I can't do anything about that now," I sighed. "I'll deal with Temple when I get back, tomorrow. Any messages from Jack?"

"Only that 'im think you a crazy woman for being out in the first place," Cilda replied. "Not'ing I 'aven't said ten t'ousand times before."

Blackmoor had left me alone to make the call. When he returned, he slid open the door of an ornate confessional and turned on the television inside. Peter Jennings was reporting the news. "Why don't you relax for a while?" He indicated the sofa.

I unlaced my boots, the ones that Richard Lewan said had probably saved me from breaking an ankle, and stretched out. Just before falling asleep I remember thinking it was a good thing there was no fireplace in the room, because I might never want to leave.

When I awoke, the office was dark except for the glow from the television. Peter Jennings had gone home, leaving Eastern Standard viewers at the mercy of a game-show host. Snow scudded the windows. The room seemed like a posh, padded, high-security cell. I couldn't see Blackmoor's face, but it looked as if he'd fallen asleep in his chair. I bent over to put on my boots.

"Are you hungry?" His voice made me jump.

"Starved."

He zapped the television with a remote and turned on a desk lamp. We both blinked in the brilliance. "Hadary always leaves something in the kitchen," he said. "But if you're feeling up to it, there's a place not far down the road I like. We could take the Rover."

The night was so quiet it was like wandering onto a blank canvas. We painted it with our footseps, making hollow gray caverns with our boots. Blackmoor had on something like a pea coat, only I could tell it had never seen the inside of an army-navy store. Everything he wore seemed to have been custom-made. Or maybe it was just the way clothes sat on him. And, of course, he'd have a Range Rover for blizzards, just as he probably had a Rolls for dress-up, and—who knows?—maybe a Peugeot for Bastille Day. I waited while he backed it out of the brick barn that served as a garage. He reached over to the passenger side, opening the door and extending his arm so I could pull myself up.

"How're you feeling?"

"Fine," I lied.

He drove slowly. The canal followed us like a sliver of mirror cut and pasted alongside the road. After about ten minutes, we turned into a parking lot that had been shoveled, but not plowed. An inn was tucked helter-skelter into the banks of the river. The sign hanging out front was covered with snow and unreadable.

We stamped off our boots before entering a small sitting room with a fieldstone fireplace. Tongues of yellow flame lapped at the perfectly stacked triangle of wood. Whoever had built this blaze definitely rated a merit badge. I'd married a man for less. An old fellow sat in a chair to the side of the fire. Hello, Dane," he drawled easily. They shook hands, but Blackmoor made no introductions.

"You serving on a night like this?"

A younger man entered the room. "Always for you, Mr. Blackmoor," he said, shooting a glance at me. He was nimble, but I caught him just the same, mentally making all the tabulations—*not a local, not a kid, not a glamour girl* . . .

"Madam," he said, with a beckoning nod. *And definitely not a madam.*

The floorboards creaked. Large historical lithographs lined the dark walls, framed in funerally ornate frames. Classical music was playing a little too loud for the empty dining room. Our table had a view of the canal. A small suspension bridge spanned the shores, its arches drippydipping ice. It looked like one of those tiny blown-glass creations sold in flea markets.

Blackmoor ordered a bottle of Ruffino, and carefully watched as the waitress uncorked the bottle and poured. Once she'd gone, I said bluntly. "I thought you were an alcoholic."

"Don't believe everything you hear from Elizabeth." He shrugged. "I was on the wagon for, oh, three years. Now I drink, one day at a time." He tilted his glass in a mock toast.

"Does that mean you're resigned to being a drunk?"

Blackmoor considered this. "I'm not sure I ever was a true alcoholic. I was one of the crowd, with a capital C, you know?" His lips twisted with scorn. "The crowd that got high in the sixties, wasted in the seventies, saved in the eighties, and healthy just as the century started to wane."

"So where was I?" The words tumbled out before I could stop them. "Somewhere between the high and the waste?" I hated myself for letting him know it still mattered.

"Look," he said quietly. "What I did was unforgiveable, coming on to a fourteen-year-old—"

"Thirteen." I couldn't help myself.

"Thirteen," Blackmoor acknowledged. "What makes it worse is I can't even say for sure whether that was the first . . . or the last . . . time. The truth is, I don't remember much of those days." His voice was thin, breakable, like glass. "But . . . I remember you—"

How many were there? Besides Torie and me? How many other little girls who loved you like a father, you fuck?

The waitress came over with her pad. I ordered the Dover sole and a garden salad. Through gritted teeth Blackmoor said he'd have the usual.

"I'm truly sorry," he said, after she'd left.

I cut him dead. "For many things, no doubt."

"People change." He offered the line, hopefully, as if he'd just unraveled it from a fortune cookie; then, embarrassed by the effort, he lapsed into his usual mocking sneer. "Except, of course, in Garner Quinn's book. The people there, I suppose, make the same mistakes, over and over."

We dug into our salads simultaneously, fiercely, as though looking for bones. Far below, on the banks of the canal, a young couple trudged along, arm in arm in the snow. When they came to the suspension bridge they stopped. I latched onto their dumb show, grateful not to have to look at Blackmoor.

The boy hoisted himself up and put an arm out for his girlfriend. She slipped twice, landing in the drifts. I watched their mouths— the girl's rounded "O," the boy's jaw like a steel trap snapping against the cold. I couldn't hear their laughter. The inn was tucked too far away for that.

The girl had somehow managed to pull herself up onto the first of the metal slats. The bridge rocked slightly. For a moment I thought it might actually break, like an icicle. The kids started racing across it, bumping and sliding into each other, picking up un- packed mittenfuls of snow, flinging them at each other. Flakes flew, haloing them like angels. The girl took another fall, and when the boy put his arm out for her this time she pulled him down, and they fell together. They kissed again, passionately. For some reason this made me feel so incredibly sad it took all my willpower not to fall facedown on the table, sobbing into my salad plate. I wondered if Annie and her married man were out on the canal now, the *zing-zing* of their skate blades slicing the night with sharp little cookie-cutter edges.

"Stupid kids." Dane Blackmoor's words seemed to come directly from his throat.

Dinner, and the ride home afterward, was passed in silence. The Rover pulled up the drive casting pie plates of light onto the snow. I hopped out so Blackmoor could park in the garage. Later he joined me on the banks of the canal, near the draped tombstones.

"Family plot?"

"My own, in a way," He lifted one of the blankets. A jagged lump of marble gleamed in the moonlight. "My mentor used to say that great sculptors like Michelangelo freed their figures from the stone. Released what was already there, just waiting to be let out."

"I like that."

"The bastard knew his stuff. He'd watch me chip away on a piece. Put his ear up to it and listen. Then he'd shake his head. *Nothing's there,* he'd tell me. *Nothing worth getting out.* So I came up with the plaster-bandage technique. If I can't take 'em out, might as well put 'em in, right?" He knocked the snowcaps off the stones. "My mentor died penniless, by the way."

And you ran off with his wife. "Why do you keep them?"

"I guess I keep thinking someday I might go back and see if the old fuck was wrong. If there might be something inside, after all." We stood for a moment, looking up at the sky. I remembered a shadow box I'd made for Sister Virginia Frances in the first grade—black construction paper dotted with Elmer's and a sprinkling of silver sparkles. Sister had given it a C; but then she'd graded on a bell curve with God as the front-runner. Same as Blackmoor's mentor.

"How's the wrist?" he asked softly.

"Better."

"Sure?"

"I'm sure," I replied, a little annoyed.

"So, you mean, then," he said, "it wouldn't hurt it if I did this—" He came closer, one hand gently removing my hat—*oh-myomy-omyo*—while with the other he deposited a big pawful of fresh snow on my head and tugged the brim down so it almost covered my nose.

I realized at that moment that I'd never heard him laugh. It was low and resonant, and it rang through the fields, sending little dustings of snow falling from the high places all around. I stood completely still for a three-count, then I threw my hat into the air. "You've had it!" I yelled at his retreating back, my fists packing powder as I moved.

And I was all over him.

14

The snowball fight was down and dirty, within certain parameters. There was no body-to-body contact. Blackmoor favored speed, which resulted in a lot of misfires—snow spraying when it should have pelted. Three harsh winters in a New England boarding school had taught me the secret was all in the packing. I got off fewer volleys, but scored the most hits.

We tracked in pools of icy water, shivering in front of the fieldstone fireplace. In old movies, this was where the male star said to the female star, *We've got to get you out of those clothes before you catch your death.* Blackmoor said, "I'd really like to do a casting of you."

So that was his line.

"As a model," I replied, evasively, "I make a better writer."

"Not a full torso," he assured me. "I'd only do the face."

I recalled what he'd once said about my mother—"I never wrapped her face . . . even I'm not that arrogant." *Well, screw you, mister, and the horse you rode in on.* He pulled off his snow-encrusted sweater. The slight paunch beneath his sweaty shirt pleased me inordinately. *Maybe I'm sizing you up against somebody else, too,* I blazed silently. I said, "Isn't it kind of late?"

But the idea excited me, more than I cared to admit.

Blackmoor crossed to the light switch, triggering a couple of floods over the platform. "The bandages are already cut. All I have to do is get the water."

And the knife.

"You could consider it part of your research," he suggested. I knelt down to unlace my boots, trying to give myself time to think. Then he added, very softly, "Unless you're afraid . . ." No dare this time, his voice concerned, and a little sad.

"I'm a mess—" I motioned to my dripping hair and clothes.

Blackmoor jumped up on the platform and tossed me something. "You can change anywhere," he said. As I headed toward the kitchen, I heard him ripping strips of cloth with his strong fingers.

I held up the long-sleeved sweater of pale lemon yellow, size XL, breathing in its owner's distinctive scent. There was no bolt on the kitchen door, so I barricaded it with a chair before stripping down to my underwear. The crew neck was wide, exposing a rim of breastbone. It hung to my knees. Leaving my clothes on the radiator to dry, I pushed aside the chair and headed for the studio, barefoot, my heartbeat ricocheting against my rib cage.

Blackmoor was slouched behind the tripod, looking through the lens of the video camera. "You're not going to tape this."

"Standard procedure," he said.

I suddenly remembered something that had eluded me all day. "What about those tapes for Donna Fry and Kimberly Arnette's sittings? Did you find them?"

"They're in the study. You can see them tonight, or take them home with you in the morning."

"The morning will be fine." I watched him adjust a dial on the camera. "Don't you need a cameraman?"

He shook his head. "I put it on automatic pilot."

"I don't want to see myself on those big screens." Quite abruptly, he took my chin in his hand, tilting it brusquely. His hands were slightly damp from the water in the basin, but I noticed that he'd towel-dried his hair. He left me sitting on the platform for a few minutes while he went to turn on some music. A piano solo drifted over the speakers, sensuous but lonely, as though the hands of the pianist were caressing the ivories in lieu of available flesh.

Blackmoor returned to the trolley, where a basin of water steamed like soup. He picked up a plastic jar of petroleum jelly, and with swift, gentle motions began rubbing it over my face and forehead. It felt warm and clammy. I sat, helpless, as his fingers roamed over my chin and neck; behind my ears, in my ears; around the back of my neck, where I happened to be ticklish. I dug my nails into the back of one hand, admiring the four angry little crescents of pain.

He walked to the trolley, returning with a can of shaving cream. "For your hair," he said.

"You've got to be kidding."

He nozzled a glob onto his palm. "Trust me." Shaving-creamed fingers massaged my scalp. It felt good. Decadently good. I pressed another set of crescents onto the back of my hand. "Later, after the mold is painted," he said, "we'll apply real hair, strand by strand. In your case, it'll probably take days."

"Did you ever do an inner casting of Torie?" My mouth tasted creamy. The Vaseline had an odorless smell to it.

"Look, Garnish, I know this isn't going to be easy for you," Blackmoor said, "but you're going to have to shut up for a while." He turned his back, and my mind began to race. *What am I doing? I should've called Jack.* Maybe it wasn't too late. I could always tell him I needed to use the bathroom.

Don't be silly, I chided myself, *he'd be crazy to do anything to me here.* Then I remembered Annie and the others, taking their leave, one by one. *"She took her car and drove off"* was all he'd have to say. *"I warned her, but you know how stubborn she was."* Was. In my mind's eye I saw those hairpin curves, deadly iced, so perfect for staging a fatal accident—

Blackmoor stood over me, a strip of dripping, wet bandage in his hand. "I'll start with your mouth," he announced. I felt myself pucker like a fish, and remembered Jack's kisses. "Relax," he said, in a soothing voice as he put the moist cloth over my lower face, deftly smoothing it across my lips, around my chin to the base of my nostrils. He looked at what he was doing, rather than into my eyes.

"One more," he said, placing a sopping strip across the bridge of my nose, stretching it over each ear. The water was very warm, and it trickled a little down my neck. He dabbed the flow, as though he knew exactly what I was feeling as I was feeling it.

"I'm going to put one over your eyes now." We locked gazes for the first time. The plaster around my mouth had begun to harden. I felt its dull tug against my cheeks and chin.

He came forward, holding another strip. "It's natural to feel some panic when you're first encased," he whispered. Or maybe he wasn't whispering. The plaster bandages against my ears muffled my hearing.

"Just remember, you're not alone. I'm with you every moment, even when you can't feel my hands." *This is supposed to make me feel calmer? That he's with me?* My eyes widened as he spread the cloth over them. His palms pressed into my cheekbones, fingers playing lightly over my eyelids until I could feel the bandage adhere and almost immediately begin to harden. From behind the plaster blindfold, I sensed him looking at me. I felt more helpless than I ever had in my life.

Then suddenly he was moving away. *Where? Toward the trolley? What was he doing?* I heard a gentle splash-splash of water, and his voice again. "You know, dentistry students practice the drill on each other, so they'll understand how it feels when they use it on their patients." He placed a small, moist strip between my nostrils, and started to shape it.

"My assistants have offered to wrap me," Blackmoor continued, "but I've always refused. I prefer to imagine what it's like, locked in, with only one's thoughts." I felt the pressure of his hand against my neck now. A small rivulet—not of water, but of perspiration— wound its way down my back, under the borrowed pullover.

"If you let it, it can be a very spiritual experience," he whispered. "You're on the other side. You know what's there . . . and I can only guess."

The face mask had completely tightened. When the first bandage was applied, I could see—or if not see, then at least, sense— light and movement. But the second layer had effectively blocked the outside world. The holes under my nostrils weren't large enough to allow in much air. I longed to drink long gulps of oxygen, with my mouth, through the pores of my skin.

Blackmoor was still talking low, but his voice drifted in and out—swelling, and falling, undulating in crazy spirals of sound. In fact, it felt as though I, too, were undulating. Surely I couldn't be sitting up straight in my seat anymore. Everything outside the mask had shifted. I tapped my toes, felt the hard floor, but even that seemed an illusion. For all I knew, I was sitting sideways, slumped over, about to fall off the platform.

He wouldn't let that happen, I told myself, remembering his words—*I'm with you every moment, even when you can't feel my hands.* A feeling of trust washed over me. It was such a visceral thing, I immediately felt warmer all over. I unclenched my fists, surrendering to the tough casing of plaster skin. Dane was in back of me now, smoothing the plaster behind my neck.

Inside the cast, where there was only darkness, brilliant colors flashed behind my closed lids, in firework patterns. Not fireworks. More like snowflakes, only not just white, but red, neon orange, and magenta. No longer could I distinguish touch as hands or fingers, but only as warmth and color exploding over me. The piano music trilled somewhere deep, in my inner ear.

Blackmoor must be at the trolley. Had he been away long? Time was a thing sealed without. Where I was, it didn't count, except— except it seemed so long since he'd spoken to me. What if he was speaking, only I just couldn't hear him? What if something had gone wrong, and he couldn't get me out? What if he changed his mind—?

A kaleidoscope of images began to turn, flickering brightly on the surface of the blank plaster wall over my eyes, replacing the gorgeous rainbow hues with bits and pieces of familiar faces. There was little Charlie Stratten, cowering in the closet, mummified in a flannel blanket that twisted around his small, stiff body, like a winding-sheet for burial. And Deirdre Purdy, from *Dust to Dust,* in that awful makeshift coffin, her fingernails torn completely off, the fingers raw, bloody stumps from trying to claw so desperately, so hopelessly, through the wooden lid. There were those rows and rows of buried cigar boxes in an animal boneyard.

Jeff—I'd forgotten to write that letter—

As in my dreams, the last coffin in the pet cemetery was bigger than the others. It opened slowly of its own accord. I wanted to turn, to look away, but the plaster mask pinioned me, cutting off escape. I stared with blind dread at what was inside. My mother. Arms folded; rosary beads trailing like flower petals out from under stiff fingers; head cushioned on a satin pillow, just shy of her body, her features embalmed in plastic, the irises gone, and in their place—a blank and terrible void.

My lungs threatened to burst, yet there was nothing I could do. He'd covered me up. Locked me inside, and I couldn't get out. I felt his hand gripping the base of my skull. "Easy now, Garner," he said, very clearly. "Breathe through your nose, and whatever you do, don't move." I felt pressure against my neck, just below the right ear. It seemed unbearable.

And then the knife broke through.

The casing came off easily. Air flooded so forcefully it took my breath away. My eyes stung. I followed Blackmoor to the sink. He pushed my head over gently and brought it down into the water. When I stood, he was holding out a towel. "Come see," he said.

His plaster pale Garner Quinn looked back at me with a haunting, dead-ahead stare. "Once the mold is made, you'll see more detail," he explained. "I'll insert glass eyes—although getting the right color for yours will be a challenge. And then, there's the hair." He seemed nervous. Excited.

"Incredible," I said, meaning it. I was tempted to tell him about what had happened to me inside the cast, but I didn't want him to know me that well.

"How's your wrist?" he asked.

"Okay." In truth, the throbbing now ran through my entire body.

He was already marking the cast with a grease pencil. "There are robes, nightgowns, whatever you need, in your room." Castoffs from the women in his life. Had he wrapped all of them?

I left him peering into the mirror image of my own face. He appeared to be totally captivated.

15

It was the fire alarms that roused me. There had to be at least four or five going off at once, reverberating like buzz saws, slicing into my sleep. The sounds grew louder and more insistent the closer I got to consciousness.

I bolted out of bed and ran to the window. My first thought was that the Mill was on fire, but there didn't appear to be any smoke or flames. I quickly pulled on my jeans and sweater. Blackmoor had to have a security system, I thought, although it wouldn't hurt to make sure. I picked up the phone.

It was dead.

The night had turned sharply colder. My teeth were chattering by the time I reached the breezeway to the main building. I stopped in my tracks. *What if this were some kind of trap? What if he was waiting in there, with a club, a match, and a can of kerosene?* The alarms cut off suddenly. Complete silence reclaimed the night. Not knowing whether this was a good or a bad sign, I kept on walking.

It was like stumbling into a surprise party and unexpectedly seeing the faces of friends. Except these weren't friends. Still, I recognized most of them. The cleaning lady with the Walkman. The bloody child. An anorexic ballerina. A construction worker, about to sink his teeth into a sandwich. I even saw a pale, unpainted Kyra, staring moonily ahead while flames licked the surface of her wooden vanity. *Such a shame*, I thought, inanely, *after all the trouble Roberto had with the mirror.*

Elizabeth Rice wove in and out of the figures, the perfect hostess mingling with her plaster-cast guests. Only instead of a tray of hors d'oeuvres, she was carrying a propane torch. Blackmoor stood on the rim of the platform, so still I thought for a moment it might be only another lifelike effigy.

"What's going on?"

Rice turned toward the sound of my voice. "You left her in town?" she shrieked. "You're such a liar, Dane! You left her in town!"

"This has nothing to do with her, Elizabeth!" He looked over his shoulder. "Get out of here, Garner. Just go—"

I wanted to go, but my eyes were glued to Beth Rice. Her hair had come undone, the pleats of her shirt wilting under the heat. She looked like one of those pre-Raphaelite paintings, of Ophelia or some other beautiful but mad woman. In the far corner of the studio, the cockatoo flapped its wings in terror, screaming, *"Hihowaya! Hihowaya!"* over and over.

"Listen to me, Garner," Dane commanded. "Move!"

I was about to obey when Rice trained the torch in my direction. The flame was low, orange and blue, like a jet on a gas stove. It failed to reach me, but the heat tickled, maliciously. I took a step back.

"That's right, Garner," Rice said. "Listen to *me*."

Behind her, on the platform, Blackmoor's painted plaster figures sat, stood, danced, crouched, and bled; but mostly they burned. Not the way wood burned—or at least not at this stage. The flames weren't charbroiling. They licked white and clean, eliciting a noxious odor that jabbed at my lungs. "Beth, please." I coughed.

"Don't worry, darling," she snarled. "I'm not about to kill another one of his girlfriends for him—"

Blackmoor took a step forward. "Elizabeth, you don't understand—" His voice sounded faint over the roar of the fire.

"Would-you-stop!" Rice screamed. "If you only knew how sick and tired I am of people saying that!" She continued in a mocking tone, *"Elizabeth, you don't understand! Elizabeth, you don't know how!"*

She turned to me. "Do you think he'd have any of this, *any of it,* if it weren't for me?" She gestured wildly around the burning studio. *"Who-do-you-think-is-responsible-for-this?"*

"You are," I replied obediently.

"You and your smart mouth and smug eyes!" She paced, within burning distance. "You think I'm nothing, don't you? Well, I'll have you know I'm a very capable woman."

"I believe you," I croaked.

"Don't patronize me," Rice said bitterly. "You ain't seen nothing yet." She reeled around with the propane torch, hosing down another sculpture with its small, mean flame.

"Go ahead, show her!" she ordered Blackmoor. When he didn't move, she shot a snaking tongue of flame, backing him toward the audiovisual cabinet in the corner of the room. *"Show her!"*

Dane picked up a videocassette and put it into the VCR. "What is it?" I asked.

Beth smiled sweetly. "It's what you were poking around, looking for all afternoon." She aimed the torch, motioning me toward the platform steps. "Sit. I want you to enjoy the performance."

Twin images appeared on the video projection screens overhead.

Elizabeth Rice, a blood-streaked smock over her designer clothes, faced front, addressing the camera as one would a friend. *"After locating the seam with my knife, and slicing it open, I'm faced with the formidable task of re-enclosing the model's head,"* she said, waving a plaster-whitened fingertip. *"Are you paying attention?"*

Her video image broke into a dimpled smile. *"I said, I'm going to* re-enclose the model's head!" She dissolved into uncontrollable giggles.

"Hit the fast forward," Rice ordered Blackmoor. "The lighting in this section makes me look lousy."

He did as he was told. The tape jerked forward. I watched in horror as Beth picked up Torie Wood's severed head and fit it inside the casing, her fingers repeatedly plunging into the basin of water, and out, caressing the plaster surface, at triple speed—*dip and sculpt . . . dip and sculpt . . . dip and sculpt . . .*

The platform steps felt hot on my buttocks. I sensed the fire at my back. But Rice was closer. "Stop here for a minute," she told Blackmoor. He slowed the video down to real time.

"*My plaster-bandage technique is much more difficult,*" Beth told the camera, "*because not only do you have to align the seams, you need to moisten the entire mold, so that you can shape it gently to the face. The final creation is less of a life mask, than a death mask.*"

The flames that had been lapping the bottom of the left projection screen leapfrogged over each other, consuming it whole.

"Damn," said Rice good-naturedly. "But I think you get the picture, right?" She started walking toward Blackmoor. "Dane didn't think I had any talent, but he was wrong. Weren't you, Dane? Weren't you?"

I stood, ready to run for my life.

"Deserting your lover?" Rice taunted. "What makes you think I want him anymore?" Blackmoor's plaster sculptures were in the final phase of destruction, collapsing toward each other in a great funeral pyre of flame. A fragment of what had been my own face—*a life mask? a death mask?*—curled under the ravenous heat. But Rice seemed to have lost interest in them, turning instead to wander back toward the burning platform.

I ran to Blackmoor, wrenching his arm. "We've got to get out!"

"Come with us, Elizabeth," he shouted.

Her crazed eyes went crackle-snap like the flames. "You think I care?" she screamed. "You think I care about anything but destroying you?"

She stepped off the dais, brandishing the torch at a scaffold. Its trail of winding muslin went up like a waxless wick. Fire had reached the trolley, skimming over the water tray, square-dancing on the floor. Trails of twisting, burning fabric created a cyclorama of flame all around. Blackmoor's figures were shriveled to scorched crisps no bigger than slivers of burnt toast.

That's what we're going to look like if we don't get out of here fast, I thought. A phrase kept buzzing through my mind—*I don't want to die. . . . I don't want to die*—and the words had a face, and the face was Temple's. "Can't you see she's not coming?" I cried.

Dane pulled away from me. "Elizabeth!"

Rice shot a rasping funnel of flame, so thin and colorless as to be almost invisible. Blackmoor grabbed his arm, wincing in pain. I latched onto his belt, dragging him toward the door.

We were almost at the threshold when I broke away from him, running back, fighting my way through the smoke. It was there, still intact, within a circle of fire. I covered my hand with the cuff of my sweater and pushed the button. The cassette popped out of the VCR. I looked up and saw Elizabeth Rice, climbing the winding staircase to the gallery.

Blackmoor found me seconds before the first explosion hit. The second and third followed immediately, increasing in force until we were propelled outside into the snow, he on top, shielding me with his body. The videocassette cut into my ribs. We struggled to our feet and scrambled toward the water.

Sirens wailed in the near distance, an insistent panoply of ruby lights reddening the white night; but I turned away from them, toward other sounds—glass shattering; a piercing scream. Elizabeth Rice, in a coat of flame, came crashing through the glass of the large arched windows. She hurtled through the air and landed on the frozen canal. The force of her descent cracked the ice into a million pieces; Elizabeth merely into two or three.

Blackmoor pulled me so tightly to him, he felt it—felt the cassette between us. "Is that what you went back for?"

"It has everything." I nodded. "Everything."

He glanced toward the trucks. Fire fighters were already jumping off, hauling hose, shouting to each other. "Throw it into the canal," he whispered to me. "Let it all come to an end, with her."

It was a strange request, and I soon forgot it in the confusion of the moment. A man in a protective uniform, the shield of his hat up, bounded over. "Anyone in there?"

"Not anymore," Blackmoor said, grimly.

"Are you all right?"

"Yes," I sobbed. "I just have to make a call. I have to talk to my daughter—"

A patrol car arrived on the scene. We started for it, Blackmoor's arm around me, protectively, the cassette nestled safely under my sweater. Later I would discover it was marked simply "3/15."

March 15. The Ides of March.

THE TRUTH

GARNER QUINN MANAGES, AS HAS NO ONE SINCE CAPOTE IN *IN COLD BLOOD,* TO TAKE US BEYOND MERE FACT, INTO THAT NETHER REGION OF ESSENCE. HER BOOK IS AS STARK AND INEVITABLE AS GREEK TRAGEDY—AN EPIC TALE THAT NEITHER JUDGE NOR JURY HAS SEEN BEFORE, AND EVEN THE VICTIM AND THE MURDERER HAVE GLIMPSED IN ONLY DISTORTED AND FRAGMENTED GLIMMERS. BY THE FINAL PAGE WE FEEL THAT QUINN HAS CHIPPED AND CHIPPED AWAY AT THESE EVENTS UNTIL THE TRUTH, AND NOTHING BUT THE TRUTH, IS LEFT.

REVIEW OF *ROCK-A-BYE BABY: THE BALLAD OF DULCIE MARIAH*
(*LOS ANGELES TIMES,* 1981)

GARNER—

HAVE READ YOUR BOOK. CONGRATULATIONS. YOU SEEM TO HAVE INHERITED YOUR OLD MAN'S TALENT FOR MAKING PEOPLE BELIEVE. I THINK IT WILL COME IN HANDY IN YOUR CHOSEN LINE, AS IT DID IN MINE. EVER SO MUCH BETTER THAN HAVING TO RELY ON THE TRUTH ALL THE TIME . . . . —D.

LETTER FROM DUDLEY QUINN TO HIS DAUGHTER UPON THE PUBLICATION OF *ROCK-A-BYE BABY*

"FUCK THE TRUTH. THE THING THAT'S IMPORTANT IS THE *APPEARANCE* OF REALITY."

DANE BLACKMOOR
AS QUOTED IN A *PLAYBOY* INTERVIEW (1993)

1

Six hours later we were roaming through the rubble of what was once the Mill. My legs still felt wobbly. "I thought this place would be indestructible," I said, lamely.

Blackmoor sifted through a pile of ashes with the hand that wasn't bandaged. "Well, the walls are still standing." His five o'clock shadow was working on a second shift, and the skin above his beard line looked unnaturally pale. We wandered around, picking up small tokens that had somehow escaped incineration: several glass eyes, dull as old marbles; a rhinestone necklace; a silver belt buckle.

Jack had wanted to come get me, but I'd vetoed the idea. My wrist was in decent shape, and although I hadn't slept in over forty-eight hours, I knew it would be hours before I crashed. Through the shattered windows, we watched the sky turn from rosy pink to blue. The local police knew where to reach me. I was free to go. If I left now I'd miss the flocks of reporters that would soon come streaming into New Hope in their network vans and beat-up rental cars. And yet I couldn't bear the thought of it ending like this.

"What are you going to do?"

Blackmoor shrugged. "I really don't know."

"Why don't you hang out at my place for a while?" I heard myself say. "I have a small guest house. It's very private. You could rest up before the inquest—" I felt compelled to stumble on. "I'll be working on the book, and I'm sure there are things we'll need to go over together."

"Okay," he said. He retrieved a studded leather wristband from the debris. It looked as if it might have belonged to Lucy Moon. "I have the insurance people to deal with. How's the end of the week sound?"

It sounded awful. Ridiculous. Frightening, even. "Fine," I said.

Temple was sitting on the front gate, looking small and cold. She wore her Lakers warm-up jacket over denim cutoffs, and her legs were bare—no socks, just unlaced Keds in the freezing weather. When my car pulled up, she didn't smile, didn't wave, but still I knew. How many times had I seen her sitting, just like this, sometimes even in her nightgown, waiting for me to come in from some airport, after a long trip, far away from home?

I managed to put the car in neutral before jumping out. She hopped off the gatepost and ran to me. "You okay?"

"I'm fine," I said. "Let's go home."

"What you need," said Cilda, setting a cup of tea down on the table, "is sugar. Blow the shock right out your system."

"What I need is about twenty-four hours of sleep." I sank down onto the hard kitchen chair. There was no use in prolonging this. "Listen, we're going to have a visitor in a few days. Dane Blackmoor."

Temple just nodded, not exactly the response I was looking for, but I guess I couldn't blame her for being cautious. Cilda's reaction was more predictable. "It's your 'ouse," she muttered. "You can ask Jack the Ripper if you care to."

"He didn't murder that girl," I told her.

"There's killing ladies," Cilda said, cryptically, "and there's lady killing." I remembered what Blackmoor had said at dinner. *"People change."* That was not a working concept for Cilda Fields. Cilda had learned all she needed to know about men like him from watching television. Her favorite program was "Divorce Court." Every morning at ten she'd sit in the old rocker, sheer righteousness in motion—crooked hands knitting and purling; the chair swinging back and forth on its runners; head nodding, tongue clucking, *"Oo-ee, 'e's an evil one,"* or *"'Er be lyin' to you now, mister!"* And when, at the very end, the white-haired judge had his say, her lightning-quick knitting needles clapped together like long, thin, pleased fingers. *"You tell 'im, judge,"* she'd holler. *"Thought 'e'd get away with it, did 'e?"*

For Cilda to accept that Dane Blackmoor had changed would be tantamount to saying that they'd replaced the cheating husband at the commercial, and they just didn't do that. During her years as a viewer, that had never happened.

The phone rang. "Emory," Temple said, running upstairs to get it.

I sipped my tea in silence. When I couldn't stand it anymore, I said, "I'm going to take a nap. Remind me to call Ben about opening up the guest house, will you?"

When I left, Cilda was scrubbing the kitchen sink. It was almost three o'clock. In a few minutes she would snap on "General Hospital," where people were not only pretty, they acted just like you expected them to.

2

I woke the next morning, still fully dressed, under a mess of covers. I felt stiff and my wrist was throbbing. The Bride of Frankenstein stared back from the bathroom mirror: hair on end; mascara raccooning my eyes; the lace edge of a pillowcase tattooed across one cheek. Showering didn't help much.

Cilda was mopping the kitchen floor when I came downstairs. "And 'ow you feeling this morning?"

"Barely alive. Thanks for letting me sleep. Did Temple take the bus?"

"So she say."

I poured myself some orange juice. "What's that supposed to mean?"

"She put me in mind of a young lady I knew in Jamaica." She clucked her tongue. "Girl who got pregnant for two men."

I was not in the mood for one of Cilda's bizarre morality tales. I threw an old cardigan over my long winter underwear. Even this slight exertion made my body protest. "I'm going to the office."

"Hey, boss," Jack smiled when I opened the door. I tried to remember whether I'd combed my hair. "You okay?"

"Sure. Swell."

"Max called." He followed me into the next room.

"I have to talk to him," I said. "With Blackmoor staying here, we should have a first draft in no time."

I watched his face change. "You're kidding."

"I didn't have a chance to tell you"—it bothered me that I felt guilty about this—"but I think the arrangement's going to work for all of us. He really has no other place to go."

"What are you, on drugs? The guy must own three or four estates, not to mention luxury apartments all over the world."

"We don't want him all over the world," I reminded him. "We want access to him so we can finish this book."

"So I'll reserve him a room in the Marriott." Jack sat across from my desk. "Dammit, Garner, the man is—"

"What? The man is what?"

He pulled on his beard. "Well, we don't know that yet, do we?"

"What do you mean we don't know? I was there, Jack. I saw the tape. I heard Beth Rice confess."

"So?"

"So?"

"I just don't think we should tie this up until we've explored every possible angle," he said.

I laughed. "That's my line you're using."

"I mean it. It just seems . . . shoddy . . . not to pursue—"

"So pursue, if you want." He got up to go. I picked up the phone and dialed. "Ben Snow, please." Jack was still well within earshot when I said, "Ben, it's Garner. I need you to do some work for me."

My agent was the only one pleased with the news.

"Darling," Max drawled over the line. "That's a fabulous idea." I could almost hear the wheels turning, as he wondered, *What's the catch? Garner Quinn can't actually be telling me she's writing a book that takes for face value the facts, as the facts.*

"I want to get this wrapped up as quickly as possible." I imagined him checking his pulse. Pinching himself. "Then I'm going to retire. Maybe try my hand at a different kind of writing."

So that was it. His money client wanted to leave a multimillion-dollar career in true crime to write slim books on gardening. Max took a long drag of his cigarette. "Darling, you know I'll support you whatever you decide to do." He emitted one of those phone sighs that went on for days, like the north wind. "But we'll have plenty of time to discuss that later."

Later. As in, after the book was delivered. After it became a Main Selection, and the movie rights were finalized. He'd represented me long enough to know that I'd probably change my mind twenty times by then.

I was walking back to the house when I heard the man. "Miss Quinn?"

He strode briskly in my direction from the enclave of heavy machinery. A worker sat in the crane, depositing huge metal jawfuls of tow stone into the gaps in the seawall.

"Tom Tolano, Coastal Engineering." He was trim and still had a summer tan. "We're trying to fix this little potential flood problem you got going here."

"That would be nice. We were evacuated twice last year."

"Goes with the territory."

I thought of the spread in *People* magazine. *True-crime writer Garner Quinn has built her home, and her career, on dangerous ground.* After finishing this book, it would be time to move on. "I hadn't realized the rebuilding of the seawall would be so complicated."

"It's a bitch. The original rocks have settled so much you got caves big enough to fit Volkswagens in there." We watched as the crane operator drove the machine up a ramp onto the wall. Another worker in a hooded sweatshirt stood on the ground giving hand signals.

"For my money," Tolano said, "there are only two men in the whole state who know anything about building a wall like this." He didn't mention if they were on this particular job.

"Would you like some iced tea? A soda or something?"

"No, thanks. I'm just checking to see how it's going." He handed me a card. "Listen, give a call if you have any problems." He sauntered off toward his men.

I shaded my eyes against the sun and looked over at the seawall, imagining a network of hidden caves in the rock, and a line of shiny little Volkswagens, parked end to end.

3

Blackmoor arrived in the Rover. He got out carrying a small leather duffel in one hand and the birdcage in the other. Moments later, a van rounded the drive.

The cockatoo squawked, *"Takeyourhat? Takeyourhat?"*

"I thought I might get some work done while I'm here."

"No problem," I replied faintly, watching as the moving men began to unload the first batch of crates and boxes. "Let me show you around."

He followed me through the front door of the guest house. "It's really just this room." I gestured toward the cathedral ceilings. "I'd thought about putting a pool in here, which accounts for all the windows." Ben had removed the shutters so there was an unobstructed view of the ocean. "You'll have plenty of natural light."

The movers staggered in with a huge hunk of marble.

Blackmoor watched me, watching them. "It's been years since I thought of sculpting stone. I suddenly feel inspired to try again." His voice was flippant, but the look in his eyes made me start to sweat.

At the door I said, "Why don't you come over to the house for dinner tonight? Meet all the hostile troops." He laughed. "No, really. I'm serious."

"I am too," he told me.

Jack, a tad overdressed, arrived early with flowers and wine. Blackmoor came after, with the bird. Cilda and Jack, the welcome wagon from hell, stared insolently as I bumbled my way through the amenities. It was a relief when Temple came bounding down the stairs, her hair still damp from being washed.

"Hullo," Blackmoor said. "I'm Dane."

I watched them devour each other's faces. Or at least that's what it looked like to me. Temple put her arm out for the cockatoo. "What's his name?"

"He doesn't have one. Or, at least if he has, he hasn't told me." Blackmoor was one of those people who didn't alter his voice when speaking to children. I should have remembered that.

"Oh, but you have to name him!" The cockatoo hopped onto Temple's wrist, cocking its head at that improbable angle.

"I'm afraid if I did, I might become attached to him," he said. I thought of the expression on his face when he discovered the bird, shivering on the snow-covered branch of a tree the night the Mill burned. He obviously didn't know when he was attached.

They sat on the love seat, Temple, Blackmoor, and the nameless bird. I recognized the look on her face, the acute way in which she was listening to him speak; but I was seeing it for the first time from the outside. The way he must have seen me.

Across the room, Jack sent out sullen semaphores; Cilda's busy anger billowed out of the kitchen like an approaching cold front. But, starboard, on that sofa, everything looked sunny.

"Could I name him, do you think?" Temple asked.

Blackmoor considered for a moment. "You could. But whatever you decide should be between you and the bird."

She broke into peals of childish laughter. At the sound I immediately tripped into action, topping everyone's glasses with more of Jack's wine.

4

The next morning I stopped by the guest house early. The door was ajar. "Hello?"

Blackmoor had already set up a worktable, and most of his tools were unpacked. It looked as though he'd been at it late into the night. "Anybody home?" I stepped toward the center of the room, wary of the bird.

On the table lay a sheaf of papers. I thumbed through them quickly. They were pencil sketches of a nude female torso, shown from several angles. A highly sexual energy charged each bold line. I felt suddenly ashamed, as though I'd stumbled upon someone's secret stash of pornography.

I walked over to the window. Just beyond the seawall, I caught a glimpse of Temple, barelegged, in a tiny foam-fringed wave of water, her hair blowing. Blackmoor stood next to her.

They appeared to be laughing.

. . .

"Hey." Blackmoor waved from the beach. His jeans were rolled up, like they'd been that first day.

Temple ran up to me. "Do you know what? Dane says I look like my grandmother. That I have her eyes."

"Does he really?"

"Can I sleep over at Emory's tonight?" She grabbed my hand and spun me around in a dizzy circle. "Can I? Can I?"

"I don't see why not."

"Awesome!" Temple immediately started sprinting back toward the seawall.

I yelled, "Make sure to leave a number—"

"It's on the corkboard," she called back, "up in my room!"

Blackmoor said, "That's a very beautiful young woman." His voice was barely audible over the sound of the surf. We fell into step together. "I was wondering if you might like to share a pizza and a bottle of wine with me tonight? Seeing that you'll be on your own."

"Okay." I added, "There are some questions I want to ask you, anyway."

We parted company at the guest house. I walked to my office, sensing him standing there, in the open doorway, his stare tracing a warm, meandering fingertip down the small of my back.

Jack was still sulking. Since we'd kissed that night, he'd been making a concerted effort with his wardrobe. Today he wore a thick wool sweater in a shade of deep emerald that brought out the green in his eyes. I felt a sudden surge of tenderness. "Hey, mister." I touched him lightly on the shoulder.

He spun around in his chair. "You and I have to talk," he said. "About Blackmoor."

And then the phone rang.

It was ten-seventeen on Jack's digital desk clock, and the men from Coastal Engineering had just started up the bulldozer. I would remember the sound of the machinery later, pinning it, specifically and forever, to that particular moment in time.

5

Dudley's longtime secretary, a large red-faced woman named Miss Eggert who'd looked middle-aged at twenty-four, and had simply gotten more florid and hunched as the years passed, retired from the firm when the Great Man first went off to Portugal. This voice was unfamiliar to me.

She introduced herself as Lindsey from Quinn, Nash, Loughlin and Verdun; she was calling because Mr. Quinn just had a heart attack in his office.

In the half-second of dead space on the line, I realized I'd already lived this moment in my imagination. Only, there, I was scanning the *Times* when the headline leapt out—

PROMINENT ATTORNEY DUDLEY LONIGAN QUINN
DEAD AT THE AGE OF—

Or, there'd be a knock on my door, and some clean-shaven messenger boy out of an old black-and-white film would crow, *"Telegram for*

Miss Quinn!"; and I'd see those stark, block letters: FATHER DEAD IN PORTUGAL STOP.

Father dead in . . . ? *Stop.* I heard myself ask, calmly, "Is he alive?"

"Oh, yes," Lindsey responded, obviously glad to be the bearer of at least this much good news. "They took him to Columbia Presbyterian." I wondered who *they* were. A lengthier silence loomed. I was on the verge of asking, out of real confusion, why I'd been called; and then I realized.

There wasn't anyone else. Geoff was dead. Dulcie was dead. Even the faithful Simone was somewhere in the south of France, comfortably married to an old man with a useless title. Who knew about the others? Dudley Quinn the Third, man of a thousand friends and a million acquaintances, knew no one intimately enough to invite to his possible demise.

"I want to drive you," Jack said.

I shook my head. "No, this is something I have to do alone." The corny line triggered a couple of frames from the old, imagined scenario: FATHER DEAD IN PORTUGAL STOP *You stop,* I ordered myself. *Your father is alive and well in Columbia Presbyterian. By now he's holding court in some posh hospital suite, surrounded by a bevy of admiring doctors and horny nurses, drinking vodka and tonics and telling tall tales.*

Cilda sat motionless on the bed while I packed. She should be going instead of me, I thought. He loved *her.* The childishness of this sentiment, and my Freudian slipping into the past tense angered me. "I wouldn't worry," I said coldly. "He's too ornery to die."

I dialed Country Day and asked the secretary in the office to get Temple out of class. A few minutes later, her voice came on the line. "Mommy . . . ?"

"It's all right, sweetie," I quickly assured her. "Your grandfather's had a mild heart attack, and I have to go see him in the hospital, that's all."

A rush of air drummed against the earpiece. Temple was crying. "I got scared. I thought maybe—"

Maybe what? Maybe something happened to me? I realized that, no matter how hard I'd tried to shield her from it, the ever-lurking presence of danger—a side effect of my career in true crime—had touched my daughter. Changes would have to be made, and soon. I cradled the receiver against my shoulder. "There's nothing to worry about, honey. I'll call you tonight."

"Tell Grandpa I hope he feels better," Temple said softly.

"I will." *I'll tell this man, whom you have no memory of ever seeing, and who never once, in all the years since you were born, has even so much as sent you a Christmas present, or a birthday card, that his granddaughter is concerned about his health. And if that doesn't break his damaged heart, then they better take a look inside. Maybe it's already been surgically removed.*

I said, "I love you," and Temple said it back. The words put little clouds under my feet, floating me out into the driveway, toward the car.

Jack jogged over as I was tossing my suitcase in the trunk. "I booked a room for you at the Mayflower." He opened my door. "Call me as soon as you know something?" I nodded.

"I want to be there for you," Jack said. "Through this."

"I know you do." Backing the 190 out of the drive, it occurred to me that I hadn't left word with Blackmoor to cancel our dinner. I saw him in the window of the guest house, a dark, faceless figure, watching me pull away.

I checked into the hotel. A light, cold rain had begun to fall, making it difficult to get a cab. It was almost four o'clock by the time I reached the hospital. There could be no more stalling—like it or not, I was faced with the situation I'd most hoped for, and feared, throughout my whole life. I was going to be alone in a room with my father. And he would not be going anywhere else, anytime soon.

The woman at the reception desk informed me that Quinn, D. L. was in ICU, and directed me toward the elevator banks. For a moment I considered making a detour into the gift shop to buy some flowers. It would postpone the inevitable a few minutes longer, and give me something to do with my hands once I got inside the room. I pictured setting the arrangement on a table near his bedside, while Dudley beamed, *Honey, you shouldn't have*.

It didn't scan, even in my imagination.

The nurse on duty was small and chesty. A name tag—E. ROSA, R.N.—was pinned halfway down the white slope of her bosom. When she spoke it dangled like a daunted climber, clinging to the side of a mountain. "Mr. Quinn's condition is stabilized," she told me. "We'll be keeping him here for the next several days so we can monitor his vital signs."

"But he's going to be okay?"

"He's in very good hands. Dr. Chuska is the best we've got," the nurse said sympathetically, not answering.

"Is the doctor here now?"

"You just missed him. But you might catch him at the end of his rounds, in say, an hour." I left a note. Then I turned toward the metal door marked ICU.

"Last room on the left," Nurse Rosa directed. "We ask that you observe the fifteen-minute time period so as not to tire the patient."

"No problem," I said primly. Fifteen minutes with my father would be a lifetime record.

He was sleeping, mouth slightly open. They'd removed a bottom dental bridge, so his lower lip had shriveled against the gum. His skin was the same translucent color as the plastic nosepiece feeding oxygen into his nostrils. The hospital gown exposed arms on which muscles hung like grapefruit in netted bags. His breath came in shallow gasps, blipping onto the screen of the heart monitor.

Otherwise, I might have thought he was dead.

It occurred to me that I should touch him. Press his hand, or brush his forehead with a kiss. The closest I could come was a pat to the edge of the bed where his feet poked up under the thin cotton blanket. There was a long pause in the beeps on the heart monitor. I held my breath—*one . . . two . . . three . . . four . . . five . . . six.*

Another jagged peak appeared on the screen.

In the corridor, doctors were being paged over the intercom. Nurses walked by, their soft-soled shoes squishing on the clean tiles. Dudley's irregular breathing roared over these life sounds. Around me, walls melted whitely into the floors, sheets into the pale hair and face of my father. Every time I moved I felt as if I were disturbing the room's ozone layer of Lysol. The sweet, acrid smell of old flesh filled the air. I needed to get out. . . .

I found a pen and a scrap of paper in my purse. *"Dear Dudley,"* I would write. *"Sorry to have missed you, but I didn't want to disturb you when you were resting peacefully—"*

Resting peacefully. Rest-in-peace. R-I-P. *Blip . . . blip . . . nothing.*

The flat mountain ranges tracking Dudley's heart snaked off the monitor, winding around my throat, cutting into my trachea. I'd started to breathe in sync with the bleeps, but there was no rhythm; and I was inhaling when I should be exhaling.

Surely fifteen minutes had already passed.

I'd forgotten to check my watch before coming in. They really should have a timer on the wall. *Better ask the nurse. Get some fresh air. Breathe a breath without a bleep.*

I had my hand on the doorknob when the soft voice murmured, "What . . . have you been doing with yourself . . . Garner?"

Caught, on the verge of a clean getaway. "How are you feeling?" I managed to ask.

Dudley raised one eyebrow, disdainfully. *There ought to be a rule about that,* I thought. *They ought to test their sarcasm levels before admitting them.*

"I mean—" Something was caught in my eye, a speck, a granule, a particle of dust. I tried to blink it away. "Are you in pain?"

"This whole scene pains me." He flailed one stringy arm, straining it against the IV. "I'd always thought I'd go out with more style."

I moved closer to the bed. "You probably will. When you finally do." He turned away from me. "Plenty of people have heart attacks. They'll just figure out which part isn't working right, and fix it, that's all."

"Don't be an asshole, Garner." Dudley dropped his head back into the pillow as though suddenly bored.

E. Rosa, R.N., opened the door, her bust entering first like the prow of a ship. "I need to take your father's readings, Miss Quinn," she said crisply. "There's a waiting room for the families at the end of the hall. You can stay there until the next visiting period."

I would have been out like a shot if I hadn't heard him call my name.

"See if you can rustle me up some scotch, will you, darling?" His smile was weak, but wicked.

"Yeah, sure," I replied.

Once out in the hallway, I had to stop myself from breaking into a run.

6

I ran the tap in the rest room, making a cup out of the coarse brown paper towel the way I used to in grade school, with the nuns. Only a little water stayed in the bottom of the funnel, warm, with a smoky taste, but it did the trick. I began to pace. In the waiting room, people were pacing, too—only slower, more aimlessly, as though unfamiliar with the workings of their own feet. They looked anxious and scared.

Not angry, like me.

"Don't be an asshole, Garner," he'd said. He always said. But this time there was no audience around to appreciate it. No houseguests. No hangers-on. Just Dudley and me. I stared at my reflection—my hair caught up in a classy Katharine Hepburn topknot, tailored silk shirt buttoned up to the throat.

I loosened my collar, and took out hairpins, one by one. Then I smiled brilliantly into the mirror. "Nurse Rosa strip-searched me and confiscated the scotch," I said out loud.

"Nurse Rosa strip-searched me and confiscated the scotch."

"No matter." Dudley smiled lecherously. "It's quite obvious where she keeps her stash." We lapsed into the inevitable silence. I picked at a small strand of thread on the strap of my purse.

The bed had been raised slightly. Dudley looked like a walk-and-talk doll tethered to a battery pack. The heart monitor bleeped and peaked. I pulled a chair over to him. "I need to ask you something."

"My will is in order," he said. "Everything goes to you."

"I don't want your money."

"Well, then give it away."

"You're not going to die."

"Don't tell me what I'm not going to do." He started to laugh but it caught, bringing on a dry spasm of coughing. The monitor went wild. The bleeps were so loud I felt sure any minute the door would be broken down by a fleet of people in white wheeling in that machine that hot-wired hearts. *And he will die. And I will never know.*

I looked out into the empty corridor. Where was E. Rosa, R.N., anyway? On a break? What about the other nurses? Were they all on breaks? How could they *allow* breaks in ICU? Didn't they realize a patient might expire while they were out, drinking a Coke, taking a pee?

The coughs subsided, slowly, and when he spoke again, there was a new softness to his voice. "What is it you want to ask, Garner?"

I walked slowly toward the bed. "I was right, wasn't I?" My voice sounded hoarse, like his. "Dulcie did it, didn't she? She killed Charlie, and convinced Ben Slater to take the blame."

Dudley stared at me. This time when the laughter came it was harsh and bitter. "You . . ." He struggled to sit up on the bed. "You . . . !" His effort to right himself was awesome. I didn't try to help. I was pinned to the floor.

"Always asking," he wheezed. "Even as a kid . . . always asking those stupid, *unanswerable* questions!"

All at once I realized what I'd done. I'd had one last chance, and

I'd blown it. *I'd picked the wrong stupid, unanswerable question*. I stood clutching and unclutching the leather strap of my bag as Dudley railed on. "For Chrissakes, she's dead. We're all . . . dead. Let it go. I won a trial and you wrote a bestseller. What else . . . goddam matters . . . ?"

At that moment I could almost believe he was right. In the larger scheme of things—of life and death; fathers and children—what *did* it matter? I tried again. "Why do you hate me so much? Was it because of my mother?" Two more unanswerable questions, both still off the mark. The one I'd wanted to ask was *"Why can't you love me?"* Always that one.

Dudley pursed his mouth to laugh again, but now nothing came out. He was dry. "Still trying to make sense of it, Garner? Still think you're going to stumble onto the one missing piece that'll make all the others fit? Mummy broke Daddy's heart, and that's why he's such a bastard?"

He shook his head but the nose tube caught him short. "When are you going to learn that life isn't one of your made-up stories? Why can't you just accept people the way they are?"

I stood at the end of this bed pressing my purse to my chest so my heart wouldn't fall out. It occurred to me that we'd had almost fifteen minutes together. *Fifteen minutes*. And I'd spent them foolishly.

"So much for patching up things in the eleventh hour," Dudley whispered, jauntily. He rolled toward the wall. I couldn't see his face, but then that was fitting. I tucked my bag under my elbow and walked to the door.

"Tell my grandchild that her grandfather sends his best," he called softly.

I stood there for a moment—a moment too long, because the unthinkable happened. A sob welled up in my throat and forced its way out. Dudley turned. Our eyes locked before I could siphon out all the love and the pain. All the humiliating love and pain.

"Garner," he began, "in my own ways I've always—"

But it was too late. Our fifteen minutes were up.

7

"Ms. Quinn! Ms. Quinn!"

I spun toward the sound of my name. The man was tall and handsome. He had deep dark pouches under eyes that were very black, and a comic-book hero chin. He reminded me of Omar Sharif. "The nurse pointed you out to me," he said.

I must have looked confused, because he continued in a soothing voice. "You are upset. It is a very emotional time for you." *Who is this guy, the staff psychic?* "But please accept my assurance, we are doing everything possible to stabilize your father's condition."

The doctor. "Dr. Chuska?"

"Here, we may talk." Chuska motioned to a small bench near the nurses' station. I wiped my nose on the sleeve of my blouse in passing, as though I had an itch.

"Stability is the key." Dr. Chuska smiled. His teeth were whiter than his eyeballs. "Once your father is stable, we can begin to pinpoint the troublesome area, and determine the extent of the damage." He talked on about two kinds of tests, one where they shot the dye, one where they blew up the balloon. He was a happy guy. They were happy tests. It was all going to be wonderful.

But it wasn't.

Chuska stopped abruptly. "I'm so sorry," he said, fervently. "You are worried and fatigued." His vocabulary was stilted, antiquated. Charming. Add to that the bucks he pulled in, and it probably made him quite a hit with the ladies.

"You must take care of yourself so that you can provide support to your father during his recovery," Chuska told me. "Later we will talk." His dark eyes twinkled. "You know I, too, am a writer, although, as yet, unpublished. Yes, I have just completed a volume of short mysterious stories with medical twist-ups at the ends."

I didn't know what to say. We stood. The doctor touched my arm. "Now, please. He is being well taken care of. Get some rest. Go out to dinner." He smiled again. "Surely a lovely lady as yourself will have no trouble finding a companion for a relaxing meal?" I nodded dumbly, backing out of the man's presence as though he were a raja. Which I supposed was only proper etiquette when taking leave of a doctor.

At the Mayflower, I put in the requisite calls. *Dudley was fine. I was fine. Everything was going swimmingly.* I told Temple that her grandfather had sent his regards. Then I sat on the radiator by the window, looking out at Central Park. The phone rang. I wanted it to be Blackmoor.

"Garn?"

The voice sounded familiar. "I heard about your old man, and I took a guess that you'd be staying at your old haunt."

"Nick! How are you?"

"Hungry like a wolf," Shawde replied. "How's about I take you out for a nice expensive dinner, on you?"

8

It was a bad idea, so bad that, for some reason, it was good. We met at a little Italian place off Columbus. Nice, but relatively untrendy, considering Nick, who flew into the dining room on polished wing tips, a full half hour late.

He stopped short when he spotted me, then dropped to his knees, as if he'd been shot.

"Is this Garner Quinn in a moderately sexy dress?" he asked, loud enough for everyone within fifty yards to hear. Shawde flicked up the tablecloth and whistled.

I put my head in my hands. "Sit down, Nick."

The waiter came over. Shawde took a sip of my drink, and decided we should have champagne. "To celebrate," he said, adding, in a rare flash of sensitivity, "and to toast the health of the Big Guy."

I answered all his questions about Dudley, a man Nick revered because, as he said, he'd once heard him described as "the most ruthless attorney alive." He pulled no punches. "So is this The Big One?"

"The doctor seems to think he's stabilized."

"Oh, they always say that." Shawde lobbed great wads of butter onto his bread. "The truth is, these things usually come in waves, you know, *bing-bang-boong*, you're gone."

"Well, gee, Nick, thanks. I'm glad I decided to let you cheer me up."

"Look, somebody's got to give you your daily dose of reality." He jabbed my arm with his loaded slice. "I figure if your dad's anything like me"—meaning, *he must be, because he's brilliant and he's a bastard*— "he'll probably welcome it. That's why I became a lawyer. It's a Type A profession for Type A types who'd rather go out like a light than hang on into doddering senility." He popped his bread in his mouth, whole. *"Bing-bang-boong."*

We ordered. Dawdled over dinner, drinking too much champagne and dishing people we knew in common. Eileen had finally asked for a divorce ("She got the house, and she got rid of me. She's never been so happy in her life"). He didn't see Maria Lombardi much anymore. She'd taken an offer from another firm, which was just as well because, according to Shawde, "her biological clock was ticking so loud, it was keeping me awake at night." I laughed on cue through a veil of bubbly, thinking Nick was really an okay guy.

"So what's going on between you and old D.B.?" He did that one-two-three hike of the brows.

"I don't know what—"

"Yeah, right," he sneered. "Listen, I got it from Gold. She thinks something's sizzling between you two."

I remembered suddenly why I'd always despised Nick Shawde. He was nosy. A gossip. A tease. "Sorry to disappoint you, Shawde," I said, trying not to slur my words.

"Aw, come on, Garny," he needled. "Now that he's been unofficially let off the hook, you can tell me—"

"I *am* telling you, there's nothing. Now will you lay off?"

He cut his eyes to the tables around us, as though I'd embarrassed him. The guy who drops on his knees in a restaurant to look at a women's legs, embarrassed by a little loudness. "Okay, okay,"

Shawde said. "I dunno. Maybe it's Diana who's hung up on him—she ever say anything to you?"

Smooth, Nick, I thought, but I caught the way you said her name. "No," I said. "We don't get along. It's one of those girl things."

Nick nodded. "She's a bitch on wheels." He stretched a hand lazily across the table, ensnaring mine. "But forget about her. I've always thought you and I should give it a go."

"Give what a go?"

"That's what I mean, Garn." Shawde laughed. "You see through all my shit. It's beautiful. You're beautiful, babe."

I sobered up just enough to say, sincerely, "And you, Nick Shawde, would be a new low. Even for me."

He sat straight in his chair, clapping his hands and tapping the toes of his spitshine wing tips with delight. "But you *know* it!" he squealed. "You *know* what a heel I am! Do you realize what a break-through this could be for you, sweetcakes? Hooking up with a guy who you realize is a lying, conniving piece of dogshit from the start! I tell you, Garn, your road to self-actualization could start right here." Nick thumped his chest.

"I'll give it serious consideration," I said, wryly. Around us, people were shooting warm, positive glances, as if we'd just gotten engaged.

When the waiter brought dessert, Nick leaned back in his chair and zapped me with one of his *I've-saved-the-best-for-last* squinty stares. "So, didja hear the latest about Susie Trevett?"

An alarm went up. "No, what?"

"Seems Sistah Cox is experiencing a major relapse in salvation," Nick drawled, with relish. "She ditched the hubby, took all his credit cards. Ran up a nifty bill of something like three thousand dollars in clothes and fine dining, and when last heard from was turning tricks and doing a lot of blow in Hot-lanta."

My mind took off through the alcoholic haze. "Has she . . . has she said anything else about Jeff?"

"Relax, babyface." He sipped his cappuccino. "The girl just got tired of wearing polyester suits and low-heeled shoes. End of story."

"I heard from him," I said.

Nick pulled himself straight in his chair. "Yeah?"

"He wanted me to write a letter of recommendation to some colleges up here." I played at folding my napkin.

"Up here?" Nick repeated, cautiously. "So, did you do it?"

"I'm thinking about it," I said. "Why not?"

"Yeah," he echoed. "Why not?" His smile was a little too tight.

After a lot of feinting this way and that, I ended up paying the tab, wondering at which *"No, I insist"* he'd bamboozled me.

Outside the restaurant, he asked if he could sleep with me. I said no. Without missing a beat, he asked if he could get me a cab. I said yes. We stood on Columbus Avenue, the cold drizzle jolting us both back into our respective lives. I thought about Dudley. From the look on Shawde's face, he was deciding whether to grab a taxi or hit another bar before heading home. He asked me how long I'd be in town. I said I didn't know, but I'd call.

We both knew I wouldn't.

He hailed a cab and managed a too-earnest kiss on the lips before I slid inside. "Take care of yourself, kid." Nick waved.

I waved back, picturing him with Diana Gold. Not a bad match, I decided. Diana would relentlessly ridicule him in public, and Shawde would cheat on her at every opportunity. They'd both be very happy.

The last I saw of him, he was loping down the street toward one of the big West Side singles' places.

The telephone rang at two forty-five. I reached for it, snapping on the light at the same time.

"Miss Quinn?" a kind voice on the other end said. "Your father has taken a turn for the worse, and we thought you might want to be here."

9

The bed was a huge white raft, and he was afloat on it, marooned by his own body. His blue eyes stared blankly. A silvery line of spittle ran down one side of his mouth.

I took his hand. It was unresisting, unresponsive. "I'm so sorry," I said.

The screen blipped. The IV dripped. The nose tube sent its invisible charge of life into his body. But he was dying, in spite of it all.

"I know this is the last thing you'd want." Not a flicker of an eyelid. Nothing. I dragged over a chair and sat close. Minutes ticked by. I realized they would leave us alone now. The doctor, and the nurses. They were no longer concerned that this patient get his rest. He was resting. He would be resting.

Little by little, I began to relax. I studied his profile from many angles. Then, very gently, I put my finger to his face and traced a line from cheek to jaw. He had the beard of an old man, slack and shiny, like worn velvet. Not once did he stir; yet it didn't matter. That I should be able to stand this close to him seemed miraculous, a gift. I'd never touched him just to see how he would feel.

The monitor skipped a few beats. I put my face on the pillow next to his. "Don't go yet," I whispered. "Tell me what you were going to say before I left this afternoon." *Garner, in my own way I've always—*

"You can do it. I know you can." I pressed his hand, hard. "Dammit, I need this—" His eyelids flickered open.

"I love you, Daddy. I love you." His eyes looked confused, then they fastened on my face and seemed to suddenly calm.

A flat buzzing sound screamed from the monitor. I scrambled to my feet as the night nurse rushed in, then someone else, a doctor maybe, but not Chuska. "Wait." I stood in their way, trying to block them from entering. "Can't you wait a minute?"

The nurse put an arm around me. "I'm afraid it's too late, dear."

"You don't understand," I told her. "We needed more time"—I clutched the sleeve of her starched white uniform—"just a little more time."

10

The whole thing took seven days. It was a Prominent New York Death, culminating in a brief, largely attended, and relatively unemotional memorial service.

Dudley Lonigan Quinn the Third, who'd lived a hedonist, died a Puritan. Neatly. Properly. Tastefully.

At the last minute I'd tried to throw him a rowdy Irish wake. I made a few calls. But they were all gone now, my father's drinking buddies and cronies, his girlfriends and mistresses, scattered who knew where—although I thought I spied a few of them among the mourners, looking appropriately chastened and somber-eyed.

Black will do that.

Jack drove Temple and Cilda up for the service. We stood together, my daughter nodding solemnly to the well-wishers as though she'd really known her grandfather, as if a relationship in her life was actually passing away. I held Cilda's arm. When the minister read the passage from the Gospel of John, *"In my Father's house are many mansions* . . . ," she swayed and sobbed a little; and I felt certain she was remembering Dudley's house. The house of my childhood.

Jack appeared overly awed by the presence of two governors; several once-were and wannabe mayors; celebrities and show-biz types; and the full ranks of the press. There were flowers from my ex-husband, and from Nick Shawde—neither of whom attended. Blackmoor sent a card to my hotel, four words, *'I'm thinking of you,'* unsigned.

After the service, the four of us had a quiet dinner. When Jack offered to drive Temple and Cilda home, I was relieved—grateful for a few hours of silence and solitude.

By the time I pulled through the gates, everything looked locked up for the night. Instead of going directly into the house, I took the flagstone path around back. The air was almost balmy. A chiffon drape of clouds hung over the moon, diffusing its glow against the darkness like a dusting of flour in a cast-iron pan. In a couple of days it would be full. Lights danced in the windows of the guest house. Blackmoor was working.

Once inside my office I slipped into the spare sweater and jeans I kept in the coat closet, then headed for the beach. The rusty metal ladder that hung from the seawall creaked under my weight. The hump of the wall was only three feet wide, and the uneven rocks made it rough going. Several feet below, the crane and the backhoe grinned wide smiles, with full sets of metal teeth.

I climbed down the other side and set off on the sand at an easy jog. After I could run no more, I sat on the slick, black spine of the jetty, fighting hard to keep conscious thought from flooding back to me.

It was no use.

I saw death everywhere. In the tangle of crushed crab shells. In the abandoned domiciles of sea creatures that encrusted the crevasses of the rocks. In the waves that beat the shore mercilously, with wicked, foamy fists. It surrounded me, leering from under the clouds with a blank, moony stare.

I leaned back, abandoning myself to a morbid little game of free association.

Father?—Dead.
Mother?—Dead.
Marriage?—Dead.

But I was forgetting the most important one of all.

Career—
Dead. Dead. Dead. Dead.

One for every bestseller. I closed my eyes, feeling the spray from the ocean on my face. Then something else, warm and substantial. A human hand.

Blackmoor's. I scrambled to my feet. "You scared me—"

"I thought you might like some company." He was wearing jeans, expensive cowboy boots, and a baseball jacket over a very white shirt. The moonlight treated him kindly. I took the hand he offered and jumped off the jetty.

"I'm sorry about Dudley," he said stiffly. This was where the person was supposed to say something nice about the deceased. *He was a good man. He did a lot for those in need. He was a great golfer.* Anything would do. Blackmoor remained silent.

We walked. He picked up shells and threw them into the ocean, where they landed in the valleys beneath the waves with flat little splushes. Halfway down the beach, I stopped. "I want to know if you had an affair with my mother," I said.

"That's none of your fucking business," he replied, very quietly.

"I think it is."

"Well, you're wrong." He left me standing in a little puddle of foam. I had to run to catch up.

"Look," Blackmoor said, when I caught up to him, "I know it's not polite to speak ill of the dead, but manners never were my strong suit." He looked out toward the ocean, hands in his pockets, shoulders hunched. "Your old man was a born liar. I wouldn't believe a word he said, especially if it had to do with Gabrielle."

I bristled. "What makes you think he said anything?"

"I just assumed—"

"There were no last-minute confidences," I said. "None of that."

Blackmoor scanned my face. "I'm sorry," he said. Then his expression hardened. "But that still doesn't change my position."

"She was my mother, you bastard. I have a right to know."

"The trouble with you is," he said, "you actually believe that line counts for something in real life."

I wanted to kick him, to scratch his eyes or slap his face. Instead I started running toward the seawall, as fast as I could. Blackmoor caught up easily. I pulled away from him. He grabbed my sweater, tackling me from behind, until we were both on the sand, fighting breathlessness, and each other.

"Stop it, Garner." He had my arms pinned. "Stop trying to shake me out of your twisted little family tree!"

"I'm not!"

"Don't give me that." His face was only inches away. I lifted my head, not admitting, even then, that I was going to kiss him, until I was in the middle of it, and it was much too late. His mouth tasted of salt and wine. I could smell his clean white shirt, and the leather of the baseball jacket, which crackled next to my ear when he moved into the kiss.

Then he pushed me away. Sand fell from the creases of his clothing into my open mouth, burning my eyes. "Let's get this straight," he said softly. "You want to find somebody to father you? Fine. You want to find somebody to fuck you? Great. Just don't keep looking for them both in the same place." He sat back on his heels to push a strand of hair off my forehead. "At least not when you come knocking at my door, little girl."

He left me there. When I was sure he had gone, I pulled my sweater up over my head, and cried bitterly in a dark, sandy tent of humiliation.

1 1

"I'll drive you to the bus stop."

"I feel like walking." Temple grabbed her backpack and Lakers jacket, pecked me on the cheek, and flew out the door.

I sat down next to Cilda at the kitchen table. "You're upset about something."

"And why not," she said, "wit' 'imself in a day-old grave?"

"There's something else. Has Temple been giving you trouble?"

Cilda stirred her oatmeal in small, vicious circles. "Why should I be upset about 'er? She's your daughter now, isn't she?" She went on, muttering under her breath. "Walkin' where she used to be ridin'. Ridin' when she used to be walkin'. Out on the beach late all times of the night. Stickin' her love letters down there in the wall."

"What do you mean, love letters?"

"Oh, she's smart, but she don't fool me. I seen her tuckin' them notes in the rocks, and next thing you look, they all of a sudden gone."

I got up to turn off the boiling tea kettle, trying to stave off the sickish feeling in my stomach. "This started while I was gone?"

Cilda shrugged. I took it as a yes. As I passed the window with my cup, a flurry of outside activity caught my eye. "Looks like they've been doing a lot of work on the wall," I commented, to change the subject.

"Better work quick." Cilda dabbed her eyes with a napkin. "Big storm tomorrow. Prob'ly take the whole place down."

She was impossible when she got in these moods. "I'm not really hungry," I told her. "I'd better get back to work."

On my way over to the office, I ran into Ben Snow carrying a wooden shutter, his trademark red flannel shirt standing out against the dull gray clapboard. "Gone t' fix that window out behind, before the nor'easter hits."

"Think we'll catch it?"

"Been a freaky winter so far." He shrugged. "With the full moon and the tides, we'll get something. You know I can put you up at my place if they evacuate."

"Thanks," I told him. "I'm just hoping the predictions are wrong."

"Wouldn't be the first time." He went on dragging the shutter around the side of the house. I glanced toward the seawall.

No notes of love were stuck in the recesses of rock today.

Jack was at me as soon as I came through the door. "We have to talk."

"Sure." I tossed my jacket onto a chair.

"I've been sitting on this for over a week—"

"Sorry. I've had my mind on other things."

His face reddened. "Of course. I didn't mean—"

I cut him off. "In fact, I'm not even sure I want to continue with the Blackmoor book."

"You're not serious?"

I sank into a chair. "I'm burnt out. Maybe this would be a good time to cut loose for a while. I need some time to regroup."

Jack walked out of the room. I heard him opening the wall safe in my office where we kept sensitive documents and research material. When he returned he was carrying a padded envelope. "I think you'd better take a look at this before you book any cruises."

I looked inside. The videocassette was marked simply "3/15."

"Allow me." He took it and walked over to the VCR, swiveling the monitor in my direction. The tape had already been cued up.

Once again I watched Elizabeth Rice demonstrating her unique talents as a performance artist. The long, white bandages draped over her arms fluttered around in the air, softening her actions, blurring all the hard edges soft, white. "*My plaster-bandage technique is much more difficult,*" she said to the camera, "*because not only do you have to align the seams, you need to moisten the entire mold, so that you can shape it gently to the face.*"

Her fingers moved quickly over the surface of the cast. The camera followed. An exposed portion of Torie Wood's polyurethaned head filled the frame, like a close-up of a new product—freeze-dried terror in a boilable pouch. I sat up straight in the chair. I'd never get used to this.

"*The final creation,*" Rice told her viewers, sweetly, "*is less of a life mask, than a death mask.*"

Jack froze the picture. "Did you see it?"

"See what?"

"You reacted to it viscerally"—he sounded excited—"but did you see it?"

My heart thumped clownishly in my chest. "See what, Jack? Get to the point!" But there was a point, and I knew it, knew even before I could put it into words.

Patiently, he rewound the tape. We watched Beth going through the grisly motions, backward this time. He stopped it and hit Play. Rice began performing on cue. "—*you need to moisten the entire mold, so that you can shape it gently to the face."* There was a tight shot of Torie Wood's head.

A tight shot.

"My God," I whispered.

"Cameras don't zoom by themselves. At least the one that Blackmoor owned didn't. I checked. Someone else had to be there." He zapped the machine on fast forward. "I found another spot where he does it again—"

"Wait." I put up a hand, my mind moving in a million directions.

Jack's calm buckled. "Don't you see? There were two of them all along."

"Not necessarily." But of course he was right. What other explanation could there be? I remembered the way Elizabeth had addressed the camera. Teasing it, instructing it, flirting with it.

"You had him pegged from the start." He pulled me off the chair, lifting me into the air. "It was her confession that threw you off track."

"But why would she have said all those things if he'd been in it with her?" A phrase popped into my head, something Rice had said—*Don't worry, darling. I'm not about to kill another one of his girlfriends for him.*

Jack persisted. "So are you going to confront him?"

"Not yet. You need to do some follow-ups on the others. Lewan. Lucy Moon. Roberto and Hadary."

His mouth dropped in disbelief. "You're not going to let him go on living here? Now that we know?"

"We don't know anything."

"Are you crazy? He killed a young girl. Maybe more than one." He caught my startled reaction. "You never did get to see those tapes of Donna Fry and Kimberly Arnette, did you?" I didn't have to answer. "And you're going to allow him to stay in your home? Near you and your daughter?"

"You know I'd never do anything that would put Temple in danger."

"Well, I've got a news flash. I've seen her go traipsing over there. It was one cozy little get-together after another while you were gone. And you mean to tell me you're just going to let it happen?" His voice lowered, icily. "Are you that hot for him?"

My slap was dead-on. The kind that left tracks.

"Sorry," Jack said. "I was way out of line."

I slammed the door behind me as a way of letting him know his apology wasn't accepted.

12

For as long as I can remember, old-fashioned hardware stores have been my idea of heaven. I've always felt there was something inherently pure in the smell of woodshavings, of paint settling on the bottom of cans. Between books I'd usually find myself spending some part of the day shuffling over worn pumpkin pine plank flooring, peering into bins of nails and screws. Most times I returned to the beach house with a waxy brown bag filled with gadgets. Why I bought them I didn't know. Ben Snow did all the odd jobs, and I've never been what you might call handy. But still I hoarded them—mat knives and ratchets; padlocks and plastic buckets of Spackle.

I think they gave me the illusion of being in control.

Maybe that's why, after my argument with Jack, I ended up in a hardware store on the peninsula.

Afterward, I just kept driving. It was after seven by the time I got home, but the sky was overly bright, the shade of iced lemonade. I parked the car, retrieving my sack of toolshed treasures from the backseat—a Snap-On Phillips screwdriver and twelve penny nails. I was trying to decide where to hide them. This was a game of cat-and-mouse I played with Cilda, who found the bags and moved them elsewhere.

That's how we'll end up, I thought. Two crotchety old eccentrics squirreling away lumpy paper bags, inside drawers, under mattresses. It made me shiver.

I found the back door unlocked.

There was an open bottle of Merlot on the kitchen table. Microwave popcorn littered the clean counters, its oily smell still lingering in the air. A few kernels had fallen on the floor. Blackmoor's bird was picking at them.

"Shoo!" The cockatoo dropped an unpopped pellet at my feet. *"Bless you!"* it squawked. *"Bless-ess-ess-you!"*

I followed the sound of Frank Sinatra, blasting from the great room. Temple and Blackmoor were sitting cross-legged on the floor, playing roulette with a makeshift wheel fashioned out of one of Cilda's lazy Susans. Temple stopped laughing when she saw me.

"Hullo," Blackmoor said.

I went to the compact disc player and turned down Frank. Temple jumped to her feet. "Dane says I'm a natural gambler."

"Don't you have homework to do?"

"No," she said. I detected an unsettling edge of defiance in her voice.

Blackmoor was already pushing chips into a box. "I have to be going anyway." He rose with the ease of someone used to spending a great deal of time on floors. Temple ran upstairs without another word.

He followed me into the kitchen. "Listen, about last night—"

"Forget it."

"Yes," Blackmoor said, finally. "That would probably be best." He put his arm out for the bird. "I hope you don't mind. I stopped to borrow a lightbulb, and Temple snagged me for a quick game."

"Why should I mind?" We were standing at the door. "She's probably always hanging around, anyway. Over at the guest house."

"No," Blackmoor said. "She hasn't come there at all."

I made a note of the ease with which he lied.

13

Temple was at her desk, writing furiously. When she saw me, she crumpled the piece of paper and tossed it into the wastebasket.

It took all of my self-restraint not to drop to my knees and go digging for it.

I said, "I want you to stay away from Dane Blackmoor."

"Why?"

"Because he's dangerous."

She got up out of her chair. "Real good, Mom." When she brushed past me, I felt sparks of anger rising from her, like static electricity. "If he's so dangerous, why'd you invite him here in the first place?"

"I don't mean he's responsible for killing the girl"—*or did I?*— "it's just . . . he"—I fumbled for the right words—"he . . . isn't what . . . he seems to be." Temple threw herself down on the bed with a sarcastic little laugh.

I tried a new tack. "Look, I understand all too well how charming he can be. And you're of an age . . . I know—"

"You don't know anything," Temple said. I'd never heard her speak to me in that tone of voice before.

My eyes darted frantically around the room. It took me a second but there it was, protruding from some papers on the floor—Dane Blackmoor's scrapbook. I picked it up. "Honey, let's be honest. You had a crush on the guy before you even met him. You only have to look through this book to—"

Temple grabbed the album from my hands. "You're so stupid!" she shrieked. "*So stupid—*" Tears were running down her face. "The book was for *you!* I made it because I thought then we'd have something to talk about . . . maybe for once you'd talk . . . to me—" She threw it at my feet.

"Temple," I started to say, but my mind was somewhere else: in the shadows of a foyer, waiting for the hustle and bustle of arriving guests to subside, so I could ask my father a question about his trial. *All these years spent trying to be a good mother—a better parent than Dudley had been to me. . . . Was it possible? Could it be true? Had I really shut my daughter out, the same way?*

I was so mired in my own thoughts that I stopped listening for a moment, but Temple kept right on talking. "—and now you've wrapped up this case," she was saying, "so it's bye-bye, Blackmoor, just like the rest of them! Like they don't matter as people—just as books! As books on a shelf!"

"Temple," I said weakly, "that's not true."

She snatched up her jacket. "You don't care!" she cried. "Not about me, or him, or anybody! All that matters to you is the next one. And the next one—"

I leaned over the stair railing, calling after her. "Temple! Please!"

But she didn't stop. When the back door slammed, I went over to the window. Temple's bedroom faced the rear of the property. The guest house was dark. Blackmoor's Range Rover was gone. I breathed a sigh of relief. At least for now, she would be safe.

14

I was sitting at a long table in a big, bright room, my favorite pen in my hand. A grade-school composition book lay open before me.

The door opened—although I hadn't seen a door before—and he walked in, wearing a hospital gown over an impeccably cut dinner jacket.

"What have you been doing with yourself, Garner?"

I said, "I'm working on this case."

"Yes," Dudley said. "Awful business."

I had my pen poised over the notebook. "Who do you think killed her?"

He put his hand over mine, over the hand that held the pen that was ready to write. "You already know, Garner."

"No," I said, "I don't." The room grew smaller around me. I felt panicky, claustrophobic. I suddenly realized the hand on top of mine wasn't my father's. It was younger and stronger. The nails bit into my flesh. I was afraid to look at him.

"Garner," a familiar voice sang. "You know who killed her." His fingers closed like a vise.

"No," I cried, "I don't!" I forced myself to look at his face. The hospital gown was covering his head like a snowy hood. He wrestled the pen from me, jabbing it at my midriff. "Yes, you do, Garner . . ." *Jab.* "Sure you do . . ." *Jab.* "You know you do . . ." *Jab. Jab.*

He poked the pen in my ribs, my breasts, then upward, toward my face. "You know, Garner. You know you know." *Jab.* The point of the pen was aiming straight for my eyes—

Shattering glass smashed the nightmare into a thousand pieces.

I sat bolt upright in bed. Wind blew fistfuls of rain into my bedroom. I ran to the window, struggling with the shutters, the dream still fresh in my mind.

It took Ben a long while to come to the phone, and when he did, his voice was falsely hearty. "Now, Garner, I don't want you to worry."

"Are you all right?"

"I was in the garage this morning, and a damn hammer fell off the shelf, clipped me on the head," he replied. "Still can't figure how it happened."

"Maybe I'd better drive you to the hospital."

On the other end, Ben managed to laugh. "Take more than that to make an invalid out of me. But the wife's laid down the law. Enforced sick day."

"Good for her."

"I heard about the bedroom window," he sighed. "Got one of my fellas comin' over there this morning."

"Don't worry about us. Just get some rest." I hung up and looked out the window. It was already raining, and the guys from Coastal Engineering were moving with fresh urgency, yellow slickers over their standard jumpsuits. Angry waves reared through the chinks in the seawall.

"They'd better fill in those gaps soon," I said to Cilda, "or we'll be bodysurfing in here by dinnertime."

"You look terrible," Jack said.

"I didn't sleep all that well. The wind."

"Sure it was the wind?" He came up behind me, massaging my shoulders. "You're one great big knot."

"It's been a rough couple of weeks."

He kneaded my neck. "Have you decided what you want to do?"

I moved away. "I'll handle Blackmoor my own way."

"Actually, I wasn't talking about him. I meant about us." He ran a fingertip down the back of my neck.

"There is no us." It came out more roughly than I'd intended. "I'm sorry. The other night was a mistake—"

The intensity of his reaction shocked me. "A mistake. A *mistake?*" he repeated. "How about all those other times? *Jack, come on over for a beer? Jack, stay for dinner. Jack, Jack, Jack.* We were a fucking family—you and Temple and me. I didn't just dream *that* up, did I?"

"We work together," I told him. "You're a friend. That's all it was." But even as I said it, I knew it wasn't entirely true.

In one sudden movement, he swept everything—the papers, the blotter, the phone—off his desk. "This is great." He rammed his fist into the wall. "So like, I've just wasted two years of my life, is that what you're telling me? Two years of breaking my ass—nights, weekends, taking the flak for your prima donna act, holding down the home front when you went off, traipsing around the country—"

"You wanted the job," I reminded him.

"I thought it was leading somewhere. I didn't know you'd use me, then throw me out on my rear—"

"I'm not throwing you out."

"Throwing me out, throwing me over." Jack shrugged as if it

were a moot point. "You'll see." His voice dripped venom. "You think you can make it without me, Garner? Well, go ahead and try. You don't know—you don't have the vaguest clue of what I do around here!" The words bounced loudly off the walls, and an echo came back: Elizabeth Rice demanding, as the studio burned around her, "*Who-do-you-think-is-responsible-for-this?*"

An insistent buzzing sound was coming from the telephone on the floor. I wanted to put the receiver back on the hook, but I was afraid to move.

Jack put out his hand to me, repentantly. "Garner—"

I couldn't help it. I recoiled from him. His face darkened. He picked up the wastepaper basket and hurled it against the filing cabinets. "One of these days," he said in a bitter whisper, "you're gonna play one of your games with the wrong person."

After he slammed the door, I walked like a zombie over to the filing cabinet. The *T*'s were in the second drawer from the bottom, on the right. Jack's file was less than a quarter inch thick. *I have only a skinny millimeter's worth of knowledge about this man*, I thought, thumbing through tax forms, our early correspondence. I remembered asking for references, and there they were—three names printed in Jack's cramped handwriting.

Acting totally on impulse, I picked up the angrily buzzing receiver with shaking hands.

15

On my way to the guest house, I noticed Cilda bringing a tray of muffins to the workers. They swooped
around her like birds, slickers flapping, hands pecking at the food.

Take your break, I muttered under my breath. *I'm sure the storm
will wait.*

Blackmoor answered the door, unshaven, in a gray sweatshirt
and jeans. "Hullo," he said.

I walked in, uninvited. Wineglasses, empty bottles, and several
used coffee mugs littered the workbench. He'd been sketching again.
When he noticed my interest, he gathered the drawings up and
stuffed them into an open carton.

The marble stood in the center of the room, under the skylight.
I squinted my eyes. The ghostly shape of a female torso seemed to be
struggling, fighting to emerge from a chrysalis of stone.

"That's quite a beginning."

"Well, it's the ending that counts, isn't it?" He picked up his hammer and chisel. With each quick thrust, a sliver of marble flew into the air, settling like soap shavings at our feet. *Chip-chip-chip-chip-chip-chip-chip*. Stop. *Chip-chip-chip-chip-chip-chip-chip*. Stop.

"Stop," I said. "Could you stop?" He focused on me with effort. His eyes were bloodshot. "How come you asked me to throw the cassette in the canal?"

"What are you talking about?"

"The night of the fire. You told me to throw it in the water. So it would end with her, you said."

"Did I?" He sounded unconvinced.

"Yes, you did."

He went back to attacking the stone with the tip of his sharp, pointy chisel. *Chip-chip-chip-chip-chip-chip-chip* . . .

"Elizabeth Rice didn't act alone." I spoke quickly, in the small silent space between sets of thrusts. Blackmoor set his tools down on the table, but said nothing. "Someone was with her the night she sealed Torie's head in the plaster. The camera zoomed in for close-ups. Some mounted camcorders can do that without a person operating them, but not the one in your studio. Jack checked."

"Jack checked." Blackmoor's mouth twisted into a flinty grin. "And I suppose Jack also has a theory about who the mystery camera-person might be. He can be quite thorough, I imagine, Jack. When it serves his purposes."

"What's that supposed to mean?"

"I don't trust him," he said. "I've caught him skulking around outside, and some of my things are missing."

Only minutes before I'd been desperately dialing references as if my life depended on it, my heart sinking with every disconnected number, every disembodied voice on an answering machine, *I can't come to the phone right now, but if you leave your name and number—*"; but in the face of Blackmoor's sarcastic innuendo, I felt strangely protective of Jack Tatum.

"If Jack came in here, it was to do his job. Nothing more."

"So where does this leave us, Garnish, now that I'm back on the hot seat?"

I felt something inside me crumble. I didn't want to believe it was my heart. "I want you out of here," I said.

Blackmoor turned the chisel over in his hand. "I suppose this is all a big relief to you."

"What are you talking about?"

"You know," he replied. A cold ripple of fear ran down my back. *You know*, the hooded man had said.

That's when I heard the scream, and the other voices—overlapping, terrible in their urgency.

Blackmoor reached the door first. "Stay back," he warned. I shrugged off his arm, rushing toward the circle of slickered men clustered around the crane.

Cilda lay on the ground, not moving. "Somebody call for help," I yelled.

Dropping to my knees, I cradled her head in my lap. "Hold on," I whispered into her ear, "I'm here. It's going to be all right."

No one knew how it happened. One worker said he'd noticed her raking up gravel near the seawall before the crane lurched forward. It had been parked on an incline, but the operator insisted he'd activated the emergency brake. No one could offer any plausible reason as to how it might have given way.

I rode with Cilda in the back of the ambulance. "Temple." She grabbed my arm. "She's all alone, with school lettin' out."

"She'll be all right. It's you I'm worried about."

Cilda thrashed her head back and forth on the stretcher. "Temple," she cried. "Temple . . ."

"Shock," the paramedic said. "Sometimes they become agitated."

I pressed her hands. They were clammy and cold, stiff as feet. "Shhh." The ambulance hit a rut. Cilda groaned. I held her tight. The seawall was just a soft blur against another iced lemonade sky.

16

"A couple of fractured ribs, a sprained wrist, and a broken leg. All things considered, she got off pretty easy." I stood at the payphone, jangling some extra quarters in my hand.

"WILL she haVE to stAY in the hoSPITAL?" The connection was spotty, probably because of the oncoming storm.

"The doctor wants her to, but you know Cilda." The line crackled. "We should be here awhile longer, though. Listen, honey, do me a favor, and pull out the sofa bed? We'll never get her upstairs."

"I was supPOSED to go to EMory's."

"Call her, and tell her you can't come."

"MOther—"

I held the quarters against my cheek. They were cool and smelled like greasy thumbprints. "We'll discuss it when I get home." A volley of static obliterated the reply. "I love you," I called.

But the connection had already been broken.

. . .

The sky lay low on the horizon, nestling layer upon layer of color over the sea, as if trying to dazzle it down. But the ocean kept rising.

I parked the Volvo behind Blackmoor's Range Rover. Getting Cilda out of the car was even more difficult than I'd expected. Between the wrapped wrist, taped ribs, and plaster cast, I couldn't figure out where to grab her. After a few attempts I leaned on the horn.

"Where is she?" The place seemed to be completely deserted. "Looks like we're on our own." I smiled through gritted teeth.

"Temple!" The name echoed in the empty kitchen.

We stopped so Cilda could rest. I knew she was in a lot of pain. "I'm fine on me own," she protested. "Go find our girl."

"I want to get you settled first."

We hobbled through the silent great room. At the bottom of the staircase I called again, "Temple?" No answer. Even the piano was tightly shut, its teethy ivories betraying nothing.

The downstairs sofa bed had been pulled out and made up with fresh sheets. "She must be here somewhere." I eased Cilda onto the mattress, taking care to keep the fear out of my voice. "It's good to be home, huh? Should I put on the television for you?" She shook her head impatiently.

I went into the bathroom, looking out of the window as I ran the water. The guest house was dark. I caught a glimpse of myself in the mirror over the sink. My hair was tangled. My cheeks looked scorched, as if they'd been pressed with the tip of a steam iron. I carried the glass of water back into the other room along with the tiny amber bottle of painkillers. "Why don't you take one of the pills the doctor gave you?"

"Got no use for that stuff." Cilda motioned me away. "Makes me dopey."

"You might need them." I set the bottle on the table, next to the water.

"Go find Temple," she whispered hoarsely. "Go."

"Temple?" The door swung on its hinges, creaking a little. I walked into the bedroom. *She's gone to Emory's,* I thought miserably, *and didn't even bother to leave a note.*

But, then again, that wasn't quite true.

Looking out the window, I noticed a piece of paper sticking out of the seawall, flapping bravely, a tiny white flag. Temple had left a message for someone, although I was quite sure it wasn't meant for me.

The wind was so fierce that it almost got away. The paper flew out of my fingers and landed in the surf, skimming the water like a toy raft. I waded up to my calves. I was afraid the ink would blur, that I'd never know what it said. I snatched it up with both hands and stuffed it in my jacket.

Pockets of air swirled around me in strong, silent currents, pasting my hair to my face, pushing me backward, toward the ocean, shoving like a pair of invisible hands. It took forever to reach the seawall.

The rusty metal stairs clapped noisily against the stone. I clung to them, feeling salt spray on my back. When I finally managed to pull myself up onto the hump of the wall, my eyes were immediately drawn to the office.

The door was wide open. It swung loosely in the wind. I lowered myself off the wall and broke into a lopey, head-down run. Were they there, Blackmoor and Temple? Or was it just Jack?

Just Jack.

The door teetered back and forth. It seemed strange that the lights should be off, unless— I found the switchplate. One quick flip illuminated a scene of absolute chaos. Papers had been strewn everywhere, some torn in half, some rolled up into little balls. The filing cabinets gaped, lantern-jawed, spewing files, upchucking folders onto the floor. The walls were splattered with India ink—black, blue, purple, and a shock of blood red—like some modernistic mural. I moved like a sleepwalker into the inner room.

A hammer stuck obscenely out of the blank screen of the Macintosh. My chair had been hacked to ribbons. I picked up the photograph of Temple. The glass from the frame showered my desk, small and glinty, crunching under my feet. Someone had drawn a pair of wide, red, lascivious lips over her mouth. When I put my finger to it, the lines smudged. It was greasy, like those pencils Blackmoor used to mark his plaster.

I started to cry.

The phone rang. I backed away from it. It rang again, and again. Finally I picked up the receiver. "Hello?"

"Is this Miss Quinn?"

"Yes," I said, tentatively.

"Miss Quinn, this is Larry Thorbes. You left a message about Jack Tatum?"

"Yes." My voice sounded ethereal, untethered, out in space. "I remember."

"Look, Miss Quinn, I'm afraid I just can't get involved," Larry Thorbes was saying. I wanted to respond, had my lips pursed and ready, but somehow nothing came out. "I mean, Jack's a friend, but I'm married now. Settled down. I just can't keep bailing him out."

"Bailing him out?" I repeated dully.

"Well, that's why you're calling, isn't it?" the man said. "He's gone apeshit again, right? Had one too many, and leveled some bar? I mean, I've been there. I know what he's capable of when somebody crosses him." My mouth fluttered open, uselessly.

"But I'm sorry," Jack's personal reference went on, "I've got a family now. I'd like to help him, only I just can't this time, okay?"

"Okay," I whispered. "Thank you, anyway."

17

The guest house was locked. I stood in the shelter of the porch, pounding the door until my fists were sore. Inside, it might have been a tomb.

Wind tapped on the kitchen windows as if it wanted to get in. My boots were soaked from wading into the ocean. They squished as I walked across the floor. I sat at the table, carefully unfolding the note. The dampness and the heat from my pocket had softened the paper so that it felt almost like cloth. Temple's big, curly writing leapt off the page, splotchy in places, but still quite legible.

> Help!
> Things are really heating up here. I think she knows something's going on. She's on my case all the time. I was supposed to go to Emory's but now I'm not sure. One thing I know is I'm not going

to give you up, no matter what SHE says. You think I'm a baby, but you'll see. It wasn't just talk (at least on MY part). No matter what I'll meet you at the usual time, in the usual place.

LUV YA, Temple

Her signature was bubbled in a heart.

I put both hands on the table, palms down, as though to steady it, and not them. A thin ribbon of fear undulated from my abdomen, up to the back of my throat. I felt light-headed, on the edge of a faint. *At the usual time, in the usual place.*

The wall clock read ten after seven. It had been almost an hour since I'd checked on Cilda. I walked through the empty great room, not bothering to turn on the lights. A huge shadow—myself distorted, tiny head, massive thighs—preceded me. My boots left damp prints on the carpet.

The door was open, the way I'd left it. Cilda was sleeping on her back. The saliva trapped in her throat gurgled a little with each drawn breath. A fringe of steel-gray hair stood up from the pillow, blunt-edged, like a broom.

"Cilda?" No answer. The water glass was almost empty. She must have taken her pills. I turned around and tiptoed out the door.

Emory's number was no longer tacked to the corkboard in Temple's room. I began rifling through the desk, keeping one eye out the window. Expecting to see what? A lantern bobbing, or the soft white cone of a flashlight? Would they meet that way? In a tempest? In the dark?

My head had cleared some. It was comforting, somehow, being up here, eye to eye with the storm. It gave me a sense of power. The rising tides had already reclaimed the beach. Waves rapped angrily on the back of the decrepit seawall. In a few hours they would swell over the shoulders of the rock, and creep inland. But there was no use thinking about that now.

I was supposed to go to Emory's but now I'm not sure. Temple's telephone book was in the bottom drawer. I found the number there, under *P.*

"Hello, Cindy?"

"Ye-es?" Cindy Pratt's voice was perky, the way I'd remembered it.

"This is Garner Quinn. Temple's mom."

"Garner! Why, you poor thing, we were just thinking about you, in this storm."

"I wanted to let you know I'm coming by to pick up Temple."

Emory's mother sounded confused. "Oh, Garner, honey, there must be some misunderstanding," she said. "Temple isn't here."

My jaw moved in jerky spasms. "Are you sure? I mean, could you check? Maybe she came in without you knowing."

The voice on the other end lowered, sympathetically. "Well, I'll ask. Emory's sitting here in the kitchen with me now, making cookies." I stabbed the front of the desk with the toe of my wet boot. *Cookies? What kind of person made fucking cookies in the middle of a hurricane? AND-WHERE-THE-FUCK-WAS-MY-DAUGHTER?*

Cindy Pratt came back on the line, apologetically. "No. I'm afraid Emory hasn't seen her since school let out."

Downstairs, someone was thumping loudly on the front door, ringing the bell. Temple! And it was locked. She couldn't get in. "I have to go now," I said, abruptly. I heard Cindy Pratt calling *"Please let us know when you hear from her"* before I settled the receiver back into its cradle.

I raced downstairs, fumbling with the knob. "Temple—"

A policeman in uniform huddled on the front steps, bracing himself against the wind. "Mrs. Quinn?" He was young, well built, a beach bum–turned-cop.

"I'm Quinn." My voice sounded loopy and drunk, even to me. "What . . . what is it? Is anything the matter?"

The officer grinned as though I'd just told a funny joke. He had very small teeth. "Nothin' much, as long as you don't mind your basic hurricane and tidal wave conditions."

I breathed a sigh of relief. "Oh. You're here about the storm."

He nodded. "Yes, ma'am. We're evacuating this end of the peninsula." My face must have gone blank, because he went on, this time more urgently. "Look, lady, you got terrific digs here, but there's nothing you can do. I been coverin' this area for years, and I'll tell you, you don't want to be around when this baby hits."

I nodded dumbly. "I'll just get some things." My *missing daughter. My crippled housekeeper. The usual.*

"Okay," the cop was shouting now, just to be heard. "Only, take my advice—don't wait too long." He jogged back to the patrol car and put it in reverse, spinning out as though he didn't want to waste a minute.

18

She was sleeping in the same position. The leg cast looked immense, phosphorescent, her crooked old toes peeking out.

"Cilda." I shook her shoulder. "Cilda, wake up." She groaned, turning a little, her eyes closed fast.

I picked up the amber medicine bottle and shook it. An hour ago there'd been five or six pills in it. Now only two were left. I scanned the label—"One every four hours as needed for pain." She must've taken too many.

I slapped her cheek, gently, and then harder. "Cilda? Can you hear me?"

"No," she cried in her sleep. "Get away."

I threw the rest of the water in her face. Her brown eyes rolled open, and then back. "No you don't." I held her up by the shoulders. "Look, we have to get out of here. Do you think you can walk?" *Walk? She couldn't even stay awake long enough to reply.*

"I'll be back." I said the words right into her ear, blowing them like pointed little darts into her subconscious. "I'm going to find Temple, and then we're leaving."

It occurred to me that the one place I hadn't checked was my bedroom. If Temple had run away, she might've left a note. Pinned it to my pillow. Propped on my nightstand. Tucked into the edge of my mirror. I took the stairs, two at a time, sliding inside my sloshy boots.

The first thing I noticed was that the pane of glass had been replaced. Sometime during this crazy day, one of Ben Snow's workers must have come up to do the job. Otherwise, everything looked the same as it had when I left this morning. No *Dear Mom* letters. No sign of Temple anywhere.

My energy drained away suddenly. I kicked off my boots, hurling them across the floor until they hit the wall. Then I walked over to the closet.

The doll swung toward me as I opened the door.

Splatters of blood covered its face and clothing, dripping onto the floor, speckling the shoe rack. *Let me out!* it wailed, over and over. *Maamaaaaa, let me out!*

I yanked the doll from its noose. A small tape recorder was taped to its back. *Let me out!* the voice shrieked from the cassette. *Maamaa, please! Let me out!* I went at the tape like a madwoman, pulling it, shredding it, until it was only a skinny, shiny, tinselly pile of silent ribbon on my lap.

The doll stared blankly up at me. It looked just like Temple.

The bottom of the sky had fallen out, releasing great, sweeping torrents of warm air. It pressed down on me from all sides, the charged particles of air burrowing deep into my lungs, cutting like spurs.

I hammered on the guest house door. There was no answer, no

sound of anything going on inside. I dug into my jeans and pulled out the master key. The lock turned easily. I fumbled for the switch, but no lights came on. The storm must have knocked off the power. "Temple?"

Moonlight shone through the bracketed skylights. I closed my eyes, trying to adjust them to the darkness. I heard a sound coming from outside—a soft, steady shuffling, growing perceptibly louder as the footfalls got closer.

I ducked into the shadows, plastering myself against the wall. From the window, I could just make out the overhang that sheltered the front entrance. A man stood outside the door, hooded and faceless. The slick dark mackintosh he wore spread like bat wings in the billowing wind. Moonlight flickered on something he was carrying, outstretched in one hand. It was long and tubular, made of metal, like a gun.

I edged along the wall until I reached the workbench. My hands groped furiously, blindly reading the tools that were laid out on the bench's surface. Then I crept to the door. The knob was already moving.

He moved into the room, hooded, his barreled weapon out. Hearing me behind him, he spun, but it was too late. I brought the hammer down, hitting him first on the shoulder; and again, more efficiently, on the back of the head. He swayed, fighting to remain on his feet for a brief moment, before toppling to the floor with a groan.

I reached down, and turned the body over. Once the hood was pushed aside there could be no doubt.

I'd killed Dane Blackmoor.

19

I circled the body, my extremities bucking. In the half-light Dane's face was waxen pale. With all the life drained from it, his features had relaxed into mere conventional handsomeness. I remembered what I'd been thinking as I swung the hammerhead.

I was hoping it would be Jack.

A stab of panic needled my ribs. I still hadn't found Temple, and I'd killed the only person who might've known where she was. I slipped my fingers inside the starched stiffness of Blackmoor's shirt collar, searching for the pulse in his neck. Day-old whiskers rubbed against my hand, erect, bristling. His skin was still warm. My foot hit something small and hard. I picked it up.

He hadn't been carrying a gun. He'd been carrying a flashlight.

It was black metal, quite long, with a nasty-looking barrel. I trained it around the room, skimming over the shadows. Everything appeared the same as before. The litter of empty wineglasses and abandoned coffee cups. Tools neatly aligned. Cartons and crates, in various stages of being unpacked. The marble.

I edged closer, wanting to believe the weak light played tricks with my eyes. But this was no optical illusion. The female torso that, only hours ago, had grappled under a cloak of stone, was now smashed. Deep veins of crushed crystal glittered like unmined diamonds within the granite. Each perfect breast had been gouged several times. The nipples were painted bright scarlet.

At the base of the mutilated sculpture I saw a rounded shape draped in muslin. I approached it, warily, crouching as I lifted the cover. Temple's face stared back at me, unblinking and—except for a thick slathering of lipstick—unnaturally white. I forced myself to touch it.

The casing felt light and fragile. *Empty.* The sudden wave of relief was so powerful it buckled my knees. I toppled into a narrow box made of plywood.

Two words—"OPEN ME"—had been printed in neat block letters on the lid.

The nail heads protruded, as though the person who'd hammered it shut had done so carelessly. It didn't take long to find a crowbar among the near-perfect array of tools on the bench. I used the toe of my boot for leverage, working the wedge-shaped end of the bar under the lip.

The box moved with each thrust of the iron, until it splintered with a loud crack. I threw aside the tool and began pulling on the lid with my bare hands. It gave way all at once, sending me sprawling, still clutching the ragged length of wood.

I shuffled forward on my knees. Blackmoor's cockatoo lay inside, lifeless. Something was tucked under his wing. I let the paper flutter to the floor. A pen-and-ink drawing, a *graven image*. The flashlight haloed the inscription—

To my lady of ladies
Love, Jeff

Something was under the bird. I pushed the carcass aside, whimpering in fear.

My own face smiled up at me. I flipped the picture over, noticing the embossed title. *Dust to Dust.* A narrow red ribbon stuck out from one page. I cracked it open to the mark, staring at the words that had been specially outlined in bright yellow crayon.

> But Deirdre Purdy had not only been kidnapped, she'd been buried alive. Somewhere, her parents knew, their daughter lay, embedded in the earth, in an airtight box, with just enough oxygen to last until morning. If she didn't panic.

A violent gust of wind smacked and battered the windows. The entire east wall seemed to shudder. I started tearing apart the book, systematically, five or six pages at a time. I remembered Jeff Turner sitting inches away from me, on that prison cot. Jeff, in prison blue, which so brought out the color of his eyes. I recalled the look on his face when he spoke about my work. I saw myself leaning toward him, in the flush of shared confidence, admitting that I was drawn to crimes that played on my own deepest fears.

But Temple—how did he get to Temple? The crumpled love note was still in the pocket of my jeans. *Not for Blackmoor. It had been Jeff all the time.* On the beach. Near the wall. In the woods. All over these dangerous grounds. I'd given up struggling with the book and was sitting in a daze when, from the other side of the room, I heard a groan.

"Jesus," Blackmoor muttered. "What'd you hit me with?"

20

"You're not dead!"

He rubbed the back of his neck. "Couldn't prove it by me."

I ran to him. "I'm so—" I was crying again.

Dane reached into his coat and took out a handkerchief, swabbing first my nose, and then the blood clotted in his hair, "Jesus," he said again. He sank against the workbench, weakly. "The last thing I remember was pouring myself a glass of wine. When I came to, the power was off, so I went outside. I don't know. I wasn't thinking too clearly."

"He drugged you," I said. "He drugged Cilda, too. And he took Temple—"

He sat straight up. "Jack?"

"No, not Jack. *Him*—"

. . .

The whole time I talked Blackmoor didn't look at me once. He walked around the room, touching things with his hands—the hacked-up marble; the bird in its pine coffin, unshriven and un-named (*would it be turned away at the gates of animal heaven, I won-dered, or had Jefferson Turner already performed the necessary rites?*); the plaster bust of Temple, her lips painted in a lewd Kewpie doll smile.

"We were going to surprise you with this," he said, picking up the cast. "The funny thing is, I knew she was seeing someone. A boy she met through her friend's brother. She made me promise not to tell you. I thought it was just one of those things kids go through." He hurled an empty wine bottle toward the wall. "Fuck me."

"What else did she say?"

He put a hand up to the back of his head. "That he was older. He was doing some kind of manual labor to pay for college."

I thought of the endless stream of faceless workers, their eyes ob-scured by hard hats and hooded slickers, parading in and out of these gates. I went over to the window. Put my head against the cool pane. The wind rattled the glass, boring a hole into my skull, where it flew around, shrieking.

Blackmoor came up behind me. "He put her in the wall," he said softly.

"Oh, my God." I followed his gaze. The fat, arrogant moon sat in the sky, tickling light over the tumbling foundation of stones, taunt-ing the waves over. "Oh, my God. My God, my God."

"Remember, he was on his own, working fast," he said. "That means he couldn't have put her down too far." What he didn't say was that when people worked too fast, things tended to go wrong. Boxes weren't sealed properly. The necessary amount of oxygen was miscalculated. A boulder could slip from the jaws of a crane. There might even be a rockslide, if one was moving, in too much haste—

I pushed these thoughts from my mind. Something fragile flut-tered against my throat, like the beatings of small wings. *Hope.* "The engineer said there were tunnels big enough to fit cars in."

"Listen, Garner." Blackmoor was choosing his words carefully.

"What I said before, about her not being in too deep—that's true . . . but still, he must've used equipment. We're talking rock here. There's no way—"

"We'll get help."

He turned me so that I faced the window again. "What do you see?"

"I can't see anything." Then it hit me. All the lights were off in the main house. "He's cut the lines," I said dully.

"The tires on our cars are slashed, too," Blackmoor said.

I clung to his arm. "We could do it together." His face was set in the same old disparaging lines. "I know we could," I insisted. "You're a sculptor. You know about things, about rock and stone—"

"I'm a fake, Garnish," he said. "You said so yourself."

I saw the tired cynicism in his eyes. "Play it any way you want," I said. "But I, for one, am not going to sit here counting the hours until my daughter runs out of air."

21

Mountainous waves shattered over the seawall. Fingers of foam probed. Over, under, in. I tried to concentrate on the hundreds of times I'd walked the slender balance beam of these rocks before, one foot in front of the other, never giving it a thought. Now I made my way slowly, looking for breaks in the stone, testing the filler to see if it felt too hard or too soft.

We had to shout at each other to be heard. "Over there." Blackmoor pointed to a section of the wall just ahead, throwing down the leather pouch packed with tools. "Hold the beam steady."

I focused the flashlight. The surf was almost directly at our backs. In a few hours the wall would be completely submerged. Had Turner calculated for that when he built the box? Had he considered the possibility that Temple might drown?

"Damm it, Garner," Blackmoor cursed. "Keep the light on me!" He ran his hands over the rocks, then took a chisel out of his pocket and began to tap.

"What are you doing?"

"Checking for movement." I could hardly hear him over the roar. "For gaps."

I watched, desperately wanting to believe that this was something more than another Dane Blackmoor performance. He moved confidently enough, but never once did he meet my eyes.

The wind filled his coat like sails. He yelled for a crowbar. I scrambled for the bag. By the time I got it to him, though, he was shaking his head. "It's solid." He pointed in another direction. "Let's try over there."

We walked in single file, me with my arms out, steadying myself against the wind. Blackmoor paused occasionally, moving his hands over the surface of the wall, tracing the crevasses, sometimes tapping. We'd been at it for maybe fifteen minutes when he stopped short.

"What?" No answer. "What? Tell me!"

He signed that I should put my ear up against the rock. "Listen."

"I can't hear anything." I yelled, frustrated.

He backtracked several paces. "Now listen over here."

"The ocean sounds different."

"That's because this section is hollow."

Still avoiding my eyes, he lowered himself on his heels. I huddled next to him, cautioning myself against a false alarm. But this time I could even see it. The irregularity in the wall. Instead of a solid bank of stone and concrete, several medium-size boulders had been stacked in a heap, and packed with loose gravel.

Blackmoor began digging with his hands. "Got anything like a shovel in that bag?" he shouted.

"There's one in the garage."

His eyes scanned the dark house. "Forget it," he told me.

He feels it, too, I thought, *senses that we're not alone.* I dropped onto my stomach, scooping fistfuls of tow stone. A wave crested, dousing us with cold salt water, but we kept on working. Minutes later, we'd cleared away the area around one of the smaller rocks.

"Get the crowbar," Dane directed. "I think we can take it out."

I found it. "Now, look," he said. "When this sucker starts to move, we've got to keep it going. We can't have it slide back, understand?" I nodded. He didn't have to explain what the falling weight could do. If the box were below it. If Temple were still alive. *Please, God, please, let her be alive.*

Blackmoor dug himself in. "Okay, on three, then—"

The sound of the surf, and my heart, pounded in my ears. I couldn't hear the three-count, but moved forward when he did, felt the dead resistance of the stone, as every fiber of my being flexed against it. For an instant it seemed hopeless, but Blackmoor pulled down the bar, and suddenly the boulder moved—rolling, at first slowly, then picking up speed and momentum.

I fell on my face, cutting my chin. When I got up, Dane was already leaning into the hole, smoothing the sand and gravel off something flat and shiny. I crawled toward him, marveling at those magic hands, which could produce a metal box out of the surface of sheer rock.

"Temple! Temple? Honey, can you hear me?" A faint thumping came from below. *Once. Twice. The third time much stronger.* I grabbed on to Dane to keep from falling over.

"Sit tight, sweetheart," he called. "We're going to get you out of there."

Just before he lowered himself into the wall, Blackmoor clapped his hand around the back of my neck and drew me toward him. I collapsed under the tent of his raincoat, allowing myself to be smothered within the folds of his shirt. His heart drummed softly in my ear.

"He's made it too easy," he whispered. Or at least that's what it sounded like. Before I could ask, he'd pushed away, telling me to train the flashlight on the top of the box.

.   .   .

She emerged from the metal coffin just the way she'd been born, shiny-wet, crying, gulping for air. Beautiful. Dane lifted her up and placed her in my arms.

"Mommy, Mommy, oh, I'm so sorry—" Her slender body convulsed.

"Shhh." I hugged her tightly. "It's over now."

Blackmoor took off his big raincoat and placed it over her shoulders. "Do you want me to carry you," he asked, "or can you walk?"

"I . . . I don't know," Temple sobbed.

He caught my eye. "We'll try for the house," he said.

The rusty staircase rattled like false teeth. I went first, followed by Dane, who half-supported, half-carried Temple, talking to her all the while in a soft, encouraging voice. Once we were off the wall, the wind suddenly abated. A mother-of-pearl sheen glazed the sky. The air had texture. I could feel it, settling in my pores, pressing against my hair, thick as wool.

"Put your arm around my shoulder," Blackmoor said to Temple.

I took her other side. We leaned toward each other, eyes fixed on the gabled outline of the house. What we'd do when we got there, I had no idea; but still, it would be something—a place I knew; a safe haven, with pokers in the fire, and knives in the kitchen; with places to hide. It beckoned us, less than two hundred yards away—two hundred yards of open, unprotected space.

I felt it even before I heard the idle of the engine, before I risked that first backward glance. The crane lumbered steadily in our direction, its headlights casting crazy ellipses over the uneven ground. We ran toward our shadows, which were tapered and distended, somber, frightening, like figures in a painting by El Greco. It was gaining on us.

"Dane!" The wind swallowed my scream.

Blackmoor had thrown Temple over his shoulder. "Stay with me!" he shouted. He was trying to dodge the ever-widening spheres of light, but it seemed useless. Whether we went left or right, the crane followed, trampling the ground, pelting us with gravel—inevitable, relentless. Bird Turner stood inside the cage, a shrouded silhouette, less man than machine.

"Watch out!" Dane yelled.

A long, menacing shadow appeared over my head. Split seconds later the metal claws lowered, pinpointing me, bearing down, snapping viciously in my ear. I was running as fast as I could. Breathing in and out had become incredibly painful. In a small, still section of my brain I considered what it would feel like—the metal teeth, making their deadly clean lacerations. I saw myself being lifted skyward, like a child riding in a Ferris wheel, imagined myself part of the sky, the air, the hot, woolly whiteness. I was just about to give in to it when a pair of arms shot out of the darkness, pushing me forcibly out of the way. I tumbled backward, with Temple on top of me. We landed in a heap, watching in horror as the three-pronged grabs went for Blackmoor, snatching him with pointy jaws, before hurling him to the ground.

The crane lurched into reverse, with Turner at the helm, coming in for the kill.

"Stay here," I said to Temple.

I crouched low, my face to the dirt. Dane was still conscious, but blood was everywhere. I took off my jacket and put it over him. "Go," he rasped.

"I won't leave you." The crane was making a wide loop, approaching lazily, toying with us.

"Don't you trust me yet?" His breath was labored.

"Of course I trust you," I sobbed.

"Then get out of here, or he'll kill all of us." He tugged on my jacket, pulling me toward his chest. His kiss was still salty, but sweet, too, on account of the blood. "Go," he whispered, hoarsely, "before he gets to Temple."

I kissed him again and ran toward my daughter.

22

Wind hootchy-kootched the windows. The big grandfather clock on the landing tick-tocked peacefully. We'd almost made it to the steps when two round spots of light appeared in the windows. They grew larger and larger.

"Get into the closet." I pushed Temple through the door seconds before the wall of glass shattered, tinkling like so many discordant wind chimes.

Turner cut off the motor, swiftly, one in a series of sudden deaths. Then he dismounted, a length of rope hanging from his shoulders like a necklace. The unsheathed knife glinted in his belt. Greasepaint flattened all the familiar lines of his face. For some reason this frightened me more than anything. I called up the memory of the boy I once knew: Jeff Turner in his pressed khakis and navy blazer; in his county-issue periwinkle blues. But I couldn't seem to get past the gleaming makeup, smearing his features, obliterating his eyes.

"Hey, lady," he said cheerily.

"Hey, Jeff."

I stood at the foot of the stairs holding the butcher knife I'd taken from the kitchen.

"So, what do you think?" he asked. "Not bad for a country boy, huh?" He edged closer. "I really had you goin', didn't I?"

"Yes," I told him. "You really did."

"Don't talk down to me." Jeff circled in front of me, his hand playing nervously over the hilt of his knife. "You know, I hate when people underestimate me." He leaned forward, just beyond striking distance. "And I love it."

He feinted in my direction. *"Boo."* I flinched, and he laughed. His eyes scanned the room. "Where's our girl?"

"She made a run for it," I told him.

"Garner, you disappoint me," Jeff said. "First that big ole knife, and now these deceptions." He began walking around, calling, "Hey, pretty baby, it's lover boy. Come out, come out, wherever you are."

"I told you," I said, "she's not here."

"She'll turn up," Turner said, "sooner or later. Didn't I tell you, it's the lonely ones that can't ever get enough of me? Sweet Temple. Little Jenny Price back home. Now she was a good one, because she couldn't talk about what I did, after . . ."

When he lunged, it was so swift and unexpected, the image registered in my head as just a blur, unsubstantial energy, not matter. And suddenly his fingers were locked over my wrist. I cried out, releasing the kitchen knife into his palm.

"Temple," he called, his face so close I could feel the warm, sticky greasepaint on my cheek. "You're not gonna leave your pretty mama out here in the clutches of the big bad wolf, are you?"

I tried not to scream *No, don't do it,* but he cut me off with steady pressure from the crook of his elbow to my vocal cords. "If you don't get your little ass out here by the time I count three, sugar," Jeff said calmly, "I'm gonna have to cut sweet mama's throat and then come looking for you. *One—*"

Temple stepped out of the closet, face ashen, her hair matted with sweat and sand. "Good girl," he said. "Now sit." He nodded his head toward a chair. She looked at me. Jeff jabbed the point of the blade into my neck. "I said sit." She obeyed.

He loosened his grip on me so completely I fell forward. "Tie her up," he commanded, tossing the rope.

"I don't know how—"

"Start with the hands." I moved slowly, mentally calculating the distance between the chair and the piano bench, desperately trying not to look at it, not to give myself away.

I felt his eyes on me as I circled the rope around Temple's wrists. "You were never totally sure about me, were you?" He came over to test the knot himself. "Even after Susie went and changed her story." He mimicked Susan's voice. *"God knows Mr. Turner is an innocent man."* Jeff signaled for me to kneel. "Man, that was one crazy bitch, huh?"

He was running the knife down my scalp. The blade snagged on the tangles in my hair. I wrapped the rope several times around my daughter's bare ankles. She had a nasty cut just above the bone there. I wanted to kiss it. Instead I concentrated on the piano bench. The bench where only yesterday I'd hidden my stash from the hardware store. The nails. The big Phillips screwdriver with the thick yellow handle.

Jeff said, "I never did it with two before. Hope I came prepared."

Out of the corner of my eye I saw him pull a condom from his pocket. It fell out of his hand and rolled under Temple's chair. "No matter." He grinned. *"I know where you two ladies been."*

I pushed Temple's chair as hard as I could. She screamed, spilling from the seat, half-tied, but immediately rolling away.

I crawled on my hands and knees toward the bench. Jeff caught me as I was lifting the lid. I slammed it down on his fingers. He howled like a mad dog, striking me so hard I fell forward; but my hands kept moving with a life of their own. On a mission, unstoppable.

His knife found my flesh somewhere above the shoulder blade.

In nomine Patris, et Filii . . .

There was a delayed reaction to the pain while my fingers danced across stacks of sheet music, clutching, grabbing, as unwilling to believe the simple truth—

. . . et Spiritus Sancti . . .

The tools were gone.

Cilda had stealthily moved them to another location. I'd find the screwdriver in an unlikely place, when I least expected to, on some other day.

Only this time there wouldn't be another day.

I twisted around to face my killer, watching his man-in-the-moon face rise above me, knife out, already bloody. Before it struck, he moved it up and down, and side to side, in the sign of the cross, the way I knew he would.

Each cut was slow and methodical.

I heard my voice crying, *Run, Temple! Run!* but inside there was an enveloping warmth, an easy calm. I wondered if this was how death had been for Dane Blackmoor. I hoped so.

Jeff was praying again. *In nomine . . .* , his mouth in a perfect O, when his greasy moon face suddenly darkened, and he grunted, falling forward on my chest.

Two long steely knitting needles were sticking out of the middle of his back, like arrows.

He struggled to his feet, trying to pull them out, moving his arms backward in wild circular strokes, like a drowning man attempting to swim. But Cilda was already poised over him, the crutch held high in her hands, carefully aiming it before she struck.

In the ambulance I dreamed that Diana Gold had sent the policeman back—something about not being able to reach Blackmoor on the phone—about needing to tell him that Lucy Moon had confessed. She'd killed Torie and the other girls. Lucy Moon and Elizabeth Rice . . .

In my dream Diana Gold dispatched that officer . . .

Someone whispered it all into my ear. And I thought, *It's not a dream*, then, *Oh shit. I owe my life to Diana Gold. . . .*

EPILOGUE

I woke out of another nightmare.

The sheets were wrapped so tightly around me that for a moment I thought I'd been tied up. I struggled, relaxing only when I realized where I was.

The hospital.

Lights were lowered in a semblance of night. Still, I could clearly make out Temple's face. "Dane's alive," she said, "but—"

I put my hand up, weakly. It was enough that I could see her, and Cilda; and she'd said the words I wanted most to hear.

For now it was all that mattered.